EARLY PRAISE

"An enchanting escape full of passion and delicious angst."
- L.R. Friedman, author of The Blaze Legacy Series

"Between the world-building, the characters, and the tension ... it's a fantasy book that you will fall into and never want to leave! I need more."

– Fay Bec, author of The Dark Curse Series

"A heart-pounding, jaw-dropping page turner. The perfect addition to any fantasy lover's shelf."
– Lauren Leasure, author of The Benevolence & Blood Series

"Magic is awake, indeed! The Heat of Seas is packed with world building, complex characters, a unique lore, and romances that'll have you swooning!"
– Elle Beaumont, author of the Immortal Realms Trilogy

THE HEAT OF SEAS

THE ASHONERA SERIES: BOOK ONE

DEANNA HILL

Midnight Tide
PUBLISHING

MIDNIGHT TIDE PUBLISHING

Book Cover by bookdesignsbyshae

Carnaxa Header Illustrations by MagicBookCoverDesign on Etsy
Dividers by MinimalMarks on Etsy
Other headers created through Canva

Edits by: Joyce Fernandez @ Rejoyce Literary Editing
Proofreading: Sarah McCloy
Sensitivity Reader: Yvonne Marie

Paperback ISBN: 978-1-958673-81-2
Hardback ISBN: 978-1-958673-83-6
E-Book: B0CKXY6J68

First edition 2024

CONTENTS

Authors Note

The Heat of Seas is book one of an Epic Dark Fantasy Romance series. It contains explicit, graphic content and is intended for readers over the age of 18. For a full list of content warnings, please scan the QR code below.

Shaston
The Cartilen Mountains
Midaeliea
Antalis
The Northern Continent

ASHONERA
THE SOUTHERN CONTINENT
LIDIENS
CORTAVE
SAN'DOMA

Dedication

To those who took a while to find their voice.

It's okay.

We eventually roar.

Playlist

Atlantis- Seafret

Falling Apart- Michael Schulte

Middle of The Night – Elley Duhe

Gods & Monsters – Lana Del Rey

Infinity – Jaymes Young

The Night We Met – Lord Huron

Arcade – Duncan Laurence

Black Out Days – Phantogram

If You Want Love – NF

Feel Something – Jaymes Young

Power Over Me – Dermot Kennedy

Bored – Billie Eilish

Power – Isak Danielson

Gilded Lily (Sped Up) – Cults

Daylight – David Kushner

Twisted – Missio

Crazy In Love (Epic Trailer Version) – J2, Wulf

Prisoner – Raphael Lake, Aaron Levy, Daniel Ryan Murphy

Lovely – Lauren Babic, Seraphim

I Wanna Be Yours – Arctic Monkeys

I Feel Like I'm Drowning – Two Feet

The Feels – Labrinth

Dust Till Dawn (TikTok Remix) – TommyMuzzic, PHAZZED

War of Hearts – Ruelle

Glossary & Terms

Character Names Pronunciation:

Carnaxa: /car-nax-a/

Thylas: /thigh-lus/

Ereon: /air-E-on/

Siphonie: /siph-oh-knee/

Rhenor: /rain-er/

·····•••◐●○●◑•••·····

Sigils Of The Northern Continent:

Antalis (An-Tall-is) Kingdom:
Blue & gold;crescent moon holding a trident above
Shaston (Sha-s-ton) Kingdom:
Silver & black;snake in the middle of the sun
Midaeliea (Mid-A-Lee-ah) Kingdom:
Green & brown;large tree in a circle with roots running deep

·····•••◐●○●◑•••·····

Lunar year: Twelve synodic months.
Moon cycles: Eight phases one after the other as the moon moves through its cycle. One month.

·····•••◐●○●◑•••·····

Antalis Structure & Titles in Antihana:

King/Queen: *Tinge / T-E-n-g-e/*
Queen: *Telae /te-l-e/*
Princess: *Su Kechni - /Sue K-E-ch-n-eye/*

Prince: *Myesh Kechni* /My-e-sh- k-E-ch-n-eye/

Lady: *Bêlit* /b-E-lit/

Lord: *Bêl* /B-E-ll/

Royal Guard: *Ke Neye* /K-e ne-ya-E/

Ground Army: *Shayi maka* /Sh-a-ya-E m-ah-k-ah/

Water Fleet: *Shayi Yengo* /Sh-a-ya-E ya-e-na-o/

Army: *Shayi* /Sh-a-ya-E/

···•••◑●○●◐•••···

Antihana -The Language of The Goddess

Mohasha **/mo-ha-sh-a/:** The afterlife

Festival of Täht /t-ah-t/ and Mar /m-are/: Festival of Stars and Seas. Annual festival in Antalis that coincides with the *Shæmi* fish to honor the Goddess.

Kosæ/ko-s-eye/: Fuck.

Nohæ/ no-h-eye/ : (You will find out.)

Na iwo /na-E-wo/: Playful term for someone who loses a game.

Mæna /m-eye-n-ah/ : Pleasure woman; woman for hire in Antalis

Noko Maki /no-ka-o ma-ka-E/ : The Shell Ceremony of Antalians, much like a wedding ceremony.

Neni/ne-nE/: Official ceremony to deny and/or break a twin drop.

Ata /ah-t-ah/: What young children call their mothers in Antalis.

*Hayæ /ha-ya-eye/:*Flowers used in Antalis to symbolize celebrations.

Pasa /p-ah-s-ah/: Flowers used in Antalis to symbolize grief.

Shæwi Koki /sha-eye-we k-o-k-E/: When twin drops are found after a Noko Maki is performed, the individuals create a family unit.

Neshæ Pekæ Ra, Lengo Ra, Noko Ra /na-e-sh-eye 'p-ek-eye ra, 'la-e-na-o ra, 'na-ok-o ra/: An Antalian Prayer. Watch over her, guide her, love her. The "ra" part can be taken out to read as: Watch over, guide, love.

·····●◑◐○◑◐●·····

Creatures:

Pesho /pe-sh-o/: Fluffy white beast rumored to bring good luck. Sign of new beginnings.

Khind: Dark creatures of the pass.

Pitongi /pE-t-on-gE/ birds: Sea gulls.

Shæmi /sh-eye-mE/ fish: Great fish, revered used during the Festival of Täht & Mar.

Wəngesk /w-en-g-e-sk/: Giant elephant squid, highly revered.

Taoho /ta-oho/ : Small, beautiful creatures that glow blue as the waves crest along the shoreline.

EPIGRAPH

"The moon herself grew dark, rising at sunset,
Covering her suffering in the night,
Because she saw her beautiful namesake, Selene,
Breathless, descending to Hades,
With her, she had had the beauty of her light in common,
And mingled her own darkness with her death."
~Crinagoras of Mytilene

PROLOGUE

Fire dances around me as the ones I love have turned on each other with hate fueling their hearts. I hold my hands out, fighting back the flames with the water within me, the magic pulsing through my veins.

He did this, because of his jealousy. He made the deal that sealed our fates – a fate I never wanted for any of them. Death was a dream that I never had, and yet it will forever be the nightmare they can't escape.

Flames lick toward my feet and I move again, casting them away with a flick of my wrist. Even if they touch me I won't burn. He stands there sneering before shouting an order to his men. His creatures of darkness slink between the shadows and flames as they bring something out. I can't tell what it is through the maddening chaos.

Men and women stand behind me as we fight for everything we believe in, a fight we have never prepared for. Their powers weren't meant for war but as gifts, and yet, they fight beside me anyway. The stench of smoke, rot, and death lingers in the air.

Shielding my eyes from the heat of the flames with my hands, I look up, noticing what the creatures brought out. My knees crumble and the rocks beneath dig into my skin as I see my beloved tied to a pole in the middle of a platform. It's for him I fight, for him I destroy those that I love. For him, I will do anything. The flames inch toward him, inching instead of swarming because the betrayer wants me to suffer, to watch as my lover dies.

Reaching my arm out and knowing it's worthless because my powers can't reach that far, but I have to try anyway. The flames wrap around him and he screams, the sound echoes all around me. It's all I can hear, but I can't look away and I scream too.

Ice sprouts from my pain enveloping me, creating a coolness amidst the heat.

"A læ t neni pe, o a læ pengæ pe wæ lomo popo ra læ," I scream into the wind, reaching for the dagger at my side. It's hopeless. I can't win this. Not now, not today. But I can give them one more gift.

ONE

CARNAXA

His ruddy fingers dig into her golden sun-kissed thighs as he thrust up into her, her skin grinding against the stone behind them. His oily hair falls onto his face as she moans against his neck. His hands come up to grab her wrists, taking them and placing them high above her head. The muscles of his back bulge and dip as he continues, their pace quickening. Her bangles clink together with each thrust, the same bangles that match my own. Different shades of silver and gold that are gifts from our mothers who are no longer with us.

The man is of no real status but this is how Siphonie wants it. How she always wants it. Quick and to the point, not saving a lot of room for discussion or getting to know one another. This has been her preference for the past couple months, while he is docked in Antalis, before he sets sail across the seas again. She buys her pleasure here at the docks because it's convenient with no strings attached. Her pale pink hair cascades down around her and finally, she grips his shoulders finding her pleasure as the man pants his release into her.

He slowly lowers her onto the ground and she straightens her skirt before tossing a few coins at the man. "Thanks!" she says over her tawny shoulder as the man bends down pulling up his trousers and grabbing the coins that lie on the edge of the wooden dock.

"Always a pleasure, Princess." He smirks, running his hand through his golden locks.

"I'm not the Princess" – she looks toward me and smiles – "she is." She takes a step back and he grabs her one more time around the waist pulling her deep into his muscled arms.

"You are my princess, at least when I am inside you." He kisses her cheek again before letting her go and heads back toward his men.

"Are you ready, Naxa?" Siphonie asks me, trying to adjust her hair. Only those closest to me call me by my childhood nickname, most call me Carnaxa Althister, Princess of Antalis.

"Do I always have to come with you? I mean, honestly, what fun is this for me? Watching you with your man of the season."

She laughs. "Well, my dear one, it's not fun for you. You are here to watch and make sure none of these men think they can get away with anything I don't wish to happen. I do have my limits, you know."

We walk across the canal and back onto the main streets of Antalis. The ocean waves crash against the bridge, shooting drops of water onto us. Antalis is one of three kingdoms that make up the Northern Continent of Ashonera.

The guards glance toward us and smile as we pass. Their golden armor glints in the afternoon sunlight, our kingdom's symbol, the trident etched in gold across their breastplate. Even though we are a mostly peaceful kingdom, the guards' swords, and shields are attached to their sides. The soldiers are trained as if war is on our doorstep. Our naval fleet, the *Shayi Maka,* is one of the best from what I hear. And according to Siphonie, our soldiers, both male and female, are trained for many other things as well, their passion in the bedroom the most widely discussed.

The ocean glitters as *pitongi* birds fly high and dip low to catch fish, the smell of it all surrounding us. The smell of home.

"Do you have limits? Because sneaking off to find pleasure with a fisherman instead of your husband doesn't seem to be one."

She sighs and rolls her light hazel eyes. "Our marriage was, and still is, a political arrangement that your father put together. Rhenor does what he does, and I do the same."

Siphonie and Rhenor were betrothed when she was but thirteen. She and Rhenor married two lunar years ago when she was eighteen, and he has been kind to her ever since.

"Rhenor is a considerate man." She hooks her arm with mine as we continue to walk down the cobblestone streets. "Your father made sure of that. Rhenor is sixteen years my senior and he told me that he would never force himself on me, nor does he expect me to love him. It's why his sister raised me when I came into their household, he thought it strange to raise his future wife. So instead of a normal wedding night, he made me that oath and it's one he's lived by. He isn't bad to look at either nor a bad lover." She raises her hand to cover her eyes from the glaring sun. "He still misses her you know, his first wife. I think that's why he never expects me to love him. I don't think he could ever love me like he did her. Maybe one day, but that day is not today." Her hand tightens around my arm and she glares up ahead. "Get ready."

I squint, looking toward where she glances, and see Ereon as he walks toward us, his chestnut brown, curled hair bouncing as he walks. His stunning white teeth show as he grins from between full lips. His warm, ivory skin glistens beneath the sun's glare. His guards stand just three steps behind him, a custom from his home, the Kingdom of Shaston, where his father King Atlas rules. The Shastonians have a harder life than those of Antalis according to rumors. They are known for their prowess both on and off the battlefield and they pride themselves on it. They have a life without the peace of the ocean's water, living in the northeast of our continent, a place rumored to be cursed by the Goddess. The Cartilen Mountains separate them from the other kingdoms, and there is only one path that leads through those mountains, only traveled when necessary due to the creatures lurking there.

"Good afternoon, Princess Carnaxa," he greets me as he bows at the hips, "*Bêlit* Siphonie." His off-white tunic is a stark contrast to the darkness of his eyes and hair. His eyes are such a deep brown, one might lose themselves in his gaze, ignoring any dangers that may be lurking within.

I curtsy. "Good afternoon, Prince Ereon. It's a lovely day for a walk."

His intense eyes look back toward Siphonie, slightly smiling as he takes in her disheveled hair and sweat still glistening against her flushed skin. She readjusts the deep-v of her neckline. "I'm sure that's what you were both also doing, enjoying a *walk*." He winks at Siphonie, and to her credit she doesn't falter. Siphonie's reputation has apparently reached his ears. When Prince Ereon's soldiers first arrived, she found her way into several of their beds. Despite my constant worry over the rumored, ruthless soldiers, she found their company thrilling.

Siphonie, my cousin, has been raised in Antalis. She worries not about the opinions of others and embraces our culture of free sexuality, which we have found some foreigners who travel to our kingdom do not understand. She smiles right back at him, "You wouldn't be on the same type of *walk*, would you? You are betrothed to our lovely Carnaxa after all."

He smirks and crosses his arms in front of him. "I am going to visit the fishing markets to see about gaining a few new members to my guard. When Princess Carnaxa returns to Shaston with me, I want as much protection as possible for her. The way home can be treacherous at times." My skin flushes beneath his gaze as he reaches out and tucks a piece of my cerulean wavy hair behind my ear, "Her safety and happiness will be my responsibility after all, not too many moons from now."

My father, the King of Antalis, made this match. King Atlas of Shaston and my father have never been able to see eye to eye. The Great War was the biggest battle between the kingdoms and we've still had our skirmishes through the years. However, no matter how hard we work to keep the peace the tension is always near, the King of Shaston, constantly in a volatile state. The kingdom between us, Midaeliea, tries to keep the peace among our three kingdoms of Ashonera. The Kingdom of Midaeliea takes upon itself the role to call a summit of our three kingdoms every three lunar years.

Antalis is not the largest kingdom on our continent, but we have the sea. We have our ancestors, we have protection surrounding us and we have the blessings of the Goddess. Leaving my home to travel to Shaston is not something I want. I don't want to leave Antalis with the possibility of our magic awakening. My father swears the magic of our land is long gone, but we've all heard the rumors and prophecies brought from the Southern Continent. People there talk of another war that approaches, one that will change the world. He remembers the stories his great-grandfather told him of magical creatures that lingered in this world and protected it, the *wɔngesk* that came to the call of the Goddess during the Great War. None of the magic has been seen since the end of that war, but we continue to pray to Her, for Her protection, and hope that She will bring the magic and Her blessing back.

"Naxa, I'm sure, is excited to see the beautiful Kingdom of Shaston, Prince Ereon." Siphonie digs her fingers into my side, pulling me back from my scattered thoughts, and I quickly smile and nod in agreement. My tutors used to have the same problem with me, I was always one to get distracted and lost in my thoughts, my dreams, and my worries.

"Yes, absolutely." I glance at the Prince, the muscles in his neck are slicked with sweat from the summer heat. "Are you beginning to enjoy our climate here?"

He wipes at the sweat collecting along his strong brow and sighs, "No, I think I prefer ours at home. It's hot and cold to be sure, but whatever makes the air so thick here, making it harder to breathe, can stay in Antalis. However" – he leans in close enough I can feel his breath on my ear – "I will miss these gorgeous dresses that your kingdom is accustomed to." He leans back and steps to the side to admire me; my cheeks heat.

As a people, we don't feel the need to cover up one's body. Our tunics and dresses are simple garments. Women are usually seen wearing two-piece dresses, our mid-drifts on display, and most of our items are made of gauze-like fabric. From what I have learned, this is not the way of the Shastonians. Their lands have sand but not water, and the sun is so hot it can burn skin within moments of exposure. The people of Shaston wear long dresses or tunics, cover their feet in layers of protection along with thick soles, in addition to special garments to protect their heads from the sun's rays. The nights in contrast are so cold, it's been said that hands would stick to iron if one isn't careful.

"Well time is getting ahead of us, I must be returning. I am sure my guard is worried sick and will come find me shortly." I lightly touch his bicep as I step past him. "I hope to see you soon."

"Oh, you will. Your father invited me to dinner tonight."

His words send a shiver of fear down my spine. We are betrothed sure, but the time Prince Ereon has spent here has not been centered around me and he is still very much a stranger. Dinner is one of the few moments I have with my father and I cherish our time together. Ereon attending a meal with just the two of us feels as though he is intruding on the precious, little time I have left, and I don't like it.

"How wonderful. I look forward to seeing you this evening," I reply, pulling myself from my thoughts. Siphonie and I curtsy and quickly make our exit, she's barely holding in a giggle as we leave his sight.

"I'm almost jealous of you, Naxa! If it wasn't for his homeland, he would be perfect." She starts jumping as she skips ahead of me, turning to look back at me. "I don't know why you aren't more excited about Ereon. Honestly, he is young, sexy, and probably amazing in bed. He has seen battle and his body is just something I could lick for days. What is there not to like?"

I roll my eyes. "Oh, many things. The fact that I have to leave you, leave Antalis just to name a few. Plus, Rhenor has seen battle."

"And I love the scars on his body from it, makes me feel protected. You know, you can request who you want to come with you. Request me, I would love to go someplace new. I've lived here my entire life. Maybe we could travel to Cortave. Wouldn't that be fun?"

"And what of Rhenor, Siph?"

"He wouldn't care if I went, he would probably come along too. He's been to Shaston a few times. Either way, let's get you ready for tonight since you'll get to see two good-looking men at your dinner table, it's going to be a formal event, I'm sure ..." Siphonie grabs my hand as we walk through the castle doors.

"Do not start about ..." I barely finish my sentence before I run into a golden breastplate and look up.

Thylas, my bodyguard and Captain of the *Ke Neye*, stares down at me with his emerald green eyes, not happy that I slipped out during his watch this morning. His midnight hair, so dark that it turns blue at the edges, is tied up in a bun at the top of his head. His eyes flame with anger because I have left him once again as I scrambled out with Siphonie this morning.

"Where the *kosæ* have you two been?" he seethes, eyeing us both.

Siphonie only laughs and walks around him. "Doing the same thing you do in the taverns during your off time." She turns around to face him and winks.

He rolls his eyes and I notice the vein along his neck pops out, a telltale sign he's irritated.

"I wasn't concerned about you Siph, I'm not your guard. You are your husband's problem, not mine." He stares at her, but she just smiles.

"Oh, go shuck a shell!" She throws up her hands at him as if she is indeed shucking a shell before showcasing her middle finger in a crude gesture and walking past him.

Ignoring her, Thylas steps in front of me not letting me pass. "Where were *you*?" he asks as he places his hand around my bicep. Siphonie leans against the wall, waiting on me as a devious smile passes her lips.

I look up at him as he towers over me. His strong jaw, covered in scruff, and his pouty lips are the reason he has women falling at his feet. I jerk my arm out of his grasp. "She told you where we were. Now I'll be in my chambers getting ready for dinner."

I don't miss the fury in his eyes at what I've suggested I was doing. He knows as well as I he shouldn't care, but I also know I shouldn't irritate him. It's hard for me not to toy with him, he used to be one of my best friends after all.

TWO

CARNAXA

The table is set with roasted fish, cooked seaweed, bread, and other delicacies from our lands. The kitchen must be showing off since Ereon is eating with us, wanting to put their best culinary foot forward. Which I can't help but think is humorous considering he's been eating from the kitchens since he arrived, just not at our table. I was raised to always respect the common folk and castle workers as much as I would respect any royal because we do not survive without the other. We don't have the fish we eat without the hard work of those who do the fishing and we don't have the meals before us, without those who serve in the kitchen. My mother always wanted to show that a title does not define your worth and instead, one should look at the heart of the individual. So with that in mind, we normally don't have this much prepared for dinner. This is all the kitchen's doing, not our request.

"Thylas said you once again went to the markets without an escort, Carnaxa," my father groans from the head of the large table. My father, King Clennom, with his stark white hair and clearly irritated expression, meets my eyes with his stern gaze.

Thylas stands on my left side, which is my father's right. My guard has an expression that never changes. He keeps his eyes distant and unmoving, but I know he is watching. He's probably smiling internally. He loves getting me in trouble, ever since we were little kids.

"Thylas, should either learn to do a better job of watching me or a better job of keeping his mouth shut." I toss a grape in my mouth and wash it down with a sip of water. Thylas' feet shuffle the slightest bit behind me and I hear a sigh come from his lips. Ereon is here and it's making everything that much more uncomfortable. Dinners are usually just my father and me, a time of connection after my mother's death. Now I have Ereon across from me and Thylas at my back. My father could have at least invited Siphonie and Rhenor to break the tension.

"Daughter, we have discussed this. You cannot be moving around the city like this when there are so many new faces in the kingdom now, including people from all over Ashonera for the fishing season. I don't feel safe with you leaving the grounds unguarded. Keep Thylas with you." His eyes flick toward Ereon. It's his men who roam the streets my Father is worried about. His men come from a kingdom that views women as property.

Ereon hasn't said a word since dinner began, after his initial greeting, his eyes bounce back and forth between my father and me. "Your Grace," he begins wiping the corner of his mouth with a linen napkin. "Maybe Princess Carnaxa has a point. Maybe we should punish the guard for not doing his job. How hard could she be to watch? My men would have no problem watching her. Would you like us to replace this one?" Ereon motions with a bob of his head to Thylas.

I choke on my drink, this was not what I wanted. How could I have been so stupid as to speak my mind in front of Ereon? Of course, he would want to punish Thylas. Father is used to our little disagreements but knows that at the end of the day, Thylas is a loyal member of the Antalian *Shayi*, my father also understands my free spirit. He blames my mother for that.

I smile at the Prince. "Prince Ereon, thank you so much for your offer, but I promise you, Thylas is a dutiful guard. We've known each other since we were children, I know my safety is of the utmost importance to him."

"As much as that pleases me to hear Princess Carnaxa, your safety is worth more than a childhood friendship. If we were in my kingdom, he would be flogged or potentially face a worse punishment for not watching over you."

Thylas stands tall but I can see his fingers tense at the sound of being flogged. He knows too well the sharp pain of a whip, even though it was long ago. The air in the room becomes tight with tension and even my father seems to dart his eyes toward Thylas to gauge his expression. The day of the flogging is forever ingrained in all our memories.

My father tosses his linen cloth beside his plate and crosses his legs. "That won't be necessary, Ereon. Thylas is one of our most trusted inside the Antalian *Shayi* and I know he has my daughter's best interest in mind. Carnaxa should be the one to blame as she knows it's not safe to be wandering during this time." He eyes me and I know not to argue at this moment. Shaston is a whole different world. "Women of Antalis are simply more independent than they are in the north. Our women are known for their tempers and will to fight, as well as their utter disregard for their own safety while in search of satisfying their curiosities."

"Then perhaps it is Princess Carnaxa who should bear the brunt of the punishment. Women are taught their place in Shaston, regardless of their station. When she is to be my queen she will do well to remember this."

I grind my teeth at his statement. Queens are not meant to be simple accessories to their king. The thought of being nothing more than a silent partner goes against everything we are taught in Antalis and against everything my mother stood for. I pop the knuckle of my ring finger to keep from speaking out, how dare he have the audacity to recommend I be punished for a simple walk around my kingdom. I should speak up, I should say something more but my father looks at me, a subtle shake of his head. A reminder that this is not the place.

I sense Thylas step just a half step closer to me, his fingers itching toward his sword. We don't talk about it, but I know he does not like the idea of me becoming Ereon's wife. Maybe it's his long-ago feelings he had for me, or maybe it's just loyalty to Antalis and my father. At one point in our friendship we would have already discussed this, but the last few lunar years we've grown more distant and I don't know how I feel anymore. As he grew and aged, he got more handsome and also more cold toward me. The dark times after my mother's death were when my father's reign changed the course of our lives with the decisions he made and as a result, Thylas pulled away from me.

It would be nice to have someone from Antalis in Shaston with me, but Thylas is a wild card. He's loyal to my father, to Antalis. But if he left to go to Shaston it would be an easier life to pledge his loyalty to the Shaston King instead of living as an Antalian on their sands. Thylas' fault is his loyalty, the unnecessary desire to show my father he is worthy of the home provided to him all those lunar years ago. Thylas never talks about where he is from, I don't know if he even remembers, but he's thankful for his home in Antalis nonetheless.

"You are correct, Prince Ereon. My daughter should be punished but you would be wise to remember that you are in my home and not Shaston. As such, you will keep that in mind as she is my daughter and not yet your queen." My father pushes back from the table and tosses his napkin onto the table as he ends the conversation, "I think it is time to depart." He walks away, not giving anyone a chance to have any other words. He glances at me over his shoulder. "Come daughter, for your punishment," he states, as he makes his way through the doorway, not sparing another glance back.

Sweat thickens across my brow and my hands become clammy. I've seen father's punishments but have never been on the receiving end of them – even when it was deserved. He's not dealt out the roughest of punishments in many moons. The times after my mother's death were rough and I often wondered if we would end up like Shaston, but my father was able to reign in his anger and keep Antalis a peaceful nation, as we've always been. However, he will still sentence punishments if the offense is significant. Those who rape or kill, those who deserve punishment.

As I stand up, my purple gown slightly touching the floor as I do; Ereon stands, and bows at the waist, a slight grin on his face before he gets in the last word, "Your Highness."

· · • ● ◑ ● ○ ● ◑ ● ● · ·

"You have to watch your mouth and your attitude, Carnaxa!" my father yells, as he slams the door shut behind him.

After leaving the table we walk down the long corridor to his personal chambers in complete silence. Thylas is behind me, his heavy boots thumping against the castle's marbled floor. The castle is one of Antalis' greatest treasures. It is not made of the grey, dull stone of the peoples' homes, but of white marble with gold and blue veining throughout. The ornate, floor-to-ceiling windows let the natural sea air and light in. The moon shines down on us as we walk, reflecting off the polished floors. Even so, this walk feels heavy with strong words that cannot be said because of the ears that might hear. Strands of cerulean hair tickle my pale olive skin as the ocean's breeze whips through the corridor. My father is not pleased by what transpired in the feasting hall, and I worry about what he will say as we stop in front of his door.

"Thylas, you are dismissed for the night. I will have someone else watch her. She will be ready to see you in the morning, as she will be there waiting for an escort before she leaves her chambers." My father turns to his personal guard and politely requests, "Eldoris, please stand outside. I'd like a word with my daughter before you take her back to her rooms."

Eldoris, wearing his own golden armor, stands tall and nods quietly to my father. He has been my father's personal guard for many lunar years, since he was a young man himself. His father was the guard for my grandfather as well as his paramore, and when my grandfather stepped down from the throne and walked into the sea's embrace, his guard went with him.

Thylas bows slightly. "Good evening, my king" – and then he turns to me with a weary smile on his face – "Good evening, Princess." He turns and walks down the hall. Thylas is one of the tallest in the *Ke Neye*. His shoulders are strong and broad, but I know the dark secrets held in the scars across his back. His arms bear the markings of what it takes to become a soldier of the *Ke Neye*. The tattoos are from the rankings he has gained in the *Shayi* along with his personal story. They swirl in dark ink around his arm, in a language lost to most. The tattoos detail the sacred oath one must say when joining the Antalian *Shayi*. The soldiers are the only ones in our kingdom to wear those specific tattoos, some have more than others. Oaths of marriage and words of honor are also seen marked on their skin. Thylas is still young, but I have no doubt he will have more markings as time goes on.

Father slowly opens his door and beckons me inside. His main room is dimly lit with only one burning candle near his bedside. I walk toward his window and peer out, watching as the waves come in and out. I take a deep breath and exhale slowly as the waves appear to do the same. The moon, high in the sky, has a small cloud in front of it, and I watch as it drifts across its face.

Father walks toward his table and grabs a glass and the dark liquor next to it. Pouring himself a finger and slowly brings it to his beard-covered mouth. He's aging and the stress of the future doesn't help. My mother and he tried to have another child, so I wouldn't be left alone in the world. Instead, they had me, and my mother was taken by the deluc.

"I'm sorry, Father," I say as my fingers begin to tremble as I remember how the loss of her affected him, how her passing impacted the kingdom.

He looks toward me and his eyes soften. "Don't do that. Don't act as if you're scared of me – I have not permitted floggings in several lunar years. I'm not going to harm you, I just want to remind you that you are not always in a place to be sharing your thoughts."

Father pours himself another finger of liquor, and the tension between his eyebrows relaxes just for a moment before he turns back to me.

"You know I don't want to do this, Naxa. I just don't know what else to do. Iviloan would have ... she always knew what to do. I never wanted this. You will be the sole ruler of Antalis and you have to have a powerful husband to defend it with you. We are in a time of peace right now, but the Southern Continent could decide at any time to challenge us. If I broke the agreement of your betrothal, Shaston could, within their contractual rights, declare war on us. I made a rash decision, one I must stand by now. Many of our young people have not seen battle, and the ones that have are too old to carry the burden alone. Our *Shayi Yengo* soldiers are strong for war at sea and our *Shayi Maka* soldiers are prepared for battles on land, but the Kingdom of Shaston lives in the blood of battles."

I walk toward my father and put my hand on his squeezing tightly. "I know, Father."

We've been through this same conversation many times over. He is lost, has been lost, without my mother. She was his twin drop. She was everything to him.

The years after her death were dark. He swore the rainbow surrounding the sun no longer had color because she took it all with her to *Mohasha*, our home after death. I remember the ring around the sun, illuminated by a multitude of colors, now it is a simple, bright-white ring. The color went out the day my mother died. That was the first sign something was wrong with Ashonera.

The myths have long told Antalis is special, blessed by the Goddess. She created Antalis, consisting of islands made up of concentric circles, two of water, and two of land with our castle in the middle on an island all its own. The canals open to the sea south of us, giving our ships access to the Great Sea for trade and also to let the water flow from the sea into our inlets. Before the end of magic, powerful creatures lurked beneath and were often there to help protect us. The Goddess created Antalis first before She created the rest of the world. The Goddess wanted companionship, people who would celebrate and love her, because she walked among them. She had been lonely for so long in the cosmos. She blessed the first Antalians with magic and life. A life free from ailments, and when the time of death is upon us, she gives us the gift of being called home, a sense of peace, of purpose fulfilled. We have never feared sickness of the body like those who live in other kingdoms.

If the stories are accurate, the ancient Antalians had power over water. They could create isolated rain storms, and some people could speak to the sea creatures of the Great Mother's oceans. Whispers of rare powers that could harness and manipulate ice or tame the waves of the sea are also written within legends of old.

My mother was the first Antalian to die from illness. According to the elders, when Antalians are called home, a sense of peace, and the Mother's voice whispering in your ear to 'come home' is what we have to look forward to. Those chosen to leave this realm simply walk toward the ocean's waves with a smile on their face. The deluc is what we are all afraid of now. After my mother's death, each moon, many others have come down with it as well.

The other kingdoms, on both continents, have their own myths; I never paid attention to the stories since I believed my life would forever be in Antalis. Obviously, I should have listened more to my tutor. The one thing I remember, however, is that the Goddess has always favored us.

I've asked my father multiple times why I couldn't rule alone and the answer is simple – because someone else will try to overthrow me. He's scared – all Antalians are – this is a time of the unknown. A time of change. We thought the deluc just affected my mother, until the oldest member of our kingdom became sick the next season. The deluc is gaining momentum and seems to be taking even the children. Father doesn't want me to be alone, he doesn't want the deluc to take me either and the Antalians to be left without a royal leader. If our royal line ends, our people would be left to the mercy of the Shastonians who would surely assume the throne. This is our safest option to try to keep some say in our kingdom.

"Will he punish Thylas?" I mumble, fidgeting my hands in the folds of my gauzy gown.

"No. He's in my kingdom and will obey my rules. However, whatever the problem is between you and Thylas, it needs to stop now. Did you think I didn't notice how close you once were and now you seem to be nothing but a hindrance to each other? If times were different, I would have considered a betrothal between the two of you for surely he would have asked by now. Since that is not the case, I need him to travel to Shaston with you. I need to know you will be safe. Shaston's laws and culture are not like ours,

Daughter, and you need to get ready for what will be expected of you. Your mother would have done better at preparing you."

"My mother would have taught me to be exactly what she was: strong and authoritative. Mother would have wanted me to find my twin drop, not just agree to a marriage because of your politics. Mother would have never forced me to marry ... "

He cuts me off sharply, "Your mother would have also taught you to be smart and to do what needs to be done for your kingdom and your livelihood. She would have encouraged you to marry for *my* politics, because if you don't, the rest of our people could suffer. A twin drop is not a guarantee anymore Carnaxa, you know that. We have to do what we must to survive."

I try to take a deep breath but my mouth is dry and my tongue feels heavy. I don't want to fight him, so I relent, "Yes, Father." My mother did her best to raise me to have a mind of my own, but through the years I've learned it's easiest to agree and go on. Perhaps it was the loss of my mother, perhaps it was witnessing the cruel punishment Thylas received, or maybe it's just the idea that even if I want to change things I can't. I wish I had Siphonie's resolve, she has my mother's mindset. She's strong and has no problem arguing for her beliefs, yet I will always be the one who strives to attain everyone else's approval. To keep the peace.

"Carry on to your rooms for the night, and try not to give Ereon a reason to have a problem with Thylas or you, again. You know what happens to the women of Shaston if they don't behave. I don't want that to happen to you when you leave here. Please, Carnaxa." His eyes look older than they used to. The wrinkles around his face and the worry lines surrounding his eyes are like a stab to the gut as he kisses my cheek.

···•••◗◉○◉◖•••···

A layer of sweat slicks my skin as I wake, confused and blinking, I try to find my bearings. I'm not one to usually dream, but when I do it's always nightmares. Sometimes they make sense, my mother's death and Thylas' whipping. The looks in their eyes haunts me. The look on his face as he took the pain, her eyes glossing over as death took her. Other times I dream of water and drowning or blood and war. Wars I've never seen, yet they torment me. Blood covers my hands in these terrible dreams and I scream, unable to escape them.

I slip my feet from beneath the covers as I run my hands through my matted, sleep-ridden hair. The candle has burnt out but there is still a sliver of moonlight filtering through the curtains, fighting with the rising sun. The steady wind moves the lacey curtains that separate me from my balcony. I yawn and run my hands across my face; it's much too early to be waking up.

I throw on my green silk robe that hits me at the middle of my thighs and walk toward my bookcase. Shadows dance from the slit under the door catching my attention and I stop moving. I tiptoe toward the door so that I can hopefully hear the ramblings of the guards or servants up at this hour. Guards and servants are always the best gossips. Salacious rumors surrounding the castle and the city, the comings and goings of people of note, and if you listen closely enough — you can learn about everything having to do with Antalis. The guards or those who serve in the castle often blend into the background well enough that many talk freely in front of them. The guard my father had positioned outside my door is new and young and I don't know his name but maybe he has interesting whispers to tell in the dark to whomever else may be out there.

I let my ear touch the cold door made from driftwood that's found on the shore and soften my breaths to better hear. Boots softly clack against the marbled floors approaching my door.

"I'll take it from here," Thylas says aptly. My throat suddenly goes dry at the sound of his deep voice and I lean further into the door. He was dismissed by my father, not expected to be seen until morning, a new guard sent as his replacement for the night. Why is he here now, and at this hour?

"King Clennom told me to guard Princess Carnaxa until the morning. I'll finish my shift as instructed," the guard answers apathetically. "Go enjoy the taverns, take a break with one of the *mæna*." The guard chuckles under his breath while he shuffles in his armor.

Thylas' voice takes on a more serious tone, "First, I am your superior and you will address me as such. Second, King Clennom has had me stationed as her guard for many years, he won't mind if I tell you to go. In fact, he might prefer it. Now as I stated, I'll take it from here."

I hear a quick mumble of, "Yes, Captain," as the young guard retreats. A steady shadow underneath my door lets me know Thylas is in place and won't be leaving. Thylas is the Captain of the *Ke Neye,* the soldiers responsible for guarding the royals of Antalis, Thylas is my personal guard. I breathe a sigh, I always feel safe when he's at my back, or in this case, at my door. I know he'll protect me, regardless of the coldness between us.

I step away from the door and light a small candle that sits on the edge of the desk near the door. The wax has already dripped down its holder and I make a mental note to replace the candle soon. I again walk toward the small bookcase on the opposite wall, deciding to read before attempting to sleep again. I run my fingers along the spines of the leather bound books. Volumes filled with myths, legends and history line the bookcase and I would love nothing more than to get lost in a book. I breathe out deeply knowing reading would do nothing more than keep me awake. I pass over my favorite stories and instead pick up my most boring tome, *The History of the Shaston Kingdom.* This book was given to me by a tutor so I could, at the very least, learn about the history of the kingdom I'll be residing in soon. I settle in an oversized, satin lounge chair and stretch out my legs, draping a blanket across me. I open the book and start on the first page.

"The Goddess didn't bless those of the Shaston Kingdom as she did those in the Kingdom of Antalis. The people of Shaston are cruel, warriors fashioned by blood and ..." is all I am able to read before I find sleep once again.

THREE

THYLAS

Walking down the corridor I listen as King Clennom's door shuts with Carnaxa inside. Of course he would dismiss me, still seeing me as the young boy who came to this castle many moons ago. The small boy who did everything right until one night, I didn't. One decision made for the right reason in my eyes, not in his, and I'll forever wear the scars on my back. I run my hands through my hair, gathering half of it up and tying it behind me with a leather band. I walk out through the tall castle doors, nodding to the sentries. Making my way to the small village across the bridge on the front side of the castle, the night becomes brighter from torches marking the path. The center island of Antalis is for the royal family and those who work in the castle along with the training yard and barracks for the soldiers. The middle ring is where many Antalian subjects run their businesses. The marketplace is full of shops, along with common areas for worship and festivals. From the middle ring, another bridge leads to the outermost ring that connects to the mainland of the Northern Continent. If I need to meet with a tradesperson, I go to the outer ring. Always bustling, the fishing markets, stone masons, blacksmiths, tailors and other merchants have direct access to the *Shayi Yengo* ships. The land that meets the Midaeliea Kingdom border is home to the majority of our people if they don't live in homes connected to their shops here on the ringed islands. The castle sends weekly envoys with access to healers, priestesses, scholars, and anything else that they might require so the people don't have to travel for necessities.

Carnaxa and I would often travel and explore the rings when we were children. Her father forbade her from leaving the inner island but she often ignored his commands. Even then, I knew I would forever protect her. She was the one who saved me the first night I washed ashore.

Regardless, her disregard to listen to reason is becoming overwhelmingly frustrating. The past couple of lunar years have been the worst, and now it seems more severe with the arrival of her betrothed. Disappearing from where she is supposed to be and leaving with Siphonie or sometimes by herself. This morning she said she was simply going to the gardens, so when I called for her and couldn't find her my temper flared. She *was* permitted to go to the gardens alone since it's still on castle grounds, but for obvious reasons, it is no longer allowed.

Carnaxa has always been one to push me, but this is not the time. Not with her marriage ceremony so close and not with Prince Ereon here. Ereon brought his men from the north, men who are trained and are as dangerous as anyone. Shaston still has to fight creatures at the edge of their kingdom, the frozen lands of the north. I always found it interesting how a kingdom as hot and barren as Shaston could also encompass land that is so cold. The last true battle was The Great War but that was over two hundred lunar years ago, my mother told me stories of the bloody battle. The people of that age wielded magic as well as they wielded a sword. A shiver skitters down my spine as I imagine a battle being fought in such a way.

The Shastonians care little for the small amount of strained peace we have. They would rather conquer us if they saw an ounce of weakness, which is in fact, starting to show. It was why King Clennom agreed to the betrothal of Prince Ereon and Princess Carnaxa. When Queen Iviloan died from the deluc, everything changed. Even the air felt different with the death of Queen Iviloan; I remember when she passed, the chill that seemed to sweep through the kingdom. Once sickness and disease were stories told to scare Antalian children. No longer were we the Goddess-blessed Antalis, we could succumb to sickness just as easily as any other from any of the other kingdoms.

Standing before my favorite tavern, I kick the wet sand off my boots before I open the rickety wooden door and walk in. The crowd is a light one tonight, with only a handful of patrons and a few ladies for hire. The ladies smile as I walk through the room, making sure to pull their already revealing tops a little lower. The ladies for hire are unapologetic in their sensuality, they are looked upon the same way any other woman in our kingdom is. Without judgment or condemnation. These women have chosen their work as *mæna* and are happy to give their gifts of pleasure to others. They aren't looked upon with disdain for their bodies as some women are in other kingdoms. No, these are respected women, choosing to embrace their bodies and the sensuality the Goddess bestowed upon them.

I walk toward the back table, pulling out a wooden chair. I sit down and adjust my sword to lay across my back instead of poking into my hip bone. The owner smiles at me, already bringing me a glass of my favorite ale. Chantara saunting behind him. He nods before notifying me, "She's been waiting for you ... " He sets down the foaming ale, sloshing a bit onto the table before retreating back to the bar.

Chantara comes up behind me, her brazen red hair falling in loose curls down to her hips. She rubs her chest against my back and begins kneading the knots out of my neck. Her long painted fingernails dig into the tender muscles. The same muscles that Carnaxa's constant recklessness likes to add stress to. Not to mention my constant worrying of what will happen when it's time for her to leave. I am anxious to know if she will take me with her or not, and then I worry about my place in Antalis if she doesn't. I've always been her personal guard since taking the oath. I would most likely remain Captain of the *Ke Neye*, I've earned that right. But I worry still, what will become of me, all I've ever known is protecting her.

"How are you tonight, Thy?" Chantara whispers softly into my ear. Her teeth gently tug at my earlobe. Her soft fingertips trail my collarbone as she does so.

"It's been a long day," I exhale, as I lean back into her embrace. While we take no vows of chastity as guards of Antalis, I am not one to sow my oats everywhere. Not that I am innocent, I did have a few lunar years after the flogging where I was more liberal in my sexual escapades. I would find anyone who would have me during that time. But recently, Chantara has become the one I seek in the dark of night.

"Want to talk about it?" she asks as she continues to knead her long fingers into my muscles. I don't want to talk about it, because talking only leads to me wanting things I can't have. I make the only decision that will help me forget.

"Not really." I take another gulp of ale, finishing it completely before turning to face her, and pull her down onto my lap. She giggles as she pushes her red-stained lips upon mine, her tongue dancing softly with mine. She tastes of ale and honey. She pulls away and kisses my cheek.

She runs her fingers through my hair and whispers softly, "Let's go up to the room, what I have in mind doesn't require talking." She eyes the stairs and I nod in agreement, not stopping to remove her from me. I stand up, grabbing the back of her thighs and wrap them around my waist. We haphazardly walk up the stairs to the room I know she has waiting, the door already open.

Kicking the door shut, I lay her gently down on the bed. Her small room is warm with a fire in the corner casting dancing shadows through the area. Her gauzy tan dress rides up to her waist as she scoots further back. Her skin flushes, her porcelain white skin now a rosy pink. I watch as her chest rises and falls while her dark green eyes watch me, wishing they were eyes of blue.

I quickly remove my armor and cast my linen shirt to a corner of the room. Sinking onto the feather bed between her legs, I trace the angle of her knee, down her soft thigh with my fingertips. Following the same path as my fingers, I kiss slowly toward her core as she moans softly. I grab her legs and drape them over my shoulders having her presented like a feast before me.

"Always the gentlemen, pleasuring the ladies first," she says flirtatiously. Her fingers curl into the blankets beneath her, my cock already pushing hard against the leathers of my pants. Looking up at her, I swipe my tongue against her center. A shiver runs down her body when my tongue softly flicks her clit. Her desire coats my tongue as I bury it deep in her, feeling her body erupt in goosebumps and a loud moan rushes from her lips. She pulls at the roots of my hair, and I growl against her. Using one finger, I push inside her, finding the spot I know she craves. She bucks against me, already wanting more. I use my thumb to rub against her clit, picking up the pace with my finger. As I am about to add another finger, she suddenly pushes me away, and I look up at her confused.

"What's wrong?" I push up to my knees and rub my hands along the inside of her thighs.

"Nothing," she breathes heavily. "I've thought about you all day, and I want your prick inside of me instead of just your tongue tonight."

She leans up, pulling the thread of my pants, and my length pulses forward as she pushes them down to my knees. She looks up at me with her round eyes and dark lashes before taking me into her mouth and I gasp as the warmth of it overwhelms me. She hollows her cheeks, taking me deep and I push against her.

"Wait," I tell her as she releases me, "these damn pants are in the way."

She leans back and smiles devilishly at me as I stand to take them off quickly, tossing them in the corner with my shirt. She races her nails along my chest, sending shivers down my spine.

Sitting on the edge of the bed, I motion for her to come to me. She climbs on top of me, her thighs straddling my waist. She leans on her knees as I align my cock at her entrance before I push myself up into her and bite softly on her chin as she comes down. Her dress bunches between us and I rip the bottom, getting it out of the way. She doesn't miss a thrust as she rides me, her moans mingling with the sounds of the streets below wafting through the windows.

I push up and into her faster as she digs her nails into my chest and I grasp the back of her neck and grip her hip. She bounces against me, her hair falling over her breast. I loosen the knot of her dress at her neck and it falls, her breast rubbing against my chest. Her pink nipples peak and I lean down greedily to take them into my mouth. She clenches around me and as her climax takes her, and I push deep inside her. Her walls pulse around me as I find my own release. It's in those moments, as we regain our breaths, I find myself still thinking of another, and I know I won't be waking up to Chantara tomorrow morning because I need to be somewhere else.

FOUR

CARNAXA

The book falls to the floor, the heavy thud waking me. I lazily lean down from the high-backed chair and pick it up from the floor. Just as I expected, *The History of Shaston* put me right to sleep.

I stand and stretch then walk toward my vanity and begin taming my Goddess-blessed mess of hair. The light cerulean blue strands are going in all directions, and the frizz is out of control. Only few remain who have hair the colors of the rainbow. Before the war it was common for babies to be born with all colors upon their scalp. Now, it's a rarity, something else that left this earth with magic. I grab my mother's golden brush and begin brushing from the bottom up, holding the ends in my fist, the way my mother taught me when I was a young girl. The memories of her have faded some over the years, but her lessons will always remain.

My father's eyes stare back at me, sky blue, deep-set and almond shaped. When I was younger many thought I was my father's twin but as I've aged – it's my mother's face that stares back at me. I could almost be considered her twin, even my pale ivory skin is the same shade as hers. Her pointed chin and round high cheekbones. My slender nose, which I used to hate, are all reminders of what we've lost.

After her death, we created her burial ship as we do for all those whose lives were taken instead of called by the Goddess. The ship was made from the white palms that cover the beaches nearest the sea. We decorated it with her favorite herbs and flowers. Then we let it go into the sea - carried by the current. The smell of salt and lavender swept back to us as we let her go. I watched for as long as I could, her ship becoming smaller and smaller until it was no more than a tiny speck against the light of the crescent moon above.

My father, in his grief, tried brutishly to take back his shell from her neck. It didn't make sense, but to him, he wanted to keep a piece of her. He scratched with his fingers until the tips were bloody and her chest was marred. But an oath of marriage is not meant to be broken, and nothing he did could get the shell back. I glance at the base of my own neck knowing Ereon will soon place his shell on me as well. Shastonians don't recognize the practice, but I would never allow my wedding ceremony to be without it.

Walking to the wardrobe, I choose a silken gown of gold, the sides are cut out and the skirt becomes sheer as it reaches the floor. I finish braiding my hair in twin fishtail braids and let it drape down my back, before I slip on a pair of thin sandals that tie around the ankles.

Opening my door, Thylas stands outside, leaning his back against the far wall, facing the door to my rooms. I eye the marks along his collar bone, he's been with a woman recently. Not that I'm jealous, that was never a path for us. It's still irritating that he can go and do whatever he likes, and yet now that I'm betrothed, I am supposed to be chaste till my wedding night. The only time an Antalian is supposed to be chaste, man or woman, is when they are betrothed, a tradition started from a superstition. The belief being, if you were tempted to be with someone after your betrothal, then a burdensome marriage awaited. But still, there was a time I thought maybe the ripples would happen. He could have been my twin drop but the ebb never occurred.

"Good morning, *Nohæ*." He bows slightly before putting his hand on the top of his sword, and his other hand sweeps toward the corridor.

"Good morning, Thylas." I smile and walk past him. There will be no losing him today, he's going to make sure he is stuck to me like algae on stone.

"Are you ever going to tell me what that means?" He's called me *Nohæ* since he learned the old language of Antihana, a language the *Ke Neye* use but is lost in most daily speech except for our prayers.

"Hadn't planned on it, no," I hear him chuckle under his breath. I've asked him since he began to call me by it, but he never reveals its meaning. I truly think it just means brat or pain in the ass. Burden might be the correct translation. I should go find a scholar and see if they can shine some light on the subject.

The sun is gleaming off the sea as it rises higher bringing the day with it. We walk in silence as servants shuffle down the halls, getting ready to clean our rooms. Like little doves, they flitter in and out of each room making quick work.

"I would like to venture into the markets today," I mention, glancing over my shoulder. "Does that work for you?"

"As you wish, *Nohæ*." He walks behind me, his boots thudding softly as he does. "Because why would you want to make my job easy and just go to the library or the gardens inside the castle walls, right?"

Ignoring him, I walk into the breakfast hall. The space is flooded with people grabbing food from the long golden breakfast table near the front of the room. My father isn't here, nor is Siphonie, but that's not unusual. My father usually wakes before everyone and Siphonie ... well she wakes when she wants to. *Bêlits* smile at Thylas and I watch as they try to subtly adjust their clothes or hair, blush crossing most of their faces. Thylas is not expected to have a twin drop since his blood is not Antalian but I have hope that the Goddess will bless him with one. It wasn't unheard of for those who fell in love with Antalians to be blessed as well, but now it's a rarity to find your twin drop Antalian or not.

"If you want, go ahead and sit down and I'll grab your food." Thylas motions toward the table with my friends, and I walk over. He knows what I eat, I've eaten the same thing most mornings since I was twelve. A piece of toasted bread with almond butter, a peach, and a glass of goats milk.

I sit beside some of the ladies that grew up alongside me in the castle. Marianna sits next to me. Her chocolate hair is tied up in a loose knot at the back of neck. The bright orange dress compliments her warm ivory skin and she smiles as she greets me, "Good morning, Carnaxa."

"Good morning, what are your plans for the day?" Marianna just got married last week. Her father, *Bêl* Taelic threw a wedding celebration to remember. She's one of the lucky ones who found her drop early in life. She's only eighteen but she told me when the matching flow to her ebb reverberated around her, it was like she could see their lives past, present, and future.

"Today ... " she sighs, "Fanon and I are going to survey the area that is to be ours on the outskirts of the rings. My father, you know, has an old home out there but it hasn't been used since he moved into the castle, years before I was born."

"So you won't be here anymore?" My heart breaks at the news. Besides Siphonie, Marianna is one of my closest friends.

"Oh, we will come back every so often. I just want a place that's just mine and Fanon's. I grew up in the palace and he didn't. I think I'll like the change of scenery, and maybe even enjoy some of the silence that comes with living out there. I've heard it's a great place to bring up children. Less chaos, less stress ... and with the deluc."

She pauses. Everyone always pauses when the deluc is mentioned since it was Mother who was the first to succumb. Many blame her like she was the one to irritate the Goddess soliciting a curse be brought upon her. I know that's not true. Mother was a full believer in the Goddess. She spoke of her daily, even making up stories to help me feel more connected to her. She spoke as if the Goddess was a friend of hers, and in a way she was. I believe Mother was more spiritual than some of the priests or priestesses. We, as Antalians, know there is only the Goddess, but the way Mother told the stories and sang the songs had the Goddess feeling real to me when I was a child.

"Here you are, *Nohæ.*" Thylas sits the wooden plate in front of me with exactly what I wanted. His own plate overflowing with bacon and sausage and eggs. "A man's breakfast," he used to call it when he was a kid. "I'll be over there. Do not even try to leave this hall without me."

He turns and walks off, Marianna leans in close, whispering, "Are you sure he isn't your twin drop? Or even just a special one night? That man is absolutely gorgeous."

"I'm positive. I have not experienced anything you've described and plus, he deals with me because he has to, not because he likes me."

"Right, let's pretend that he can't switch positions, or ask for a change or just work as a sentry. He still doesn't have to bring you your breakfast." She eyes the plate in front of me. My cheeks heat with embarrassment. I look around the hall and see other members of the *Ke Neye* and none of them are bringing their charges a plate, instead they are fixing their own and sitting down to eat, some with their charges, others not. Thylas is the only one who seems to serve the one he has vowed to protect, me.

"Are we going to the market today?" Siphonie asks, appearing out of nowhere. Her question draws me back from my thoughts as she plops down beside me, the ever-graceful one.

"Well good morning, Siphonie." Marianna leans forward to look down the table from me. "Long night?" She smiles, knowingly.

A telling smile breeches Siphonie's face. "It was." She winks toward us as her husband, Rhenor, walks in. His eyes drift to Siphonie and a small smile twitches the corners of his thin lips. The man isn't bad to look at. He looms over most men of the palace, his broad shoulders stretching the fabric of his stark white tunic. His light green eyes, with a hint of yellow around the pupils, have small wrinkles at the corners, evidence of the full life he has had. He is often quiet, which is funny considering Siphonie is the complete opposite. His short-trimmed hair once was red as flames but now has white streaks throughout. He keeps his body in shape with rigorous routines of habit that being a soldier requires.

"And with your husband no doubt?" I laugh at her. "That's a happy look from a man who wears a scowl resembling the face of a dead fish most of the time."

She smacks my arm lightly. "Shut it."

Marianna snickers, "Don't worry we won't tell anyone your secret, imagine the horror of someone sleeping with their husband. The people would never stop talking about it."

"I never said I didn't. I said we don't love each other, not that he's not good in the bedroom. I just prefer to have a taste of all that's out there. I'm sure he does the same." She steals a piece of bread off my plate. "So are we going to the markets today?"

"We are. Thylas will be tagging along. We got into a bit of trouble yesterday after the whole fiasco you got me into."

She runs her hand down her pale pink hair and sighs, "Oh, that's unfortunate. I didn't think you would find yourself in trouble. I didn't get you into anything." She tosses a small piece of bread in her mouth. "Plus I thought you liked the trouble with Thylas. You normally love to irritate him."

"I'd like to irritate him," Marianna chortels. "I mean … if I wasn't already married, of course."

"I'm serious. Ereon came to dinner and found out. Wanted to whip him for not being able to do his job, then when Father said that wouldn't be necessary – the Prince suggested I be punished."

The two women fall silent, eyes looking down at their food. We know that Shaston's women aren't allowed to speak their minds freely, they are controlled by their husbands or fathers. We don't know to what extent this controlment is, and it's probably something I should learn more about before leaving. Before Ereon's mother died, she was the only one who had traveled south to visit us. And even then, she remained shrouded and was only allowed to speak when the representative from Shaston allowed her. Without her husband there, she was expected to submit to the judgment of the man sent with her, regardless of her royal status. To our knowledge, no other women have made the journey.

I change the subject to break the silence asking Siphonie, "Will you be ready to go to the markets after breakfast?"

Her face flushes as I notice her attention has drifted back to Rhenor. He's looking at her in a way I can only dream a man will look at me someday. She may not be his twin drop, but he does love her. That is plain across his face.

"I think I'll stay back," she murmurs, smiling softly before looking back at me. "Rhenor did promise we weren't finished this morning and I want to make sure he is a man of his word. He looks like a man on a mission."

We all burst into laughter. This is what I'll miss the most when I leave to go to Shaston. The familiarity, the friendships, the feeling of being home.

·····●○●····

The markets on the middle ring are bursting with colors and smells. Roasted fish along with kelp that is slightly salted and turned into holders for the fish are the most fragrant. It makes my mouth water even though I'm not the slightest bit hungry. The awnings, now faded from being in the sun, were once as bright as the rainbow that once circled the sun. The canvas flaps in the soft breeze, brought in with the soothing swish of the ocean waves greeting the shore.

Thylas is a living shadow today. Walking in step with me, to what has become our normal, a lack of conversation between the two of us. He exhales deeply in annoyance every so often due to my inability to sit still or make his job easy, his eyes rarely stray from me. I curl my toes, feeling the gritty sand between them as the awkward silence between us grows.

"Princess Carnaxa, can I interest you in something new for your wardrobe?" a vendor, Ilis, asks as she sidesteps to let me see behind her. She sells the prettiest silks and dresses from the Southern Continent. Ilis' sons are known to go there to trade, and her daughter Vailles, who was a member of the *Shayi Maka* before deciding she wanted to pursue other things, helps her around the shop. The woman knows I will always purchase something when she's open, her asking is just a formality.

The sun hits the tent and casts a blue glow over everything inside as we enter. Her silks range in colors. I let my fingers graze across the fabrics, touching them and the variety of textures.

"See anything you like, *su kechni*?" Vailles stands in front of me, her round belly stretching her grey gown taut. I smile at the old term, one of the few I know of Antihana that means 'princess.'

"I see many things I like, as always." I sigh, as I let a silk fabric slide through my fingers. "How many more moon cycles until your sweet one is here?"

"About three, and it can't come fast enough. She's our third, so I know what to expect and I'm ready for it to be over."

I smile to myself, I have never met her husband or the other two children in their *Shæwi Koki*, but the way Vailles speaks, she seems happy. While some Antalians have twin drops, there are times when two people marry thinking they are, usually those in the throes of their first love, and it isn't until they meet their actual drop that the true connection happens. In this case, since *Noko Maki* already happened, they create *Shæwi Koki* or family units. It must be agreed upon and is just as lasting a pledge as a twin drop. It also seems to provide significant comfort as the elders in the *Shæwi Koki* age, always having friends and loved ones around even as the children leave the home.

"Are you so sure it's a girl?" I smile at her coyly.

"Well, no ... but the last two were and Elian has two girls as well. Our husbands feel blessed by the Goddess each time we have one. Although, our men wouldn't mind having at least one boy." She laughs and rubs her palms lovingly over her swollen abdomen, smiling down at it. She looks behind me and smiles. "You know, Captain Thylas, if you ever want a woman, Elian has a sister who would be a perfect companion. She's currently attending training for the *Shayi* and I think you would like her."

I hear him scrape his boots across the dirt, a nervous gesture he's had since we were little. "Thank you, but no. I plan to see if the Goddess will bless a foreigner with a drop instead." His eyes flutter to mine and I see the softness in them as he studies my face. Many would say that look is because he loves me, but it is one of pity, at the fact that I will never have the choice of a twin drop once I make Shaston my home.

"Well, it worked out well for me, not having my own drop. I love having our large family, I'm not sure what I would do without any of them; and should I ever find my drop, I know we will all be thrilled to let them join our *Shæwi Koki*. If you change your mind, let me know. I'm sure she would be thrilled to get to know you."

He grunts a response, "If you don't mind Princess Carnaxa, I'll wait outside for you."

I nod toward him and continue my way around the tent. My eyes focus on something I've never seen before. A white wrap in the corner of the shop and my fingers itch to touch it. The thick fur runs through my fingers and I chuckle at the rough, yet soft feeling of it. "Vailles, what is this?"

Ilis walks toward me, bringing the wrap down and placing it on my shoulders. Its golden clasps close at the base of my neck. "This is called a stole, it's a wrap worn around the shoulders." Instantly, sweat dampens my brow and the heat of it makes me uncomfortable.

"Why would anyone need such a thing? It's impractical given the temperature here."

"My sons tell me, not everywhere has such lovely weather as we do here in Antalis. They say most of Shaston is so hot water evaporates as it touches the ground, however, at the northern end of Shaston it's so cold water freezes before it makes impact with the ground."

"I vaguely remember the stories from my tutors about such. Can't even imagine it. Vailles, have you ever witnessed the land freezing over or do you still claim your mother makes up strange tales?" I smile at the old woman. She once told me, had the Goddess not blessed her with children she would have considered becoming a priestess. Ilis is known for her stories and myth retellings as much as she is for her silks. When Vailles had children of her own, she realized her mother had been twisting stories to threaten obedience when she and her siblings were younger. Had Vailles known her mother wouldn't have been able to follow-through with her creative punishments, she would've raised a lot more hell; fabricated consequences or not, her mother is a wise woman.

"She speaks the truth, I've heard talk of Shaston's extreme temperatures. I've never seen it, but ask your groom, I'm sure he has," Vailles speaks and as she does a hush goes over the tent. Another reminder that my time here, in my home, is limited.

"I am just telling you what I am told, Your Highness." She takes the stole from my shoulders and studies me before saying, "Why don't you have this?" She looks at her daughter who smiles back.

"Ilis, it's beautiful! How much is it?"

"It doesn't matter, just take it as a gift. Something this rare shouldn't be for just anyone."

"And what makes it so rare?"

"Simply because of the fur. It's said to be from one of the last *pesho* having graced Midaeliea." She runs her hand through the fur. "The *pesho* were seen, before The Great Wars, as a sign of new beginnings and luck." She shares a look with her daughter. "And I think it befits you."

"Thank you," are the only words I can come up with as Vailles removes the white fur from her mother's hands and begins wrapping the beautiful garment.

"I've watched you grow up and you will be missed when it is time for you to go. It'll be nice to know you have something from me, even when you are far away."

I simply nod, and take the bag from her. It seems that I'm not the only one who is not pleased with my upcoming nuptials. Except my father, the one who agreed to this arrangement. No. I can't dive into those thoughts, the pain. He's doing this for the betterment of our people, and I have to follow suit. To maintain the peace. It doesn't change the fact I would prefer a life living in Antalis.

Leaving the tent behind, I notice Thylas crouched just outside. His eyes squint as he looks toward the sun where a little girl has called his attention. Her pale white hair glistens. She's playing some game with him, laughing as he throws a rock into a circle trying to knock her rock out. He glances back toward me when he hears the flap of the tent open and sighs, "You win again Lauralie, as always. Now I have to go do adult things."

"You have to keep the Princess safe?" Lauralie is a social butterfly, always flitting around at the markets. Once when she was little, Thylas was in a grumpier mood than normal and she refused to accept it. She coaxed him to play with her until there was a smile on his face, it seems any time he is in the market – so is she.

"I do," he agrees and stands up, dusting the sand off his knees.

"Will you marry the Princess?" She stands, twirling her hands in her silver gown. He looks at his feet, kicking the pebbles across the sand. He glances at me, but I can't stand the look that passes through his eyes, so I look away, pretending to be eyeing literally, anything else.

"The Princess is going to marry a prince, Lauralie. Not some *na iwo* like me. You beat me four times in a row. Who would want someone so unworthy?"

Lauralie laughs, "Well have a good day, Thylas! Mother will be wanting to have lunch soon anyway."

He pats her head, ruffling her hair a bit before she takes off running home, dust clouds following in her wake. Thylas quickly turns back to me.

"I see you had a good time in Ilis' stall, found things you liked?"

"I always do. And I'm not done yet. We have a few more places to stop."

Thylas follows me all day as I shop. He makes sure I'm okay, and asks if I need food but the topic of Lauralie's question is never broached. We walk through the corridors, finally arriving back home as the sun begins to make its descent, bringing in my shopping haul when I hear my name, taking me aback.

"Princess Carnaxa." Prince Ereon stands with his shoulder against a doorframe looking at me with his deep, brown eyes. He stands just a few inches taller than Thylas, his presence towering over me. "I see that you had a good day, been shopping in the market have you?"

"Good evening, Prince Ereon. I was, and am now exhausted. How are you?" I curtsy slightly before him, the edges of my dress touching the floor as I do.

"I am doing much better now that I see you are taking your father's warnings to heart. Glad to see the Captain also doing his job."

There is a popping sound behind me and I glance back to see Thylas, with a very tight scowl across his face, his jaw must have made the sound.

"Thank you so much for your consideration of my safety, you and my father were right. The *shæmi* fish season does bring many newcomers to our shores and we can never be too careful, can we?" I reply, while smiling at him and internally rolling my eyes. I have never been scared in my own city, however, with the deluc tearing through our kingdom, it makes people think the royals are weak. We can't control the deluc, or protect the people from something we don't understand, as much as we may want to, and as much as it's expected of us. The *shæmi* fish season has always brought in newcomers, normally harmless fishermen supporting their families but this year, who knows if those who wish to take more from our kingdom have arrived? Lidiens, for many moon cycles, has been trying to send the people who have been banished from their kingdom to Antalis and father continually turns them away.

"That's so good to hear, your safety as my future queen is important to me. Alas, I didn't come here to find you today, although you are a breathtaking sight. I want to have words with your guard, if I may."

My hands become balmy as I watch the sneer that spreads across Ereon's face. Will he punish Thylas even though my father said not to? I can't let that happen.

"Anything you have to say to Thylas, I assure you I can be privy to. We prefer not to have too many secrets between us." I hope he doesn't see through the deception. Thylas keeps many secrets from me, as I do him. I don't need to know future battle plans or how the *Ke Neye* train. He doesn't need to know who I visit when he's not around.

"This may not be proper speech for your ears, Princess," Ereon counters, smirking.

I laugh under my breath, if Siphonie was also his cousin, he would realize I've been hearing 'not proper spe*ech*' since we were young, thanks to her. It's a challenge though, because if I argue with him about this, he'll wonder why I'm so close to a *Ke Neye* captain and it will make me appear even less like a future Shastonian queen. I'm supposed to be laying low, arguing with my betrothed in the corridor definitely wouldn't qualify as minding my tongue.

Thylas finally breaks the silence between us and snaps his fingers to a sentry nearest him, commanding, "Take Princess Carnaxa back to her chambers and wait for me there. I will speak to Prince Ereon and then be on my way to relieve you." He whispers something to the man who nods in response.

"Very well, I have many things I need to put away from today's trip anyway." I smile and try my best to sound carefree about the dealings of men, "I hope to see you again soon, Prince Ereon."

"Oh, I'm certain you will, Princess." He bows low as I turn and walk away from him, my neck feeling hot from the eyes I know are watching me retreat. I can only hope Thylas comes out unscathed.

I walk down the hall, fidgeting with the folds of my dress as I glance back. Thylas stands just to the side of Ereon, watching me as I go and I bite my lip. I don't like leaving them alone, but I know that Ereon won't speak until I am out of earshot. That is one thing I have learned, as charming as he may be, he doesn't see women as his equal. The months that Prince Ereon has been here should have been a time of us getting to know each other. Instead he is almost like a rumor, constantly heard of but never seen. My father says they are in meetings discussing the betrothal or Ereon is procuring men who will help accompany us to Shaston. With the creatures of the north, they lose as many people as their kingdom births in a moon cycle, each time they make the trek across the border, so I hear.

I should try to get to know him. My hope is, if I ignore my impending marriage, then the wedding won't happen. What a foolish thing to do. Perhaps I should start spending more time. As it is, we have only a few more moon cycles until our wedding.

FIVE

THYLAS

Carnaxa moves swiftly through the corridors, her eyes subtly glancing back as she does. I've known her too long to not read the subtle, anxious cues she displays as she walks. To everyone else, she's calm and collected, but I don't miss the fidgeting fingers in the folds of her dress or the biting of her lip as she leaves.

Ereon has done a great job of making his presence known in the capital without actually getting to know her. It's bothersome, why wouldn't he want to get to know his future queen? The thing is though, if Ereon wanted to hurt me it wouldn't be here, in front of witnesses in the castle.

Ereon watches Carnaxa as she walks, his eyes seemingly glued to the bottom half of her and I know what he's thinking. She has a beautifully shaped ass, heart-shaped and full. Any man, or woman for that matter, would have to be blind not to notice, and prince or not, at the end of the day Ereon is a man. From what I hear, he is a man with an over-inflated ego who likes to have multiple women around. He's constantly seen with women in the taverns, even allowing his men to enjoy the *mæna* he has paid for.

Ereon says nothing until Carnaxa is out of sight. He turns toward me with a look on his face that should be a smile, but comes off looking more like he's pained, or wants to kill me. I've seen the same face on men in both scenarios. It's probably the latter.

"I see she was not too much trouble for you today," he sneers, fixing the collar of his tunic.

"Princess Carnaxa, while a handful at times, is a pleasure to guard." I would throw myself on my sword before I let him think that I would ever betray her, or that I would let a negative word fall from my lips about her before him.

"I hear you like to visit a woman of the taverns." He leans against the wall, crossing his feet at the ankles and arms across his chest.

His remark surprises me and I have to take a moment to settle my thoughts before answering. Normally those of royal status do not concern themselves with the whereabouts of their soldiers in their off time, unless someone is interested in where the taverns are. He already knows.

"Yes, we in the *Shayi* are allowed to do what we please when we are not actively on duty."

"Good. Keep your dick there and don't get any ideas with the Princess. I have no doubt her maidenhood is not intact, as is the case for most Antalian women. You all don't believe in keeping control of your women."

I curl my fist, the sword at my side heavy on my hip. To speak of Carnaxa this way makes my blood boil and my head rages inside with thoughts that, if he wasn't a foreign royal, I would strike him down in the blink of an eye. The women here aren't controlled, especially when it comes to their bodies and their sexuality. I dart my eyes around looking to see how many others have heard his words, but besides a handmaiden brushing beside us, no one is here. Maybe he does intend to kill me. I would prefer to have our showdown now, rather than later, I think I can take him.

"I can assure you, Prince, my *dick* knows. I am, however, unsure why this is a topic of conversation between us."

"I'm a man, I see how you look at her. The negotiations with her father about who will travel with her to my kingdom as she becomes *my* queen are still underway, and I will make sure you are not a part of our return home. You will stay here, despite whatever tiny friendship you had as children, you will not cross the kingdom's boundary." He spits on my sandals as he speaks, his brown hair casting shadows over his eyes ... the same eyes that I would very much like to gouge out right now.

"I just want to make sure we understand each other man-to-man," caution lacing his tone. He pushes off the white marbled wall and walks away without waiting for my reply; his guards trail behind him.

I stretch my shoulders and roll my neck, if he doesn't want me going with Carnaxa – I will absolutely find a way to accompany her. So before going to relieve the poor soul I have watching her rooms, someone she's probably already snuck out on, I am going to go have a visit with the King.

·········●●●◑●○●◐●●●···

Walking into the throne room, I kneel at the King's feet waiting for the chance to speak. He's known me since I came to this land and once I would have considered him like a father. He and Rhenor took on that role when I came here.

The throne room is magnificent, with high ceilings and decorative, floor-to-ceiling windows that let the salty, sea breeze in. His throne is one of dark grey coral and white shells with a light coating of beeswax to make it comfortable and not rough. The King's throne is tall, towering over him as he sits, with an identical one empty on his right – that was the Queen's. The room is filled with his select members of the *Ke Neye*; they stand in armor matching mine, saying nothing. Ready to lay down their life for him at any time.

He looks down at me, a smile coming over his face.

"Tell me she hasn't run off again," King Clemmon queries, motioning for someone to grab the parchment from his hand.

"No, my king. She is safe in her room, under guard." At least I hope she is. I continue to kneel as I tell him why I'm actually here, "I wanted to inquire if you made the final decision on who would be accompanying Princess Carnaxa to Shaston. After speaking with Prince Ereon, I wanted to double-check her safety measures."

"As if I would not protect my only daughter, Thylas." He eyes me. "Do you still hold grudges of the past between us? You know I would never harm her, if I could I would find a way out of this arrangement. Even though it appears I can't, do not insult me by acting as if her safety isn't my top priority."

King Clennom has always been a strong man. The years after Queen Iviloan's death were a dark time for him, and he did many things I'm sure he regrets. My flogging is one of those regrets. I was but a young man at the time and did what I thought was necessary, however, the scars still mark my back and I'm not sure if the trust he broke can ever be fully repaired.

"It was not my intention to sound as if I doubt your concern for Princess Carnaxa, Your Highness," I quickly state and glance up to meet his gaze, one that always seems to see more than he lets on. "I am simply asking as her friend, not just her guard."

That makes him stop, a short expression that I can't recognize passes across his face before he adjusts in his throne and beckons me closer, "Come here, Thylas."

I rise slowly and walk toward the throne, separated by three marbled steps and sitting higher than the rest of the room. I walk to the first step and he ushers me even closer with a twitch of his hand. And now here I stand, but one step below the king.

Speaking quietly so the others do not hear him, "I am very old Thylas and I know many things. I am thankful for your friendship with Carnaxa, despite prior actions. However, I also see how you look at her. I worry you will forget her fate is with Ereon, and I need to know you will not do anything to damage this alliance between our kingdoms. It's barely stable and so much of the future is still unknown."

"My loyalty is to this kingdom, your majesty. I would never do anything to jeopardize my oaths, or to displease you or Antalis. I just don't want Naxa to be viewed as property by him. I don't know if I can handle watching her be abused." Her nickname slips from my lips before I can stop it and the King eyes me questionably, a small twitch at the corner of his lip showing the smile he's suppressing.

"As I said, I know many things." He runs his wrinkled hand along his jaw. He sighs, "I want to send you. I know that you will protect her. But I also need you to remind her of her place in Shaston as she was not raised in the same conservative culture as their women are. You know how different that kingdom is."

He looks around the room before sighing and turning his attention back to me. "I have an idea but I need you to make me this vow: keep her safe, but keep her on her path."

I would do anything to keep her safe, even if that means reminding her of the path she must follow. What her father says is true, Antalis' relationship is unsteady with Shaston. As the deluc cases increase throughout the kingdom, we worry about how much longer we have until it reaches epidemic proportions. If it takes hold of the *Shayi Maka* or *Yengo*, we will quickly perish. So I do the only thing I can, I bow before the King, kiss the hem of his robe, and make my oath.

"I swear to the Great Goddess above, on my sword and my life, to protect Princess Carnaxa, now and forevermore. I will defend, honor, and serve her as we travel. I will guard her in the Kingdom of Shaston as she becomes, and reigns as, their queen. I pledge to be at her side while she walks a path known only to the Goddess, and to uphold her best interests at all times, denying my own wants. If I should fail, may I never feel the Goddess' presence again." The words taste bitter coming off my tongue, because it's a half truth given to her father. The oath that will be marked on my skin with the others is one I know I'll forever upkeep. If all I can do is protect her as she walks this plan then that's what I will do. I still can't help but wonder, what if fate has another path for her, for myself, for all of us?

Six

CARNAXA

The moon rises high in the sky, and Thylas still isn't back. The guard he sent me with is still standing outside my door. I can just barely hear his breathing through the door. The guard was told it wouldn't be long and yet, here we are.

I pace back and forth across the room, fretting more than I should. Father wouldn't let anything happen to him right, not by Ereon's command. Father only punished Thylas that once, and he swore to never do it again, at least not so brutally. He once was like a father to Thy; I remember my father reading books to him in the gardens when we were young.

Ever since I saw Thylas, all those lunar years ago, he immediately became family. We were tutored together and we were friends. He would steal cheese from the kitchens for me and then we would sneak out of the castle to roam the middle ring. Even then, he had my full trust. Not only did he take cheese to keep me happy, he went with me into the dark market streets so I could explore, unencumbered. While we may not have gotten caught sneaking out, we were constantly in trouble ... Siphonie too. Her and Thylas would argue often over who was the leader of the group. Siphonie didn't always join Thylas and me on our many adventures, but when she did, she was a force to rein in.

I walk out onto my balcony, the smell of salt invading my senses as the warm breeze gently blows my hair. The sound of waves crashing against the stones at the edge of the shore below reminds me of the night I found Thylas.

· · · • ◑ ● ○ ● ◐ • • ·

Thirteen Lunar Years Ago

The pitongi birds swarm the coast, catching crustaceans as the daylight slowly starts cresting the horizon, soon they'll go back to their nests to sleep for the day. The world is starting to wake up and I walk lazily across the shore – I snuck out again, all the way to outer rings. I wanted to see the sea along the horizon as far as the eye can see. I know Father will be furious if I don't return before anyone notices. I love twilight hours best, the oranges and pinks of the day bleeding with the retreating darkness of the night.

The water comes crashing around my toes, foam slipping around them. I dig my feet into the sand letting it glide in between my toes. Looking out at the deep blue ocean, I wait, hoping to get a glimpse of any of the creatures my mother has told me about. The ones that used to live in these seas, but don't anymore. But I still have hope. I don't have long till daylight breaks so I turn back toward the castle, when the shoreline catches my eye. Something isn't right. Piles of seaweed and sticks clutter the normally pristine beach. Among the debris is a black cloth that looks unnatural against the golden sand. The cloth clings to a mass beneath it, which moves the tiniest bit, and I wonder what sea creature might be trapped underneath. Curiosity, getting the better of me, I walk slowly toward it, grabbing a big stick, just in case.

Poking at the cloth with the end of the stick, a slight moan catches my ear. Poking it again, it's definitely not a creature, but a human. Quickly, I grab the edge of the dampened blanket, revealing what's underneath. It's a boy. He's older than I am, but I don't think by much. His pale skin is soaked, and blood is dried and flaking from the matted dark hair on the back of his head.

I lean down and put my fingers in front of his nose, he's breathing. He's also shivering from being in the sea for so long. I look around, searching for anyone else, or answers about where the boy might have come from. I don't see anything- just the crabs on the beach and the birds in the sky. He's alone, and from the looks of it, not doing so well.

"Hey ... " I gently try to shake him awake and his eyes flutter open meeting mine. The deep-green orbs are like the lands of Midaeliea.

"Are you ... are you ... the Great Goddess?" he whispers hoarsely, I barely understand him. He grips the sand, his hands fisting to try to pull himself up before he collapses again, looking up at me.

I shake my head. "No ... I am Princess Carnaxa Althister of Antalis."

"Antalis? The sea kingdom?"

I nod, struggling to pull him further out of the water, he tries to help but he is weak. I continue to struggle with the dead weight of his conscious, yet limp body, before falling on my backside in the sand. "I'm going to get help, okay?" I mumble.

He nods feebly before his eyes close again from exhaustion. I don't want to leave him here, but I must go get someone who can help. I run as quickly as I can over the damp sand and return to the castle for my father and mother. They will know what to do.

· · • ◗ ● ◖ ○ ◗ ● ◖ • · ·

Present

The door opening catches my attention as Thylas stands in the doorway, frustration on his face. He looks at me and his eyes check me from head to toe as mine do the same. A simple way to see if the other is okay. Leaving the coolness from the balcony, I walk to him. He leans just inside the doorway, his hand still holding onto the doorknob.

"Princess Carnaxa, I wanted to tell you that I am back at your door should you need anything." He bows and turns as if he will walk out the door. He probably will, he never has been one who wanted to give up a lot of information. But I can't let him go, not yet.

"Thylas" – I grab his arm before he can walk further from me – "are you okay?"

His eyes dance down to where my hand is on him, and his face softens a bit. "Yes. Prince Ereon only wanted to talk about your upcoming nuptial arrangements and travel. Then I had an audience with your father. Nothing more."

He tells me one thing, but I can see the doubt playing in his eyes. "I don't believe you." I stand a bit straighter and cross my arms. "That look may work on others but I have known you for thirteen lunar years of my life. I still remember the boy who washed up from the sea and I can still see when you lie. So do us both a favor and tell me the truth. I'll stop worrying and you can stop keeping secrets."

His emerald eyes meet mine, a soft smile playing at his lips before he shakes his head. He steps inside my bedroom, closing the door before letting out a sigh and leaning against the door.

"You always were more observant than people gave you credit for. Nothing is for you to worry about, I am fine. You are fine. We were just discussing who will be a part of your entourage when you go to Shaston."

"Why did Ereon want to know about that? Isn't it my choice? I was told it would be my choice." I stand, twirling my hand in the fold of my dress. The only choice I still have to me is choosing who will come with me, would they take that from me so quickly?

"Of course, it is, *Nohæ*. Your father, however, also has a say. As to why Prince Ereon wanted to know – he was wanting to double-check on what type of supplies we will need for you and those whom you decide to bring," he explains, smirking at me. I notice his hesitancy as his foot scrapes against the floor. He's nervous, but why would he lie?

"Well, that makes sense, but I don't fully believe you. I think you're hiding something."

He runs his hand along his scruff on his jaw. "Why would I be hiding something? It was nothing, truly."

Deciding I'm not going to get any answers I continue, "So who will be accompanying me?"

"I'm not sure about all of the arrangements, but your father ... " he trails off as he looks at me, then back toward the balcony, before finishing his sentence, "he wants me to go with you. If that's agreeable to you, of course."

I sigh a breath of relief. I was on the fence about wanting Thylas to join me, but I also can't imagine him not going with me. I know he will protect me, and I will feel safer with him. Many things about Shaston are going to be new and scary, it will be nice to have someone on my side. Someone I can depend on.

"Do you want to go to Shaston?" I ask.

"I have no more choice in this than you, not really. I'm sure your father will give you the final say with regard to whom you want to accompany you, so if you choose not to bring me ..." There it is again, that look of brief sadness that flickers through his eyes. "If you choose not to bring me, I am sure you could tell him and he would oblige."

"I want you to have a choice. I want you to have something I don't have, Thylas. I want you to be able to stay in our home, find a woman and carry on in your life if that is what you choose. I don't want you to feel like you have to because of our past. I don't know why you haven't asked for a position change already."

His feet shuffle as he pushes up from the door. The space between us feels so much smaller as he steps near me. He reaches out, but quickly puts his hand back down at his side. "Why would I want that?"

"So you could be free of me, it's not like you care in the same way you did before my mother died. You signed up to be my personal guard years ago when you were young, but things change and there are many who would probably be less infuriating for you. This is your home, you shouldn't have to leave it. So I'll talk to Father if you want."

His mouth opens and shuts, reminding me of fish in the ocean. Shaking his head subtly as if deciding whether or not to say anything. He turns and pulls the door toward him. Halfway through the door he stops and glances back.

"Naxa, I don't want to be free from you. My home has never truly been Antalis. I pledged my loyalty to you, and it's you I will follow. You are my home, not the sands or seas of any kingdom." Then he walks out the door, shutting it quickly. I hear the scrapping of his boots as he stands guard at my door.

········•●○●●●•·····

Siphonie stands in a pale-blue dress against her balcony window, the sunlight illuminates her faint-pink hair and it appears to be glowing.

"Oh, Naxa ... I wish I could go with you to Shaston. I am so bored with Antalis," she laments, as she plays idly with a strand of her hair. "It would be an adventure, even if it is a bit scary."

Siphonie is the closest person I will ever have to a sister. She thrives on the unknown and I'm happy to stay with routine and tradition. She proudly wears her carnality on her sleeve and I shy away from the fact that I've not yet been with anyone.

"Ilis, from the market, said that it's so hot in Shaston that water evaporates before it touches the ground. Can you imagine? It's hot here, admittedly, but a place so hot to be without the Goddess' presence, I would happily stay in Antalis for all my life. Hopefully, find my drop and have kids. Antalis is my kingdom and home."

She laughs. "I keep thinking that maybe my drop is out there, but as time passes ... I'm still stuck in the same boring life."

"Your life isn't that boring. Rhenor accepts you for who you are. For all that you are. He waited for you to initiate anything between the two of you, even after you two were wed. He also knows what it is like to have a twin drop, if you found yours ... I know he would let you embrace it. Are you sure you aren't just denying a bond? I know he loves you. I can see it."

Like my upcoming marriage, my father also arranged Siphonie's. When her father, my Uncle Seliun, perished due to an unfortunate incident of being thrown off his horse during a festival, she was left alone. Her mother was previously killed by a jealous lover whom she rejected when she found Seliun. My aunt's murderer was caught and banished from Antalis the same year my mother died, the year my father's rule decided our fates. The year he made many decisions, for many of us, that we can't go back on now. Siphonie and Rhenor's marriage was one of those decisions.

She flicks her hair over her shoulder. "I don't think I am. Who's to say? But maybe you're right. So what else did old Illias have to say about Shaston?"

"Not much, honestly. She did mention that somewhere in the north of Shaston, it's so cold, there are ice covered mountains. How odd for a kingdom to have both – extreme cold and extreme heat."

I chuckle and roll onto my stomach, stuffing a pillow underneath my head and gazing at her. "I'll have to ask Ereon the next time I am graced with his presence, surely he'll have more details on how to survive the extremities of both. Maybe some of the stories and rumors of Shaston and the war are true."

The war is a time that isn't spoken about much anymore, the stories are conflicting and confusing. Lots of rumors have circulated since no one is alive that can tell the truth from fiction. One story will tell you the war was a fight simply because new land emerged - presently Shaston. Others say it was a war for the Goddess' heart. The Goddess' priestesses, who mostly congregate in Midaeliea where the scholars are as well, tells the story of both. The other being, the Goddess fell in love and it ended cruelly so she banished those who were against her and they were unhappy about it. From what my father told me, the stories change in the scrolls every few lunar years and the oldest ones aren't to be found anymore. Lost to time, like many moments from history.

"I have something I need to tell you, Carnaxa." The sudden change in Siphonie's tone catches me off guard, and I gaze back at her. Her face is paler than usual, she has worry lines across her face. She smiles but there is a hint of sadness behind her eyes. She fiddles with the bangles on her left arm, the clinking the only thing breaking the silence between us.

"You aren't sick right, Siph? Please, Goddess. Tell me you haven't had any symptoms of the deluc," I blurt out as I start looking at her eyes, for the circles that always form. The whites of her eyes don't show any blood streaks, the tell-tale signs that come with the deluc.

"No, no. It's not the deluc." She walks toward her bed with white silk sheets and sits beside me, the bed sinking beneath her. She grabs my hand between her own, breathing deeply before she begins, "I'm pregnant."

I sit up immediately, wrapping my arms around her in a hug so full of relief, I know she must have a hard time breathing. "Siphonie, you had me worried! That's fantastic news!" I exclaim, squeezing her tight, but she doesn't return it. Her shoulders are stooped and her bottom lip trembles as if she's holding in tears.

I sit back again, keeping my arms on her shoulders. "Why is this bad? I don't understand."

"I don't know who the father is. It could be the sailor's or Rhenor's."

Therein lies the issue. Rhenor may accept her choice of having multiple lovers, but that doesn't mean he'll accept a child, one that may not be his. This is what the tonic is for. The priestess brings it to the castle so it is readily available.

"I thought you always used the tonic to prevent pregnancy?"

"I do ... I did ... for all of them, including Rhenor. But, I might have forgotten a few times."

"So he doesn't know? How many times did you forget?"

She shakes her head and a tear slips down her cheek. "I ... I don't know. I don't feel bad for seeing others. Rhenor is fully aware that I do. He knows he wasn't my first choice, but I don't want him to hate me because this child may not be his. I don't want him to hate the child either. I just ... forgot for a month. That's all. One month."

One month, with two lovers. It could be either man's. The fisherman she was with on the docks or her husband. Children are rarely seen as anything but a blessing in Antalis, but as always, there are exceptions to the rule.

"Turn around, I'm going to braid your hair, and we'll pray to the Great Goddess." She turns and I let the strands flow in, and between, my fingers as I braid her hair that reaches past her thighs. She sings a song of prayer in the ancient language of Antihana, the language when there was but one kingdom. The language that the *Ke Neye* use to tattoo their oaths to their skin, only the highest among them actually learn from priestesses and scholars in Midaeliea. As royalty, we are required to learn the prayers and songs in the Antihana language.

The marriage she has with Rhenor is everlasting. The shells are set on each of their breastbones, at the top of their sternums, embedded and shimmering forever ... but that doesn't mean Rhenor won't hate her. He never had children with his first wife. She was haunted by the voices in her head and walked into the sea early, blessed by the Goddess even though her blood wasn't Antalian. Rhenor tells my father, as much as it pains him – he is happy to know she is with the Goddess and safe again.

Siphonie finishes the prayer we've memorized since we were children, the one for protection and strength. She turns toward me and gives a half smile.

"I feel a bit better," she sighs, "I'll tell him tonight, I promise. What better night than the Festival of *Täht* and *Mar*?" She kisses me on the cheek. "It's our favorite night of the year."

SEVEN

EREON

This kingdom is something else. It feels like my sweat is sweating. The humidity in the air is something I don't think I can handle for the rest of my life, and the stink of fish that wafts through the air, I know I can't. Antalis is a beautiful kingdom, its women even more beautiful than the land itself. Soon though, I'll be returning home. Home to my father, my one-day kingdom, and then I'll finally be back in her embrace.

The people seem alive today as they hustle and bustle around me as I make my way toward the docks. I'm still looking to hire more men to accompany us to Shaston. When the day finally came that I needed to travel to Antalis and meet my bride, I didn't waste any time gathering a small party to get me down here. The return trip, however, will need more soldiers. We will have those from Antalis, but that's not why I need more people. Most of the time I have been here I have been acquiring people for my father, and it's getting hard. Shaston's life is not for those who are weak, and admittedly, that doesn't always get the best people.

"How many men are you looking for, Prince?" the dock master asks as he sees me approaching. I've been here a few times when new crews come in. His sunburnt skin shows the signs of spending days on the water as the sun beats down on him, his missing teeth show his lack of nutrients while also on those seas.

"As many as anyone can spare and as many as will come," I respond in kind, smiling at him. The sea is truly beautiful, even I can't deny that. The waves create a song all on their own that makes even the hardest hearts want to dance. The *pitongi* birds move across the sky as the sun sends its glow across the reflective blue.

"Having a hard time finding those who want to make the trek?" He smiles smugly. He knows who I am. It's only the cutthroats, thieves, and rapists who usually choose to willingly travel to Shaston. Who would want to leave their homes for what we have to offer?

"Something like that … " I answer, tossing him a bag of silver. "If you find anyone worthy of my time and you think they can make it, send them my way, I'll be around."

"Yes, Your Highness. Tonight is the big festival, I'm sure I'll have more men coming in this afternoon who will be happy to join your caravan. Just be sure you remember who sent them your way."

Antalis and their festivals, it seems they are always having some celebration or another. It could be for their goddess, their marriage ceremonies, death rituals ... whatever it is, they have a lot.

"What is today?"

"It's the Festival of *Täht* and *Mar*," he states with a grin.

"Is that supposed to mean something to me?" I glance at the ship, about to make berth, I don't have much more time with him before he'll have to get to work.

"I guess not to a *Myesh Kechni* from Shaston, no. But you'll see why it's well attended. The celebration starts in the afternoon, the real festivities start after that. I wouldn't recommend missing it." He nods his head toward the ship. "There's my cue to leave. I'll spread the word. These people are from Lidiens; they won't care about where you're headed since I'm under orders from King Clennom to send them back to the Southern Continent – that is the last place they want to go."

I tilt my head in his direction as he walks off. This festival, I might just have to attend. See what has everyone stirred up about. I shake my head, walking away from the docks. The rumors of Shaston are going to be the death of our kingdom, although if I'm particularly honest they aren't rumors.

The heat is dry, life is hard, and more than likely people will be sent up north to the ice caps to fight monsters. The monsters that the beautiful Kingdom of Antalis doesn't have to worry about because they are safe inside their little rings of a kingdom. Safe from the life that I had to grow up with because they are *goddess blessed*. That is a luxury Shaston never had, but it doesn't matter. We don't celebrate their goddess simply because in our stories, she's the villain.

EIGHT

CARNAXA

The Festival of *Täht* and *Mar* is one of our favorite celebrations in Antalis. It always coincides with the gathering of the *shæmi* fish and is a time for us to give thanks to the Goddess. It is a time of enjoyment for all those of age. It's a time of feasting and drinking, of love and sex – a celebration of all, for all.

I gaze at my reflection in the silver-edged mirror. I have a round face, but my chin is sharp. My breasts are round and full and my hips are even more so. I'm not as thin as Siphonie, but not as robust as Illias. I'm just who I am, pieces of my mother and father and generations past coming together to create me.

The skirt of my dress is paneled with teal and gold fabric that flows all the way to the floor, with thigh-high slits. Diamond cutouts trim my waist. The strapless top has crystals of blue and white all the way around. Turning, the skirt billows around me. I love the way the fabric clings to my voluptuous hips. I waited until the last minute to pick out my outfit for tonight, but this couldn't have been more perfect. I've let my hair hang long in its wavy form, half of it tied up at the top of my head with trident pins keeping it in place. I've let thin cerulean strands frame my face.

My mother's frame, that's what I have. A body that resembles the hourglasses we have to keep track of time. A body as thick as the waves that crash the shores, but tapered at the waist. She was told she resembled the Goddess because of the few engraved images we have of the Goddess — her full hips and large breasts, as she raises her hands toward the sky above.

Siphonie knocks on my door before entering. Her salmon hair is high on top of her head and curls hang beside her ears enhancing her heart-shaped face. Her cheekbones are high, like mine, thanks to the familial genes we share. She wears a sheer dress of bright yellow, leaving little to the imagination. Her nipples have been covered with a small bra made of sea shells and a similarly-styled undergarment rests low on her hips, never one to shy away, I love her confidence. I smile at her. "You look lovely, Siph!"

"Thank you." She smiles back and twirls around, making sure to show off her whole outfit. "Are you ready to go? You look ravishing as usual ... you'll be certain to find someone tonight."

"Psh ... you know I can't."

"Says who?"

"Tradition ... " My eyebrow raises as I look at her. She knows once a person is betrothed they aren't supposed to seek out the affections of others until the ceremony is complete and both agree to the *Noko Maki*. "You know this, you were betrothed once upon a time."

"Those are details. Not to mention, that is Antalis' tradition, but Ereon isn't Antalian, maybe he does not know that tradition." She smiles surreptitiously, and I see the corners of her lips tilt up ever so slightly. She mumbles under her breath, "I'm sure Thylas would be more than happy to be yours for the night."

"Stop! He'll hear you, he's right outside and you are extremely loud. Before you get us in any trouble, let's just go." She laughs under breath and links her arm with mine. Opening the door, Thylas and Rhenor stand outside talking to one another.

Thylas stands, his broad chest stretching a silky blue shirt with flecks of gold throughout, paired with black leather pants. His boots are also black, and he stands with a look I'm unfamiliar with as his eyes dance across my body.

Tingles shoot across my skin from the places his eyes skim over slowly and I flutter with self-consciousness, something I'm not used to, placing my hands over my chest to try to hide some of the skin. It's not normal to worry about the showing of skin in Antalis, but the look in Thylas' eyes makes me feel like some prey about to be eaten. It's not a look I have seen from him ... in a very long time. He cocks a half smile before catching himself and bowing, "Good evening, *Su Kechni.*" He is certainly being formal tonight.

Rhenor also bows. He is wearing a matching set to Siphonie's yellow, bringing out the color of his eyes — even more so tonight. I look toward her with a curious expression, she catches and kisses the air toward me as though nothing is amiss.

Usually, couples wear matching colors while attending the festival, and it's that thought that makes my eyes shoot toward Thylas. His outfit coordinates with mine and as I look more closely, the seams of his shirt and leathers are gold, and the material is the same exact shade of teal as mine. His hair is pulled high on his head with a leather tie that is intertwined with strips of gold, silver and black. We look like a couple. I chose this dress two hours ago, there is no way he could have known, it must be a coincidence. Maybe his companion will be wearing the same fabric, it's not unheard of, we all find our outfits around Antalis.

Siphonie pulls me forward and out of my thoughts as we find our way toward the festival.

· · • ◑ ● ○ ● ◐ • • · ·

The lanterns are made of sea glass in different shades, casting a multicolor shadow through the streets as we walk. The moon is full and high, helping shine light on the patrons and celebrations before us. The activities are pretty mild right now since children are still awake and enjoying the festivities. Bobbing for apples, pin the fin on the fish, and a game of finding the flower are being played by children and families. As the night progresses, the activities will become more adult centered.

The vendors have many delicacies available for purchase ranging from roasted fish, lobster tails stuffed with garlic and other herbs, kabobs that have different types of meats from animals raised on land, and so much more. The kids run with their sky candy, a special sugary treat that looks like clouds. Sky candy is a favorite of mine, but I only eat the pink kind.

Dancing is in the center while families play and laugh. Those looking for entertainment tonight are already perusing others who are marked with a silver clam shell around their neck- a symbol of being open to more for the night. The necklaces can be picked up at any of the taverns, as well as ale for the night.

This is our first stop of the night, the first ale house we see. Siphonie and Rhenor smile at each other as he grabs her hand and leads her in. He pulls her into his side and kisses the top of her head.

Thylas glances at me asking, "What's going on?" It's not new information that those two aren't always super close, so I just shrug and head inside with them, Thylas following behind.

The tavern is busting with the noise of voices and laughter, ale flows freely tonight. A cloud of smoke from tobacco pipes wafts around us, the air becomes even hotter as so many bodies are pressed into each other. As we walk in, the patrons realize I just walked in, stop and bow slightly.

"Don't stop on my account, continue." I bow back toward them, respect given is respect earned.

The patrons continue back to their business and the four of us head toward the far table in the back corner. Thylas pulls a chair out for me, situated deep in the corner. He claims I'm easier to guard, only having to worry about what is in front of us not behind us. He sits beside me on my left, making the chair creak beneath him as he does. Siphonie sits on my right with Rhenor sitting across from me.

A red-haired woman, topless, except for the necklace between her breasts and the shells pasted on her nipples, immediately comes to take our order. Her sheer, red skirt drapes down her long legs ending at the silver bells wrapped around her ankles. Her eyes land on Thylas and I don't miss the way he quickly looks down, scuffling his feet as he tries to appear less than interested. It's a lie.

"Can I get you anything, Your Highness?" She smiles at me but her eyes constantly dart toward Thylas.

She's obviously a *mæna*, and it's obvious that Thylas has visited. A heat I've not felt before flares inside my chest. I know of his trysts outside his watch hours, but having a woman who he must have visited here, in my face, is something I've not knowingly experienced. I rarely feel jealous, but right now, it's as though there is a knife deep inside me, slowly twisting.

"We need some necklaces please," Siphonie interrupts my thoughts. With a quick glance toward her, Thylas adds, "And some ale."

The red-haired woman walks off quickly to gather what we requested, and I can't help but hide the smile that crosses my face as I look toward Thylas. "A friend of yours?" I tease.

"Don't" – he shakes his head – "whatever you are wanting to say … just don't."

I chuckle to myself as she returns, tossing the necklaces onto the center of the table and walking off again to fetch the ale.

Rhenor grabs a silver shell and ties the small strands holding it around Siphonie's neck before placing one on his own. Siphonie grabs one and fastens it quickly on my neck.

"You know I don't want this … stop." I start to tug the necklace off but she places her hand on mine.

"This is the last Festival of *Täht* and *Mar* before you are taken away from us, shouldn't you enjoy it?" Her eyes plead with me and the truth of her words hurts. This will be the last festival that I will be simply, Princess Carnaxa. Next year, I will be Princess Carnaxa of Antalis, the future Queen of Shaston.

I hesitate for a moment before nodding and letting the shell rest along my collarbone. The woman returns with ale for us, smiles like a fox toward Thylas, and grabs the last necklace on the table, fixing to place it around his neck when he catches her hand.

"Not tonight, Chantara," he says simply, before grabbing his ale and taking a drink, not looking at her again.

Hurt momentarily flashes across her features before she quickly nods and walks away. Chantara glances back at him, her expression full of sadness, until she looks at me. Then her facial features show nothing but fury, before she turns again, disappearing into the crowd.

"What's gotten into you?" Siphonie asks Thylas, while she moves the ale in front of her toward Rhenor. "Last year, from what I hear, you were all the women could talk about."

"And you were all the men could talk about," Thylas retorts before he mumbles to Rhenor, "Sorry. That was uncalled for."

Rhenor smiles. "The past is the past. Every day is a new chance to create something better. Now, let's not start the night off this way. Leave all the shit behind us and let's just have a good night." He takes a gulp from his ale.

Thylas follows suit and I just laugh. We may be a dysfunctional group at times but I will miss them. I will miss all of this as I look around the room. Just for tonight, I'll ignore the past and the future and focus on the present. I take a drink of the warm ale as Rhenor is already motioning for a refill.

NINE

CARNAXA

As the moon peaks high in the sky, music and laughter have carried from the taverns, outside, to the entire market. The streets are roaming with people of various states of undress. The ale is flowing like the water from our cool springs. Couplings are happening in private areas as well as on street corners.

The night started with us in the taverns and lots of awkward silences until the ale started hitting our bloodstreams. I notice a shift in the mood of our group once we've all had a couple of pints of ale. I don't miss how Siphonie hasn't touched the ale and yet subtly asks for water.

Rhenor takes a long swig of ale, a smile spreading across his face, before saying, "Princess Carnaxa! I ... or well, my wife and I, have some great news we would like to share with you." His voice is joyful, and he rubs his hand through his tangled, greying beard.

Siphonie's cheeks redden and I catch her eye. "I am going to give Rhenor an heir." She smiles a real smile that touches her eyes, an expression I haven't seen from her in a while.

Rhenor leans down and kisses her scarlet cheeks. "She sure is!"

Thylas reaches over and pats Rhenor on the shoulder and they clink cups together. "I would say congratulations Rhenor, but we know it's the women who do the work during pregnancy – while you got to have all the fun. "

We all can't help but laugh.

"I'm happy for you both." I smile up at them as they truly do look like two people perfectly happy at this moment in time. Siphonie leans in close, giving me a hug, "I'll tell you more about it later." I wink at her as she pulls away and takes a bite of a strawberry pastry that made its way to our table at some point.

Thylas, the drinks turning his normally serious expression into one full of glee and joy, places his hand on my upper thigh obviously by accident and he quickly removes it. "Let's go find you some sky candy *Nohæ,* I know it's your favorite." For a short moment, the boy I knew is behind those eyes. The boy who would always find me a block of cheese or my favorite sky candy. The boy who held me the night the world stopped.

Quickly jumping from the table, I excitedly agree, "Absolutely!"

The ale has morphed its way into our bodies now and the past few hours have been like old times. Thylas is beginning to relax, allowing himself to enjoy the ambiance, and yet still refuses to put on the clamshell necklace so that he too, can find someone to spend his night with. The four of us have our fill of sky candy, crab claws, and ale as we gather around the huge bonfire inside our sacred stone circle to wait for the ritual performed by the priestesses. The celebration will start with the first carving of a giant *shæmi* fish.

As we wait for the ceremony to begin, acolytes bring out bright blue and gold paint, passing out small bowls to the crowd. If any-thing, Antalis has plenty of traditions when it comes to tonight. But this is one of my favorites. Siphonie grabs the bronze bowl from one of the small boys' hands and I turn toward her. Every year, we paint each other. It's supposed to be done with a partner, but since we never really had them, we have always been each others.

She turns to Rhenor who smiles at her, dipping his fingers in the paint before placing them on her shoulders. I bite my bottom lip, looking around daftly. I didn't think about how her and Rhenor trying to mend things between them, would impact me.

"If I may, *Nohæ*?" Thylas grips a bronze bowl of his own be-tween his palms. "I know Siph is usually your artist, but she looks ... " – he smiles toward them as she's laughing, while Rhenor runs his hands down her thighs, leaving streaks of blue and gold as he does – "occupied."

Letting go off my lip, I smile up at him and concur, "Sure, why not?" For many reasons, I'm sure 'why not.' But what am I supposed to do? I guess I could paint myself but as the words start to take form, I feel his fingers softly brush down my arm. He swirls the colors softly down my arm, and motions for me to turn. His fingertips are searing as he passes along my shoulder blades and I notice then he is using the same placement of his own markings.

His lean fingers swirl around and a shiver slips through me as he does. He hums as his fingers trail down to my left thigh, making the same motions and my breath hitches as he brushes against the inside of my ankle. He looks up at me, beaming from ear to ear. "I think you're finished." He stands handing me the bowls.

Looking down, I notice the most beautiful design. Blue *shesæ* flowers with gold leaves are branching from one wrist to another, across my back, down my sides, all the way to my ankles. The flowers he chose are those that bloom only at night. I glance toward the shore where they grow and see the *shesæ* flowers reaching up toward the moon overhead.

"I didn't know you were such an artist, Thy," I jest.

"I am many things you may not realize" – a smile tugging at his lips – "but it's your turn. Hurry or we won't get there in time."

I let my fingers run along his corded arms, making stripes of blue before adding dots of gold. My designs aren't as impressive as his, but they'll do. He looks down admiring my work. "Well we know which one of us won't be drawing pictures in the scrolls for the scholars," he laughs, and I push at his shoulder with my palm.

"Are you two done? Rhenor said we better hurry ..." Siphonie yells at us, "He is also going to grab you both an ale before the ceremony begins so come on." She holds out her hand to me and I grasp it, before turning and grabbing Thylas' too. He delicately grips my hand as she leads us into the crowd.

Thylas stands behind me and I sway slightly with the breeze, it seems I have had enough ale. Almost tripping over my own feet, his hands grab firmly around my hips to keep me standing on my feet. He whispers into my ear, "*Nohæ* ..." – his breath tickles my ear and I laugh – "I do believe you're drunk."

I turn and swat at his arm playfully. "I am not ... just simply enjoying ..." The drums beat loudly, slow and steady, cutting off the rest of my sentence. The drums signal the priestesses who walk in their light blue gowns, short veils cover their heads, falling to their chins. They walk toward the fire in sync with the beating of the drums.

The women circle the fire and raise their hands above their heads, making the shape of a triangle with their forefingers and thumbs. The crowd quiets and squeezes together, not wanting to miss a single second.

"The Great Goddess gave us life," the matron priestess begins, only noted by the gold circlet in her hair, before she dives into the story we hear every year. "She was alone in the cosmos for many millennia before she decided she was lonely. She created us – the Antalians – people to worship her and never forget her. She walked among us, giving the rainbow around our sun its color. The rainbow was our constant reminder of her love."

I take a deep breath, the day my mother died, the rainbow disappeared. There has been much speculation about why. Are we as a people now cursed? Was my mother the harbinger of death? It certainly appears so given the deluc. I quietly take another drink of ale from my cup and Thylas rubs the lower part of my back, he knows what I'm remembering. It was a day that changed his life too.

"When the Antalians forgot their mother and instead started fighting among themselves, She created Midaeliea to give the Antalians additional company, fearing her presence alone was not enough to satisfy their need for companionship." She smiles, the love she has for Midaeliea and the Great Goddess obvious in her countenance. The priestesses train in Midaeliea, some choose to live there for the rest of their lives.

"She gave us power to avoid sickness of the body. She gave us a way to escape death by calling us home as we walk into her waters. "

The smell of sandalwood and sage filters through the crowd and I lean back further into Thylas' embrace – his smell is always intoxicating, but more so right now. His tattooed forearm curves around my waist and his thumb traces small circles on my right hip bone.

The drumbeat stops and the priestess starts again, "When the Mother watched as her creations fell in love, she became lonely again and created a man from a single drop of Her sea – and that's why we call our bonds with each other twin drops. Rarer now as the years continue, but not impossible. He and the Goddess loved each other very much until She was betrayed."

I hear Siphonie gasp, this part of the story always gets to her, since we were kids. I watch as she leans against Rhenor. He wraps his hand around her and her head rests lightly on his chest. Thylas' grip around me tightens and I let it, slipping even more into his strong chest behind me.

"The traitor was banished from Antalis, and Shaston was created, a land so hot Her seas cannot exist there, and her magic cannot be felt. Her powers, now gone from the world, as is She. But as Her chosen people, we do not forget Her. We will never forget Her. Not even with the deluc plaguing us. Not even if other kingdoms say She has abandoned us in our greatest time of need. With this *shæmi* fish, our prize of the sea, we honor Her for all that She gives us daily, we honor Her, by honoring our desires."

Two young priestesses in training, dressed in white, hand the matron a gold knife with the image of a trident on the hilt. The matron priestess walks to the fire spit, and slowly slices a piece of the *shæmi* fish and takes it to the shoreline letting it disappear in the surf before she returns.

"Let us remember the Great Goddess tonight. Be fruitful, be merry, and honor her in all acts this evening."

Applause sounds loudly around the fire as more timber is added, making it larger. The priestesses silently walk away- their job is done and the music begins. Thylas quickly releases me and I instantly miss his heat.

Thylas grabs my hand and asks, "Would you like to dance?"

"Yes, she would," Siphonie answers for me, pushing me slightly toward him.

He wraps his arm back around my waist and sparks feel as if they shoot across the path. His heavy scent of sandalwood and sage drifts through the air mingling with the smell of sweat from the others near us. The intertwining smells should be less than appetizing, but at this moment I wouldn't change anything. As we dance across the sand-covered area, his emerald eyes meet mine and a smile cuts across his face.

"What?" I find myself whispering.

"I just ..." – he sighs and pulls me closer to him, our chests melding together. "I forgot what a joy it is to be in your presence when you are this happy."

"I'm always happy."

As the music changes to something slower, he takes a hand and slowly tucks a piece of hair that's fallen in front of my face behind my ear.

"You always pretend to be. But I see you, *Nohæ*. I see the look on your face when no one else is watching, I see the want in your eyes for things you cannot have now." I have a hard time finding my words and I know my mouth is open as I just stare at him. He never misses a turn, keeping with the beat, keeping us in time with music. His eyes dart to my lips and I want to say something, anything, but his remarks remind me that he will always see me, the me I try to keep hidden. He has known me since I was a child; he knows me better than most.

"Thylas, then why be this way toward me? Why keep up your attitude toward me, keep me on a leash instead of enjoying time with me."

"It's for the best." The music stops and he lets go of me, taking a few steps back. "Let's enjoy tonight. I think I still have some more dances left with you, and I know Siphonie is expecting at least one." He nods his head toward her as she is already heading our way.

· · • • ◐ ● ○ ● ◑ • • ·

After the moon has traveled higher in the sky, many people have wandered off the streets. Including Siphonie and Rhenor, once they found another couple. Most folks went smiling back into the castle or their homes leaving very few left with Thylas and me.

The sweat drips down our faces and fallen strands of hair cling to my face as my arms wrap around Thylas' neck, his hands dancing across my body and up my back. His fingers feel like fireworks as he touches bare skin. He's not said much since our conversation earlier, and I'm too worried to say much for fear I might ruin the memory of this night. When Siphonie made me wear the necklace, I had zero intentions of finding a suitor for the night and so Thylas is a good buffer for anyone who thinks of approaching me.

The music stops and he pulls me into his chest mid-twirl, stopping me. "Want a drink?" he questions, gesturing toward the few remaining open ale houses.

"Yes, but one to go. I think I'm ready to get back to my rooms. I'll sit here and allow you the honor of getting me one."

His chuckle under his breath is genuine and gravely. I can't hold my liquor as well as some, certainly not as well as him. I watch as he walks away, seeming to sway a bit but it could just be my eyes. I sit sharply on the sand and groan as I come down a little too hard. The stars are beautiful as they twinkle in the sky, lit still by the full moon. I run my hands through the sand and let the emotions I've been keeping at bay take over me. I don't have much longer here, after the ceremony I'll be in Shaston. I won't be surrounded by the pale sand of Antalis but sand of red and orange — of Shaston. I won't have the coolness of the sea breeze kissing my cheeks but I will run from the sun's rays in fear that I'll burn.

Huffing out a breath, that is certainly not the thought I want to have tonight. Thylas is taking too long to return with my much needed libation so I look toward the direction he disappeared to and that's when I see him, a woman pressing against him.

The same woman from the tavern earlier, Chat? Chane? Chanteriea? He called her something like that. She's rubbing her bare breast across his chest as she runs her slender hand up the hem of his shirt, along the abs I know he has there. He runs his hand through her hair as she backs him up to a wall, and heat coils inside of me. Watching them is a breach of privacy but I can't force myself to look away either. He leans down to her and I wait for the meeting of their lips, but he simply whispers in her ear and walks away, removing her hand from under his shirt.

I look away as he walks toward me, appearing to have been watching something else. He hands a glass to me. "Sorry about that," he mumbles, sliding down beside me. His thigh touches mine as he sits beside me, stretching his legs out.

"About what?" I take a sip, the warm brown substance drifts down my throat with a slight burn.

"Chantara, she ..." he fumbles for words, "she is someone I see on occasion."

"Ahh, so she's the reason you didn't wear the necklace! I wondered if you had turned into a chaste man these past few years," I laugh, trying to play off the jealousy I felt just moments ago.

"No, that's not it. She's a pleasure woman, we are not pledged to each other."

"Then why didn't you wear a silver shell? I see women looking at you, you could have your pick tonight." I give him a slight jab to the ribs, a familiarity we've not had in so long coming back to us. I've missed this.

"Why did you wear one, knowing you're betrothed and yet you have not sought the attention of anyone?" He looks down at the necklace before his gaze drifts a bit lower – for too long – before slamming his stare back at me.

I grab the necklace from around my neck and break the chain before throwing it into the sea which slowly hums as the waves go in and out with the tide. "Siphonie wanted me to wear it, my last night as a single Antalian after all, my last Festival of *Täht* and *Mar*, before I go to Shaston."

"*Nohæ*, look," he interjects, pointing toward the sea, where the *taoho* are gathering. Such small, beautiful creatures that glow blue as the waves crest along the shoreline. With every passing wave, they glow brighter and brighter. Soon they'll take flight, like stars lifting from the sea.

Along the crests I can see shining lights under the waves, illuminating the dark depths. Like the rainbow that once surrounded the sun, the waves glitter with varying colors. The pink of jellyfish, yellow from the squids, purple from the small seahorses, it's breathtaking.

His eyes drift back toward the sea mesmerized by the lights, before his words, barely above a whisper, reach me.

"I can't believe this will be our last," he whispers as he pulls the leather band from his hair and lets it hang loose atop his shoulders. He runs his hands through the damp, stricken mess of hair.

My fingers itch to run through his hair and probably could have at one point. He was the first boy I found attractive when I was growing up. It was innocent then, my intentions, and yet I knew... I knew the feelings that grew in my chest for him.

We watch in comfortable silence as the ocean comes and goes. The *taoho* take flight, blanketing us with soft light. I watch as the creatures, each one no bigger than a couple grains of sand, fly around us. I lean my head on Thy's shoulder, inhaling deeply the sandalwood and sage that seems to always linger on him. He wraps his arm around my shoulders and pulls me in tight.

······●●◐●○●◐●●···

We sit on the shore a while longer before we stand and begin to walk back to my rooms in the castle. I'm exhausted from the dancing and the adrenaline I had running through my system is slowing down. Now, all I can think of is sleep.

Thylas walks me to the doorway, but when I walk in he follows behind me instead of staying outside the door as per protocol. I am sure he is exhausted and ready to hand off protection duty so he can find himself elsewhere.

"Everything okay?" I ask, turning toward him. Realizing he's but inches from my face I search his expression looking for anything. Maybe he senses danger? Surely I didn't miss a threat as we walked back.

The fight in his eyes snags on my lips and my mind registers too late what he has planned before I feel his long thick fingers wrap around the back of my neck pulling me toward him. His full lips crushing against mine, his other hand wrapping in my hair, giving me no way to escape even if I wanted to. But I don't. I kiss him back, opening my mouth slightly letting his tongue explore. I run my hands up his back, underneath the tunic, feeling the scars.

He doesn't stop for us to take a breath and I know, as soon as he does, this moment will be over. He moves his hand from my hair to the small of my back, causing my body to line up flush with his, and goosebumps pebble my flesh. His rough fingers dig into the back of my neck as if it's the only thing holding him to this world. I let my fingers drift into his inky locks like I've wished to do so many times before. Deep inside me a coil heats and I rub my thighs together, his obvious desire presses against me. I want him more than even I dare to admit, and I start to lean into him more, pulling him to me. My fingers dig into the skin of his back, I'm sure I am leaving crescent-shaped marks from my nails, but I don't care. I can let him have me here and now, and would forever be happy that he was the one I chose to be my first. But I feel his fingers loosen on the back of my neck.

As quickly as he started the kiss he pulls away, leaving me breathless. I stand motionless, unsure of what to say or do. A look of regret and sadness passes across his features as he looks down at the floor, his breath equally as labored as mine before he turns and walks toward the door. I rush to him before he can get out the door and put my hand on his shoulder stopping him, "Why?" I mutter. It's the only thing I want to know, why now?

Without turning toward me I hear his breathless tone, "Because, *Nohæ*, it's your last festival in Antalis and I would be a stupid man not to taste you at least once." And then he walks out the door, leaving me standing in an ocean of my own thoughts.

TEN

THYLAS

Standing outside Carnaxa's door, I rub my hands down my face. I shouldn't have done that. *I should not have done that!* I want to punch the wall beside me, but that would only cause alarm. I kissed her. I fucking kissed her, knowing that I shouldn't, knowing that she is betrothed, and the worst part is, she kissed me back.

I felt her hands running through my hair, the sweet taste of her mixed with ale, as her tongue explored mine. I thought she would push me away, tell me no, and then I could move on. I would respect her decision, I would leave her be and never try again. But instead I found myself ready to throw her down on her bed and see what she would feel like underneath me. I pace the hallway trying to decide when in the night I decided I was going to take my daydreams this far.

I made the decision to stay away from her years ago, it's a decision I felt fine with, until tonight. Going out of my way to request what she was wearing so we could match, making sure I didn't take a clam shell. It was all for her protection, right?

·· • • ◐ ● ○ ● ◑ • • • ··

This Morning

"What has Princess Carnaxa decided to wear?" I ask one of Carnaxa's handmaidens. I should really know her name, but I don't. Her flaxen hair is tied at the back of her neck and she smiles with brilliant, white teeth, a gap between her bottom, front two.

"She hasn't yet decided, Captain."

"When she does, let me know immediately, please."

She eyes me and her smile goes sheepish. "Are you two planning to wear matching threads?" – her eyes drop to the floor – "I'm sorry ... I shouldn't have asked that it is none of my business. I will let you know immediately."

The handmaid knows what wearing matching attire means, and while it does stand for a couple joining the celebration together, my intention is to help ensure Carnaxa handles herself as her father would want. I want to make sure the men don't see her as free game, because Siphonie will make her wear the silver shell necklace. I know she will. I vowed to her father I would keep her on the path the Goddess has planned for her. I'll do what I can tonight to keep her safe and keep my promise.

"Just let me know, thank you." I walk out quickly, not sparing a second thought.

$$\cdots\bullet\bullet\circ\bullet\circ\bullet\circ\bullet\bullet\cdots$$

Present

Everything was for Carnaxa's protection, even chaperoning her against Siphonie's carefree influence. I've been around Siphonie just as long as I have Carnaxa, I knew she would have Carnaxa wear the shell tonight. The pregnancy announcement was unexpected but I'm happy for Rhenor and Siphonie. They've been married for two lunar years now and it hasn't always been the happiest of marriages, but I know how long Rhenor has wanted a child of his own. I also know how Siphonie is at celebrations, she lives each moment to the fullest and pushes Naxa to do the same, which is both a blessing and a curse. Although tonight, even I have to admit, Siponie was different and her behaviors of the past might be changing. I garner a small smile as I think of the happiness I hope she'll find.

I knew men would know the Princess would be there tonight, hoping to catch her eye and bed her, just like they hope for every year. I have to subtly remove them from the vicinity before they can even approach. But this year was even more important, I swore an oath to her father to keep her on the right path, the one pointed right at Shaston and Ereon, and until just a few moments ago I had done exactly that! I had succeeded … until the beach.

As the night went on, Carnaxa had given into the ale's influence and wasn't entertaining the idea of trying to disappear with some lucky bastard, or bring anyone back with her to the castle. I don't know how I would have handled it if she had. Would I have wanted her to have her freedom for one night? Could I have handled seeing her with someone else? My *Nohæ*.

Naxa told me I was the first to call her by that nickname. I have always meant to tell her what it means, but as the years passed, I have come to enjoy how much not knowing the meaning irritates her. I've kept it a secret. While I was in *Shayi* training I learned the old language, the name fits her. It still does, even if she doesn't know it. It's the one thing I say so she knows I still care, I'm still here for her, even if I'm not the same person I was once.

Tonight though, something was different. Perhaps it was the ale or the realization that tonight would be our last. The dance in and of itself had been torturous, her full hips under the palms of my hands as her own fingers searched my body. Her light sky-colored hair clung to her pink pouty lips as she twirled around me, and I enjoyed every minute of watching her have her fun, especially when I saw jealousy etch across her face.

·····••◑●○●••···

Earlier That Night

Leaving her on the beach, I went to fetch ale. Probably not the best decision since we'd had more than enough, but that was the only way I could catch my breath after dancing and being so close to her.

As I walk toward the tavern, Chantara saunters up. Intoxication is plain in her eyes and she wraps her arms around me, pulling me into her.

"I thought you weren't coming back for me tonight," she coos in my ear as she turns me slowly and brushes herself against my chest. Her chest is flushed and sweaty as it glides against me. She runs her hand up my shirt and pushes me against a wall.

Looking up for a quick moment, I catch Carnaxa on the beach. Her hair blows in the wind but she's no longer looking toward the sea, she's looking at me. The look in her eyes is something I haven't seen from her, at least not so boldly. It's the look of desire and ... is that ... jealousy? I caught the same glance from her earlier in the night when Chantara tried to place the necklace around my neck, but it was so fleeting I couldn't truly decipher it.

I want to see, no ... I have to see if I'm right. Is Naxa truly jealous of my understanding with Chantara? She has never mentioned it before or shown anything but indifference, not that I've flashed my "understandings" in front of her. I run my hand into Chantara's flame-red hair and watch as Carnaxa grips the sand in her fists

tighter, her lips parting slightly. Yes, that's certainly jealousy. Lean-
ing down into Chantra's ear I whisper, "Not tonight."

She huffs and I pull her hand from my shirt, Chantara doesn't
own me like she wishes she does. She's beautiful but she knows we
aren't anything more than any of the other suitors she entertains as
a mæna. It's not her fault I'm frequenting her more often the past
few months, and maybe it's time I stop. Perhaps, I am giving her the
wrong idea.

I grab the mugs of ale as I return to Carnaxa, who's looking back
toward the crashing waves.

····•••◐●○●◑•••··

Present

Watching Carnaxa's expression at the exchange between Chantara and I had not only clouded my judgment, but fueled my
desire for Carnaxa I kept so cleverly, or so I thought, hidden. I
am her protector first and her lover, never. I found out years ago
that I could never be, because it would be her who I protect and
emotions can get in the way of my duty to her. I serve and protect
her, not the kingdom, not her father ... only her. It's always been
her.

The moment we discussed this being her last festival, something
inside me broke. That small part of myself I keep tucked away
pushed its way through. This is a celebration of everything Antalis
believes in ... and yet, next year she will be gone. She will be the

Queen of Shaston and Ereon's wife. I have remained silent, keeping my urges under control as always, until her room. I couldn't and wouldn't let her last memory of *Täht* and *Mar* be one of sadness and jealousy, no she deserves more than that.

I chose to let her last memory of the festival be of me and maybe that was wrong. I wanted to walk out of her room, maintain the normality between us, and I almost saw myself out, until I didn't. I pulled her toward me kissing her pink-tinged lips, wanting to be completely surrounded by her. She tasted of sea salt and sugar mixed with ale, the memory alone causes my cock to stir again. She would have let me go further, I wanted to. I wanted to pull her thick thighs around my waist and carry her to the bed. I wanted to see if she tastes as sweet between those thighs as her lips did. But it's easier to walk away from a kiss than be left alone as the sun rises, feeling regret. We can't be anything more than what we are, that much is truer now than it's ever been.

I rub my temples with my fingers, pressing deeply, hoping the headache forming will ease. I barely hear the rumblings from Lenion, the guard sent to relieve me of my duty, before I'm already walking down the hall. If I stand outside her door any longer I know I will change my mind and go back to finish what I started. Hopefully tomorrow, she'll wake up and forget the kiss happened, or perhaps hope it didn't, and I'll be the only one to carry the burden of what happened here tonight.

·· • ● ◑ ● ○ ● ◑ ● • ··

The sunlight starts hitting the white and gold marbled walls. I was awake before the sun rose, having barely slept. Tossing and turning all night, even after coming into my own hand as I thought of her, loving that I still bare faint evidence of her passion on my back. I noticed the marks as I took off my shirt last night, and I'll be sad when they completely fade.

I can't go back to the tavern now. I often bury my want for her inside of Chantara, but now that I've tasted her ... Now that I know what it's like to have her, even if just for a moment, nothing will ever compare.

I decide to go on a run, the only thing I know that will help me think of her less, but when I leave my rooms my thoughts are still running rampant.

A new recruit, I can't remember his name, starts up the corridor. His armor is too big for his thin body, that's how we all started, with nothing but legs and arms, but with the training, he'll bulk up. His head hangs toward the floor and I can already see the sweat glistening on his brow as he approaches ... he's nervous. I tilt my head watching him before he finally stops in front of me.

"Captain ..." he huffs out. Has he been running the whole way here? Taking a deep breath and talking way too quickly he adds, "You and Princess Carnaxa are being requested immediately in the throne room."

"Why?"

"I ... I don't know Captain, but Prince Ereon is there and I could hear him shouting from the hallway before the King called me to come to fetch you."

"Very well," I say as I pat the boy on the shoulder. "Thank you. Please tell the King we will be along shortly."

Eleven

CARNAXA

I always dreamed of waking up to Thylas. I dreamed of his moss-colored eyes and his dark-as-night, curly hair as I would lie awake at night. I never, however, dreamed of Thylas bursting through my door early in the morning demanding I hurry up and get ready to go to the throne room to see my father.

He does not give me many details, just that we were requested and Ereon is there waiting. So I guess we will just forget last night and I'll try to calm my erratically beating heart that decided to get excited when he entered, foolishly thinking he was coming to finish what we started. But, fair enough. I knew that is what he would do – become cold again, emotionally distance himself from me. I had hoped not, but what chance do we have? A captain and a princess … are there not tons of legends about such an ill-pairing finding love? Normally they end up with children running about and a home of their own, but that won't be our story. It can't be, because *my husband-to-be* is waiting for me.

It's quiet around the castle this early in the morning. The few people we meet are either soldiers protecting their charges inside the castle walls, maids scurrying to clean after the festival, or cooks preparing the morning meals.

Walking through the large, marble rounded doors, Father sits on his throne of white coral and grey shells. My mother's matching throne is beside his, empty. Her tall crown of silver and blue once resided there, but Father gave it to me last year. He said she would have wanted it to be worn, not just placed on a vacant throne. I rarely wear crowns or diadems because I find them cumbersome, but hers is one I cherish.

The high, floor-to-ceiling windows normally reflect the sun's morning rays and cast small rainbows across the room, but today the sun is covered by large grey clouds requiring torches in the throne room. Ereon is standing at the bottom of the dais, his fists curled in on his sides and his left foot tapping lightly. His guardsmen, dressed in all black, stand three steps behind him, their eyes downcast but their hands rest on their swords near their hips. No one turns to look at me which is fine, because right now I can't help but look as nervous as I feel. I breathe deeply trying to compose myself. Thylas grabs my hand so quickly and squeezes it before letting it go.

My hands feel clammy as I walk through the doorway, and Thylas takes a step back to let me lead. The lines on my father's forehead are scrunched together and his fingers are steadily rubbing at his temple. Well, he's not happy and my heart starts beating even more, now that I see the seriousness of the situation.

I stop at the bottom of the dais, not even looking toward Ereon but I can feel his stare as I approach beside him. He smells of citrus and rain as if he's freshly showered. He doesn't seem to be bothered, but of course, who would be nervous when you are the one causing the problem. I have no doubt this is something of his doing.

"Good morning, my king." I bow, and my emerald green and yellow dress touches the tops of my brown, leather sandals. It was the first one I could find this morning with Thylas rushing me. I run my hands over it trying to smooth out wrinkles from it being shoved in the armoire for too long.

"What is the meaning of the rumor I heard about you being out last night?" Ereon bellows from beside me causing me to jump, his voice louder than customary in the throne room. I straighten my shoulders and smile, turning towards him, I will not allow him to make me feel less than in my own home. I have also been made aware, time and again, there is little I can do if I am to play my part of his future wife and the future Queen of Shaston.

"Good morning, Prince Ereon." I curtsy before confirming, "Of course I was out. The whole kingdom was out. You could have joined the celebrations as well, it was a festival for all." I turn back to my father, my father is the ruler here, not him. And as of now, I don't have to answer to him. Not yet. Another reason I don't want to go through with this marriage. Ereon cracks his knuckles and Thylas moves one step toward the left, a clear barrier between Ereon and me.

My father clears his throat before chiming in, "Prince Ereon, as I have explained" – his ice-colored eyes never faltering from the intense gaze of the Prince – "last night was the Festival of *Täht* and *Mar*, a yearly celebration of the Great Goddess. I am aware you don't have this particular festival in Shaston, however, Carnaxa was accompanied by her guard, Thylas, and did nothing more than she has for her entire life last night. I have reports that she returned home alone and has been alone all night if that is your concern." He shifts in his seat, his face full of irritation until he turns to me in greeting, "Good morning, Daughter."

Before I can utter a word, Prince Ereon is speaking again, "I understand you have your traditions here in Antalis but she was seen wearing the clamshell necklace. From my understanding of *your* traditions, once betrothed an Antalian is not to wear a silver shell until after their marriage ceremony is complete. Yet, she was. Did she also whore herself out like I saw many doing in the streets? Perhaps she didn't bring him to the castle, but fucked him in the alleys."

"That is enough!" my father bellows from the throne, standing abruptly. In his younger years he was just as fierce as any warrior, today it shows. "Prince Ereon, while you are a guest in my kingdom, you will speak to both my daughter and me with respect. If you would let Carnaxa speak, I'm sure she can explain herself, as I also have assurances that she did not *whore* herself out. However, you would also be wise to remember that the women of our kingdom do not have to live up to your modest expectations, nor do we hide the fact that sex is a blessing from the Goddess, not something to be ashamed of – regardless of how it is shown."

Ereon rolls up the sleeves of his black tunic to his forearms, as if he did not just offend my father or me. He exhales loudly and turns my way in expectation, "Let's hear it then."

I look directly at my father. I twist my fingers together, fidgeting before running them along the silver and gold bangles on my wrist. They clink together softly, and I exhale trying to find my confidence so that I show no fear.

"Prince Ereon is correct, I did wear the clamshell necklace, but not because I was looking for pleasure with another." My breath hitches as I remember that I did in fact find pleasure in another last night, even if the moment was brief. Thylas' feet shuffle a hint beside me. "Your niece, *Bêlit* Siphonie, suggested I wear it since this was the last time I will attend the festival for some time, as next year I will be the future Queen of Shaston. Her husband, *Bêl* Rhenor, was also in attendance with us and can tell you I made no such actions toward finding anyone. Thylas was the one who brought me back to my rooms, alone, and the other guard on duty last night will tell you that I did not leave until this morning when summoned here."

My cheeks heat as I recall Thylas' hands around me, pulling me into him. The way his fingers explored, the way he tasted of smoke and ale. The way his tongue danced with mine.

"See, there is nothing to worry about," my father proclaims, sitting back down on his throne, tapping his fingers along the arm. "Just a young girl having fun in her kingdom for what could be the last time, she did nothing wrong."

"Be that as it may, King Clennom, I would like to propose that the marriage ceremony take place in Shaston instead of here in Antalis so these types of miscommunications can be prevented. We wouldn't want rumors of what did or did not happen here to reach Shaston and for the people of Shaston to think badly of their future queen *consort* would we?"

I take a step forward, as I try to catch my breath. What he is asking is preposterous. Not be married by a priestess in our temple? To not be surrounded by the sea and the people of my kingdom? My eyes plead with my father, he would never agree to this, he can't. That was the agreement and the agreement was to be married here, under the strawberry moon, as is the tradition.

"Prince Ereon, surely you know that it is important for those of Antalis to be married by one of our priestesses. Marrying in Shaston would break our traditions, our peoples' heart, and furthermore, the agreement made three lunar years ago."

"Actually, the contract states we will be married after I come to Antalis to retrieve her. Not that we would remain here for the ceremony. We have a priest in Shaston, we aren't heathens after all. We can be wed there, I'll even allow your shell ceremony there, our priest knows the words and we have something similar anyway. I just don't think, under good faith, I can continue worrying about the trouble Carnaxa will find herself in, here in Antalis. First, it was leaving the castle grounds without her guard, and now this. What else will she do to further embarrass herself in the people of Shaston's eyes?"

The room is silent and everyone looks to my father. Thylas' breath behind me is ragged – like he's on the verge of losing control of his anger, and he probably is. My hands are sweating and I can't speak. There is no way our customs will be disregarded just because of a simple misunderstanding, is there? My father's constant tap of his index finger against the arm of his throne is the only sound that can be heard.

"Carnaxa," my father begins and I hold my breath, "return to your rooms while Prince Ereon and I discuss this."

"But Father ..."

He looks down at the floor, instead of at me as he repeats, "Go to your rooms." His eyes dart to Thylas' in a silent command. Thylas' hand grips my elbow pulling me toward him and the door. Before I can pull my elbow out of Thylas' grip, my father subtly shakes his head no. This is not the place, not in front of Ereon. I nod towards him and maintain what composure I still have as I walk back silently.

·· • • ◑ ● ○ ● ◐ • • ··

"There is absolutely no way your father will agree to this, Naxa," Siphonie exclaims, sitting on the edge of my bed. Her skin glows from the sun's rays that are starting to leak through the sheer curtains of my room now that the clouds seem to have cleared.

"Then why did he send me away if he is going to object to a wedding in Shaston? Why couldn't I be there?" Running my hand along the railing of my balcony, the wind picks up and kisses my skin. Goosebumps flare along my arms. The *pitongi* birds soar across the bright blue sky and cry to each other in a harmony I've heard since I was a girl.

"I do not know. We are equals here alongside men, but not where Ereon is from. Maybe your father thinks he will have more pull without the presence of a woman?"

"That's idiotic." I walk back toward her and fall onto my bed, wrapping the blue silk blanket around me. "I don't want to get married in Shaston. I don't want to marry the man at all, but especially not there. Can I not have that? I don't get to choose and I have to leave everything I know ... can I not just be married in the same temple as my mother was?" Tears threaten to spill from my eyes. From the moment I was a little girl I've always envisioned being married beneath the stars and the moon at the temple where my mother and father were married. Where she went from a baker's assistant to a queen. Where the ebb of a drop ripples with the flow of another.

Siphonie wraps a hand around mine and lies down beside me. "I didn't want to marry Rhenor, but ... it seems to have worked out for the best. The Great Goddess always has a plan. I never gave Rhenor much of a chance before now, but it seems we have more in common than we expected."

Leaving my land of seas and salt for a land of sands and heat breaks my heart. I just wish things were different. I want to do right by my people of course, but I also ... I want what my mother had with my father. I want love. I want passion. I want too much. I want more than I can have. I could throw a fit, pretending to be a spoiled brat but would that help me? No, in fact it would only have Ereon and his men see me as even less than. I can only do one thing, and that is to hope my father can keep me in Antalis longer.

"Do you wanna hear about what happened before the festival?" Siphonie releases my hand and rolls onto her stomach, kicking her legs criss-crossed in the air behind her. She smiles down at me, trying to change the mood. I can't bring myself to speak just yet, still trapped in my own thoughts but I nod, thankful for the distraction.

"So I'll give you the short version. When I explained to Rhenor that I was pregnant, he was excited. I had never seen him look so ..." – she bites her bottom lip in contemplation – "full of life. He was so happy, like I was the Great Mother herself blessing him from *Mohasha*."

"And he's okay with the fact that it may not be his blood?"

"Not bothered by it one bit. He said he knew I was with others, but I was still with him, and any child born to me – he will always accept. We still aren't sure where we stand, and in fact, it's a bit odd at times not knowing how everything will play out. I can't say I am in love with him, but perhaps there is love forming. We recently discovered we both have a love for music. Did you know he can play the lute? He's quite good at it and his voice is beautiful when he sings."

Imagining Rhenor singing and playing a lute does bring a smile to my lips, not something I would have expected. Twirling a piece of hair between my fingers I look up at the inlaid ceilings, contemplating out loud, "So you won't be sleeping with others anymore? Just like that, you're okay?"

"*Mohasha,* no. I mean I don't plan to visit the sailors or soldiers anytime soon ... but Rhenor is still fine should I decide to do so. We both are. That's why last night we chose a couple together for the night. I was happy they chose us in return. We had a good night. The first night in a long time we have been more of a couple rather than two souls stuck together." She mindlessly traces the pink shell embedded in her skin, the object of their marriage.

When two people are married we have a ritual in Antalis, *Noko Maki,* the wedding and shell ceremony. The night before the two betrothed are wed, they walk with their closest companions along the shoreline looking for the perfect shell or the one that calls to them. When it's found, they take it back and carve it into the shape of a teardrop. On the day of their marriage, a priestess gathers the shells and places them at the top of their sternums and it becomes embedded in their skin. A reminder of the bonds and oaths they have placed that day, and a hope for the future ahead. An outsider would probably think inserting an object like that into one's tender flesh hurts, but the feeling is described as pleasurable as long as the other party is willing; it's one of the few tangible reminders for our people that magic once covered this kingdom.

"Naxa," Thylas' voice breaks through my thoughts. How long has he been standing there in the doorway? His eyes dart from side to side and the panic in his voice causes my heart to beat fast. His lips are moving but I can't hear him. I can already tell the news will not be what I want. I can see it in his stance, in the way he's holding his head in defeat. The way Siphonie sits up quickly and squeezes my hand even tighter, tears brimming the edges of her lashes. I sit up on the edge of my bed, trying to focus on what he's saying. But there is only a buzzing in my head, the sound of the blood rushing through my veins.

"Are you listening?" He steps toward me, putting his hand under my chin and forcing my eyes to look up at him. He bends down to one knee, his face directly in front of mine as his hand cups my cheek.

"Your father ..." His eyes glance toward the open window before he takes a deep breath, finding his words and looking back at me, licking his lips before continuing. His finger swipes back and forth across my cheek.

"Your father has decided that you will be wed in Shaston. We leave in a fortnight."

TWELVE

EREON

Carnaxa walks out of the throne room, basically stomping as she does, her round ass swaying from side to side with every step she takes. King Clennom doesn't look happy as she walks away, rubbing circles on his temples. The old king is as stubborn as my own father, my father who still refuses to step down despite his increasing age. Though they must be close in age, King Clennom has aged better than my father, who has more wrinkles and scars than anyone I've ever seen. Doesn't matter, eventually, with the joining of Carnaxa and me, both kingdoms will be mine to rule over.

"King Clennom, I will continue to insist that the marriage ceremony be in Shaston. I will not change my mind on this." I walk toward the center of the dias, now that Carnaxa is gone, I'll make my presence known, front and center. This is not a topic of debate.

"Prince Ereon, I am not trying to cause disruption with you or King Atlas. However, what happened last night was simply a misunderstanding, and it is not a reason to change the plans that have already been set. If you were worried about the affairs of my daughter, perhaps you should have made her your ally before now."

To have the wedding in Shaston has always been the plan, he just wasn't aware of it. I was dispatched with the intent to bring her there quickly one way or another. My father insisted the wedding be done on Shastonian ground, not on Antalian. Since I left Shaston, I knew this was always going to happen, I just got lucky and she actually wore the clamshell at their little festival last night, and how fun a festival it was. What an absolute stroke of fate for me. Watching her as she danced with her guard round and round, his arm over her shoulders on the beach. I know that no one was brought to her rooms from what I was told, although he spent a considerable amount of time in there. But, it's enough of an excuse. Enough to get myself and my men, the few I brought and the ones I've acquired back home. What I've done should be enough to get me back in her arms, I hope.

"I don't need Princess Carnaxa as an ally. Let's not pretend that this is something it is not. This is not a marriage of love or one of your peoples' rumors of 'twin drops.' You made the alliance and I care not for the circumstances around why you did. However, as the next king of Shaston and Antalis, I refuse to have my future queen consort be the talk of Shaston's gossip. If she is to be my wife then she is to abide by our customs and traditions – not those of Antalis."

He slams his fist down on the throne, an angry vein marking the path from ear to collar as he growls, "She is heir to Antalis, you need to remember that. She can rule here without you or your kingdom. I am under the impression she will be Queen of Antalis, an equal to you for her kingdom, not queen consort while you rule both. "

"Yes, she is heir, and as such she will be *queen consort* to both kingdoms, but I will be ruler as the rightful king. Do not forget the promises that have already been made. Oaths to upkeep. Your impression of the conversation and what is written on the scrolls are two different things. She can rule here ... without me, but for how long do you think she will last against our armies if we want to challenge her rule? When was the last time your men saw true battle? Because my men have been raised in battle, you might have us on the sea front but that wouldn't help you if we descend via land," I quip. I can't help but smirk and look him directly in the eyes. He knows of our armies. Our vast army, the *Prel*, is larger than their *Shayi*, an army mostly trained for war at sea, it's what they are surrounded by. Surely they have training on land but would it be enough, is he brave enough to find out?

Since the death of Antalis' former queen, the kingdom has been shaky as the deluc take more of their people with each passing season. Once favored and now no longer, just like the rest of us, they are no longer superior. Shaston has forever been out of favor with the Goddess, if one exists that is. Antalis craves peace within their borders, but Shaston ... Shaston was built on war and disruption and King Clennom knows this. He knows that while his fleet may be great, they have not seen real battle in some time. The Shastonians bathe in blood from early ages. Our men are always prepared for battle, since we still fight along the northern border against the monstrous creatures that lurk there. As heat melts the ice that encases them, their now rotten bodies descend upon us, never ending it appears.

Running my hands through my beard and shifting my weight from one side to the other, I watch as he tries to find a way out of this. A few small grains of sand catch my eye as I swipe them from the sleeve of my shirt, a perfect picture of someone who will not give in. His brow scrunches and he peers out the window as his hand rubs his jawline. Probably praying to his goddess for some sort of help. She hasn't been here for a while, she's not going to help you old man.

"Why is it so important that she marry in Shaston?" he sighs, and I already know I've won. He can't argue and risk the alliance, I'm sure he regrets the actions he made when he was experiencing such immense grief after the death of his queen, but oaths have been made and must be kept.

"Because, as you've mentioned, she will be their queen. We will live there, why shouldn't our life as a married couple start there? What is the purpose for your people to see her married when in fact after your death, it will be I who will rule both Antalis and Shaston? We agreed to leave your people in peace after this alliance, but do not test our limits."

He straightens in his seat. "I'll agree but only with conditions. First, she will be accompanied by Thylas. He has guarded her since she was young and I trust him fully with her safety. I also want my niece, *Bêlit* Siphonie, to act as the Antalian representative. *Bêlit* Siphonie's husband, *Bêl* Rehnor, shall accompany you to Shaston for the ceremony. They can return home when they wish as I know they will, but they are to remain as ambassadors."

Popping the knuckle of my index finger I consider his proposal. "No." He looks at me, shocked that I would dare continue to argue, but I will. My father will never allow a woman to hold any title with power, King Clennom should know this. "*Bêl* Rhenor can be ambassador, but not the *Bêlit* Siphonie. Women do not have that kind of power in Shaston. And the two *ambassadors* must stay in Shaston. We will not entertain the idea that we have to wait for their arrival each and every time to hold political meetings; if you want an ambassador, make them stay." In fact, the less native royalty in Antalis, the better. More Antalian royals in their home kingdom will perpetuate the peoples' hope that Antalis can be under its own rule again; having them in Shaston keeps them out of sight and out of mind.

King Clemmon smiles, as if remembering a joke from long past. "Well, since you refuse to let women have power and you want someone there who can be in Shaston, I propose Thylas – he can become ambassador for this kingdom at the wedding. He will remain the Antalian representative even after my death and shall be included in all meetings concerning the Kingdom of Antalis. If his death should happen before he can name a replacement or if he would like to step down from his position, it will revert back to my niece *Bêlit* Siphonie and her heirs. She and her husband, *Bêl* Rhenor, will accompany you to Shaston for the wedding ceremony with permission to leave when they wish. Thylas will remain as Carnaxa's guard and will stand as the ambassador for our kingdom as I just laid out, do you agree?"

Fuck. I should have known his next option would be that captain. I was hoping he would go for the *Bel* Rhenor, but he wants them to have the freedom to come home. The Captain will be a problem.

The Captain thinks no one notices as his eyes trail her body every time she passes by or that no one watches him as he smiles just the smallest bit when she laughs. But I do. I didn't miss the look on his face as they danced last night, the way his hands stayed barely above her ass, just enough to keep it proper. If given the chance I have no doubt he would take their relationship further. That is not my father's plan and it is certainly not mine. It is important to make sure that any child from her womb comes from me and me alone.

I roll my eyes and lick my top lip. I have to give him this, because unfortunately, he has a right to name a representative, we just hoped he wouldn't. Foolish of my father to not omit that option from the contract. If Thylas is his named ambassador I have no choice, but I might have more options when we return.

"Fine. We leave in a fortnight," I conclude, bowing slightly. I walk out of the room, my guards following behind me. The door slams shut behind me and I let out a breath. We walk quietly to our rooms and I can't help but let my mind wander. I hope that this will not infuriate my father, I did as I was told. I'm getting Carnaxa to our kingdom earlier like he wanted and the ceremony will be performed on Shaston land.

He won't like the new deal that I struck, never giving us absolute control of Antalis, but I can't help that. I just hope he takes the punishment out on me and not her. I think of her soft skin beneath my touch and the way she always has the right words. I shake my head, clearing the thoughts away, because right now I have to focus on what I was sent here to do.

THIRTEEN

CARNAXA

"Your father has decided you will wed in Shaston. We will leave in a fortnight." Thylas is on bended knee in front of me, his finger softly swiping my cheek. My heart breaks at his words and I slip off the bed and my knees collapse cracking as they hit the marbled floor. This couldn't be. Father wouldn't agree to this. He couldn't agree to this. This has to be a trick, a cruel joke made by Thylas surely. My right to choose who I marry has already been stripped of me, surely now my father wouldn't take away the ceremony too. It was one of the few things that would connect me to my mother who is no longer here.

My breath comes in rigid breaths and my hands start to shake. I can hear those around me speaking and have a faint notion that Siphonie has leaned down beside me, but I can't move. Leaning further over my knees, and placing my hands over my ears I start to rock. I try to count and focus on my senses, but all I hear is, "We leave in a fortnight." over and over in my head. I clutch at my chest. I can't breathe at all, not anymore. Trying to take short shallow breaths my head begins to feel dizzy as the room starts to shift.

Siphonie yells something, and I feel strong hands grip my shoulders, legs coming around me and pulling me into a tight broad chest. The smell of sandalwood and sage comforts me, and I know Thylas is the one holding me. His hand wraps around me, pulling me further in, and his other hand brushes the back of my head. He's whispering but the words don't make sense. The light touch of his lips tickle my ears. He holds me tightly and the words seem familiar. It's a prayer, one he learned in his training. The same one I heard the night my mother died.

"You have to breathe, Naxa. You have to breathe." He pulls away from me to grab my face and bring it to his. Only inches away, he pleads, "Look at me." I keep my eyes shut, hoping that when I open them I'll wake from this nightmare, but he tells me once again, his voice full of concern but also commanding, "Baby girl, you have to look at me."

I open my eyes to find his deep-green eyes staring back at me, his fingers run a trail softly across my cheeks that are now tear-stained.

"I swear to you, Naxa, I will not let any harm come to you. From here on out, our past is the past, I had my reasons for keeping my distance from you – but they don't matter anymore. You have me for this next adventure of your life. You have me for the rest of your life if you should allow it." My breath starts slowing down and he leans in to kiss my forehead. "I promise you, *Nohæ*, you will not be without me."

Siphonie sniffles behind me, reminding me that she is still in the room. She stands just behind us, a tear still slipping down her cheek as she looks our way. "That was beautiful, Thy ..." – she wipes the tear from her cheek – "And I hope you know that I will expect you to keep those promises. I'll be here, full of wrath, to remind you if you don't."

I expect her to say something about our intimate embrace or the words that were spoken. But she doesn't. She just looks at us smiling, before going to the balcony to give us privacy or so we don't see her cry as she is realizing what is happening.

I try to pick myself up off my knees and decide my legs still aren't ready for standing. I lean against the bottom of my bed as Thylas does the same beside me. He runs his hands through his hair and then down to his side to remove the sword poking him somewhere.

"What am I going to do?" I can't help but ask, not that he'll have any answers. He runs his fingers in circles across my back. Tingles spread through me.

"There is nothing you can do, besides try to make the best of what you can. It's all any of us can do." He kisses my hairline and I lean away from him. I can't take Thylas being so near to me, not right now. I shuffle to relax my back against the footboard of my bed, and try to calm my breathing even more.

"I don't want this," I openly admit, probably for the first time to someone other than myself.

His feet shuffle. "I don't either."

Siphonie walks back in, her face clear of tears, and sits beside us. "What else was said?"

Thylas huffs, "That you were going to be the ambassador of Antalis."

"What?" She straightens up and looks across from me, to him and exclaims, "But I'm not the heir."

"No, but apparently, since Carnaxa will be the Queen Consort. The King wanted you to act on behalf of Antalis. Prince Ereon said no, because you're a woman but... that's what he wanted."

"So who will be?" I have to know. It breaks my heart that everything I was raised for is now slipping through my fingertips. I won't be a queen. I won't even be an ambassador. I try to think of who else my father trusts, I understand his trust in Siphonie. She is full of life, and underneath all of that, she's wise. She's caring. She would have been amazing.

"Me, apparently." He looks at me and says exasperated, "I had no say in this, and it's not something I would choose. And I have the option to pass it on at any time or upon my death, it goes to you, Siphonie. I'll be happy to pass it on before then though, after things settle with Shaston." He smiles weakly. "Hey Siph, the King said you and Rhenor will be coming with us too."

"Thylas is an ambassador, Naxa is going to be a queen, and I'm getting to see a new kingdom and have a baby." Siphonie laughs, "Who would have thought, all these lunar years later we would still find ourselves sitting on the floor planning a new adventure. It seems we are all preparing for one these days."

·· • • ◐ ● ○ ● ◑ • • ··

Ten Lunar Years Ago

"That's not fair, Thylas, you always get to choose what we do, and every time it gets us in trouble," Siphonie screams at him. Why is she screaming? Probably because it wasn't her idea.

Thylas is in his fourteenth lunar year and our time with him is slipping away. Soon he will start training as a soldier and guard, and it will be just me and Siphonie to go on our adventures.

"Yes because your 'adventure' included running to the kitchens to steal extra pastries. We've already done that and this time I want to go on a real adventure," he retorts, sitting beside me on the floor with our backs against the bed. "I have to get ready to become a guard. I want to become Captain of the Ke Neye, so I need practice!"

"He's right, Siph. We've already gone on your adventure. It's Thylas' turn now."

"You always take his side, Naxa!" She sticks her tongue out at me and humphs, crossing her arms across her chest. "I'm your cousin! You are supposed to be on my side."

He smiles down at me. "But, she's my savior," – he winks at me and I feel myself blush – "that trumps cousin."

"She should have let you drown." Siphonie rolls her eyes as she submits, "Fine. We'll do your adventure. What's the plan?"

••••◦●○●◦•••

Present

Reliving that memory, we sat there for hours that day forming a plan to do whatever it was that Thylas had planned. I don't remember what it was now, but I do remember that we, as usual, did get into trouble. Thylas stood up and took most of the blame for it as always, claiming it was his right as a future guard to protect us. Those were the good times. The times before he changed and everything got so complicated.

Tonight, we sit on the floor talking about the new paths laid out in front of us, and we make a promise. One that doesn't really have to be spoken, but one we all know is there. No matter what happens, we will always be there for one another.

Thylas will be ambassador, that was the biggest shock. From an orphan found on the shores of Antalis, to the kingdom's first ambassador, I know he will do what is right for our people. But I also know he meant it when he said if Siphonie wants the title, he would hand it over.

Antalis has never needed to have an ambassador in this capacity. Not one who would essentially have rule over the kingdom no ...

not rule as Thylas pointed out, but have a say in its affairs. Someone to have a pulse on the internal and external politics surrounding not just Antalis, but Shaston and Midaeliea as well. This is the first time since the formation of Antalis that it will be ruled by a king not sitting on a throne on Antalis' soil.

·····●○●●●····

"Princess Carnaxa," the deep voice startles me. It's been three days since Thylas had to tell me the news, and I'm still mad at my father for not having the gall to deliver it himself – he's asked to speak with me but I'm not ready yet. I want to, I know my time with him is limited. I am just not ready for what he has to tell me, I still feel betrayed.

Today I thought a trip to the beach would help me escape the mental thoughts and worries dancing around in my head. But turning around I see my idea of escaping my problems here on the beach is not happening. Ereon stands just behind me, he doesn't wear the furious look he did in the throne room that day, instead he has a slight smile on his face.

"Prince Ereon," I address him as I bow slightly at the waist, refusing to take my eyes off of him. I don't trust him, and I never will, not now —now that my last dream was shattered just nights before. "What brings you to my side of the beach this afternoon?"

He runs his hand through his hair which cascades to his shoulders. His toned arms are showing through the sheer tunic of black that he wears, and those long legs shown in the loose flowing pants could easily make him a part of any woman's dream. He is a man of woman's dreams ... but my dream is a nightmare.

"I didn't know I had my own 'side of the beach' ... Forgive me for trespassing. I just happened to be walking and saw you here, alone, again. No guard today?" He falls in line with my steps as we continue walking the shoreline.

"One is not needed, as stated, this is my personal beach. Well, the palace's I guess. No one but those of the palace can find their way here. Your door should have been directly beside it when you came on the beach."

"So that's why we were asked to stay on that side of the palace," he chuckles, "to keep us from finding the secrets of this beautiful beach?"

Is this an attempt at humor? He's been here long enough to know his way around, he knows this is a private beach and there are, in fact, walls marking the boundary. He also knows that he was positioned in the guests' part of the palace, none of this is news to him. He's been here for months, what he was doing in that time I don't know – nor do I care because it did not concern me.

"I see that we are not in the spirit of laughing today, or perhaps my humor is just terrible. I could try a riddle if you prefer?"

It's then I notice a nervous gesture, he's biting his lip. His eyes can't seem to figure out if they want to look at me or if he wants to stare at the ocean.

"I'm sorry, I was just unprepared for the company. Do forgive me. I just ... well I honestly was just thinking of the journey ahead of us." My steps quicken just a bit because this is not a discussion

I want to have with him. I've not said many things to him, this shouldn't be the first conversation we have.

"That's actually why I wanted to speak to you. If you would slow down." He reaches out and places his hand on my forearm, gently pulling it toward him to halt me. "I know what is happening is not what you want. However, the people of Shaston are different. They will want to see their prince wed."

"And what of my people?" I yank my arm back from him, curling my fingers into a fist as the anger bubbling beneath the surface takes hold. "What of my people, Prince? The people who have watched me grow from birth. The people who never expected to be ruled by another, the people who didn't expect *their princess* to be taken away so suddenly. I know that many have already started preparations for the wedding that was to be here near to our seas, not on your sands."

He sighs and for a brief moment, his eyes relay a kindness I can't place.

"Your people ... will be mine as the tides turn and the moon continues its cycle. No, it won't be now or maybe not in a year ... but they will be my people as well. I don't do this to disrupt them, but it would be good if you would understand that now, because if you don't it will be harder for you when we get to Shaston. You have to embrace Shastonian laws."

I want to retort, I should respond, but before I can, I watch as his dark-brown eyes look past me and toward the waves crashing against the rocks out in the bay. He grabs me once again by the wrist this time, tight enough I can't pull it away. He looks down at me as he replies, "Let's not forget you aren't the only one in this situation who is being wed to someone they did not choose. I have no more say in this than you do."

He releases my arm and turns back toward the palace. His steps are heavy, denting the golden sand as he stomps back from where he came and I'm left with more questions than answers, pity, and anger coiling inside me. It hadn't dawned on me that I am not any more his choice than he is mine. I assumed he had chosen this, or at least is in favor of it. I look up to the moon, if he didn't ask for this what will we do with the path that fate has laid out for us?

·· • • ◐ ● ○ ● ◐ • • ··

"Did you know the King of Shaston has women used only for sex?" Siphonie leans across the table, thrusting a book in my direction. We sit in a large library that none of us have been in since we were children. Marianna is back from the trip she took with her husband, Fanon, to the kingdom's outskirts.

Marianna looks up from her own book that has her enraptured as she asks, "What are those?" She twirls her dark brown hair with her pinky as she talks.

Siphonie comes around the table as I try to figure out what she is reading, and where she is even at in the book. "Like our *mæna* women near the markets, but they are forced into sexual relations by whomever they are beholden to says."

"And who thinks they can have the rights to someone else's body?" I finally see the spot she's reading from. I take the worn, leather book from her hands and flip to the front *of The Mysteries of The Shastonian Culture.* I roll my eyes, of course, she would choose the interesting book- meanwhile, I've been stuck reading about the lineage of Ereon's line. Which reads about as exciting as it sounds.

"The Shastonians, apparently." She grabs the book back from me a little too forcefully and I gasp at the fact that one tug too much and it could rip. "Listen. '*I was shocked to find that the King of Shaston keeps a harem of females, sex prisoners, to use as he pleases. The women do not have agency over their own bodies, their lives, or even the children they birth. Females are for the pleasure of the male – be that their father, their husband, or anyone else who pays enough coin to obtain them.*'" Siphonie stops for a moment, pacing back and forth as her golden gown sashays in the silence. "Eww ... his father has dominion over them, even who they have sex with?" We all shiver at the thought.

"Does that mean that Prince Ereon will have control over you?" Marianna looks at me, sorrow filling her eyes.

"Surely it is different for the royalty there. Who would force their wives into something so ... brutish. They can't possibly expect a queen to be used that way."

"But you won't be a queen, Naxa, you'll be a queen consort," it's Marianna that lets that slip out, quiet enough as if she hoped I wouldn't hear it. But I did, and she's right. What is the status of a queen consort? And prior to that, what power will I hold as just as a princess? A foreign princess.

I clear my throat. "It doesn't matter, I am a child of the Great Goddess and she always has a plan, she will protect me." At least I hope she does, but even I'm starting to worry if she can protect me in such a land.

FOURTEEN

THYLAS

A smirk spreads across my face as my left fist connects with Rhenor's jaw. It's short-lived as a sharp pain pierces my ribs as he lowers himself and hits me there. My heartbeat thumps loudly in my ears as adrenaline pulses through me.

I lean down, narrowly missing another punch from Rhenor, as I sidestep out of the way and throw my hands up in defense again. Unfortunately for me, the man knows my routine and simply kicks his leg out, tripping me.

I fall flat on my back and suck in air, unable to find any.

"And they say I'm getting old." Rhenor sticks his hand out to help pull me up and I crouch with my hands on my knees trying to catch my breath.

"You are." I wipe the sweat from my brow.

Rhenor laughs, "But you know what they say, 'with old age comes wisdom.'"

He grabs water from his canteen and throws mine at me, I catch it mid-air. The arena is not what many would expect from a peaceful nation. It's large, towering actually. The walls reach high into the sky with the opening at the top letting in the light as the sun makes its way into the sky. It was built during the Great War, but now is only used for training in the event war is needed again. Peace doesn't just happen, it's forged through blood, and we try hard not to forget that.

"What's gotten you off your game today?" Rhenor asks as we gather our things for the day.

I side-eye him and pull my hair up to the top of my head securing it with a leather band.

"Do you really have to ask that, *oh wise one?*"

Rhenor laughs and shakes his head. "No, I guess not. Worried about the trip to Shaston? I've been there before, it's like a different world but you should be okay. Or is it your new title?"

I just roll my eyes, I didn't choose to be the ambassador. I don't want it, and would love for Siphonie to be the one to take the title. She truly would do what is best for Antalis, despite her free-willed nature. She is family and the position should be hers. "I still don't understand why he chose me."

He shrugs. "You're smart, you're young, you've been raised by him and me, so he knows you can be trusted. Plus, you're a man, that'll go a lot farther in that society than being a woman."

"Which is bullshit." We walk toward the door, kicking the sand off our boots before walking onto the cobblestones of the city roads. "How can a woman belong to a man when it is the Great Goddess who gives us all life and life comes from women? It should be Siphonie in this position. As soon as I am able, I'm giving it to her."

Rhenor wipes sweat from his brow with the back of his hand. "For now, I'm happy she isn't. Shaston really doesn't tolerate women in power. She'll be safer without the title, just like you will be safer with it. I hope you heeded my advice about learning about the culture and people before you go north. I told Siphonie the same. If we are to follow Carnaxa there for the wedding and all, I need Siphonie to know what is expected of her. I know she took the girls to the library the other day."

"So I heard. They came home speaking of sex women and how apparently the King of Shaston only ever has one heir or something." I swat at a fly buzzing near my ear, the pesky things coming out because the weather is showing signs of rain. They always seem to know the weather better than anyone else, but then again most of the animals do.

"That's not a lie. Shastonian kings only ever have one son, and the current king does have a harem of women. But all the women there have no say over their own sexual endeavors. And there is nothing the women can do about it, they aren't even allowed to leave the borders. Heads up." He tilts his head forward, and I see the reason for his pause.

Prince Ereon and two of his guards walk this way. *Kosæ*! It's too late to turn around, he's already seen us. He stands a little straighter and his eyes connect with mine. Yeah, he's definitely seen us.

"*Bêl* Rhenor, Captain ..." He stops in front of us.

We bow and I have to grind my teeth to keep from wanting to spit on his shiny, black boots in front of me. And yet here I am about to follow him across kingdoms and live in his homeland.

"What a beautiful day already, I think I will miss this land at times. *Bêl* Rhenor, will you be accompanying us?"

"Yes, Your Grace, I will. My wife, *Bêlit* Siphonie, and I will be a part of the traveling company with Princess Carnaxa. Captain Thylas, as you know, will also be attending as ambassador."

He grunts at the mention of my name. The way I wish my fist could do the talking instead. He smirks at me before acknowledging, "Oh yes, I have heard how you are the new ambassador. That's a lot of control for someone so ... inexperienced. I mean, from what I've heard you aren't even from Antalis so why is it that King Clennom feels the need to put you in such a position of power?"

Rhenor places his hand on my shoulder in solidarity. "Thylas isn't from here. Princess Carnaxa found him when he was a boy, but this is his home. He grew up in this castle, and I see him as a son and as a brother of Antalis, but most importantly someone who is as loyal to Antalis just as much as anyone born here."

Looking toward Rhenor, he knows I'm thankful for his support. Over the years I've had my fair share of bullying from others because I'm not from Antalis. I washed up on the shore like a clump of seaweed when I was only eleven, the first moment I saw my *Nohæ.*

"And where are you from?" Ereon steps toward me. "Maybe it is time that you find yourself back home, surely they miss you." His face shows his arrogance. Because of his title, he thinks he can get away with saying far more to me than I would let most men. I can't argue using my fist, so words will have to do.

"I am home. Antalis is my home. I don't remember life before washing up on the beach here, but I hope to make Shaston my home as well, hopefully I'll be just as welcomed there as I have been here."

It's the only thing I can say to remind the Prince that he won't be getting rid of me anytime soon. He stares at me and I stare right back. I am not royalty, I'm not even a *Bêl* ... but this man will not make me feel less than because of my birthplace or lack of status. My birthplace, my one secret that I've kept hidden from everyone else. The one fact of my life I claim not to remember. But I do.

I remember my mother's face, and the sound of her voice as she sang me to sleep. I remember being stripped from her arms, and the way she screamed my name as everything went black.

"Forgive me, but I must take my leave. I need to see if the dock master has found more people to join us on our return journey to Shaston. We will need them all if we are going to arrive home safely." Ereon pushes past me, his shoulder meeting mine but I don't falter and he doesn't look back.

Once he is gone, Rhenor looks at me and declares, "This is going to be such an exciting trip, stuck between two boys with egos larger than their heads."

· · • • ◐ ● ○ ● ◑ • • ·

A soft knock on my door stops me as I'm packing my belongings, what few I have anyway. The moon is already breaching the sky and I expect this to be one of the new soldiers needing directions to their charge. Opening the door, I blink at the sudden arrival of the last person I expected. Her fire-colored hair is braided and wrapped at the top of her head and she's dressed in a red dress that hangs to the floor, it's just a shade or two darker than her hair. I lean against the doorframe before she pushes her way through.

"I heard you were leaving with the Princess." Chantara walks to the center of the room before turning to me. How did she find my room? I have no clue, I've never once brought her here. I never would, because that would have blurred the lines that were so clearly and easily drawn. I shut the door behind her and take a deep breath.

"What are you doing here?"

Her eyes look down before slowly coming back up to meet mine and she breathes out, "I want to go with you."

The words hit me like a punch. "Why in *kosæ* would you want to do that? Shaston is not somewhere any woman would choose to go."

She wraps her arms around me, pulling me into her before her full lips crush mine. Her hands wrap up in my curling, inky strands as she pulls me even closer to her. I run my hands up her bare back because of the low dip in her dress, and find her shoulders before pushing her away.

"Chantara," – I step back, away from her, and watch as tears threaten to spill from her eyes – "I can't do this. I'm sorry if somehow I made you think that we were more but I have other things I have to do, other oaths to uphold. I did not intend for you to get attached to me. I thought I made my intentions and expectations clear."

"I thought ..." – she shakes her head – "I thought you were my drop." She rubs her hands up and down her arms as if she's cold.

"We both know that if I was your drop there would be no thinking about it, but I also know I am not. Not for you, not for anyone." I can't help but take a step toward her and pull her into my chest as the tears start to flow. I never wanted to hurt her, I never wanted to lead her on. But what I said is the truth, she's not my drop. I don't even know if I'll ever have one. That is for those of Antalis and I am foreign born, I am not Antalian.

"Look at me." I lift her chin up, her eyes staring into mine. "Shaston is not your future. You'll be much happier if you stay here." She looks up at me and the look on her face is crushing. "I promise. You will be safer here."

She nods her head. "I'm sorry for thinking ... I don't know ... I'm sorry for ... I'm just going to go." She turns on her heels. Her red dress has tear stains on the collar around her neck. Without looking back at me, the door slams as she leaves and I'm left in the center of my room wondering what I can do to make this better, but the answer is clear.

Let her go. If I chase her down or even if I bed her, nothing will make the pain of me leaving go away, and I don't want her to think I've changed my mind. I am leaving, I don't love her. I can't, the part of my heart that could love someone is already broken and bruised because I dared to dream.

I don't want to go to Shaston, I would never want to go there. I would live the rest of my life in Antalis if I had the choice. I remember waking up on the beach feeling as if I had found the afterlife. The feeling of peace that surrounded me was something I had never felt in all my eleven lunar years. I sigh deeply, slowly reminding myself this land isn't my home. My home isn't a place like everyone else's, but a feeling. It's the same feeling I had when the girl with the ocean-colored hair and eyes found me. The feeling I have every time she is around, even though she'll never be mine.

I run my hand through my hair and already know tonight will be a night where I drink myself to sleep and find myself fucking my hand to thoughts of things that can never be, and the memory of the night I had her in my arms.

FIFTEEN

CARNAXA

"Princess Carnaxa, do you have everything you need?" Mira, one of my handmaidens asks me as she enters my room. Her weathered hands softly land on my shoulders as she leans in to kiss my cheek. I've packed the trunks and collected my things, so I smile at her trying hard to keep the tears from escaping.

"Very well then Princess, I'll leave you to say goodbye. I'll meet you when it's time to leave."

She leaves, quiet as a mouse. The excitement of the festival just two short weeks ago has faded as the kingdom has returned to its dread-filled state. My people know I am leaving. Will I return? That's still a hope I hold dear to my heart, that one day I will return.

Combining two kingdoms in such a way is something that has never been done. The world, according to myths, started with only Antalis, then the Goddess created Midaeliea, followed by the nightmare of Shaston. The stories surrounding the beginning of the Southern Continent are confusing from what I remember; the continent, seeming to have appeared overnight at some point during the Great War.

I take in my room one last time, now looking foreign with the lack of my belongings. The room where my mother tucked me in at night and weaved intricate and beautiful stories of the Goddess, the room where I had so many memories with Siphonie, Marianna, and Thylas, now bare. It is the room where I've cried because my mother was gone, laughed so hard my ribs hurt with Siphonie, and woke from nightmares to find myself safe.

There is a soft knock at my door before Thylas slips in. His dark hair is tied low at the nape of his neck, and his armor shines to perfection. His face is grave as he steps into the room. "Are you ready?"

His emerald eyes peer into mine, not flinching, not looking away. And I shake my head, tears begging to be let free. He quickly shuts the door and comes to me, wrapping his arms around me and holds me against his chest.

"There is nothing to fear, *Nohæ*. I will be there the whole time. So will Siph and Rhenor. Just like I promised you, I will never let anything happen to you." His lips graze the top of my head. "Plus, I have something for you in the hopes you'll feel safer."

He lets go of me and I instantly miss the feel of his heat surrounding me. He pulls out a brown cloth from behind his back. Pulling the cloth apart lies a small, silver dagger, just a bit longer than my hand. It glints in the sunlight shining through the windows. The jewel at the top of the pommel catches my eye. The blue stone has lines of silver webbing across its surface, reminding me of the ocean waves cresting. Reaching out hesitantly, I trace the fuller, the deep groove that runs down the flat side of the blade, and breath deeply.

"Where ... where did you get this? It's beautiful," my voice quivers, my body still fighting all the emotions I'm feeling right now.

He lifts it carefully by the tip, pointing to the stone as he expounds, "This piece, I discovered the night you found me. I don't remember much." He looks away, licking his lips before returning his eyes to me. "But I remember, before exhaustion took me, I pulled myself up just barely on the shore, and I felt this stone. It was the first thing that made me realize I was truly on dry land. I held on to it. I don't know why, not really, but I suppose it reminded me that even though all seems lost it's not."

He flips it over, catching the grip in his palm. "The dagger, well I just thought you might like one. So I had it made for you. Seems appropriate you have a way to keep yourself safe, in the event I'm not around. There is always a shark in the waters even if it can't be seen. I want you to be the shark."

"It's ... thank you." Taking the dagger from him, it hits me that this might be the last time I know true safety. I grab the dagger and place it delicately in my trunks.

He comes up behind me, his voice a sea of calm, "It's time to go, Naxa."

Turning toward him, I can only shake my head as the tears that wanted to be free escape down my cheeks. His hand presses to the back of my head. His scent of sage and sandalwood rushes over me and I want to stay here. Just like this. What could have happened in a perfect world? A world like my mother had, a world where I was free to choose. My mother was nothing more than a baker's assistant before my father found her. But they had freedom back then, to be able to choose.

He grasps my chin and turns my face to look up at him, his thumb wiping away the tears. His breath dances across my lips and I slowly stand on my toes, wanting the fireworks I felt the other night to come back for just a moment, wanting to forget what's ahead of me.

"We can't do this, baby girl. Not now." His eyes search mine and it's as if all time stops. I push myself forward letting my lips take over where words can't. In this moment, I don't care what is right or what is wrong. I want the last memory of this room to be positive, to be breathtaking, to be overwhelming.

His hands find their way around my waist as he pulls me in closer, his teeth nipping at my bottom lip and I can't help the soft moan that escapes. I run my hands up his back, the cold of his armor beneath my fingers. He pulls back, out of breath and utters, "Naxa, we can't do this … we have to go."

I shake my head, tears still falling down my cheeks. "I don't know if I can."

"You can, I know you can. But we can't do this." He kisses my forehead. "If we are caught, *Nohæ* they will kill me. Would be within their right to kill you, especially once we leave your father's kingdom. I won't let that happen to you because of me." He steps back, adjusting his armor and sword at his side. I know he is right, I am not his betrothed. I am not his woman. I am Ereon's and if he was to find out … I can't help but shudder at the thought of what would happen to Thylas.

"Okay, give me just a moment." He wipes the tears from my cheek with his thumb. He hesitates, but takes a step back and then walks out the door, waiting for me on the other side.

I take one last look around my room, my home, and what I can see of my kingdom before I walk out the door closing this chapter of my life behind me.

•••••◐●○●◑●••••

Siphonie, Rhenor, and Mira wait next to the carriage, at the bottom of the steps leading out of the castle, that will be my home for the next several moons before we reach the Doorway of Aka. The doorway is how many priestesses and scholars travel to Midaeliea. The total trip would take half a moon's cycle but with the doorway, it's simply a few steps.

Thylas stands behind me as we walk through the large marbled doors. Ereon stands beside my father at the top of the stairs. This is it, this is the time to say goodbye. My father looks at me as my hands begin to shake. I can feel the hives already making their way up my chest as I try to remember my breathing and keep myself from breaking again.

"Daughter" – Father walks up to me, wrapping me in his arms and holding on for longer than normal, – "I know this isn't what you wanted, but I am proud of you."

I lean back and he keeps my hand in his; I realize this could be the last time I ever see my own father. I make a mental image of him as he looks now, his wrinkles and white hair, his kind eyes, and the way he doesn't stand as tall as he once did. I want to remember everything.

"Always remember that your mother is still in your heart. She never walked into the Goddess' embrace, so I truly think she still lives among us. She would be proud of you too."

I kiss his cheek. "I love you."

"I love you too."

He grips my hand as he looks to Ereon who stands in his Shastonian gear of his kingdom's colors, black and silver predominantly displayed. He wears his hair down, it lightly blows in the wind. His double, crescent moon-shaped blades are attached to his back. He runs his hand down his freshly trimmed beard before reaching out to me. I take his hand, unnerved at the coolness I feel.

"Today we start our new life, Princess Carnaxa." He nods toward my father and we walk toward the blue and gold carriage with the Antalian sigil engraved on the side. The crescent moon holding a trident above. The moon represents the Great Goddess and my family's symbol is the trident. It's a reminder that She will always protect us. I take a deep breath and lift my gown so I can step into the carriage. Ereon kisses my hand and my eyes immediately dart to Thylas who now stands beside Siphonie and Rhenor. He shuffles his feet and I can feel the heat from his glare on where Ereon's lips lingered. Siphonie catches my gaze and subtly tilts her head toward the carriage and softly nudges Thylas to call his attention to hers. Ereon breaks away and opens the door, helping me inside.

I slide onto the silk seat and scoot all the way to the other side, waiting for Siphonie who will be joining me. I look outside at the people gathered on either side of the cobblestone road as they wait to catch their last glimpse of the last Princess of Antalis. Mira tries to smile, but sadness touches the wrinkles around her eyes. I realize how much I'll miss her, she has become like a mother to me after my mother's death.

My mother once made this trip but it was the reverse — the people lined the streets to watch a baker's assistant become the Queen of Antalis. Now instead of *hayæ* flowers lining the streets showing their joy, the villagers have *pasa* flowers to symbolize their sadness. Siphonie slides in beside me and Rhenor, who I'm sure will eventually leave us to ride a horse later, gets in across from us.

We've all dressed today in the colors of our kingdom. Rhenor wears his silver tunic embellished with dark blue, while Siphonie's dress is dark blue with silver embellishments. Her dress is similar to mine in the fashion of the crop tops with billowing skirts that hit us right at the ankles.

I wonder if I'll have to stop wearing them now that I am leaving. Thylas stands just outside Siphonie's window, his hair pulled tight. His armor glistens in the sunlight and quickly he looks toward me and then proceeds to retreat to his horse that will be his ride for the evening.

I see my father standing proud at the top of the stairs before I hear Ereon yell at our entourage and the carriage begins to jostle forward. Making our way down the grey cobblestone streets from ring to ring of my home, I see many children I will never get to see grow. I watch as the villagers lay down their flowers on the road as we pass.

It's then that I notice Ilis and her daughter Vailles, standing beside each other. Ilis smiles at me and motions with her hands like she is putting something on over her shoulders. I nod my head toward her to indicate that I did indeed pack it. She smiles wider and lifts her hands above her head, like a priestess in honor of the Great Mother above us. My face flushes and I can feel prickles behind my eyes as I try to hold back tears. I won't let them see me cry, I won't let them worry. For this is a time of unknown for all of us, and as my mother once was, I will be strong for them.

Sixteen

EREON

"Today we start our new life, Princess Carnaxa." I kiss the top of her hand as she meekly enters the carriage. Her hand shook as I held it, which doesn't surprise me, considering I'm the villain here. I didn't miss the flush of her cheeks or the tears she held back as she walked across the grounds to kiss her father goodbye. I'm the one taking her from everything she's ever known, I'm the monster she never wanted.

I watch as her cousin and *Bêl* Rhenor follow behind her and step into the carriage, then I subtly look around for the guard she has coming along. He'll be a problem, especially after ... well, he'll just be a problem. He wants her, whether he has admitted that to himself or not, I don't know. However, you would have to be blind not to see it.

"Prince Ereon, we are ready when you are," declares Ryul, the General of my own guard, who stands behind me. I've kept him with the men in the barracks for the mark across his face is rather unsightly, I didn't want to worry the Princess more than she already is. The mark is a former cut, slashed diagonally across his face, the puckered scar now weathered and healed. It's a battle wound from the monsters, the ones the Antalians never have to worry about.

I nod in Ryul's direction and he turns his back to me as he finds his own horse to ride. My stallion stands tall, waiting. He's larger than most of the others in our company and is as black as a starless night sky. He throws his mane back and forth, stomping his feet with impatience.

Walking toward him he calms down and I run my hand down his thick coat checking the saddle fittings.

"Shiw, my old friend, are you ready to go home?" He brays softly in answer and I feed him a sugar cube I stole from the kitchen.

I mount Shiw and look toward Thylas riding right behind Carnaxa's carriage. He looks at me and I don't miss the hatred that crosses his face. I'm her monster and I guess I'm his nightmare.

I nod toward the lead and he shouts for us to take our leave. I observe as King Clennom watches his daughter pass him and then he looks up to the sky. Their goddess has abandoned them and it would be best if he accepted the fact that Antalis is weaker now.

The people here are strange, they are lined up on all sides of the cobblestone road as far as the eye can see. They have white flowers with a purple center and they place them on the ground as she passes, a farewell of sorts. The people of Shaston welcome us home, probably more because it's expected of them – not for any true love for us. These people are crying though, people are crying because the prince of darkness is stealing away their princess of light.

If only they knew everything, knew what was planned for her and in turn, them. I don't know if they understand that when their king is dead, I will be the sole ruler of both kingdoms, not Carnaxa.

I can't see the Princess from here, but I'm sure there are tears. Oh, how I know I will get tired of the tears from her. It's one thing to be sad, it's another issue to show such weakness in Shaston, she cannot show weakness there. Not in front of my father.

It's a few short days' ride to the Doorway of Aka, and one destination closer to home. The Doorway of Aka, another slap in the face of those who don't have the Goddess' favor. It connects Midaeliea and Antalis, but of course, Shastonians must traverse the Cartilen Mountains filled with monsters after leaving Midaeliea to make it home. A fail-safe to try to keep us separated from the rest of the perfect continent, a way to keep us locked within our borders. Unfortunately for them, we've learned our way through it – blood and fighting at the worst times, and at the best of times the beasts let us go right on through. Perhaps like calls to like.

"Are you ready to be home, Prince?" Ryul questions, as his brown horse walks beside Shiw.

"That is a complicated answer, for many complicated reasons," I jest, smirking at him. The closest thing I have to a friend, he's been around since I was but a boy. When I started making trips to the other kingdoms, he volunteered to come and has every time since. He's one who I can trust, and he's proven it many times.

"I understand, my Prince." He waves toward some of the on-lookers as he mentions, "The women here really know how to please a man, something about them having their freedom really does make sex with them sweeter."

"Maybe one day in Shaston we should consider giving the women some of their freedom too if it's that much better," I propose, eyeing Ryul. The idea of all women free in Shaston is a foreign thought.

"While you know, I would support that idea, there are many, including your father, who absolutely do not believe in that way of life. Also, you know to keep those ideas to yourself."

"It is just us here, the half-wits aren't listening anyway." I look around at the soldiers, still getting themselves ready. Some are stretching to prepare for the long ride, some are packing up extra food they scavenged during their time here, others are just pacing.

"But one is." He nods toward Thylas, only two horses in front of us, besides the carriage.

"So you've noticed it too?"

"I may be an old man, but I'm still a man. I've noticed it since we first arrived in Antalis. You are right to keep your eyes on him."

I rub my hands down my beard, after the night of the Festival of *Täht* and *Mar*, I asked Ryul to keep an eye on him. It was obvious the night at the beach he wanted her. I was worried when I demanded to move the wedding date up that he would try something.

"Has he done anything?" I would love a reason to be rid of him. I'm not dumb to the idea that an Antalian woman's virtue is probably already gone. They don't value womens' sexual purity like we do in Shaston, but her lack of maidenhood doesn't need to be blatantly displayed to those of Shaston.

"Not that any of us have seen."

"Good, keep an eye on him."

I can't help but sigh, there is so much to worry about, and yet, here I am worrying about Thylas, when my real concern should be on her and returning to her.

SEVENTEEN

CARNAXA

We left the salty air and the crashing waves. We will soon trade it for a forest of green and hills of the fog of Midaeliea. I kept my promise, not a single tear fell in front of my people. I've plaited my hair in a braid that cascades down my left side, but stray wisps fall in my face and I blow it away. To no avail, it clings to my sweat-slickened face, it's hot in this carriage and hotter still, when anxious and stressed.

From his horse beside the carriage, Thylas takes a sip of his green canteen before closing the lid. His dark hair is pulled high at the top of his head, he's down to wearing nothing but his leather pants and a thin, sleeveless tunic that highlights his muscled shoulders, his tattoos showing. I've often wondered about the language they are written in. I only know a few words. Those ranked highest in the *Shayi* and those in the *Ke Neye*, along with priestesses and scholars are the only ones who use it daily or in their daily lives. The soldiers use it as a way to honor tradition and to speak to each other without potential enemies understanding commands, battle formation, and strategy. The scholars study the ancient text of our mortal realm and the priestesses use it for religious rituals as well as prayers to the Goddess. The old language swirls around his forearm, traveling above his shoulder, and across his back to his other arm.

The carriage wheels trample the flowers that grow through the dirt roads. My heart hurts knowing our entourage is destroying this beautiful landscape because it's a visual representation of how my spirit feels. I thought I would find another option, or perhaps my father would, to get me out of this marriage. There isn't one, not without hurting my people in Antalis.

Siphonie sits across from me, fanning herself, her luscious locks of pink piled high on her head. "This heat is going to be the death of me. I always knew Antalis was hot, but this is sticky hot. I hate it. How can we just barely be away from home and already the climate is so different."

Rhenor laughs under his breath as he turns to her to explain, "Siphonie, Shaston is hotter than this. It won't have the same sticky feeling, but it is most certainly hot. I've been there and it's not somewhere I would choose to live."

His eyes jerk to mine, sorrow filling them. Siphonie and Rhenor can leave after the marriage is complete, and return to Antalis. But me? I'll be stuck, as Queen Consort of Shaston. The trip will be dangerous for them to make, it's probably too dangerous now, they won't make it more than necessary. When Rhenor speaks of visiting Shaston, it was when he traveled there years ago with *Shayi* soldiers in an effort to keep the peace between Antalis and Shaston.

"I think it will be a lovely place, despite what he says." Siphonie smiles at me, leaning across the carriage, squeezing one of my hands as she wonders aloud, "What do men know anyway?"

Rhenor laughs. "She's right, what do I know? I was just a young man, excited for the prospects of battle, the last time I went. It will be your home and I know you will make it a wonderful place."

"How long do you think you will stay?" I ask, wanting to emotionally prepare myself. I know they can't stay forever and I need to know so I won't be disappointed when the time comes.

"We will stay as long as you need us to, right Rhenor?" She smiles at him and he wraps an arm around her shoulder kissing her temple.

"Absolutely, my dear."

Looking back out the window, I wonder how my mother would have handled this situation. Would she have been meek and mild, doing what she was told? Would she have fought to remain in Antalis? Would she have approved of the marriage between Ereon and me? We'll never know, because the deluc took her. She didn't even have the chance to be called home, to walk into the ocean's waves. She withered away little by little as the moons passed until she died.

Ereon sits on his black horse, the glorious beast strides along with the rest of our entourage. He is a handsome man, no one can deny that. He sits tall as he lightly grips the reins, rolling his shoulders to get more comfortable. His eyes are deep and dark, the color of chocolate. I know he is older than me by five lunar years. His body is chiseled and sharp. Why am I not happy to be his wife? I've heard rumors of his sexual exploits, but every man in Antalis visits the pleasure women at least a few times before marriage, and sometimes even after, depending on the circumstances. I assume he can't be anything different than what I've already known. I've heard he is very stubborn and strict, but the moment on the beach, when I heard him truly laugh, I can't help but wonder if there is more to him. I'm not naïve to his wanting to put me in my place — we will work on that. I am the heir to Antalis, I will be Queen of Antalis and I refuse to be forced to ignore that fact. I will be a good wife and hope we can come to some sort of marital agreement.

"HALT!" a loud booming voice commands through the windows.

Peering around, I notice the entire caravan has come to a stop. "What's going on?" I ask Thylas, as his horse appears closer to our carriage.

"I'm not sure, probably someone needing to relieve themselves or we are just taking a break. I'll go check it out. Rhenor do you mind keeping watch?"

"With my life, as always," Rhenor replies, nodding as Thylas rides off on his steed.

Rhenor pats the sword at his side, a habit from when he was a soldier. Siphonie sighs and leans back again. Twisting the bangles on my wrist, I worry about what could be stopping us, anxiety always getting the better of me.

"So what do you know of Prince Ereon?" Siphonie looks toward her husband. "Will he be a good husband to Naxa?"

Rhenor runs his hands through his salt and cinnamon hair, sighing loudly, "I don't know a lot. I saw him a few times when we went to Shaston but he was a boy, and then of course, I heard rumors."

"What rumors?" I ask impatiently.

"He's stern. He's a great soldier. He is known to always have a woman in his room. He holds traditional, restrained beliefs, similar to many in his kingdom, and the laws of Shaston reflect those beliefs and values."

"'Traditional beliefs? Laws?'" Siphonie asks, fanning herself with her hand. "Would you care to elaborate or do you enjoy being cryptic?"

"You know what I mean, Siph. Beliefs like women are to be quiet. They aren't allowed to show much skin, which doesn't matter anyway considering it's so damn hot there, any exposed skin will burn. Because of these beliefs, the laws that govern women differ significantly from ours. Always believing women are the weaker sex and should stay beneath a man's control is one thing but with laws strictly forbidding women from speaking up, the women are stuck with their lot in life. Not to mention, Shastonians don't worship the Goddess from my understanding, so therefore, they don't see women as the life givers." He rubs his hand across her upper thigh.

"That's an awful way to live." Siphonie side-eyes me as she irritatingly questions, "Who would want a woman who doesn't think for themselves? Seems boring."

Siphonie could never assimilate to Shaston's way of life, once upon a time I wouldn't have thought I could either but now, I must.

"It may be boring and wrong, but it's the way it is. Has been as long as anyone knows. It's even spoken about in the first stories of our world that have been passed down through the generations. Has to do with their twisted myth of the Goddess."

Both Siphonie and I look toward Rhenor. "Well, are you going to continue?" Siphonie asks while pushing his hand off her playfully. "I could get someone with an oath of silence to say more than you do at times."

"You two really should study other cultures more," he chuckles. "Their story of the Goddess is a lot like ours but with a small difference. The Goddess is seen as the Mother of course, but She isn't the loving and nurturing deity we know Her as. The Shastonian's swear She is conniving and controlling. They say the Antalian story of Her lover is false and She in fact, was just a woman toying with the men. Vilifying the Goddess justifies how they treat women in their kingdom."

The carriage falls into awkward silence, no one sure of what to say. The loving Goddess, our Mother, could never be anything but the great awe-inspiring creature that She is. That wouldn't make sense. Why would She have created us all? Shaston must be mad because everyone knows the Goddess banished the first Shastonian and that's why their land is so miserable, it's a simple fact.

"We are making camp," Thylas says from the window, scaring us all.

"Goddess' name, Thylas! You could have announced your arrival before giving me heart pain." Siphonie clutches at her heart as if she truly is in pain.

He just gives her a coy smile. "Go ahead and get out and stretch your legs if you want, I'll start helping with your tents."

··•●◐◉○◉◑●•··

"I think we should switch tents, I do have a husband after all." Siphonie winks at me as she falls against my furs in the makeshift bed in my tent, practically rolling herself up in them – which it is certainly way too hot for. However, the furs are extremely comfortable.

"I'm the Princess, but also, I get the bigger tent because Thylas has to sleep in here with me. Apparently, it's protocol in case he's needed to defend me in the middle of the night." I roll my eyes. That's exactly what I need, Thylas in my tent at night, after what happened after the festival.

The whole trip he's acted normal, at least the few times we've stopped for small breaks. Thylas has always been great at holding, and hiding, his emotions. I remember once when we were children, I watched him get into a fight with another kid in the palace. Thylas didn't win the fight, but through the whole thing and after, he refused to cry or show any emotion. The moments we shared are like raindrops, drying up as soon as the sun hits them. Beautiful and gone too quickly.

"Sleeping so soon with Thylas are we? I've heard he's amazing. Never got around to trying though. I don't think he would have, even if I would have asked."

My eyes jolt up and the feeling of jealousy seeps into me. Why had I never asked if Siphonie had been with him? Why wouldn't she have tried? It's not that I thought he had no one, but to be with someone so close to me ... how many women have I spoken to that he has been in their bed as night came.

"No man can turn you down." I smile at her, but it's not a smile that's genuine. My jaw actually tenses as I try to play it off lightly. "And as stated, we are sleeping in the same tent. Not the same as sleeping together."

Her face shows confusion before she speaks up and assures, "Thylas has never once tried with me, Naxa." She smiles at me, seeing through my fake smile. "I think it's because of you. Even the women he has been with say he's a great night but they can tell that he's not thoroughly enjoying himself. And after what I witnessed the other day, I can tell why."

"How in the world can you not be 'thoroughly enjoying it'? Honestly, I think sex is either, you are or aren't into it, kind of a thing."

She smacks my arm, giggling, "Well obviously, he's into it … but they say it's his eyes. His never meets theirs, he never truly looks at them. I've heard even his kisses are shallow, and I've been with enough men to know when a man worships me or uses me. Usually, because I'm the same. I'm just using them for my relief, to hide my unhappiness. Sex was, and still is at times, how I cope."

"What pain could Thylas possibly have? He is the Captain of the Antalian *Ke Neye*? He could literally have any woman of any rank, he is well liked in Antalis is he not? He should marry and settle down."

"Right, so that he could uproot them to Shaston because he always knew his path would be where you went?"

The words slap me across the face. It's my fault that Thylas has grown so closed off, and is sometimes so cold. How could he get attached to anyone when his job is to protect me? His job is to follow me, daily. Here he is having his life uprooted just as much as mine is, and yet I've not stopped to truly consider him. How can I expect him to have a wife and a life? The plans for my betrothal were made so quickly after my mother's death. Even then Thylas reminded me he would never leave me, he would be my safety.

"Don't look like that Naxa; he knew what it meant to be your guard," she tries to console me.

"How could he? He's been my guard since he was a child. He went to training to become my guard, ever since I found him on the shore, I've controlled his life."

The tent flap opens up and Thylas walks in, "Whose life have you controlled?" His boots are muddy from walking around camp and he shakes bits of leaves from his hair. Dirt covers his face and his clothes. He stumbles around, holding a cup full of what I'm assuming is wine or ale. I really should have had some myself tonight. Then I could have drank and gone to sleep without having to deal with him in my tent.

"Have you been ... wrestling?" I ask, unsure why else he would have leaves in his hair.

"As a matter of fact, I have. Some of the men and I were bored. We started a wrestling ring," he chuckles, rolling his shoulders. "Siph, my apologies if *Bêl* Rhenor is a bit sore in the morning ... or now."

Siphonie rolls her neck, exasperated, "Tell me he didn't."

Thylas' smile broadens as he confirms, "Oh, he did."

"Well, I have to go check on that man. Carnaxa, I'll see you tomorrow. Thy, keep our princess safe." She kisses me on the cheek and taps Thylas' shoulder goodbye as she leaves the tent.

The golden-hued tent seems so much smaller now than before, with his broad shoulders filling the space. Thylas ruffles his hair with his hand, pulling more sticks and leaves from it as he shuffles his feet. I suck in a breath as I recognize there is only one bed in here, covered in my furs.

"Where are you going to sleep?" I ask almost too quietly to be heard.

"I'll sleep on the floor, *Nohæ*. I have my bed roll. Now back to my question – whose life have you controlled?"

"No one's, don't worry about it. That was girl talk. Won't sleeping on the bedroll be uncomfortable?"

"There are more comfortable places where I would rather sleep, but as things stand right now, I don't think there is another option." His eyes dance from the top of my head to the floor and back, and his meaning is clear. What would it be like to be with him, just once?

He walks to me, his hand lingering inches from my face before tucking a stray hair behind my ear, as he leans down. His breath still tainted with wine, brushes against the shell of my ear. "If you find yourself in any danger tonight and feel safer with me in the bed, please just let me know." A small shiver tingles down my spine and I can imagine what his heat would feel like wrapped around me, in me.

He stands up straight, then instructs me, "Go ahead and get changed into your night clothing if you wish and I'll do the same. Want to do it like we used to at the shore? Turn our backs toward each other or do you want me to leave?"

"Just turn around." Had I truly thought this through I would have changed while Siphonie was here, I didn't even think about this. He turns his back to me, now snickering. My cheeks heat and all of a sudden, I'm worried about what he would think of my body. Would he enjoy it? Would he find me attractive? Truly, without the clothing, without the jewelry, if I was just bare before him would he still want me? Would he want me if he knew ... No time to ponder, I have to change before he loses patience.

I quickly remove my two-piece, dark-blue gown and shimmy into the sleep slip I brought. The silky, grey material hugs my curves like an embrace. Once again, had I known I would share a tent with him I would have brought something less ... I don't know ... maybe something more. I should have thought of all this before I left. "May the tide take me," I mumble beneath my breath, trying to calm my nerves. "Okay, you can turn back around."

His eyes graze my skin as goosebumps do the same. His meadow-colored eyes seem to take in every inch of me and I cross my arms across my chest, feeling self-conscious.

"You are beautiful." His eyes move swiftly back to mine and he shuffles from foot to foot. "Forgive me. I'm saying a lot of things I shouldn't right now, it's probably the wine I had before we decided to start a wrestling match."

I laugh, "So I'm not beautiful?"

He runs his hand through his hair, exhaling deeply, "Of course you are, I just ... should be controlling my mouth better than I am tonight. I made your father a promise, to keep you safe and on the Goddess' path. I need to go to sleep, as do you. We will have another day of traveling tomorrow before we reach the Doorway of Aka. Do you need me for anything?"

Well, that was a lot. What oath and path? Even if I ask, his loyalty would take priority and he would deny me answers to any questions I have.

"No, thank you. Let's get to sleep." I quickly blow out the only candle in the tent and find myself on top of the furs pulling a thin blanket over me before he even moves. I don't know why I blew out the candle so quickly, except for mindless nerves. He chuckles softly, probably at me and my scampering onto the pallet to get out of sight. I can hear the clink of his sword and armor that he places on the floor. Then the sounds of the threads of his trousers, before the soft rustling as he pulls them down. I ache to turn and look at him, but I know what a dangerous game that is. It's best to leave things alone.

I listen to him get onto his bedroll, his soft breaths filling the air, his scent of sage and sandalwood overwhelming me. I find myself remembering the fleeting moments we've shared over the past few weeks.

"Hey, Thy?"

I hear him roll over to face my bed, "Hmm?"

"The day we found out about all this, you called me 'baby girl.'" I twist a piece of hair, the same one he tucked behind my ear earlier. "Do you remember the first time you called me that?"

"Yes, you were being a brat that day and I was being an ass. You couldn't have been more than what, eight lunar years, running around and following me everywhere that day, even though I didn't want you to."

I laugh in the darkness as I remember, "You called me a 'baby.' I was so mad. I just wanted to hang out with you and you were so mean."

It's then that his laughter comes crashing around me, and I hear him put his hand over his mouth to stifle the sound. "You kept telling me, 'I'm not a baby, I'm a big girl now.' I think you even stomped your little foot, stumping your small toe in the process."

"I did, and you told me to sit down and we would come to a resolution. You would just call me 'baby girl.' I haven't thought about that in a long time." I smile, the air of the tent becoming even warmer now.

"I've thought about it and many other things over the years, but it's getting late and we need rest. Not all of us get to ride in a carriage all day. Goodnight, *baby girl*."

"Good night." I roll over and fall asleep to the memories of good days, days filled with sunshine, smiles, and a sweet boy who dealt with a stubborn girl.

Eighteen

CARNAXA

The sun breaks through the fabric door of the tent and I rub the palms of my hands into my eyes trying to clear them. It takes me a moment to realize where I am, but I know it's not my home. The air smells different and it's then I look over to where Thylas slept the night before. He's gone already and I can't help but let out a small sigh and prayer, thankful he isn't here.

I sit up and pull the covers from me, letting my toes flex in the furs below the bed. Slipping off my night slip, I shift through some of the trunks at the end of my bed until I find a light orange halter dress to slip on. The shawl catches my eyes and I pull it out, running the soft fur through my fingers, before my eyes catch the present from Thylas. The small dagger feels heavy between my fingers as I pull it out. The sun catches the edge of the blade, and I love how beautiful it is. The stone shines brightly as I hold it up to the light. Maybe now would be a perfect time to keep it on me. I find a gold ribbon and wrap it around my upper thigh, patting it to make sure it's secure. Maybe I should ask Thylas for official lessons, he may have gifted it to me but I would love to know how to actually use it. I lean down to tie my sandals when I hear a shuffle outside the door.

"Naxa," Thylas' voice comes through the tent flap. "Are you dressed?"

I run my hands through my hair before tying it into a loose bun at the base of my skull, securing it with a ribbon. "Yes, come on in."

He walks in, the sunlight creates a halo around him. A smile reaches from ear to ear. His hair is half up, the ends curling from the humidity of this place. Despite the circumstances, he seems to like being outside the boundaries of the castle and kingdom.

"Good morning. I've got the travel plans. We will make it to the Doorway of Aka today. After we go through, we will make camp for another night and arrive in Midaeliea the next morning. We will stay there briefly before finishing our travels." He places a silver platter on the bed, full of ripe pears and apples. The cheese on the tray has my attention and I quickly grab a piece and let the taste flush over my taste buds.

He chuckles and shakes his head. "I grabbed extra cheese for you, and put some in your traveling pouch. I know how much you like it." He smiles at me as he pours a glass of water for me, holding it out. "They didn't have your normal breakfast but they should have all of that in Midaeliea when we get there. I hope the cheese will make up for the lack of your favorite breakfast items today. "

I take the glass from him and acknowledge his kindness with a, "Thank you." Taking a sip of water I glance at the floor, unable to let the words Siphonie said last night leave me. "And in case I haven't said it, thank you for coming with me. I'm sure you would have loved to do anything else."

I've never been good at speaking from the heart while looking directly at someone, I don't mean to come off disrespectful; I struggle to find the words when I look someone in the eyes.

"That's not true, there is nowhere else I would rather be. I told you this the other night and I've told you this before. You have me until you wish me away. I'll always be here for you, Naxa. I'll be your safety."

"I'll be your safety." I can recall the night those words were first spoken, the phrase filtering through my head as the images replay themselves.

· · • • ◑ ● ○ ◐ ◕ • • ·

Four Lunar Years Ago

Thylas stands at my mother's door, he has already advanced in the rankings of the Shayi quickly. The Captain says that he thinks Thylas will become one of the greatest soldiers Antalis has ever seen, but all I see is my friend.

When I found him on the shores of the Great Sea, I immediately ran to get my mother and father. They took him in, and the rest is history. We've grown up together. However, in the last few months, he's changed. Maybe it's my age. Maybe it's his new position. We used to be inseparable, getting into trouble for stealing cheese and running around the rings at night. Now he is such a rule follower.

"Carnaxa," my mother's weak voice breaks my thoughts. "Hunny, I need to tell you something," she persists as she grabs my hand. My mother has been sick in a way the healers say they have never seen before.

"I'm going to go soon," she coughs. Once full of life and curves, she's nothing but skin that clings to bone. Her skin was the same pale olive as mine, but now it is so pale her veins shine through. Her hand feels dry and cold when it was once full of warmth. Her eyes, however, remain just as they were, large and ever-watching.

"No, Mother." I climb up into bed with her and hold onto her. "The healers will find a way to make you better."

She kisses my hairline and pulls me in even closer, wrapping her arm around me. "I love being here with you and your father. But it's time to go. You have to know, I will always be watching over you. Don't forget that. Your destiny is only just beginning when my own ends, Naxa. The Goddess has plans for you, my dearest."

"Are you getting the call from the Goddess? Will you walk into the sea?" As much as it would hurt to see her called, it would be better than her not receiving her summons at all. This type of death is unheard of. She calls us and we walk toward Her embrace; our smile is the last thing seen before the waves take us to the Mother. But I'm not ready for her to leave. Maybe I can ask the Goddess to let her stay, maybe She would make an exception for her.

"No, Naxa." She coughs again and holds me tighter. "The Goddess won't call me home. She can't."

I feel wetness at the top of my forehead and I know she is crying. Thylas stands and turns, giving us privacy. I can't imagine a world without my mother. She was, still is, in my mind, so beautiful and kind. Her blue hair is so pale now, it looks like ice.

I hope to have a love like her and Father someday. They love each other so much. I love hearing stories of the two of them. Who will tell me stories if she goes?

"I love you, my gift," her voice barely above a whisper.

Her breath starts to become more rapid and I sit up, her eyes ... they look different, and then she shuts them. "Mother?"

"Ata?" I revert back to what I called her as a child, panic rising, as I shake her.

"Ata!"

"Mother! Wake up!"

I don't feel her breathe beneath me anymore. Thylas runs to my side, trying to pull me off of her while yelling for the guards and the healers. I grab Mother's hands tightly with one of my own and fight

Thylas' grip around my waist with the other. "NO! Mother! Let me go, Thylas!"

He pulls me away just as the healers come running into the room, their light-grey robes twisting around them as they do. "We need Princess Carnaxa to leave so we can take care of the Queen." Their faces are grim, the one beside the bed already shaking her head toward the one speaking.

Thylas grabs me around my waist again and picks me up, turning me so my face fits into the side of his neck. "Shh…" is all he says as he pulls me against him, rubbing the back of my head.

He carries me into my chambers just down the hall. He takes my anger and sadness the whole time. Letting me scream, cry, and hit him as I try to get back to my mother. When it seems like hours have passed, I sit on my bed and Thylas guards the door from inside.

"You're…" I'm sniffling, and my throat is raw from screaming. "You're supposed to go get Father if something happens."

He sits down on my bed, pulling me into him. He speaks as if he is praying while rocking me back and forth. "I'll get him later, I'm not leaving you."

"What am I supposed to do Thylas? Without her? How will I know how to be a queen? Father is the King, he can't take care of a daughter, he can't always be here for me when he needs to be available for the kingdom. What will happen to me now? How will I have safety from all the things I don't know?"

Thylas kisses the top of my head, letting my tears dampen his tunic. "Me. I'll be your safety. I'll always be here for you. I'm not a king and I don't know what life may bring, but I'll be your safety."

We sit that way for the rest of the night until I finally fall asleep, exhausted from the screaming, and wake to the sounds of my father yelling.

·· • ● ◐ ● ○ ● ◑ ● ● ··

Present

"So spill it, did you find yourself with company last night?" Siphonie interrogates as she sits across from me. Her pale-pink hair hangs loosely against her shoulders. Her sky-blue, linen dress cascades to the floor. The neckline plunges to just above her navel and a beaded wrap of sorts, showcases her thin waist. She wears her bracelets that match mine, along with teardrop earrings adorning her petitie ears.

"Goddess, no. Do you ever think about anything else besides sex?" I have my feet up on the bench beside me. I'm thankful Rhenor decided to ride a horse beside Thylas today – said he couldn't handle the clucking of two women anymore.

"Well I do, yes. But I'm certainly more interested in why the two of you fight this. I've seen this play out since we were children. Why don't you both just accept it."

"What would be the point, Siphonie?"

"It would help you know what it's like to actually be with a man for one, for two, when you get with a man you have less stress. It's proven by the priestesses and is one of the many reasons it's encouraged for everyone."

"I have been with a man, and is that your secret to how you just let everything roll off your back?"

"Better than being stressed all the time." She smiles and bats her eyelashes at me, before she continues, "You have not been with a man — you would have told me. I don't mean just kisses here and there, I mean actually *being* with a man, having one inside of you."

My cheeks flush and this horrible heat isn't helping things. Siphonie knows that I've never technically had sex. A few hurried moments with fumbling hands and lifting of skirts, yes, but I've never truly found someone who I want to be with in that aspect, yet.

"It doesn't matter. He slept on the floor and I slept in bed."

She leans back into the cushion of the bench again and sighs, "Mood killer. I'm ready to get to the Doorway of Aka. I've heard it's a beauty to behold. So much quicker than traveling by horse the whole way."

I nod but don't respond. If I do, she probably won't stop talking for the rest of the trip. The whole morning has been full of her talking about this or that. Normally I enjoy her talking, it helps keep me out of my own head, but right now I'm enjoying my last few glances at my kingdom.

I saw Ereon this morning. He winked at me but didn't approach, appearing to be in conversation with someone in his guard. The man had a horrible scar across his face. Ereon looked happy though. He normally looks so serious, but he seems excited about going home. I've often thought about our moment on the beach.

The way he looked, the way he spoke. It wasn't until then that I had ever thought, maybe I wasn't his first choice either.

Will we be walking into Shaston, a woman waiting for him? Will she know about me? What if he continues to see her even after our wedding, what of the children that could come from such a union? Stop. I can't do this to myself. Those are tomorrow's problems and I'm still trying to get through today. But I'm trying to reconcile the Ereon who laughed and joked and seemed insecure, versus the one who wants punishment dealt for the slightest miscommunication.

The carriage comes to a halt and I look out the window, the Doorway of Aka just in front of us. Thylas appears beside the carriage's window, already off his horse that follows behind him. I open the door quickly, too eager to stretch my legs and he helps me down.

"Wow."

The Doorway of Aka isn't so much a door as a portal; it appears to be made out of a white stone with symbols etched around the round archway. The edges are covered with pink and blue flowers that seem to grow into the mountain behind. Through the archway, you can see a large tree beyond. The earth and grass are so vivid and bright, I feel the need to squint just looking at the picturesque landscape. That is Midaeliea.

"Princess," Ereon calls, appearing beside me. I feel both Siphonie and Thylas shuffle a step toward me. Siphonie may like to pretend that looks are all she cares about, but she's still worried for me. "Isn't it beautiful?"

"It is. You've seen it before, I assume?"

He takes a step toward me, holding his arm out in a gesture for me to walk toward the portal with him. "I have, a few times on my trips to Antalis. Not that I've been to your kingdom much, as you know, but each time I see the Doorway of Aka, I can't help but be amazed."

The symbols seem to glow a light white and I notice it's our old language, Antihana, the same language that Thylas has marked on his body.

"Do you know how to read Antihana?" I can't help but ask, maybe he can help me understand the words better.

"I don't. I would have assumed you would have learned the dead language of your ancestors."

I shake my head in response, "No, very few are trained in it. I was not one of those few."

As we walk toward the portal, the air around us seems to vibrate. It's like small little bees are buzzing all around us. The air is physically humming. My hands start shaking and butterflies awaken in my stomach.

"Are you okay, Your Highness?" It's Thylas from behind me. Damn him for watching me so closely.

"She's fine. Everyone's always nervous the first time they walk through the door. I've got you, Princess." Ereon smiles down at me, but I don't miss the death glare he sends toward Thylas. I glance back as Thylas clenches his jaw. Rhenor simply pats his shoulder and grabs Siphonie's hand.

Since no one has entered yet, I'm assuming they are waiting on Ereon and me to be the first. It's strange seeing two different places at once the closer we get. I stop just steps away from the entryway and take a breath.

Ereon reaches for my hand. His calm cool hand holds mine softly, and he smiles toward me. "I've got you, Princess. The whole time." He seems sincere and it's better than walking through on my own. He's done this before I try to tell myself, but it does nothing to ease my fear.

Putting on a brave face, I smile and straighten my shoulders and we walk through the Doorway of Aka together.

Nineteen

ANARA

I think there was a time in my life when I was happy. I remember the smell of my mother's hair, and the lull of her voice as she sang me to sleep. I remember my father's rough hands as he worked so hard everyday. I remember the sounds of the ocean outside my room and the *pitongi* birds that sang high in the sky.

There are no birds here, or water for that matter. The space is small and dark and full of things that go bump in the night. My wrist burns from the obsidian chain that's been placed around them, a way to make sure I don't escape. I couldn't even if I wanted to. My power was lost to me the moment I was thrown on this land. It felt as though something had been ripped from me.

I hear him coming down the halls and I try to catch my courage. What will the punishment be today? Assault of my body perhaps, or more beatings? It's sad that I almost hope it's the beatings. When he thrusts into me, I dream of running through our woods and the fire that didn't burn. I don't even pretend that I enjoy it anymore, not that I ever did. I certainly don't now.

He never touched me until he knew, and it's our fault we didn't hide it well enough. It's my fault for blushing, and his for glancing too long. I was supposed to be a toy, one used and abused, forgotten and replaced.

I wasn't that, we were more. I sealed my fate before I knew…

His boots scrape outside the door and I take a breath. Soon this will be over and he'll be back. I just hope I can survive that long, but of course I will. I'm the price if he doesn't return. I'm only alive now because of what I already gave, and the answers I hold.

The door creaks open and he walks in, his black hair haloed by the light from the hall. I squint at first, not being able to put my hands over my eyes since they are chained securely to the wall.

He leans down and smiles at me, grabbing my chin, forcing me to look up at him as he sneers, "What a beautiful whore you'll be today."

TWENTY

CARNAXA

A tingly sensation washes over my body as we walk through the archway, like little moths fluttering across my skin. It's as if time slows, but as soon as my foot touches the ground everything returns to normal. My eyes adjust to the sunlight that filters through the tree canopy. These trees are massive, their branches sprouting up as if praying to the sky.

The grass is green ... in fact, everything is so green here. Flowers in every shade I could ever dream of are scattered along the edges of a dirt path on this side of the portal.

"This is beautiful." I smile and quickly realize Ereon's hand is still holding my own. He squeezes a bit and then releases his grasp.

"Welcome to Midaeliea, Princess." He continues walking, and I notice the others are finally coming in behind me. "We'll set up camp here tonight and then be at the castle tomorrow," Ereon announces. He looks behind me and I watch his expression change to something more stern. "If you should need anything, feel free to come find me." With that, he walks toward his men who have already come through the archway with the horses and our possessions. Thylas comes beside me, his fingers squeezing my own quickly before releasing. His eyes take in the beauty before us and his lips turn up in a soft smile.

"This is amazing!" Siphonie squeals beside me. "I'm so happy I got to come."

"Yeah, just remember this beauty when you are complaining about Shaston's heat," grumbles Rhenor from her side. "Thylas, I'll help you set up camp."

I turn looking at Thylas who looks just as awe-struck as I feel. His emerald eyes take in everything around us. "Yeah, okay. We should probably do that."

· · • • ◦ • ○ • • • • · ·

The men finish setting up camp and Siphonie and I still can't get over the beauty we see here. Even though we are traveling as a united front, we can see the lines that are clearly drawn. The men of Shaston on one side and the small group of Antalians on the other. Thylas already informed me that he will, in fact, be staying inside the tent with me again. Having him so near is like a sweet poison, slowly trying to kill me.

"That is something else isn't it, *Nohæ*?" I gasp and look beside me, it's like my thoughts conjured him up. He sits down beside me near the fire, stretching his long, muscular legs out. The heat from his body combined with the fire before us is suffocating. Sweat trickles from my brow and I wipe it away with the back of my hand.

"It's beautiful. I hate that we don't live in a world with magic anymore. I think it would have been beautiful." I finish plating my hair as I shuffle a step away from him.

"Beautiful and more dangerous. I know you heard the stories of the other types of magic, not all of it was Goddess-granted."

"Still, it would have been beautiful. And of course, it was all Goddess-granted. Who else would have it been from? The Goddess cannot control what the free will of people do."

He smiles at me before reaching out to feel the heat from the fire, before acknowledging, "And the firepower that was seen during the Great Wars. What of that?"

"Rumors or something, I don't know. Maybe we should ask the scholars when we get to Midaeliea."

"I doubt we will have the time, we will just be stopping for the night before carrying on. Then through the Cartilen Mountains. Speaking of, we should get to bed. Siphonie and Rhenor have already found their way to their tent and the rest of the men are probably not far behind. I don't want you around those who will be up past then. Some men are starting to grow restless."

I nod my head and stand up, dusting the back of my gown off. The men of Shaston are what he implies. They've been nice, pleasant even, but we know the truth from the false pretenses they hide behind. It's known that Shaston will accept anyone who crosses their borders, including those who are cast out of Midaeliea and Antalis. Some I'm sure, are innocent of their alleged crimes except for being born of course, however, that doesn't negate the fact that these men aren't all blameless.

Walking back to the tent, Thylas' hand touches the small of my back. Inhaling deeply, I turn to look at him, but he's staring at the men in the shadows of the fire. The one's staring at me. I know that look, I've seen it many times before. They are hungry, and not for food. Wrapping my arms around myself, suddenly feeling cold, I let Thylas lead me to the tent.

"I'll stay out here until you get comfortable. I ..." He adjusts his broadsword and tries to smile. "I'll stand watch for a little while and let you get to sleep first." Lifting the flap of the tent with my hand, I walk quickly inside without a second glance back.

· · • • ◐ ● ○ ● ◑ • • · ·

I fell asleep quickly, but the nerves wake me up again. The room is much the same as it was last night and I'm ready to have my own bed back again. I toss on fur-lined crates, trying to be as quiet as I can so as not to wake up Thylas who I'm sure is asleep on the floor,

I can hear his breathing from here. I don't remember him being one to breathe this loudly last night.

I turn again so I can make out the faint outline of his body from the fires still burning outside. He's on his back, muttering in his sleep. Is he having nightmares? I start to stand to wake him up, moving my blankets slightly.

It's then I notice he is most definitely, not asleep. I notice his hand moving beneath the covers before they fall to the side. He strokes himself in long movements, and I stop moving. Instantly my cheeks flush and I feel sweat come over me. I sink lower into my blankets, pulling them tight around me, worrying that he'll notice I'm awake. Do I want him to stop? Yes, of course, this isn't something I should be seeing. There is a reason he waited until he thought I was asleep, and yet I can't find myself to look away.

His fingers curl around his girth and his strokes increase along with his breathing. I can just barely make out his face now that my eyes have had time to adjust, his hair is matted with sweat and his eyes are closed. He mumbles to himself, his voice nothing but a small whisper in the silence of the room.

He palms himself faster now and as much as I should want to move or look away, I can't help but imagine what he would feel like inside me. My core feels like it is on fire as I watch, my fingers eager to find themselves beneath my dress to search out my own pleasure.

In his last moments, he groans loudly and I let go of a breath I didn't realize I was holding. He turns toward me, a smirk across his face. "Was that you I heard, baby girl?" he whispers softly.

Quickly shutting my eyes, I pretend I'm asleep and listen as he shuffles around. The smell of him quickly envelops me as I feel him beside my bed. He leans down and pushes hair out of my face before softly kissing my forehead. "Good night, *Nohæ.*" He returns to his own bed roll and turns to his side.

Maybe I got lucky and he believes the farce. Regardless I refuse to open my eyes and stay like this until sleep takes me.

······●●●○●●●●●······

Arriving at Midaeliea, the people seem so much like Antalians. They walk around the streets in mostly happy spirits. The children laugh and play. The women walk with woven baskets hanging from their arms and smiles on their faces, as they glance and wave toward our caravan. We are gathering a crowd as they all stop and walk toward the cobblestone road. When they wave at us, I can't help but wave back.

The green and brown banners of Midaeliea line the street, embroidered with an emblem of a tree with roots running deep. The kingdom of Midaeliea is nicknamed the "peacekeeper" of the Northern Continent. Legend has it they were created when the Goddess thought Antalis needed new people to provide community After the wars and given their unique geography, being stationed between Shaston and Antalis, they hold a summit every three lunar years. Well, they did, until the deluc.

Very unladylike, I stick my head outside of the window and peer out. The town is surrounded by forests on all sides. The castle is a marvel to behold. It's not as large as Antalis', but it's still massive compared to the small wooden homes and shops around the city. Being built of mostly wood and stone, the castle almost appears as though it is an extension of the forest. The high windows are the only hint that it is not a tree itself.

Ereon is at the front of our party, his face lacking emotion as he sits stoic on top of his night-colored stallion. He guides his horse to the side, letting his soldiers pass, waiting until he is beside our carriage. I glance at Thylas as he smiles at the children, I watch as he slows down to let the smallest ones pet his horse. This morning was awkward for me, and yet Thylas acted like nothing happened the night before, bringing me breakfast and more cheese. We had to gather things quickly for the rest of the journey here, and I'm thankful he seemed to stay busy.

Glancing toward Siphonie and Rhenor, she is smiling so wide her cheeks have to hurt. Rhenor keeps his hand on her lower back and she is about an inch away from sticking her own head out of the window beside me.

"Look at how adorable this place is!" she exclaims. At least someone understands my excitement. Rhenor just shakes his head and laughs under his breath.

"How long will we be staying here?" I look toward Rhenor, but it's Ereon beside my window who answers me.

"We will stay for the night, just enough to rest a bit and pack food and things for the trip through the mountains. We have to be prepared." He smiles down at me, his chestnut hair loosely framing his face.

"What kind of precautions will we take? I've heard many terrible things about that passage."

"I've got you, Princess." He winks at me. "You're right, the lands can be a bit treacherous if you don't know what you're doing or where you are going."

"And you do?"

He runs his hand through his beard before responding, "I am well aware of the cave-dwelling creatures we will do our best to avoid, and I know they prefer to come out during the dark."

"So, can't we just stay out of the caves?" Siphonie pipes up.

"That would work if the mountains didn't make the one path through them so dark it always appears that it's nighttime. Don't fret though, we have been through the mountains multiple times."

A shiver travels down the back of my neck, feeling unsafe because of creatures unknown is something I've never known before. Those of the sea are our companions as well as our nutrition. It's a give and take and we never feel threatened by them. The jellyfish help the fishermen given their luminescence at night, they are one of the most poisonous creatures in the Great Sea, they don't harm anything unless attacked first. Even the legend of the *wongesk,* the largest animal to have inhabited the sea, was peaceful until the Great Goddess called on it during the war.

The caravan arrives at the Midaeliean castle and I take a deep breath, steadying my nerves. Thylas stands outside, opening the door, with his hand atop of his sword. Ereon dismounts his steed, placing himself between me and Thylas. He puts out a hand to assist me down.

I grab his cool hand and step out, smiling at the ones waiting to greet us. Panic seeps into me and my heart rate picks up. My nerves take over, and I cannot remember their names. I know the names of Midaeliea's King and Queen. I learned them, repeated them daily, thanks to my tutor. But now I stand here, my mouth hanging open as I'm unable to remember their names.

Thylas stands beside me, always a comforting presence. He can't help me though, not without giving away my subtle lack of diplomacy and tact. He's not to speak right now unless spoken to anyway — stupid rules of society. He probably paid better attention to his tutor.

"Princess Carnaxa, welcome." A beautiful, deep-ebony skinned woman with the most glorious, dark-green hair fused with silver approaches me. A bronze diadem sets on her brow, an emerald, teardrop stone dips between her eyebrows between her almond, deep-set, brown eyes. No, they aren't brown, they are gold. Her nose has freckles that look like stars in the night sky.

"Thank you ..." I curtsy and Ereon catches my hesitation, bowing along with me.

"Queen Natala," he finishes for me, giving me a side smile and a wink, "and King Elino. Thank you for welcoming us into your home."

"Prince Ereon, you are welcome here anytime you pass through. We are happy that you — both of you — honor us by taking time out of your travels to visit our kingdom. We did not expect your arrival for many moons, have you and Princess Carnaxa already wed?" King Elino glances toward my throat, noticing it lacks a shell. His midnight skin is in contrast to his bright yellow tunic, and his dark hair is braided in small braids that reach the middle of his back, golden beads woven through them. He's older but his frame is still one that shows strength, and his own eyes shine with wisdom.

"No, Your Highness," I say quickly, still feeling embarrassed having not remembered their names. Hopefully they didn't notice. "We are to be wed in Shaston, plans changed. We are on our way there now. May I introduce, my cousin, *Bêlit* Siphonie, and her husband, *Bêl* Rhenor." I glance toward Siphonie as she and Rhenor step forward, bowing slightly.

"Welcome," King Elino says in his deep voice that seems to deepen as he speaks. "We welcome you all to our home. What has happened for the plans to change so suddenly? Has the deluc expedited your journey to Shaston? "

"Let's not bother them with so many questions, darling. They just arrived." Queen Natala smiles at me. "Let's get them inside. I'm sure they are exhausted from their trip. We began preparing as soon as we saw your banners. Your rooms should be ready now. Go on ahead and the servants will show you where you'll be staying. Again, welcome to Midaeliea."

TWENTY-ONE

EREON

Walking toward the rooms prepared for me, thoughts of Carnaxa overtake me. She shouldn't be as beautiful and kind as she is. It's honestly very frustrating. Growing up I heard many things about the people of Antalis. I heard about their preferential treatment by the Goddess, how they were blessed in the same myths and stories that condemn my people. I heard rumors of the Princess too. I was told of her stubbornness and her beauty, her affinity for never thinking of her own safety, but no one told me she was so innocent. No one told me how much she cared, or how naïve and in the same breath, how kind she is. The stories I was told painted her as a spoiled brat, and yet I've found nothing but concern and compassion.

Carnaxa doesn't know it, but I've watched her these past few weeks. I watched her in her own palace of course, which proved difficult when she was constantly running off into the city or away to her chambers where I wasn't allowed. I had my own things to do during the months I was in Antalis. I found more soldiers to add to my rank, some sanctioned by King Clennom, some not. I lied as I answered questions about the wedding ceremony I knew would never happen in Antalis. But most importantly, I watched her. I wanted to see who she was when she thought no one was watching.

I didn't want to get to know her, I didn't want to form a connection. I intentionally avoided putting myself in situations with her that would require more intimate conversation than I was willing to be a part of. She was just supposed to be a means to an end. Then at the beach, I didn't mean to run into her. I was out there concerned about my own problems, and there she was and she was upset. I tried to make her laugh, and I'm still not sure why, I ached to see the smile she so often bestowed on others. Then it was time to go.

Since our journey started she's not been too far from my sight. Despite what everyone thinks, I know her guard is in love with her, that much is obvious, it's why I didn't want him coming along. He shouldn't have been allowed to, but alas, my hands were tied. It's also not uncommon for people to mysteriously die in my land and accidents do happen. I don't want his feelings for Carnaxa to get in the way of what I have to do when we return home, for all of our sakes.

Despite the fact that I thought she would run off on our journey to Midaeliea, her curiosity getting the best of her, Carnaxa has stayed close to her companions and hasn't done anything out of the ordinary. It almost makes me hate what will become of her in Shaston. I know the men who travel with us want a taste of her. My men are ruthless and don't care about her title, only the pleasure they'll find with her. They probably expect to have their way with her, but I can't let that happen. I once thought I would, it's not like I haven't let them have captives before, but this is different. She's different. I won't let that happen to her, and I've already started trying to spread the word that she's off limits.

I watched as she was greeted by the people of Midaeliea and how she embraced them. Watching Carnaxa fidget and forget the royals' names would have made even the darkest hearts smile, and I couldn't help but want to save her from the blunder. The Princess of Antalis is a great blessing for those of Midaeliea. They tolerate Shaston, but they love Antalis, considering most Antalian priestesses come here for training. Sometimes it seems as though Midaeliea and Antalis are of the same kingdom, even though their kingdoms' respective lands look different, their cultures are similar, yet there are borders that separate the two.

Midaelieans are raised in forests and along streams. Their homes are simple, made from the trunks of the trees that surround them. Midaeliea does not fight within itself, having even less crime than

Antalis. Queen Natala and King Elino are two people I would consider friends, even though I know what is coming. They won't be able to put up a fight when my father's plans come to pass; they will have to bow or be conquered. These are all Father's plans, which are my plans regardless of how I feel about them, he *made me* see things his way.

There is a reason my father sends me in his place to the other kingdoms of the continent. I may be an asshole, but my father is a different monster entirely. I've heard elders of Shaston whisper about how every child of our bloodline becomes as hateful as the man who sired them. One day, I will become just like him if I'm not already. I will become a monster if that's what it takes to save her. Everything I do is to protect her.

Carnaxa will have to keep herself meek and mild in order to stay on my father's good side. A side that not many of us are able to see if you can even call it a good side. I'm his only son, and yet I know the lengths he will go to break a person.

"She will be a beauty to watch ride, " a soldier says. Two soldiers stand outside my door before they notice I'm walking toward them. He shuts his mouth quickly when he finally sees me and shuffles to appear taller.

"Who are we speaking of?" I ask, stopping in front of him, staring him down.

His too-wide eyes are a mix of green and brown as he tries not to meet my gaze. He coughs, clearing his throat. "No ... no one, my Prince."

"No please, I love to talk of women riding, I would just like to know who we are speaking of. Is it one of the women here? If so, I would certainly like to give her a try."

I've not had anyone for years, but the one who waits for me back home, I don't want anyone else. It's why the men believe I'm accustomed to sharing women, assuming I would share the woman who frequents my bed, but I'm too possessive for that. The women who have been seen with me, never truly make it to my bed. I often encourage them to tell my men their company is a gift from me. I can't imagine my heart with another, someone else hearing her moans of pleasure. She is the only one with whom I want to fall into bed with at night. At least, she was.

"He was speaking of your betrothed, Princess Carnaxa," the blonde, young, stocky boy beside him says. He is new to the guard, but showed promise in Shaston's fighting ring so he got to make the trip with us.

"Interesting," I say derisively. Unwarranted rage fills me and I look toward the man with lewd thoughts of Carnaxa. Before he realizes what I'm doing, I grab his throat and shove him against the wall. I close my fingers around his jugular, his breath starts to come in shallow takes. "Princess Carnaxa is *mine* and as such, will be riding only me. Please take note and do not speak of her like that again, she is not a whore, she is to be your queen consort. This is your one and only offense as I realize I am a man who will usually share a woman. They are nothing more than pockets of warmth for me at night, but you would be wise to remember your place. And you would be wise to remember she will be *my wife*."

His eyes bulge and sweat beads down on his brow before I release him. He drops to the ground coughing and gasping for air. Kicking his booted feet out of my way, I look toward the younger one who visibly cringes, and I warn him, "They'll beat you for being a tattle-tale, you should prepare yourself." His face pales, but it's the only kindness I'll show him.

Slamming the door shut behind me, I throw a vase across the dark room. How dare the men so openly speak of her in such a way. We've traveled only a few days. Do they think that no one will notice here in Midaeliea, if she is used?

Running my hand through my beard, I lean down putting my palms on my knees. I have got to get a handle on myself. I don't understand the anger that floods me, she will be my wife, but that doesn't mean anything, not in Shaston. My mother was proof that many lack respect toward a titled woman. I clench my fist trying to find my breath, trying to tame the fury inside.

What is happening? I shouldn't care, I don't care. But then I see her eyes flash inside my mind and remember the day I met her and the pull I felt — it was a pull I've not felt in some time.

The people of Antalis whisper about twin drops, but the Shastonians have no such notion. Many marry because they are forced to or because it will advance their family's status. A few I have learned are married for love, but twin drops don't happen in my kingdom. A cruel way in which the Goddess made sure we realized how cursed we truly are, even her drops burn in this heat.

I light a candle next to the doorframe now that I have caught my breath. The emotions that floored me while I was with Carnaxa were the same I felt the night *she* came into my life, unprecedented and leaving me in a state of uncertainty.

･･●●●◑●○●◐●●●･･

Seven Lunar Years Ago

"A son of mine should know how to handle a woman properly. You are a man now and I've already heard rumors that you have yet to have a woman. I won't have that. It's a sign of weakness, as though something is wrong with you. Something wrong with your ability to produce an heir?" my father snaps as he walks in. His dark hair matches his soulless eyes and matching black outfit. He's dressed in his normal apparel of black leathers, heavy boots and a black, long sleeve tunic with his cape and matching hood. "So now, I found one for you."

He drags a woman around my age in. Her hands are bound by obsidian chains in front of her, and her dark sable brown hair falls in loose waves around her face. Dirt and mud cover her honey-beige skin, at least I hope it's mud. She smells of her travels here — the sea sickness that takes many on their trip to Midaeliea, the mud they climb through to get past the patrols and into pass. If Midaeliea knew we smuggled in prisoners, they would call it an act of war since we use their land to get people here.

Blood coats her in places across her arms and down her wrists where the chains dig in. But her eyes, the almond-shaped pools of dark brown with hints of gold catch my attention. I can't look away and neither does she. Father pulls the rope he holds connecting to her chains causing her to stumble, but her eyes never falter and her head remains high. He hasn't used the obsidian chains on many, she must have put up a fight. "Here is a toy. She's untouched by anyone in Shaston, at least that's what I was told. She's from one of the southern kingdoms, I didn't ask which."

He runs his finger across her bottom lip and smiles. "If she doesn't please you ... I'll add her to my harem. I think she would be a beautiful addition after a bath." She pulls her face from his grasp. He tosses the rope to me, turns, and slaps her across the face. Her neck snaps to the left and a single trail of blood slides from her lower lip. Fury floods my veins and I ball my hand in a fist to keep it from connecting with my father's jaw. Something I would absolutely suffer for later.

"Make him a man, or it'll be me riding you. I promise I won't be as gentle." He takes a step toward the door, but before he exits, he turns back to badger me, "And Ereon, don't disappoint me. You won't have a second chance. I'll have guards outside." His black cape trails around him as he walks out the door.

Dropping the rope, I immediately run to the young woman, trying to check her face. Pushing her hair back, my fingers feel the heat from the slap.

"Get your hands off me," she yells. "I can take care of myself." She pushes against my chest, the best she can with her hands chained.

I walk to the other side of the room, grabbing a rag from the basin on the table. "I'm not trying to hurt you, let me help." I hold my hands up and show her the washcloth.

She spits at my feet before derisively adding, "I said I can take care of myself. Just do what you are going to do, and send me to wherever I'll call home now."

I roll my eyes. "You sure have a lot of attitude for someone in your situation, trying to bite the hand that's trying to help." I can't help the way my heart feels as I look at her, like a wave of emotions pulling me toward her.

"I can handle myself. But just know, if you force yourself on me, I will find a way to gut you in your sleep. So if that's what you're going to do – let's go ahead and get it over with, so death finds one of us much quicker." She wipes the back of her hand across her cheek, smudging dirt that's already there.

I can't help but laugh. Never has a woman been so bold to speak to me like this. My father's wrong though, I have been with women. I just don't take them against their will, they leave my room happy. And here, if you want to stay that way, you keep quiet.

"What is your name?" I ask the woman, untying the rope from around her chains. I don't have the key to them, my father has the only one, but maybe I can give her some relief. "And I'm not planning on forcing myself on you, when a woman screams I want it to be my name on their lips in pleasure, not pain."

She stands a bit taller, her chainless shackles around her wrists dig into her skin as she brings her hands up, pushing her hair behind her shoulder and answers, "Anara."

TWENTY-TWO

CARNAXA

The room has a rounded wooden door and a square window opposite the entry way. I'm without a balcony but the window provides much to see. From the large window, I can see the village outside the castle gates and the forest that surrounds us. The village seems to already be awake as sounds of music and voices, along with smells of bread, drift through the air. Nothing happened yesterday after our arrival. Many of us preferred to have dinner inside our rooms after the journey here. While it wasn't a long or terrible trip, I've never needed to sleep anywhere but my own bed before, so I was eager to see a large, plush and inviting bed waiting for me.

"Good morning, Princess Carnaxa." A young woman, probably close to my age, walks in with a tray of fruits and a goblet of water. "My name is Lanie and I will be more than happy to get you, or anyone accompanying you, anything that's needed while you all stay here."

"Thank you, Lanie. Can you tell me if anyone from my party is awake yet?" I pop a ripe strawberry in my mouth.

"Yes, my lady, Prince Ereon and Captain Thylas were seen earlier this morning heading to the training yard. *Bêl* Rhenor and *Bêlit* Siphonie have not yet left their rooms, but are awake as I served them breakfast myself before coming here."

"Prince Ereon and Captain Thylas are in the training yard? Together?" My mind remembers the strong words Ereon spoke to Thylas just days before our departure. It would be a worthy fight between the two, but the thought of them harming one another makes me flinch. May the tide take me, I need both to help me survive the days to come.

"Can you help me get dressed and then escort me to the training grounds please?" I gulp down the water quickly and begin dropping my sleeping gown on the floor.

"Yes, Princess Carnaxa. However, I must warn you our training grounds are not exactly a place where royal guests are normally seen. The training grounds are brutal. Queen Natala rarely ever finds herself down there, we have no female soldiers at this time, and many women don't wish to see the bloodshed. The soldiers who train are few, as our kingdom rarely sees battle-so it's usually just men with grievances toward one another. They like an audience."

"Either way ..." My mind drifts toward the trouble the two men could find themselves in. If Ereon was to hurt Thylas, who is now also Antalis' ambassador, that would anger my father. If Thylas hurts Ereon, the mistake would anger King Atlas. "Take me."

Lanie helps me get into a floor-length, grey gown, a Midaeliean style commonly worn. The gown is heavier than I am used to with ribbons that tie up the back. The dress hangs loosely around my waist and has sleeves that are attached separately, going up to just under my shoulders and tying with more ribbon. My shoulders are exposed, but I find the garment comfortable while also being surprisingly airy. Lanie's nimble fingers tie my hair in a variety of braids that cascade down my back. She adds a wooden hairpin, shaped like a tree, to complete the look.

For a quick look, she did great. I put on a pair of loose slippers and my Mother's crown. In Antalis, I rarely wore any crown. But today, I'll happily wear it while it reminds me she's still with me in my heart. The shells that sit atop each other create the crown, coated with silver to keep them everlastingly beautiful. Along with the shells, sapphires and pearls are scattered throughout. I adjust it a bit more but it still feels heavy and I feel off balance.

Lanie smiles at me, her hair twisted and held together by a ribbon on the side of her angular face in a beautiful way. She's a lovely girl as she opens the door for me, her deep-olive dress is in a similar fashion to mine but hits her mid-thigh instead of going all the way to the floor.

"Are you ready, Princess?"

Taking one more glance toward the mirror, I tuck a piece of stubborn hair behind my ear and nod toward her, before following her out the door.

·· ● ● ◑ ● ○ ● ◐ ● ● ··

Inside a wooden dome is a large open area with grass and dirt. There are seats around the area for those wanting to witness the training or fighting. The top of the dome has an open circle in the middle allowing light to filter through while the sides of the dome are also open.

In the middle of the circular area stands Ereon and Thylas. Both are covered in dirt and sweat. Thylas' midnight hair is twisted at the base of his neck, strands escaping around his face as he stands in nothing but his leather breeches and boots. He holds a sword in his left hand and a short dagger in the other.

Ereon stands on the opposite Thylas, his wild curls bouncing as he sways from foot to foot, waiting for Thylas to make a move. *Mohasha* save me. Ereon wears nothing but leather pants and laced boots as well. He however, holds two large, curved swords that look just as deadly as the expression on his face.

Neither of them notices as I enter and I don't say a word but instead hide in the shadows, Lanie following me. The coolness from the shade surrounds us and I motion for her to stay quiet, she smiles and nods. Her eyes drift toward the men circling each other. Others stand to the side watching as it happens, some even taking bets on who will be the winner. Lanie rubs her chest with her hand, obviously getting excited by what she sees, I can't blame her.

Ereon advances toward Thylas, as he clangs his two swords against Thylas' broadsword. They both grunt and try to push against each other, kicking up dirt. I can see their mouths moving, but can't hear from here what is being said. Ereon drops one sword suddenly, startling Thylas as he brings his left hand to connect to his jaw. Thylas face turns to the side and he loses balance. He tumbles to the dirt, but rolls away and is quickly back on his feet.

"If you would have been born in Shaston, you could have been a decent warrior, Captain." Ereon spits at the ground as they circle each other again, twirling his remaining sword in his right hand.

Thylas says nothing as he advances again, kicking toward Ereon's feet trying to trip him, as Ereon jumps, his sword in the air. He brings it so close to Thylas' face that I gasp and Lanie grabs the bend of my arm. The short dagger is still in Thylas' hand, the only thing separating him from death by Ereon's blades. Thylas moves his head toward Ereon, headbutting him, and Ereon scrambles back a few steps. Thylas loses no time before kicking Ereon in the side and throws a punch across his face. He then brings his dagger toward Ereon's throat but Ereon grabs Thylas' wrist.

It's then that I notice Thylas' back. The scars that mark it. The scars that are all my fault. It's been years since he's displayed them so publically. His tattoos flowing across his shoulder blades are beautiful compared to his back. The scars are faded now, but the whipping was one caused by a broken heart and pain, the physical scars reflect that emotional trauma. Lanie takes in a breath beside me, noticing the scars the same moment I do; not many see such a mangled back from someone of importance.

The two men continue to struggle for the upper hand until Ereon glances my way and winks. In the middle of fighting and the man winks at me! He pushes against Thylas who is still on top of him with his dagger almost touching Ereon's throat. Ereon pushes hard enough that Thylas falls backward and Ereon quickly pushes to his feet, and announces my arrival, "My princess, we weren't expecting to see you here."

At that, Thylas turns around, meeting my gaze, and quickly bows. He grabs the cotton shirt he haphazardly tossed on the ground, putting it back on. He blushes, then stares at my feet avoiding my gaze. "Princess Carnaxa, forgive me. Time must have gotten away from me as I meant to be back before you awoke."

"It's certainly alright. Thankfully I have Lanie here to assist. What, may I ask, are you two up to?" Both men look like children caught stealing from the kitchen, but Ereon speaks first.

"We were simply making sure we stayed up to par with our training. I didn't find many who would spar with me, and your captain here said he would. Nothing more than men being men." He smiles and despite the dirt that covers his face, I notice he has dimples. How have I never noticed them before?

"Princess, if you would allow me to gather my things, I'll be happy to escort you for the rest of the day." Thylas looks down, grabs his sword, and twirls his dagger in his right hand, putting it into the leather sheath strapped around his muscular thigh.

Ereon steps in front of him and says, "I'll escort her. It will give you time to make yourself presentable." I don't make a mention of how Ereon is just as dirt-ridden. "I'm sure this woman" – he stops to smile at Lanie and I don't miss what seems to be a silent message between them – "wouldn't mind helping fetch some water for you." He nods to Lanie, who has become so quiet I forgot she was even beside me.

Lanie bows her head slightly. "Yes, whatever you need."

Thylas looks toward her, then back at me. "If that's what you wish, *Su Kechni*." I nod in agreement and he walks away, glancing back at me as I stare after him.

As Thylas walks away, Ereon grabs his shirt and slips it on, next he drapes his swords' sheaths criss-cross, behind his back, followed by his swords. "Do you not wish to wash your sweat off as well?"

He wipes a rag across his face. "And miss getting to know you more? Never. I will bathe soon, I won't make you suffer my stench for too long. And Princess Carnaxa, what if we stop with the pleasantries? We are to be wed soon, after all."

I twist the bangles of silver and gold on my wrist before continuing, "Then what would you like for me to call you?" I don't know why the man makes me so nervous, but he does. I am not one who is known for being strong-willed, but I would also never call myself meek, but in his presence, I am.

"How about Ereon? That is my name, you know." He gestures for us to walk and holds his arm out so that I may wrap my own around it.

I laugh. "Yes, I do know that much my ... Ereon."

"Oh, I'm yours am I?"

My cheeks twitch in embarrassment at the blunder and I lower my gaze to the ground. Trying to change the subject, I probe, "Are you ready to return home?" This is the same conversation I seem to have with him, but each time I do he tells me just a bit more about himself. It's the only time he seems to want to talk, and I really have nothing else to speak about.

"I am ready to be back ... mostly. Are you ready for a new kingdom?"

"If I'm being honest, I am excited and also scared. Who wouldn't be? I have been made to leave my home, marry someone I don't know, and rule a kingdom that is not the one I grew up in."

His eyes darken as he looks down at me, maybe I was too honest with him.

"We will get to know each other Carnaxa, I won't always be a stranger. You will be my queen consort and you will be perfect at my side. When my father steps down, of course."

Queen Consort. I want to roll my eyes, what a nice way to say, I'll have no power. If he thinks I will also take that stance when it comes to Antalis, well ... he has another thing coming.

"Are you ready to see your father?"

His arm tightens slightly around my own as he shrugs in response, "Sure. He is the King after all. Just a word of advice, when you meet him, always remember: you are not in Antalis. Antalis is not your home anymore and what I said to your father is true. You will be held to the rules of Shaston just as much as any other woman, if not more intently. My mother was always held to higher, almost impossible standards."

His tone has changed, to the one he used with my father – not the same one that started this conversation joking about formalities. His eyes look distant, searching the tree line as he quickly changes the subject again, "I do believe we will stay an extra day or two here, in Midaeliea. The trip to the mountains takes but a half day, and I think you would enjoy this kingdom a bit. Plus the Queen asked that we stay."

"That would be lovely."

We walk into the gardens, when Siphonie approaches.

"Prince Ereon" – she bows – "Princess Carnaxa."

"This is where I leave you, Princess, to go take *that* bath. *Bêlit* Siphonie, how good to see you." He pats my hand, untwirling our arms as he walks away. I let out a sigh and give Siphonie a look of annoyance.

"What was that about, Naxa. Are you okay?" Siphonie slips a hand to my brow, I don't know why she thinks I would have a fever. I suppose she is just worried for me, and I can understand that.

"I'm fine, what are you doing out here?" I fidget with my hands and the bracelets along my wrist.

"I passed Thylas and he said you were alone with Ereon. Normally I wouldn't intrude on betrothal business, but the way he said it, I thought I would come check. I didn't mean for him to leave."

She sighs and looks to where Ereon disappeared to and remarks, "It really would be good for the two of you to try to get to know one another before you're wed."

"It's okay, our conversation was finishing up anyway. I think we are working our way towards knowing more about each other, slowly. But can we go find the eating hall? I'm famished."

"I'm eating for two, so I'm always famished. Let's go." She wraps her hand with mine and pulls me toward the eating hall.

··•●◐○●◑●••·

After eating breakfast, Siphonie and I make our way to the village, wanting to understand more about what Midaeliea has to offer. The cottages and shops, along the cobblestone road, are made of wood beams and bark. I see some have large, round, brown rocks built into columns to help support the buildings.

The people of Midaeliea are extremely sweet, they smile at us as we walk past. There are many things to purchase, food, drinks, trinkets, and clothes. Siphonie walks arm in arm with me, taking it all in beside me. Many people are out and about today, enjoying the sun as its rays filter through the thick tops of the green trees above us.

Siphonie has a smile on her face, her hair blowing slightly in the wind. She stops in front of a vendor selling small clothing for children. She reaches out to touch the fabrics in various shades of dark green, bright blue, black, and white. She is happier than I've seen her in a while, not that I have seen her much since *Täht* and

Mar. It's been a whirlwind and everything has changed. I thought we would talk more during our travels, but I guess we remain in our thoughts about our changing lives more than anything.

I wonder if I will have the same luck as Siphonie and Rhenor. Sure, they didn't have the best start, but they seem to be more satisfied and happier in their relationship now. While they may not be twin drops, there is love between them for the growing blessing in her womb and I think love may also be blooming for each other. Maybe Ereon and I can find our way to one another. We may not be affectionate now, but he is charming and handsome. Our children would be heirs to both kingdoms, in a way uniting the whole of the Northern Continent, with the exception of Midaeliea.

"Is one of you expecting?" An older woman appears, her grey hair piled high on top of her head, loose strands fall down against her neck. She nods toward us in a quick bow, seeming to recognize us but kindly not wanting to draw attention. Our hair makes us stick out; I'm sure everyone already knows who we are, but I appreciate her consideration.

"I am," Siphonie answers as she looks down the table at the items laid out. "You have beautiful creations."

"Thank you, dear. Is this your first?"

"It is. How can you tell? Do you have any children?"

The old woman laughs, "Oh, dear, I have six. Twelve grandchildren, and a few greats roaming around here. I have a sense for these things, I can always tell when someone is expecting. You give off a glow."

"Six children? Of your own?" I can't help but interrupt.

"Yes, child. Six children all from my womb. Four boys and two girls. My youngest girl helps me around the shop, my other daughter is in the *Shayi Yengo* in Antalis. One of my boys became a priest, another, a soldier for Midaeliea, and my other two help out around here, as well as hunt for the kingdom."

"That's amazing, you have truly been blessed by the Goddess." I put my hand into my pocket checking how much silver coin I have on me, because I know I am already going to buy something from this woman, even if I don't need anything. I can purchase something for Siphonie.

"Blessed by someone that's for sure, given it was the Goddess who granted me my drop, but heavens if it wasn't the God who blessed my husband. The fire that burns inside of him is unmatched, that man still can't get enough of me, even in our old age." She laughs.

A god? I've never heard of anyone claiming a god. Maybe their stories have been twisted and bent out of shape. Perhaps, like my own mother, they like to weave their own stories. We all know that the Goddess created us because she was alone in the world, but who am I to tell one of my elders she is wrong? She reminds me a great deal of Ilis and her children from back home. I miss Ilis, but it brings me comfort knowing the white stole she gifted me is in my trunks back at the castle.

"Are you okay, child?" The older woman stares at me.

"Oh yes, I'm sorry. I got lost in thought for a moment. Can I ask for your name? In my kingdom, there is someone who reminds me of you."

"My name is Emi. And you are Princess Carnaxa of Antalis, correct?" She gestures toward my cousin. "And you are *Bêlit* Siphonie?"

"Emmy?" The word is strange on my tongue. "Yes, you are correct in your observations of who we are. We try not to call a lot of attention to ourselves, but I am sure our large caravan didn't help."

She sits down on a stool behind her, placing her hands on her knees. " E-may is how you pronounce my name, dear. But honestly, you can call me whatever you like. I've had many names over the years, wife, mother, daughter, friend, and I'll be happy to add more. Yes, we all watched you arrive, plus your hair is a beautiful sight. When I was young it was more common, now we've all turned gray and only a few are born with the colors. Upon your arrival, I heard you and the Prince of Shaston are to be wed."

Her eyes squint and wrinkles form deeply in the corners as she stares at me, as if she can see through my eyes and into my soul. Her wrinkled fingers twist around each other as she pops her gnarly knuckles from years of dressmaking. She reaches out to take my hand in hers. Her face contorts and a look of concern crosses her features.

Siphonie speaks up against the awkward silence, "She is. And will she not make just the most beautiful bride?" I smile at her tentatively.

"She will be a beautiful bride, no one could doubt that. However, you should know," nerves lace the old woman's voice as she looks around before her eye catches on something behind us, and she stands up releasing my hand. She fumbles around, laying out more clothing before mumbling, "Oh, nevermind. Just old words from an old woman."

I almost call out to her as Ereon appears at my side. His hair is still damp from the bath he took and he smells of earth mixed with a sweet smell I can't quite place. He wears a black tunic that molds to his body, the gold snake of his kingdom embroidered in it. His leather pants show off his trim figure and his golden boots lace up to just below his knees. My heart races at the sight of him. Goddess, he is beautiful. His deep-brown eyes meet mine as he smiles down at me.

"Princess." His hand touches softly on my lower back. "Hello again, *Bêlit* Siphonie."

Siphonie pulls on my arm and we bow in sync and he just shakes his head. "I thought we talked about formalities." He laughs under his breath, "What are we in the market for today?"

"Nothing really, just wanting to stretch our legs and get an idea for what all Midaeliea has to offer." I turn my attention back to the old lady.

"I think I'm going to buy a few of these, Emi – the one in deep-green, black, and the light-blue one. One for each kingdom that I will have traveled."

"Yes, Your Highness." That's all she says before gathering the garments to give to Siphonie. Her wrinkled hands shake as she gives the bag to Siphonie. I step out of Ereon's grasp and edge closer to Emi, finding myself standing in front of Siphonie as I face the old woman. Emi reaches out to me and I grab her hands in mine, having snatched a few coins from my purse, I give them to her.

She leans in closely grabbing the coins from my hand. "I must tell you something," her voice is barely a whisper. "Upon the day the moon turns bright, the loyal heir's death awakens eternal night. The waters will rise and the fires will blaze, then only the sacrificed can save." Just as quickly as she says the words, she turns and walks toward the back of her shop.

"Where is that guard of yours?" Ereon's smooth voice spooks me from my thoughts.

"Last I remember, you sent him to take a bath." I smile at him. "Siphonie here is a perfectly good guard."

"Yes Prince Ereon, I may not look like much but I think I could protect our Naxa if I needed to." She pretends to show off her limited muscles. My face lights with joy and she smiles at us both. "See, perfectly capable."

He smirks as he replies, "While I am sure you can protect her, I somehow managed to have enough time to walk with her until we ran into you, *Bêlit* Siphonie, bathe, and find you both again, all before he finished washing up. You should never be left alone Carnaxa, especially in a place in which you are a stranger."

We walk toward a tavern, the smell of roast meat filling the air. While I feel the pit of my stomach churning, if he is to be my husband I must learn to speak up during moments worth speaking up for. I bite my lower lip before inhaling quickly.

"You underestimate me Ereon – I might also be capable of taking care of myself. I have found no reason to fear anyone here. We couldn't find Thylas before we decided to leave, although we did leave a note. He is most likely searching for us now, but it might take him some time to find us in such a busy marketplace. He is just as much a stranger to this land as I am." The words spill from my lips in a quick and hurried manner making me sound less confident than I feel.

Ereon's lips turn up in almost a smile, but not quite; a low chuckle escapes him. He slides his hand along his baldric that holds his two curved swords against his back, and runs his other hand in his brown hair. I catch myself wondering what it would feel like to run my fingers through the mahogany curls. The thought shocks me. Perhaps the moment Thylas initiated but never finished, has my body frustrated. Soon however, I will know exactly what it's like to have Ereon's hair between my fingertips and his body on mine. It'll be my marital duty.

"I would never underestimate you, Princess. Regardless, I will speak to your guard, *again.* Not only is he your guard, but he is an ambassador. He should take his duties more seriously or I will have to take action."

"There is no need for any of this. Let's not rehash old conflicts — *again.*"

"There is no need for you to constantly protect him when his job is to protect you. You will need protection when we reach Shaston." He looks ahead of us and smiles, nodding toward a vendor. "I think the two of you will enjoy these." He stops to purchase, what I assume is a treat, something that smells like chocolate, and hands each of us one.

I accept the food and take a bite, the sweetness overtaking my tongue. "Will I need protection in Shaston because I'm to be your wife or is there something else I should fear?"

Using his thumb, he wipes off a crumb from the corner of my mouth. "Because ... I didn't expect to actually enjoy your company and I'm starting to. I would prefer nothing nefarious happens to you, so I'll need your guard to protect you when I can't."

TWENTY-THREE

THYLAS

I turn the silver door knob and walk through the rounded doorway into my room. It's sparse but not uncomfortable. A fireplace sits in the middle of the room with a large hearth attached to it, and a bed with a large grey comforter is at the far end in front of large, square windows. A private washroom is attached to the room as well.

Sitting down on the edge of the bed, untying the laces of my boots, I place them under my bed. My toes curl and uncurl as they relax and I inhale deeply. I take off my cotton tunic which smells of dirt and sweat, and throw it on the floor. I need to make this quick, I'm sure Carnaxa will be looking for me.

Water is waiting for me in a basin in the private washroom, it's still warm and I quickly pour some into a wooden bowl beside the tub and begin to rinse my face. I'd like to take a bath, but I'm simply too tired. I take a cloth and begin wiping down my body. Running the cloth across my tattoos, the language of the Goddess revealed across my skin. It's stated that when the Goddess created the first Antalians they spoke the language learned from the Mother. Over time, the language changed as the population grew to what is used today, but I'm one of few who is fluent in the original language, trained by Rhenor. It's something I take pride in, being once a child no one wanted and now having a gift that unveils so many things.

The words that swirl around my arm and across my shoulders tell of my story, my hopes, and my dreams. They portray a small happy boy, who was torn from his mother, and drifted away on the sea, who eventually found his way to the shores of Antalis. The words convey my struggles of trying to cope and learn who I am. The last of the words is the story of my whipping and even now I don't regret it for one moment. I did what I did for Carnaxa, and I will always sacrifice myself for her, to be her safety.

A soft knock on my door startles me. I open it to find the same woman who escorted me back to the castle, along with two other women who stand just behind her.

"I need you to follow me, Captain. You have been requested for a special meeting."

·····●◐●○●◐●●··

When a woman finds her lips around my cock I am usually happy, even excited. But here I am in such a predicament and wishing to be anywhere else. I need to get to Carnaxa. Their note was delivered stating they were going into the village. I don't like the thought of her alone in this kingdom. I don't know what I have to do to get her to understand, not everyone has her best interest in mind. I roll my eyes, I'm sure Ereon is with her, the one who fanangled this situation, probably so he could play the savior and blame me once again.

Lanie is on her knees in front of me, her hand wrapped around my base, her head bobbing up and down on my length. My hand slightly rests on her dark curls that have come undone from the updo she had on display earlier.

Two of Ereon's soldiers stand behind her, each with their own female for companionship. "A gift from Prince Ereon," I was told as they all came to me outside my chambers when summoned by Lanie to follow her. A gift. I laugh under my breath and she stops for a moment, before returning back to the duty before her. I'm more like a hostage at this point.

He sent her to keep me away from Carnaxa and the two soldiers here are meant to keep an eye out and make sure I don't send her away. I'm not dumb to the games of high-borns, I've played them before. I tried to pass off Lanie's advances as best I could. Lanie, nor the soldiers, wouldn't hear of it, reminding me it is rude to ignore a gift given from their prince. I've been stuck with the two of them and the women for a while now and I'm just ready to get this over with. Lanie isn't unattractive, and if this was prior to having had a taste of Carnaxa, I would be in *Mohasha,* but right now ... she's not who I want.

"Captain," Lanie's soft voice pulls me from my thoughts as she subtly rubs at her jaw. It's taking me forever, which is something I normally pride myself on, because I would give the women a great night to remember. However, right now, it's just annoying both of us. "Would you rather us do something else?"

No ... Goddess, no. She's hoping it would speed things up, but I just can't. No fault of hers of course, but after knowing how Naxa felt beneath me, I'll wait forever to have her again if I have to. The guards across the room, one plunging into a woman with large hips and auburn hair, the other man's face deep into the blonde, they both take a moment to stare at me.

"Looks like Antalian men can't finish the job," one mumbles before going back to the feast in front of him.

I shake my head at Lanie and she wraps her plump lips around me once again, but this time I close my eyes and imagine it's Carnaxa. I imagine her hands being the ones wrapped around my thickness. I imagine her tongue, the one licking the tip before swallowing me. I imagine her throat being the one that I now pound into.

"Thylas!" I hear Carnaxa's voice calling from the hallway. *Kosæ!* I try to push away from Lanie, but she doesn't realize that and in- steads digs her fingers into my thighs pulling me closer. A tingling at the base of my spines has me wanting to moan at being so close to release.

Just as my hand's fist in her bark-colored hair to pull her away, my release finds its mark down her throat, the creaky door opens and there, my *Nohæ* stands. Her beautiful ocean-colored eyes staring right into mine before her eyes dart from my eyes to Lanie on her knees, as she drinks me up. Carnaxa stops, her hand still on the door.

"I'm ... I'm ..." she turns around flustered and leaves back the way she came, slamming the door so loudly the windows shake in the panes. The other guards snicker across the room, and I glare back daring them to say something, as I pull my leathers back into place quickly tying the laces.

Lanie wipes the corner of her lips, smiling up at me. She has no idea what game she's a part of. I feel bad, she might think I am not attracted to her, contributing to the extended time I needed to find release, but it has nothing to do with her. I'll apologize later.

I push past her and walk quickly after Carnaxa. She walks briskly down the hallway, her bangles around her wrist jingle with every step she takes.

"Princess Carnaxa." I try to catch her attention. She doesn't stop, in fact, she starts walking faster down the barely lit hallway. "*Nohæ*! Please!" I yell, but she continues ignoring me as she passes other soldiers, who quickly move out of her way. Smart men. I can't help but yell at her one more time, "Baby girl! I need you to stop."

Finally, that spurns her attention and she turns around, her grey dress fluttering behind her. A flash of hurt assaults her eyes before she composes herself, straightening her back and folding her hands in front of her. "Captain Thylas, I am sorry I interrupted your activities, please go back and enjoy."

"It's not what you think, I was ..." I take a step toward her and she quickly takes one step back. She pushes a piece of hair behind her ear as she takes on a more regal tone.

"It doesn't matter. I was simply trying to see why you were not on duty today while Siphonie and I traveled the village, but as I have my answer, I'll go now."

"I tried ... I promise, I was coming."

"Well that was obvious to *everyone* in that room," she interrupts me. While her cheeks show a splash of pink, she never breaks eye contact. She motions her hand back down the hall, "And feel free to go back."

"*Kosæ!* That's not what I meant and you know it. Ereon, he's the one who sent them. He's the one who wanted to keep me away from you." I reach out to her but she moves nimbly out of my grasp. "Please, listen to me. I didn't want to be with her."

"What's the point in listening, Thylas? I'm not your woman, it doesn't matter. I'm sure Ereon was forcing you to get your cock sucked when he was at the village with me. Because you were always celibate in Antalis too, right? The woman at the festival was just a friend? The other women I've heard speak about you, giving them nights of pleasure they'll never forget. That was all Ereon? But it's fine, just finish up what you were doing. We have dinner with Queen Natala and King Elino. Please find your way there on time."

Before any more words can leave my lips, she turns and stomps down the corridor, around the corner, and out of my sight, leaving nothing but her scent of vanilla and coconut suffocating me. I punch the door beside me, the wood splintering and leaving marks along my knuckles. I hit it again and again, not caring about the damage to the door or my hands. Midaeliean soldiers appear and try to pull me away. My heart feels like it's being ripped out and it's my own fault. I didn't mean for her to see this, I don't want her to feel less than, to feel like I would choose someone over her. She's known about my dalliances in Antalis, but now things have changed. All because I had to know what it was like to just hold her, to let her be the one wrapped in my arms.

The men pull me back and I push them off. "I'm fine!" my voice is more of a growl and all I want to do is run after her.

How do I fix this? I can't deny that I wasn't enjoying it when she physically walked in on me mid-release; I can't stop that any more than a wave can stop coming to shore. She saw the look on my face as I thrust my essence into Lanie's mouth, but how am I supposed to explain it was to the image of her that I came? Damn Ereon, and his role in this. I know he planned for this to happen.

I don't know what his plan is, or why he wants to keep me away from Carnaxa. He knows we can't legally have a relationship, she's betrothed and she will be married in Shaston. He doesn't know about the hidden moments that should have never happened. Moments I will ensure never happen again. Will I serve her? Forever. But he has no reason to worry about me.

Leaning against the wall I slide down and sit on the cold floor. Ereon's men and the women leave the room we were all in, the women giggling and the men smirking at me. I run my hands through my hair, currently wanting to pull it all out. Carnaxa has always called up my emotions, having me act in ways I wouldn't normally. I used to ignore much of my duty because of her. That's why I put distance between us after the whipping. It had to happen, she is my weakness, the one I can never have. Perhaps the Shastons are correct and the Goddess loves playing cruel games with her creations, me most of all.

Four Lunar Years Ago

I had to pull Carnaxa from her mother's body. She clawed at my neck and arms but finally, she gave up. We've been sitting on her floor now for what seems like hours and I've whispered the prayers I learned as a child. I may not have been born here, but I pray to the Goddess just as much as anyone in this kingdom, if not more.

"Neshæ pekæ ra , lengo ra , noko ra," I whisper into her hair. Watch over her, guide her, love her. The only prayer I can think of to help during this time. I hold her tightly against my chest. She shakes from the tears that pour down her round cheeks, her cerulean-blue hair cascading down her back and over my hands.

I should have fetched the King at his wife's first sign of distress, but surely someone else will. As Carnaxa's guard, I'm sworn to her and she needs me. Since she found me on the beach, we've been close as we've grown up together. I find myself giving into her playful ways and enjoying our interactions more than I should. Interactions that go against my training but make her smile nonetheless, like sneaking extra cheese for her from the kitchens or leaving the castle when we've been told not to so we can see the taoho *dancing along the waves at night.*

She rocks against me and I hear her soft breaths and feel her body rising and falling slowly. She's fallen asleep, which is probably for the best given the current situation. I stand up slowly, my hands under her knees and around her back. I lay her softly on the bed and kiss her forehead. She smiles briefly at the gesture. I turn to leave when she grabs my sleeve.

"Don't go," her soft whisper fills the room.

"I'm not going far. I'm going to see what's going on and I have to go get your father."

Tears well in her eyes. "Please don't leave me, Thy. I need you."

"I have to Naxa. I'll be back soon, okay? You're safe here."

"You'll be my safety?"

I kneel down on the edge of her bed, wrap her hand in mine, and kiss her knuckles gently. "I'll forever be your safety, Nohæ. I'll always be here for you."

A sad smile crosses her lips. "What does that name mean?"

"I'll tell you one day. But right now" – I push her hair back behind her ear – "go back to sleep. I'll be here when you wake up."

I watch her roll back over and snuggle deep into her covers. Through the window I notice the moon has moved across the sky; I've definitely been in here longer than I meant to be. Quietly leaving her room, I've barely shut the door without a sound before hear-

*ing the King's booming voice from the hallway, "WHERE IS HE!?
WHERE IS THYLAS!?"*

TWENTY-FOUR

CARNAXA

Images of Thylas and Lanie assault me as I pace my room. The sun is slowly setting in the distance creating a beautiful display of pinks and oranges. My heart pulses as the anger and jealousy take over me once again. His grunt of reaching his peak and his hands wrapped in her hair plays on an instant loop. The look of desire that flickered through his emerald eyes at that moment. Does he not want me anymore? This is not a feeling I'm used to and one I don't like.

Sitting on the edge of my bed I push my hair back from my face. I want to be Lanie, I want to be the one with his essence flowing down my throat, and I want his strong hands wrapped in my hair. I shake my head and pace the room. This cannot be, we cannot be. He stopped us before, he's the one who pushed me away. He is the one who accepts that we can't be. And why shouldn't he? I'm betrothed to another, I will marry another. I will marry Ereon.

He claimed Ereon sent her, but I didn't see Ereon with his pants down. Thylas just needed an excuse to get his dick sucked. I know firsthand that pleasure from yourself can only get you so far. I still thought something between us was real. Maybe. I don't know anything anymore it seems like. My emotions feel tangled up reconciling the way Thylas is hot and cold in his interactions with me, the way Ereon is charming and yet rumors come and go of his cruelty. I thought everything that happened between Thylas and me meant more, but obviously, it didn't. Running my sweaty palms down my dress, I sigh deeply, I hate this. I hate all of it.

I wasn't happy when I was told I would be married to Ereon, but I have come to accept it. Then Thylas' behavior changed the night of the festival. He had me wanting more, wanting him. To go from years of perfect behavior to abandoning it all ... am I just a conquest? He's never been one to put feelings before duty and now because of Ereon he does? Perhaps he never wanted me until someone else held the title of being mine.

I don't have time for this, Queen Natala will be expecting me at dinner soon. I roll my shoulders at the thought of seeing Thylas. I don't want to see him, my heart can't take it anymore. As much as

I want to follow my heart, I know I must continue forward with my betrothal, for my kingdom.

·· ● ● ◑ ● ○ ● ◑ ● ● ··

The dining room is full of people as I walk in. The square, large, ornate doors open before me into an opulent room full of Midaeliea's royal court, dressed in a multitude of colors. There are wooden tables placed about the room full of different foods, some I have never seen before. Many square windows let the setting sun's light in and cast rainbows about the room. Thylas is already sitting on the Queen's left, a seat in the middle between them for me. To the King's right sits Ereon. His dark eyes are already on me as I enter the room, searching me from the top of my silver crown, to the curves that the deep-green, lace gown shows, to the tips of my toes that peek out my sandals. Thylas keeps his attention on the Queen, who seems to be telling a story — one of fascination as his eyes never leave hers.

My stomach clenches and nausea flows through me, he's probably trying to find his way into her bed as well. My heels click against the wooden floors as I glide across. Blushing, I look down. I didn't realize that I was the last one here. Great first impression, I forgot their names and now, I'm late.

"Princess Carnaxa," Queen Natala's voice rings like a song through the room. "Don't think you're late. Everyone got here early." She smiles at me as one of her guards pulls back the dark, oak chair beside her.

"I thought to arrive early, apparently everyone else thought the same." I sit down as a guard pulls out the chair for me.

"Everyone arrives early, they all want Mrs. Prinstean's special rolls. Don't worry, I saved some for you." Her deep-green hair is wound tight into a high bun on the top of her head. Her dark-black dress clings to her thick, voluptuous frame. She has painted gold across her collarbones and in between her large breasts. She looks like a goddess walking among us.

Deciding that food can help take the edge off the nausea blooming in my gut, I take a bite of a sweet roll she places on my plate, the butter drips from it onto my lips as I lick them clean. Thylas inhales deeply and I can't help but give him a glance. His deep-green eyes focus on my lips and I know I shouldn't taunt him but I lick them again just to hear his inhale.

His hand grips my knee and his eyes meet mine. Sorrow fills his eyes, but I no longer have time for his game. I run my hand along his before casting it off and give him a "what" face and roll my eyes before grabbing strawberries, roasted meat of some sort, and another one of Mrs. Prinstean's rolls because they really are delicious.

"How are you finding Midaeliea, Princess Carnaxa?" the Queen calls my attention back.

"Well, my cousin and I went into the village today, it reminds me a lot of home. Peaceful. And your people seem very happy."

She smiles and takes a spoonful of the soup in front of her. Where did she get that because it looks delicious? I look around the table, maybe that's something special for her because I can't see it.

"Oh, that's what I love to hear. The Goddess did intend for us to be the peacekeepers of the Northern Continent, and it's a responsibility we take seriously. We can't help other kingdoms if we don't set an example."

Prince Ereon meets my eye and winks at me, his smile creasing his face and showing his dimples, while Thylas' once again finds his hand on my knee. I squeeze my knees together, smashing his fingers and he jerks his hand back. I turn toward him and mouth, "What are you doing?"

He's never been one to show affection in such a way, and here is not the place. He shakes his hand before leaning in and whispering in my ear, "We need to talk."

I roll my eyes. "Not right now we don't."

Siphonie and Rhenor come in through the doors, smiling and laughing like they know a secret everyone else is unaware of. By the look of Siphonie's brow and Rhenor's usual pristine clothing now rumpled, I'm assuming they found time to find each other this afternoon.

Rhenor takes a seat beside Thylas and Siphonie sits beside him. She smiles at me before grasping the cup of water before her. Thylas leans over and whispers something to Rhenor that I can't hear. Rhenor tries to hide a laugh under a fake cough.

"Happy you could make it *Bêl* Rhenor and *Bêlit* Siphonie," the Queen greets them, a knowing smirk on her face.

"I'm sorry for our late arrival, we let time get away from us," Rhenor says simply before loading his plate full of meat.

"No need for apologies, we all know well enough, when you're having fun, time is known to disappear." The Queen winks – actually winks at them – before taking a sip of her wine.

Siphonie chokes a bit on her water as her face hints with pink in embarrassment. Rhenor just smiles and shakes his head, a youthful look of pleasure and pride displaying across his features .

"Princess Carnaxa," the Queen garners my attention once again. "If you are feeling up to it, I would love to have you join me in the gardens tomorrow before you all depart for the remainder of your journey. *Bêlit* Siphonie, you can join us if you'd like. I would like to have my own time with the ladies of Antalis."

"I would be honored," Siphonie and I agree at the same time.

Dinner continues on with idle chatter between us all. Thylas stops trying to speak to me, but I feel Ereon's eyes on me often during the night. Every time I feel his stare, I look up to see him smiling at me before turning away. His smile is subtle, but it is there.

Making our way back to our rooms, Thylas stands behind me. His breathing and footfalls are the only sounds between us. He walks in, shutting the door, the subtle click echoes through the room. I turn as he runs his hand through his hair, defeat in his tone. "*Nohæ,* I would like to apologize for what happened today. I didn't mean for you to see that, I didn't even want it to happen, nor did I mean to ignore my responsibilities as your guard. It won't happen again."

"That's the line you are going to go with right now? As you've reminded me, I'm not your woman. I am not the one who will hold your shell on my sternum, and I don't care who warms your bed. The moments we've shared recently have been nothing but curiosity and maybe even a bit of fear of what's to come." I try to take a step back, wanting to get away from his heat, but my feet feel as if they are stuck in the floor. The words I spoke, I know they are lies. I want nothing more than to be everything we can't be, but I won't let him see the weakness or the tears take over me.

His hands flex at his side, but when his eyes meet mine, I can barely breathe. His gem-colored eyes brim with a sorrow he rarely shows. "I am sorry. I am sorry for today, but don't pretend what's happened the past few moons has been nothing."

I put my hand up and shake my head. Anger fuels my voice as it gets louder, "Stop, Thylas. Just stop. Don't do this. Don't make things more complicated than they already are. I don't know what I'm doing. I'm to marry someone I barely know. Just go back to being the silent one who stayed broody and mad. Go back to being the guard who only saw his honor and oaths. I don't have time for this."

He takes a step toward me, practically begging, "Give me just tonight. I have to explain myself, I can't let this be the reason you can't look at me."

Music and laughter from the kingdom below filter through the window as a breeze sweeps through the room. A place of freedom and merriment; what a stark contrast to how I'm currently feeling. Shadows from the torches dance and cast darkness across Thylas' features. His emerald eyes look as if they are glowing and the heat from his body sweeps around me. My skin is already sweating, and this dress is suffocating. I need to get him out of this room.

"Say what needs to be said, so we can get on with everything."

"I ignored you, or at least I tried to. Since the night of the whipping. I stayed with you. Do you remember? I stayed with you when your mother died. I went against my king, and in his rage, he beat me for it. I realized then that I would do anything for you and it was a weakness for us both. I didn't want either of us to have to deal with the consequences. I knew you would eventually be married, and become our queen and what would I be? Your guard, or a childhood crush, quickly forgotten? I figured it was easier to walk away." He sighs and takes a step toward me. My traitorous legs, still refusing to move away from him. "But tonight and nights before, thinking of Ereon and you, watching him want you as he did throughout dinner tonight, it's eating me alive. It's getting harder to ignore. But even these past few years, everything I have done has been to protect you. I've only ever wanted to protect you, and that's what I have to do now."

Tears I can no longer hold back stream down my face. This infuriating man, proclaiming something close to love, yet knowing we can never be. "You speak as if you are a jealous man and only became interested in me once Ereon arrived. Never once did you try something before he arrived to collect his prize at the palace door." He grabs my wrist, pulling me toward him. Our faces are inches from each other, and his breath tickles my skin. "Would it have been better to have come to you, just to have you ripped from my arms when your betrothed showed up? I thought the night of the festival if I tasted you just once, I could get it out of my system, stop wanting you."

He closes the gap between us, pulling me into him by the back of my neck, and inhales deeply.

"But you are the tug the ocean feels toward the moon. Regardless of what phase of life you are in, I want to follow you. I want to let you go, but I want more. I know I can't have you ... but maybe just one more time ..."

His full lips caress mine deeply, his tongue pressing against my lips asking for permission to enter, I give it easily without thought. His hands roughly wrap around my hair. The smell of sage and sandalwood swallows me as his kiss takes my breath away.

The pommel of his sword digs into my hip, but I don't move. I'm too caught up in this world. The one we are creating right now, this is the only thing I can focus on. His hand releases my hair and slides down my sides as he slides to his knees. His mouth trails down my body, between my breasts, across the fabric of my abdomen and then he looks up at me, his eyes burning with desire. His hands leave my skin just to remove his sheath and scabbard, the metal weapons clinging to the ground.

"*A am rehi kæ a telæ,*" he exhales the old language before looking at me, his hands softly cupping my face. "I am forever yours, my queen." His hands trail to my legs, slowly running underneath my dress and up my calves as he grabs under my knees and lifts himself up, wrapping my legs around his waist.

My skin is flush and my heart feels like it will beat out of my chest. This isn't right, I should be angry. I should be upset. I should be a lot of things, but right now all I can think about is Thylas and my body curled around him as he walks us toward the bed. He lays me down gently, the pressure of his body on top of mine, the evidence of his desire pressed against me. He kisses the side of my neck and the three freckles that lie there, fireworks spreading through me as he does.

My dress has slid up revealing my thigh and his hand lingers there, watching me as it trails upwards. "Just say the word, and I'll stop," he mumbles before sliding his hand under my dress. I don't stop him, I don't even think of stopping him.

His hand lingers near my undergarments, unlike most Antalians I never did give my maidenhood to anyone. I never wanted to be with anyone. Have I kissed? Certainly, but this is beyond anything I've let anyone else do. He kisses my neck gently, before nipping it slightly with his teeth. I close my eyes enjoying the feel as his fingers dance up and down the thin fabric, and a growl rumbles through him as his fingers play a song against my skin.

He bites my neck rougher, leaving marks where he does and I want him to claim me, to show the world who has taken my maidenhood. He pushes the thin fabric to the side, our hearts racing against each other, pounding so forcefully it's like they want to touch. He teases my clit, and I grab the sheets, twisting the silk between my fingers.

Pushing a finger inside me gently, a moan catches in my throat and I arch my back wanting more, wanting him. Looking down at me, his green eyes search mine for any sign of discomfort or regret. He will find none. His finger slowly starts to gain rhythm and I find myself moving with him.

"'Baby girl, you are perfect." His breath tickles against my throat as he raises up, making sure he can see all my reactions. He adds another finger, stretching me even more. My hands reach up, grasping at his back. I put my hand under his shirt that has ridden up and feel the marked skin there, leaving my own marks as pleasure takes over me.

His breath catches as he feels the tightness and then he pumps quicker into me. My body shakes beneath his touch. The pleasure takes over my entire being and stars dance in my sight. A loud moan I can't control erupts from my lips, but he catches it with his mouth before biting my bottom lip and withdrawing. He waits just watching me as I catch my breath, brushing the hair from my face.

"I love watching you come around my fingers." He quickly slides his body against me, using his knees to push mine further apart, and begins to untie the laces of his leather pants. "Now to see how beautiful you are with me inside of you." Worry takes over me at his words, Thylas has been with women before. Many women if I had to guess. What if I'm not what he wants? I won't know how to please him like those other women have.

"Thylas, stop ... I ..." the panicked words leave me before I can stop them and he stops completely. I look away from his stare, embarrassment inching into the places desire had once explored.

"Did I hurt you?" his words come out as a whisper against my skin.

"No."

He leans over me and smooths my hair, looking down at me. "Then what's wrong?"

"It's not that. I'm ..." I can't meet his eyes, so instead I stare up at the ceiling wishing the bed would swallow me whole, along with my confession. "I'm still a maiden."

He kisses my forehead, breathing deeply and taking in the scent of my hair. With one last kiss, he removes himself from me, and a frown crosses my face. He doesn't want me because I don't know what I'm doing. I'm not like the women he has been with. They know how to pleasure a man. Surely, with a little time, I could figure it out. But we don't have the time.

"Thylas, I want this ..." I reach toward him, but he is already off the bed, fixing his rumpled clothing.

"I want this too, Naxa, but not like this. Not as a secret, not so rushed. I won't have that, because if I am the first one to claim you, I won't be able to let anyone else have you. At the end of the day, I must remember you aren't mine to have. Just add this to the rest of the mistakes I am sure to make."

Pain flashes across his expression and I gather my dress around me, feeling extremely vulnerable right now. He proceeds to attach his sword back to his hip before sitting beside me.

"Is there something wrong with me?" the words slip out. I have to know, for myself. "Would you want me if I was like a *mæna*?"

"There is nothing, absolutely nothing wrong with you. I just ... I refuse to treat you as a *mæna*. If I have you, I will want to keep you, and I can't. I won't do that to either of us, it was stupid of me to think I could have just one more moment. I shouldn't have done anything, you told me to go and I should have. If you're ..." He roughly wipes his face, holding back tears. He breathes out slowly, "If your future husband found out, or his people, my death would be instant, yours too, most likely."

I pull myself to my knees, my hands hang limply in my lap. Tears again stream down my face, back to where we were when this started tonight. "He wouldn't ..."

He shakes his head. "Maybe not. But I know the Shastonians, I won't risk it. If it was just my life – I would forfeit it in a moment, but I won't risk yours. Goodnight, Carnaxa." He kisses my forehead again and leaves before I find the words or courage to say anything else.

The soft click of my door is all it takes for my heart to break. I want to scream. I want to curse the Goddess for letting me have these feelings. Instead, I lie down on my side and pull my knees up to my chest and watch the moon in the distance, wishing to be back home. To be back in the land of my Goddess, even though right now, she seems angry at me. A land where I could have been with Thylas.

The crescent moon watches over me, casting shadows through the room, and I give into the pull of sleep. The shadows are the only ones who will know the truth of tonight, after all, shadows are made for secrets.

TWENTY-FIVE

EREON

There was a time in my life when I wanted the fear of everyone, and most days I still do. I want the fear of my men, I've done many things over the years to ensure that fear. I want the fear of my people, Shaston knows nothing else but fear. It has proved itself useful. If you disobey, you die. It's simple, and if I'm honest, the fear has created a kingdom of amazing soldiers who I know are lethal.

Knowing the plans my father has laid out for me, even if I wanted to do something different, it wouldn't matter. The old man refuses to step down as it is, he won't step down at all if he thinks I will change Shaston. He likes ruling and the power that comes with the position. To make sure I comply, he found my weakness. Anara's almond-shaped eyes and thick lashes haunt me tonight. The fear of what is happening to her by his hands. To make matters worse, my feelings for Carnaxa are getting in my way, seeing how radiant Carnaxa looked tonight, wondering if she tasted as good as she smelled. But I can't think like that. I'll ruin her, I'll have to. Never in the years since I was *gifted* Anara have I wanted another person, and I can't explain why I would want one now. I will fall on my own sword for Anara, and I will if that's what it takes. But that annoying rush of emotions I felt when I first saw Carnaxa is getting stronger and harder to ignore.

·· • • • ◗ ● ○ ● ◗ • • ··

Ten Months Ago

She walks in behind her father, her hands visibly shaking. Her plaited, cerulean-blue hair lays softly on her left shoulder as she walks with her head lowered, and I can see her nibbling on her bottom lip. The purple gown she wears fits her so well that it leaves little to the imagination, but I know the truth of what this is. It is an arrangement, that is all. I am here to get her back to Shaston, and that's what I will do.

"Prince Ereon, we were not expecting your arrival so soon." King Clennom walks past me, taking his seat on his coral throne. "But, I knew this day would come soon – so we welcome you back to Antalis."

She walks up the dais, never once looking at me. A man, her guard, stops just at the steps but I don't miss the look of disdain he sends my way. He'll be one to watch. She steps beside her father and he reaches out to hold her hand. "This is my daughter, Carnaxa."

She looks up and her eyes connect with mine. The beauty of the sea does not compare to the sight of those eyes. I greedily drink in the view with awe as my heart triples in speed. She's beautiful, more beautiful than my father told me. She smiles softly at me but her eyes flick to her guard, and I can feel a tightening in my chest as my heart feels as if it's rushing toward her. A gold-something snakes into my vision, but before I can make head or tales of it – it's gone.

"It's nice to meet you, Princess Carnaxa," I can hear my voice, but I'm not sure how I'm speaking. I feel as if my breath has been taken from me, a moment I've not felt in a very long time. But it doesn't matter, I have arrangements to make and plans to keep.

•••••◑●○◐●•••••

Present

I roll my neck back and forth, throwing the plush covers from over me, and step toward the window. I will miss the weather here. I will miss the relief from the heat and the sun. Running my hands through my curls, I try to tame them the best I can. My mother used to say I always looked unruly because of them. Putting my forearm on the window ledge, I lean out, enjoying the cool night surrounding me.

I'm not ready to return to Shaston. Partly my father's rule and partly the torrid weather that never gives relief. If I were to believe myths, it's the curse of the Goddess. The curse of banishment for something or another, I never did pay much attention. Who wants to live in myths of the past when you have to focus on surviving the present?

The village is quiet now, with no laughing or music as it was earlier when I first came to my rooms. The rumbling of my stomach has me wanting a bit of something to eat. I really should have paid less attention to Carnaxa and more to the meal that was before me. Watching her lips as they grazed that roll had completely taken my attention. I survey the room, looking for something I can escape to the kitchen in.

Foregoing a shirt, considering no one will be awake but servants anyway, I grab loose-fitting pants that sit loose on my hips, a short-sleeved, black, silk robe that I leave open, and my leather sandals. Opening my door, I nod toward the guards who stand there. They'll follow me, as always, three steps behind. The downfall of being a prince, you're almost always followed. I could turn them away but that would lead to questions from my father when they report back. I don't trust any of them. Thankfully these aren't the same two from earlier.

The palace is quiet and much darker at night. Lit torches line the walls of the wooden castle. From marble in Antalis, wood in

Midaeliea, and then we have sandstone in Shaston — to all be on the same continent — the further north one travels, the more our differences show.

Thankfully, this castle is relatively easy to navigate, and I don't get lost heading toward the kitchen. I open the door and peer in, moonlight streams through three windows on the ceiling. A way to ensure the entire room can be used by allowing in natural light. I like it, maybe we could add one to my rooms in Shaston. I start walking to the giant, wooden table in the middle of the large space; it appears to still have fruits, cheese, and bread on it, but I stop suddenly when I hear a whimper.

Turning sharply to my right, I notice a small figure sitting in a chair next to a round table in the corner. It's Carnaxa. What on Ashonera is she doing here at this hour? She could be hungry, like me, but why alone and where is her damn guard again? I motion to my own guards to stand at the door as I look at her again.

"Princess Carnaxa?" I step toward her as she spins, wiping tears off her cheeks.

"Oh, Prince Ereon. I'm sorry. I didn't think anyone would be here."

My stomach decides to make its emptiness known and rumbles through the quiet room. A small laugh escapes her. "I thought we were done with the formalities. We have to be now that you've heard the sounds of my stomach. Can I sit with you?"

She nods. "You started with the conventions first, you called me 'Princess Carnaxa.'" A hint of a smile touches her lips. I'll hate when she no longer does that in my kingdom.

"You're right. My apologies. But you do fit the name 'Princess.'" I grab a few strawberries, a chunk of bread, and what looks to be cinnamon butter. My favorite. Sitting beside her, I can't help but let my gaze take her in. Her pale blue hair is cast in a haphazard bun on the top of her head, tendrils hanging down around her face. She wears a short top that shows off her stomach and loose-fitting pants in the colors of her house, dark blue and silver. Her eyes are puffy and red, it's obvious she's upset and has been crying.

"Are you okay, Carnaxa?" I dip a piece of the bread into the butter, placing it on my tongue, I want to smile. Definitely cinnamon butter.

"Oh, it's nothing." Through the dim moonlight that filters through, I watch as her cheeks take on a pinkish tint, she's not used to being seen upset. Or maybe, it's because of me. The fate she's had to sign herself to. I probably wouldn't be too happy either.

"I am sorry that you have to leave your home if that is what the problem is. This is your first time leaving its borders, yes?"

"It is. I just ... am a little homesick. That is all. I will be fine." She continually wipes her hand over her neck and the three dark freckles that mar her skin there. The action draws my attention, I've recently had dreams of those marks beneath my lips and. It's then I see it. The mark of a lover across those stars, like a cloud covering. She's had a lover ... recently. Did he spurn her tonight? My eyes flash across the room – the Captain. Thylas is no doubt the reason for her tears. It's obvious to any man when another tries to lay a claim on a female. But to take her and leave marks of their coupling, that's bolder than I expected.

I try to keep my face neutral and continue to eat the bread that now feels like it's choking me. I know the laws of Antalis and their frivolous ideologies concerning maidenhood. She probably lost her virginity long ago, that doesn't bother me. It's not like I'm a virgin either. However, to think they have something and spend so much time together. He spends so much time with *my* woman. Regardless of if it's now or later — she is *mine*, just like Anara.

Her eyes catch mine and for a brief moment, a look of fear flashes across her expression. She pulls her legs more into herself, her hand pushes a piece of hair behind her ear. Tears pool at the corners of her eyes, and I realize she is scared of me. Do I want that? Do I want the woman I'll be married to to be scared of me? Not truly, Anara isn't. That's how she worked her way into my heart. It's why this is so hard now. Even before her, women weren't scared of me. They enjoyed it when I called them to my bed, but I don't want Carnaxa to think I'm her savior either because I can't be.

"I know I've asked before, but I have to ask once more. Is Shaston a place I will like?" her small voice breaks the awkward silence. She's asked about Shaston multiple times now, a safe topic perhaps, or maybe it's fear underneath it all. I'm not helping anything by continuing to lie to her, it's better to delay her fear and allow her moments of peace, for now.

I grab a drink of water and twist my neck back and forth before I answer her, "There are certainly things I will miss from the rest of the continent but there are things in Shaston that can't be replicated elsewhere, no matter how hard I try. I'm sure it will be the same for you when we arrive in Shaston. I do hope that it becomes a home for you, I don't want it to feel like a prison."

The words leave my mouth before I can stop them. Of course, Shaston will be her prison, it's supposed to be. She won't have the freedom she is accustomed to or the adoration of the people, and she won't have the love of the husband she truly wants, no matter how my feelings might mature. The thought of what I will have to do is almost as heartbreaking as what will happen if I don't.

"I am excited to see your home, Ereon. But I have to know, is it so hot the skin will melt off if it's exposed. That's not really the truth right?"

I laugh. "Shaston isn't paradise, but it's not all deadly. As far as the heat exposure, there are precautions we take. We all wear a lot of long-sleeved clothing, we are covered from our heads to our feet. Inside the men have many other options, but the women are still expected to remain more clothed than what you will be used to seeing or wearing."

"There seems to be many protocols in Shaston from what I've heard and read. I hope you'll help me remember them all once we are there, like you did with the King and Queen's names, here in Midaeliea."

"Certainly, Princess. Considering our predicament, I'll be at your side from now until we pass on. That's a lucky stroke of fate for me." I try to make light of the situation, but sadness still clings to her. I want to keep her smiling for as long as I can before her faith in me is ruined forever. Our wedding ceremony will ruin her, along with everything else my father has planned.

I stretch out my legs and cross my ankles. "Tell me something, anything. Tell me something about you. A favorite memory, a favorite food." I run my hands along the wooden table, my appetite sated.

She glances up toward the skylights and there it is … her smile. She has such a beautiful smile, this one isn't for formality's sake but one bloomed from pure joy. Her eyes light up just the smallest bit and she twirls a piece of hair between her fingers. She lets her legs back down to touch the floor, and I realize she's barefoot. Her bangles chime as she stretches.

"Before my mom died, we would often go to the village. She loved walking around each day and one night a month was more momentous than the others. The night of the full moon. She said the full moon was when the Goddess was awake and watching all night long. Sometimes, the Goddess has other duties to attend to, but when the moon is full and bright, she's there the whole time. We would dance in the light of the moon along the shore. I remember her in her favorite red dress, twirling and laughing as the surf crashed against the sand. I swear I watched the waves change shape and dance with her too." Carnaxa likes to speak with her hands, and I put my hand over my mouth to keep from laughing. It's cute to watch her hands as they make the ebb and flow of waves. "She would create the most amazing things out of the sand, and to this day no one has ever been able to recreate them. I don't know how she did it. Many have told me it was just the imagination of a child and her creations would always be gone by the time the sun rose but when it was just me and her – she made the world come alive. She was beautiful, caring, and so loving. Did you ever meet her on any of your journeys to Antalis?"

"I met your mother once, long ago when I was but a child." I smile at her and lean in close whispering, "She scared the shit out of me."

Carnaxa's melodic laugh fills the room, and I can't help but laugh with her. I may be older than her, but right now she makes me feel like a child, laughing in a kitchen late at night. I haven't done something like this in a long time; I can't remember when I last laughed without abandon, without fearing someone would catch me enjoying myself. Shaston doesn't let children be children, we are taught to grow up quickly. We don't have time to sit and laugh, to just be children.

"How did my mother scare you? You must have been taller than her when you were but a child. She was very tiny."

"Tiny and intimidating. I remember looking at her and thinking that if I messed up she most certainly would whip my hide 'till I couldn't sit anymore. She just had this presence about her. She would look at me like she knew exactly everything about me, I was scared to even talk to her."

"She did have that about her, she could always tell when Thylas and I were lying."

She bites her bottom lip at the mention of the guard. So it was him that she was with tonight. I should ask for his whereabouts, but right now I don't care. I'm glad he's not here. I don't need the reminder that she will never give me her heart, but if I'm honest will I ever be able to give her mine?

"It's getting late, and my stomach seems to have stopped rumbling for the time being. Thank you for letting me be a part of your midnight excursion. Would you like me to escort you back to your rooms or do you plan to stay here a bit longer?"

She considers the words for a moment before standing, her robe flowing to the floor. "I'd like the escort, I almost got myself lost finding my way here." She smiles at me and I stand, making sure to put the remains of our late-night snack away before I open the door for her.

My men stand and surprise flashes across their faces upon seeing her, I don't miss the look of lust either, as their eyes trail down her. I grunt and their eyes immediately shift back upwards as we pass. I know they are going to be staring at her ass the whole way back.

The men will change the closer we get to Shaston. The darkness we all hide inside of us gets unleashed upon Shaston borders, the place where those evil instincts are expected to run and rule. Some have already been complaining about the lack of entertainment available to them.

"I want to thank you for reminding me of the Queen's name the other day. I don't know why I couldn't recall it. I was panicking. I studied and prepared, but I guess I'm still trying to figure everything out." Carnaxa looks up at me. She is a short thing, at least two heads below my own, and I smile down at her.

"No trouble, I have been here many times over the years. Queen Natala and King Elino have known me since I started coming to the kingdoms' summit when I was seventeen. I should have paid more attention to my own studies as well, but I think part of the journey of youth is not listening to our tutors." I can't help but laugh at the memories of my own accidental, royal fuckups. I've had many.

The remainder of the walk is in silence until we turn the corner where her rooms are and I see Captain Thylas standing at her door. He is leaning down, his forearms on his legs. He looks like he got hit in the gut – I hope he did. When he hears our footsteps he turns quickly, his eyes dancing from me to Carnaxa and back. He rights himself, standing strong, and clears his throat.

"Princess Carnaxa" – he eyes her – "I was not aware you left your chambers."

"So how did the Princess walk out her only door and you did not notice? Honestly, I am starting to truly question your skills as a guard." I shouldn't provoke a fight, but her safety is left open so many times that it really is concerning at this point. He will have to do a better job of protecting her if he wants her to survive Shaston. Sure, I was the one who kept him away today, but that was so I could be in her presence without him. I think we'll continue our little sparrings in the mornings.

"When you went to the toiletries I stepped out," she answers quickly, her tan cheeks turning crimson. She puts her hand back across the lover's mark and never meets his eyes, instead turning to me.

"Thank you, Ereon for the escort and conversation. Perhaps I'll see you tomorrow." She tilts her head ever so slightly, turning away, and I can't control myself as I grab her by the wrist. She turns back toward me and looks up.

"Goodnight, Carnaxa." I lean down and kiss her cheek, making sure my eyes never leave those of her guard. The fury that blazes behind his eyes is immiscible. I watch as she goes through the door, while Thylas' eyes never stray from me. I can feel his rage, I know he wants to act on it, but he can't.

As I return to my own rooms, I can't help but smirk. I may never gain her heart, but he'll never fully have her either. All of us are the same, our desires and duties divided.

TWENTY-SIX

ANARA

The sting from the leather whip radiates from where it connects with my back. My hands are bound by these ridiculous obsidian cuffs as always, I don't know why he keeps them on me. He knows I'm powerless to do anything here, just like he is. Well ... mostly anyway. I guess he did retain a small amount of what was left, didn't he?

Another crack in the air and the pain again. He's been doing this for what feels like hours. He's being gentle in his mind. Creating small breaks in my skin, ones that won't leave scars. I've been lucky that he seems to forget me for days at a time, only to try to break me once more.

"What is taking him so long?" King Atlas questions no one in particular. "Messengers disclosed Antalis' people are reporting the deluc is spreading rapidly. I need her here before it spreads to Shaston," he snarls and drops the whip beside him. My knees buckle and my hands are pulled tight by the chains. I close my eyes wishing for the darkness to take me, at least it would be a reprieve from seeing this room. It's bright with the many torches that line the walls. He wants to see the pain he inflicts and the blood he spills.

"And this little plan of yours better work, or there will be blood to pay." His footsteps thump behind me and I feel his hands grasp the back of my head, twisting my hair tightly. His breath, smelling of wine and goat, envelops me. "Do you think he's already fucking her?" He licks up the side of my throat and I know I should fight back, but I'm tired. I'm so tired.

A king Atlas may appear, but a monster is his real form. I was young when I came to this land, and just wanted to survive. I was also naïve. He releases my hair and my head falls forward. His boots are all I can see as they step through my blood.

"Look up, Anara."

I can barely feel my face, and I find what little strength I have left and do as he commands. Why? Because I have to, I won't let this be the end of me. Not by his hand. I've lived too long for this to be how I die, by a king still wrapped up in the past. He grabs my chin roughly and leans down close to me.

I bet he was handsome once before hate and war changed him. His dark hair was once full and lush from the paintings I've seen, but now, it's oily and missing in patches. His eyes that once might have been green? No, maybe they were brown, either way, they are dark and lifeless now. He's as tall as Ereon and has similar broad shoulders but he doesn't have his dimples. I miss those dimples.

"I'm going to give you a choice today." He pushes hair gently behind my ear in almost the same way Ereon does. "You choose how this will play out. Do you understand?"

I nod softly, or at least I think I do. My knees are growing numb and warm blood still drips down my back and I try to think of home. San'doma. The city is unlike any other as far as I'm concerned. I remember what it was like to be with my mother, running free through the forest. This is my last chance, I've already messed up once. Atlas slaps me across the face drawing my attention back to him.

"Oh, there you are. I thought I lost you for a moment. As I was saying, I can either fuck you like a whore on the mattress here or I can take you to my room, take care of you, and you can treat me like a king."

I glance toward the mattress. How many women have been taken there? The blood and fluids that stain the mattress have it almost unrecognizable. I've been on it before because I refuse to give him what he wants. I refuse to break in front of him, and I will never be with him like he wants. He wants me to pretend he is my king. He is no such thing. I have no king. I couldn't live with myself if I abandoned what I know to be true. Whirling my tongue in my mouth, I gather all the moisture I can before spitting every bit of it onto his face, hitting him right below the eye.

"Tsk ... tsk ..." He wipes his cheek with his thumb before shoving it into my mouth. He pushes so far back that I gag, but he doesn't stop. "That's not very ladylike. I will never understand how Ereon was able to tame you. I guess you made your choice then."

He pulls out his thumb and grabs me around the throat, using his other hand to fetch the key to release me from my shackles. He squeezes tightly, before tossing me onto the mattress. My back aches as it touches the stiff fabric. For a brief moment, I want to go back, I want to make a different choice. But if I had, I would never have felt Ereon's love, and that's not something I want to lose.

The king steps behind me, grabbing my ankles roughly. "Act right, Anara or I'll make sure to do this in front of him too, while I let him know all your secrets. Because let's remember I am not the one who actually put you in this situation, and I would hate to break his heart. "

TWENTY-SEVEN

CARNAXA

Siphonie's gorgeous, purple dress billows around her slim frame and when combined with her pink hair, she creates a lovely mix of colors.

"You look like you haven't slept all night." She eyes me, coming closer. Her hand grabs mine and she squeezes tightly, concern lacing her voice, "Are you okay?"

She can always see through the façade I try to keep. She was made to be a mother, she has the instincts and always has. She comes off as being uncaring but she honestly sees everything.

"Just had a long night after dinner, that's all." I watch as her eyes glance at my neck. I knew the mark Thylas left would be visible, I just didn't find it in me to care at the time, but now? Now, I feel stupid. I shouldn't have even let him go as far as he did last night, regardless if we both wanted it. It won't happen again. Having Ereon show up last night in the kitchen was another surprise. I know he saw the evidence of my betrayal of our betrothal, he didn't get mad last night but will today be different? Will he publicly punish me for it?

Shuffling in my seat in front of the vanity, I grab a large, silver necklace from my jewelry box and hook it around my neck and mark. The chain drapes across the front of my chest tapering into a triangle ending between my breasts. I've chosen a simple dress in dark grey to go along with it. The freckles on my neck won't be visible, but I'll suffer the bulky necklace if it means I can keep the mark hidden. The small marks are a reminder of my mother, she had two of them. I always thought I was lucky to get three.

"Do you want to talk about it?" Siphonie releases my hand and slides down the wall, her back against it and stares up at me as she situates herself on the floor.

Huffing, I roll my eyes and take a sip of water before I get into whatever this is. She could be excited or mad. I was stupid for letting him gain my forgiveness, but I was even more foolish for allowing things to go as far as they did. My chest tightens as emotions swirl, contradictory to each other. So taking a deep breath, I get ready to unleash it all.

"It was Thylas," I confess, not meeting her eyes. In my peripheral, I watch as a smile spreads across her face.

"Well, I knew it had to be one of them. Did you finally give up your chastity? Not that I'm going to judge, Goddess knows where I stand on that."

"No ... it didn't get that far. He stopped when he found out I am still a maiden. I thought he wanted it as much as I did, but I was wrong."

She nods her head and purses her lips. She twirls a piece of hair. "Well ... never mind."

"What?"

She looks at me and grabs my hands. "Just be happy, Carnaxa. That's all. Forget everything else and forget your duties for a little while. Be happy before you are told what you can and can't do. Everyone knows you will be with Ereon in the long run, but you should take advantage of the time you have now. But, Thylas should be kicked in his balls for leaving you like that."

She looks like her mother, her round eyes and pointed chin are an exact likeness. I remember her mother as she was, right before her untimely death. It's who she gets her tawny skin from, her mother was from Midaeliea, and my uncle was from Antalis, obviously. She carries the same wise-beyond-her-years look, those of Midaeliea have, in fact, the glow around her seems to have blossomed more since we've been here. She's happier, relaxed, and overall just different than she was in Antalis. I debate if I should tell her about Ereon, but decide to keep that piece of information to myself.

"Is he outside?"

"Yes, your captain is outside waiting on us. He looks like someone stole his candy too, by the way. So I already figured something had happened."

Of course, he does. He can't hide what happened any more than I can. The look in his eyes last night when I arrived back to the chambers with Ereon ... I could see so many emotions. His hands tightened at his side in anger, his eyes meeting mine with sadness. It was all etched across his face. Furious I had snuck out, but he wasn't at his post. We needed the space, it wasn't my intention to meet up with Ereon.

"Well, let's get this over with, we've got a long day."

· · ● ◐ ● ◉ ○ ◉ ◑ ● ● · ·

As we walk through the rounded archway that creates a walkway through the forest here, I can't help but be in awe. I expected gardens like those in Antalis, filled with exotic and colorful flowers, along with plants that soaked up the sun. In Midaeliea there are large trees that block out a lot of the light, mushrooms that cover the ground, along with fallen leaves. Streams flow naturally in, and around, the walking path, the ones that flow through it have large stepping stones we use to cross.

Queen Natala stands and then brushes her hand toward her guards, as well as the Thylas who is moping and has not said a word or met my eyes the entire walk here. "Find yourselves elsewhere."

Thylas hesitates, but her men follow through immediately. He looks toward me before I nod and he follows them back through the entrance. He probably won't depart completely, but he'll leave us alone enough to talk among ourselves.

"Beautiful, isn't it?" Queen Natala speaks up.

"It truly is," Siphonie answers before I have the chance, my eyes still taking in the landscape around me. Siphonie drapes her arm through mine as we walk behind the Queen. Her dress today is one of gold making the Queen's eyes stand out. Her dark, mossy-green hair hangs down, the coils moves freely in the breeze. Her beauty is breathtaking.

"This is a part of our forest that has always been sacred. While all of our forests are revered, in this place, you can feel as if you are walking among the Goddess again. We've kept the garden's grounds this way for a long time, since the creation of Midaeliea. A place for us to go when we need guidance, clarity, or just need to be alone."

"Thank you for sharing this wonderful place with us," my voice is quiet, barely above a whisper.

"I will not lie, I brought you here so we can be alone. I don't always have so many new people in my home and I want to speak with you, Princess Carnaxa."

She leads us to a small, rounded, white, wrought iron table with intricate designs cast into the iron. A canopy of white flowers bloom from the trees above. She motions for us to take our seats and we do.

"It is my understanding that the marriage between you and Prince Ereon is arranged. How unorthodox for Antalis to have arranged a marriage for their only heir," she speaks frankly, her shining eyes fixed on me, a knowing smile crosses her lips as she pulls her dark-green hair over her left shoulder and begins to plait it in a large braid.

"It is unusual for my people, yes. However, I am happy to serve Antalis in whatever ways necessary." The words are beginning to taste like ash, how many more times must I remind myself that I am doing this for my people? I know this arrangement is right, but the emotions inside of me are starting to wage a war I don't know how to win. The closer we get to Shaston, the more I just want to be home. Why can't the kingdoms find sustainable peace without a marriage?

"And you, *Bêlit* Siphonie, are also in an arranged marriage?"

"Yes, Your Grace. I was betrothed to Rhenor when I was young and was not wed till I was eighteen."

"I find it interesting that your father, King Clennom, married the late Queen Iviloan because of love. Was she not, but a baker's assistant when he met her? Her family history is still unknown as well, correct?"

"It is true. My mother did not have any relatives here or any who she knew of. She said she didn't remember much about her time before she was old enough to start work in the baker's tent. All we can assume is that she was orphaned and did what she needed to survive and blocked out much of her earlier life to cope. It is also true that my father, walking through the village, went into the baker's tent to buy a sweet cake and when he set eyes on her he immediately fell in love. He said he instantly saw the ebb and flow of their currents connecting them."

"So your father knows and understands the meaning of a true twin drop and yet forces the women under him to do without. Interesting. Your mother wouldn't have approved."

A breath catches in my throat, to speak so boldly of both my mother and my father ... If she knew what my father has been through, what happened when the light left the rings of the sun, what happened when the deluc began infecting Antalians, she wouldn't be so brazen.

She doesn't let me speak a word before continuing, "The deluc is now ravaging your kingdom is it not? People are no longer being called home, but are left to slowly decay till they die? Your father should know what this means, but maybe he does without realizing it."

She sighs and straightens her shoulders. "I knew your mother, you know." She takes a sip of her tea, her dark slender fingers wrapping around the cup. "You look a lot like her, I would wager you have her spirit too."

"I have been told I look like her, but I've also recently been told that she scared people just by glancing at them. That is a trait I don't believe I possess."

"Oh, don't worry about that dear, that will come with time. Always remember, your mother is always near you. Trust that truth, and yourself, for what's to come."

Siphonie speaks up at that, "And what is to come, *Your High-ness?*"

"Only what must. As the keepers of truth and peace here in Midaeliea, there is a long story about gods and goddesses and the different lands they created. Sometimes becoming bored with the one they have only to start a new one. While our land was shaped by the Goddess, not all have been or will be. However, the creation stories almost always have prophecies that no one heeds until it's too late. Your mother told me the story of one such prophecy, it was one we discussed often in her last days."

Siphonie picks at her fingernails, I can tell how uncomfortable she is. I take her hand in mine under the iron table, rubbing my thumb across her knuckles. This is not the conversation I thought we would be having. Perhaps a talk about wedding plans or attire, but not my mother.

"Upon the day the moon turns bright, the loyal heir's death awakens eternal night. The waters will rise and the fires will blaze, then only the sacrificed can save," she says the words from memory and shrugs her shoulders. "The small, old scroll from our main library had the same words written on it, but your mother told them to me first."

Chills break down my spine and I can't help but feel my hands shake along with Siphonie's, still interlaced with mine. The Queen just smiles. "I see someone has already let this slip to you. Oh the subjects of Midaeliea, they really do like reciting it. Probably one of our older subjects who most likely worked at one of the libraries."

The way she talks with so much knowledge, without fear, without falter – I can only hope to hold her grace when I am queen, or rather, queen consort. She pauses looking at me and takes another sip of her tea. She seems to be done with the conversation, but I don't understand why this prophecy keeps being repeated to me. "And what does any of this have to do with me?"

She smiles, sitting her cup back down on the saucer. "Everything. At least your mother thought so. She told me the prophecy would soon begin. She told me many stories, in fact. Some you aren't ready for, others you already know. I want you to be vigilant and prepared, as things are not always as they seem, and to always be guarded both by the sword as well as the mind."

A guard walks toward us, his dark hair hanging to his waist in braids. He nods to us as he approaches and leans down close to the Queen, whispering in her ear. She tilts her head in agreement slightly and pats her lips with a cream-colored napkin.

"Ladies, I'm sorry but apparently, there is some urgent business I must take care of. If you'll excuse me. I'll be waiting to wish you goodbye, your party is about ready to leave as it is." She stands gracefully, her small steps make her appear as if she is floating instead of walking across the lawn. Her words circle around in my head like a song.

·· • • • ◐ ● ○ ● ◑ • • • ··

Queen Natala and King Elino stand at the top of the castle's steps looking toward the caravan of horses and carriages. Queen Natala stands tall, a golden dipped crown of entwined antlers has been placed upon her moss colored hair. Her umber skin is reflected from the more formal, gold dress she has changed into since our time in the garden. King Elino stands in matching colors, he has his hands clasped in front of him, and a smile graces his face. They are a beautiful couple and power radiates from them.

The Queen smiles as she sees me and I stop next to her. Ereon is below us helping to direct the men, including those who are packing our luggage. Thylas stands behind me, still mute after what happened last night. I know tonight we will need to camp and I'll have to be near him, but right now, I want to forget our lapse in judgement.

"I'm so happy you were able to stay with us, Carnaxa. It's been wonderful having newcomers to the area."

"The pleasure was all mine, I'm happy to have seen a piece of your beautiful kingdom."

Lanie is speaking to Thylas behind me and I try not to let the jealousy in my gut take over. I watch as she points and talks, she's telling him what is packed where in order to make sure nothing gets broken. It's not like they are having a lover's conversation. And yet it reminds me that one day, I'll have to watch him with another woman, a woman who will be his wife.

The Queen glances in their direction, before speaking, "Don't let what happened between them come between the two of you."

My eyes narrow at the Queen, as I'm sure an obvious look of confusion marks my features.

"I know many things, Carnaxa. I can see more than you realize, and I know more than one mortal should. I blame that on your mother. Understand, no matter how things happen, it's all the way it should be, even the heartbreaks of life."

Time is ticking and everyone is getting ready to go. I don't doubt the truth of Queen Natala's words, one look into her eyes shows the depth of her secrets and knowledge. Her eyes peer into my own like she's reading the writings of my soul. My time to ask questions is limited so I ask the only one I can think of.

"Did my mother tell you anything that could help me right now?"

She readjusts her crown that slipped slightly to the right.

"Your mother told me many things. She told me you would be the one to change everything, to bring change to the continent, and to fulfill the prophecy I recited to you. At the time, I thought she was rambling, but now ... now I see. Make sure to look at the gift I put into your belongings."

Ereon appears at my side, his hand slipping around my waist as he looks down at me. "We need to be on our way soon, we have a long day of travel. "

"Yes, just saying my goodbyes."

"Thank you for your hospitality, Queen Natala and King Elino. I appreciate it and hope to have your continued friendship. I'm sure we will see each other again soon."

"You will, Prince Ereon and Princess Carnaxa. I will pray to the Goddess that she blesses you with safe travels," the Queen says and

King Elino smiles softly. "Safe travels," he repeats, and nods toward us.

With that, we walk to the carriages, but I notice the elderly woman from the village in the crowd watching us leave. She stares at me and then glances toward Ereon, lastly her gaze flips to Thylas and her expression turns dark. Her face pales and she appears to want to run but stands there a moment longer. As quickly as the fear flits across her face it disappears and she retreats into the crowd as I get into the carriage.

·····●○●●●····

"When will this rain let up?" Siphonie moans from beside me. She has her legs draped over me. It's hard to be comfortable and proper inside a carriage. Poor Rhenor has decided he preferred the rain on horseback compared to listening to us whine about being cooped up again. Maybe I should learn to ride a horse like they do, and after talking with Queen Natala, maybe I should learn to wield a sword as well. I instantly remember the dagger still in my belongings, that is what I should start keeping on my person. I'll make sure to find the blade tonight and keep it on me.

"I don't know, maybe we should enjoy the rain before arriving in Shaston." I smile as my hand is outstretched through the window catching the drops.

The rain pelts on the carriage roof and I can hear the men outside talking loudly to each other, the rain making it hard to hear. We will probably be stopping soon. The sun is retreating and the rain is getting heavier and I know everyone outside of the carriage is soaked to the bone. We have to be getting close.

I hear Ereon's voice yelling over the rain, "Halt!"

A hard rasp draws our attention to the door. Thylas shakes his soaked, raven hair as he opens the door. His skin glistens from the rain that falls and he looks exhausted.

"We will be making camp shortly. Rhenor and I will make sure our tents are set up before you leave the carriage. Don't need either of you getting sick." He leaves just as quickly as he arrived and instantly the air feels cooler.

I can't help but blush at the insinuation of our tent. I'm dreading this evening, I don't know if I can be near him anymore.

"You know, Rhenor really isn't all that bad. I was stupid and young to have spit on our marriage so quickly." I look at her wondering where this topic of conversation came from. She's looking out the window at him as he rides and talks. A small teasing smile plays on her lips. "He told me a story he learned in Midaeleia and I thought it was clever. He was doing research on twin drops, you know because he lost his and I've never met mine." She leans back into the cushion of the seat and pulls her hair up to fan the back of her neck. "Old scrolls that go back to the time of the old language, hard to understand because of the missing words in places. They seem to be a record of what we nowadays consider legends. He said the sentence structure is twisted and confusing. He mentioned some of the text foretold of reincarnated twin drops finding each other again. We all know a twin drop doesn't always equal a relationship because it has to be accepted, but still, it's an interesting idea."

There are so many tales I've never heard of and honestly, I'm exhausted from it all. I will always trust the Goddess, I will believe in Her, but prophecies, stories of gods and goddesses, and now reincarnation. I don't have the mental endurance to think about it all. I have more real-life concerns than worrying about things that may never be.

The men work around the camp, setting up shelters and some poor soul tries to build a fire. I notice Ereon with a group of men surrounding him. His shoulders are tight and I can tell by his stance that he's arguing with them.

It makes sense the closer we get to their home, the more they'll be ready to get there. I can only imagine if things were reversed, I would be so irritable to get back to my own home too. But Ereon's voice booms through the camp, "I said no!" Siphonie jumps up, and looks out the window with me. Ereon has a man by the collar and tosses him to the side, before walking away, running his hand through his beard and muttering to himself.

Thylas comes to the window, informing us, "The tents are ready."

"What's wrong with the Prince?" My first words spoken to him today, and they are about Ereon. But I'm starting to think that Ereon has a side he doesn't let the others see. The person I saw on the beach, the one who laughed with me in the kitchen.

"Who knows? Probably Shaston business." That is all he says before he walks off. Well tonight is going to be *splendid*.

Twenty-Eight

THYLAS

Swinging to my right, Ereon's steel meets mine. His body is rigid as he tries to deflect my attack. Our swords cling to each other as we walk around in a circle. His predatory eyes are on me, the spot he drew blood from on my forearm is aching.

Every day, since we arrived in Midaeliea, we have had our little contest, our seemingly insignificant duel. It comes off as sparring, making sure our bodies stay in shape but I could practice with any of the men brought on this journey with me just like he could. No, this is us sizing the other up. We didn't this morning before leaving the castle, so since the rain finally stopped we figured this was a good time. The mountains glare down at us and the pass will soon be lurking upon us. It's darker here, the air tense with worry, as the Cartilen Mountains stretch high above us and we can hear the sounds of the beasts that roam the pass.

Ereon knows I have never seen a real battle, not any fault of my own. A few tavern brawls, a few drunken arguments but a real battle? It's true that Shastonian soldiers have seen battle. That doesn't mean I'm going to let him beat me if I can prevent it.

Ereon lunges toward me, almost kicking my feet out from under me as I jump and bring my sword down. His curved blade easily meets mine and he bares his teeth before pushing off me. We begin to circle each other like vultures.

"I won't lie Captain, you are much better than I expected." He twirls one sword in his right hand the other gripped tightly in his left.

I grip my sword tighter as sweat rolls into my eyes. "I don't know why you thought I wouldn't be. I am a captain in the Antalian *Shayi* after all." I smile at him.

He laughs deeply and then quick as lightning, punches my left cheek with a clenched fist still wrapped around the hilt of his sword. The punch has me falling into the sand, and I quickly stand back up. I flex my jaw to work out the pain that is still radiating. This is the second time he has surprised me with that move, it will be the last.

"You're good as long as the rules of combat are being followed, but the funny thing about those rules – they are never used in combat."

I taste iron from my split lip and take a step back. He's cocky, and I don't like it. If he wants me to fight dirty, I will. I know his feelings toward Carnaxa are changing. He once looked at her with irritation, now, when no one is looking he looks at her with a feeling I can't place. Maybe it's passion or lust, or maybe it's just knowing that he will soon warm her bed.

"Prince Ereon," a soldier from his crew calls out. He turns toward him before placing his swords in the double baldric that creates an X on his back. He walks toward the soldier and I see Rhenor leaning against a tree, a smirk on his face.

Sheathing my own sword back on my hip, I walk toward him. Grabbing a canteen of water that is on the ground.

"What's so humorous, Rhenor?"

"Nothing, just laughing at boys who are trying to see how big the other's dick is."

I take a swig of water from my canteen and roll my eyes. "We are just sparring to stay in shape. Maybe you should consider it. How long has it been since you've been inside a sparring ring?"

"Don't worry about my sparring days. They weren't that long ago, son. However, Ereon does have a point."

"And what is that?"

"You are too formal in your fighting. You still care too much about rules and proper fighting etiquette. You don't know how to fight dirty, how a battle would be fought if you found yourself in one. You'll have to learn to throw punches, throw sand, whatever you need to do to survive. I've been telling you this since you came into my arena, nothing but long arms and skinny legs."

I turn toward him and he looks in Ereon's direction. "I know why the two of you are fighting and I'm telling you to stop. No matter how many times you win the sparring match, she cannot be yours and you should watch your eyes when you are around her, your eyes will always betray you."

Gathering a bit of water in my hand I run it along my face, wincing as it touches the cut on my cheek. Rhenor treads the line between friend and father figure. King Clennom might have let me remain inside Antalis and become a part of the *Ke Neye,* but it was Rhenor who was there for me after the whipping, when my trust with King Clennom was broken.

"Don't you think I know that? I am well aware of what I can and cannot have. I know she's a weakness."

He leans in close to me, intent I understand him, "She's not your weakness, she is your strength. She is everything to you, but you can't let that get in the way of what has to happen here. And why do I have to remind you? Because the marks Carnaxa has been trying hard all day to hide are evidently not of her own doing."

Kosæ! I had seen them and just hoped that everyone thought ... I don't know what I had hoped they thought. Leaving her that night was the hardest thing I have ever had to do. For hours I could smell her on me, still taste her on my tongue.

"It was a mistake," is all I can say. What else can be said? I could easily be slaughtered if the Prince found out my hands had been on his betrothed. That my fingers had been inside her, that I had almost taken her for myself.

"Mistake or not, you need to get yourself under control. We are far from home and I can't protect you here. Not like I could in Antalis. You need to be smart. If you have her, remember you'll have to let her go."

"She's never been with someone ..." the words slip from my lips in almost a whisper, a secret meant for only his ears.

He straightens and realizes what I could have done. "Does Ereon know this?"

I shake my head at him. "Not that I know."

Rhenor nods his head. "Leave her be then, Thylas. If Ereon was to find out she was untouched and that you took her maidenhood from her ... He won't allow you in his kingdom. You know this. You know the culture of Shaston is harsh. Don't put her in a position where she has to choose."

"But what if her choice is me?" I shouldn't have even let the words leave my mouth. It's a constant battle of head and heart. What I shouldn't do, what I want.

"Don't ruin her life, don't make it a choice. Ignore the feelings you have for her."

"Could you have ignored your feelings for Balenia?"

I know I shouldn't speak of her. His first wife was his twin drop and yet had an illness inside her head. She was from the Southern Continent, and not of Antalis blood and therefore, not blessed. She often dreamt of magic that is no longer in this world, and of creatures with tales and wings, monsters birthed from fire. The more the images in her head attacked her, the more she pleaded for the Goddess to take her home. Eventually, the Goddess did, she called her home and Balenia walked into the waves like any Antalian, a smile on her face. I remember the pain Rhenor experienced in the ring after her death. I was a young man, but I remember watching him crush many soldiers in the sparring ring. He finally seems happy once again, despite losing his drop. Despite her being gone from this world. He's found love again with someone else, maybe not the same as it once was. But it's there.

"She wouldn't have let me. She figured it out first. I was the one who took my sweet time maturing to realize what the ebb toward her was. You know, twin drops are like that, they have an echo of sorts. I've never once heard you say you have an ebb toward Carnaxa like that. I'll say it again. Don't ruin her by confusing her. Carnaxa does not have the luxury to let her heart lead, and neither do you."

I see Ereon walking toward me in my periphery, one of his guards behind him. "*Bêl* Rhenor." He inclines his head slightly, as Rhenor bows deep in front of him. "It seems we're needed to discuss the road ahead. We will continue our match later Captain, but for now, we have to figure out how to keep the women in our party safe. Gather your men and meet with me and my soldiers in the council tent in a few moments."

And then he walks away. His walk is one of determination and strength. If I didn't despise him so much I might have even looked up to him for the power he seems to exhale upon every breath. If it wasn't for his homeland, how his society treats women, I'd feel better about letting her go. But I do not trust him, not yet. I still believe he will always choose his kingdom over her.

"Just keep my words in mind, Thylas. Balenia and I were in a different situation. A different time."

His words hurt deep inside, I know I've not had that pull toward her. Not in the same way he's speaking of, I used to hope it was because she wasn't acknowledging the current between us. But I love her just as much as anyone can. I would die for her and she wouldn't even have to ask. However, I know I'll never find a twin drop, that is for those of Antalian blood and Rhenor forgets sometimes that I am not. Or maybe it's not forgetfulness but hope that the Goddess will bless me anyway, she used to do that for even those, not of Her blessed bloodline. But he knows as well as I do, drops are rare even for those in Antalis, why would the Goddess bless an orphan not of Her shores.

Rhenor pats my shoulder before we make our way to the council tent.

·· • • • ◗ ◉ ◯ ◉ ◖ • • ··

"The main issue getting through the Cartilen Mountains will be something the Shastonians call *khind*," Lelfait, my commander and for overall purposes unofficial scholar, addresses the room.

"And what exactly are they?" I ask. I've heard tales of these beasts, but it's best to get the real story before giving into gossip. Men who had long journeys usually like to exaggerate what they had to overcome to get to their destination, which they think makes the women more eager to jump into bed with them.

"Terrible creatures. Taller than three horses if they stood atop each other. Similar to a wolf in appearance with bear-like paws and flames along the tips of their fur. They are black as the shadows, and their howl sounds like a woman crying but their growl is more akin to a lion."

That description is exactly as horrible as the gossip I've been told of them.

"And how do we defeat them? It's been some time since I've made this journey. I've heard there are more now," Rhenor asks, standing beside me, his right hand rests on the pommel of his sword, but a small look of fear flashes across his eyes. Of course, it does, his wife and child are among those we must protect. He's battled these creatures once, the scar across his left bicep, evidence of that journey.

"It's hard," Ereon states, standing to my left. As much as I hate being in a room full of so many Shastonians and their opinions, it's imperative we come to an understanding about the rest of the journey, plus this is my life now. "Not impossible, but hard. As mentioned, they are large and powerful, their fur can't even be touched unless you want to return with a smoldering limb. The only sure way is to stab them in the brain or heart just like any other animal. Their advantage is that they usually stay hidden among the mountains and rarely come out during the day, especially when the sun is high. We have made the trip with zero sightings before."

"And how many days does it take to travel through the pass?"

"Just one, and if we are lucky, we won't have any troubles."

"So ... we hope for sunlight. And what if we can't make it through in one day?"

"Pray to your goddess, Captain," Ereon's snide comment grates on my nerves. But if what he says is true, then that will truly be the only answer. Pray and hope that we don't encounter them.

As the soldiers filter out of the tent I follow suit, making sure not to catch anyone's eyes as I look around camp, hoping to find Carnaxa again. The firelight cast shadows along the trees. In an effort to give both Carnaxa and me some space, I've asked other Antalian guards to watch over her today, something I'm sure added to her discomfort. I know she's furious with me, and I don't blame her. I'm irritated with myself. But tonight, regardless of the varying tensions between us, I won't let anything get in the way of keeping her safe. So tonight I'll be in the tent as I have been during our entire journey thus far. She can stay mad at me, she'll get over it. She asked me to be her safety, and that's what I'll be.

I would have never put her in that position had I known of her innocence. Of course, does that make it better? Would it really have been better to have had her once and never again? My heart certainly thinks so. It aches for her, as it has for years. Since the moment I realized she was everything to me. The day my loyalty changed from her father ... to just her.

······●○●····

Four Lunar Years Ago

"I don't wish to do this, but it must be made apparent that the law of the King is the law of the land. When something is asked of you soldier, you must follow the command as though it is law. Regardless of your other inclinations."

King Clennom stands behind me, his arm holding the nine tails that will soon lash across my back, but I regret nothing. I do not regret for one moment holding Carnaxa in her time of need. Because it was during that time I felt my heart slowing down to match her heart's rhythm. I felt my own heart break as she sobbed against me from the loss of her mother. I know she is not my drop, I won't have one, but I don't care. I don't think I could ever feel for someone like I do her. Or maybe, just maybe, the Goddess is blessing the orphan boy who knows too much.

"Do you have anything to say for yourself? Because of you, I did not get to wish my wife goodbye as she left this world. You were told to get me as soon as anything changed because I trusted you and yet you disobeyed me."

I stand there with my arms pulled tight around the column because I've already told him I was with Carnaxa. That I was taking care of her. It wasn't what he wanted to hear, and so I'll say nothing now. I'll take my marks with pride. I'll wear the scars as a reminder of everything I would do for her.

"Thirty lashings then ... if you have nothing left to say."

The whip whistles through the air and meets the flesh of my bare back, making marks as the knots in the leather plunge against my skin. The king quickly adjusts his arm and strikes again. I refuse to give him the satisfaction; I refuse to cry out or pretend to hate where I was that night. I don't understand the pain he's going through, but I can imagine. I can imagine how it would feel if Carnaxa was taken from me, because I realized something that night. She is everything to me, I'll always protect her. But the point remains, as the pain lances my back, I won't scream, I won't cry out.

Sticky blood flows down my back, and his arm picks up speed. It infuriates him that I'm not screaming. He wants to make me hurt like he is hurting right now. He's wanting my back to match his ravaged and raw heart.

"How about twenty more then, huh?" The anger seeping through his voice is unmistakable, making him sound unrecognizable. Proof of his complete and utter despair, of his anger. But anger not truly aimed at me, his anger at the world is being taken out on my flesh. Never would I have imagined that he could inflict this type of pain on someone.

I stand there until my legs give out from the pain, gritting my teeth as much as I can. As my knees crack against the stone beneath me, I hope it will signal him to stop. I don't know how much longer I can stay this way, black specks already lining the outside of my vision. He continues. I would scream at this point if I could, but I'm stuck somewhere between being asleep and awake or maybe it's dead and alive. He's definitely exceeded thirty lashes, I know that and so does every guard surrounding me, but not one of them can stop him any more than I can. The smell of vomit hits my nostrils, my own or someone else's, probably from seeing the scraps of flesh that hang from my back, I don't know.

I hear a scream from the window overlooking the courtyard, a blood-curdling scream from the only one who could wake me at this point. The scream I heard the same night my fate was set in motion. Carnaxa, she shouldn't be here. I heard him say that she was to stay in her rooms. But there she is, screaming and crying. I barely lift my head as her ocean eyes meet mine and I watch as she fights the guard who's trying to pull her away from the balcony's railing. She spits in his face, and I struggle to stand.

"Remove her!" the King yells from somewhere behind me.

She's screaming my name and I can't help but twist my wrist, the ropes digging in even more as I try to get to her. The soldier, Marcus, grabs her waist and throws her over his shoulder. But she fights him the whole way.

I chuckle, probably from delirium, in addition to knowing she is about to give him a battle worthy of any soldier. Her father's whip digs into my back again, and then I hear it fall to the ground.

"You can't love her. Her mother's death changes everything. The Shastonians will know we are vulnerable and she's the only hand I have left to play."

I don't know if he meant for me to hear that, but I did. And he's right, I always have and always will love her, but she's a princess and the only heir to Antalis. Her father will probably force a betrothal, the only thing he can do to keep Shaston from raining down on us. But I won't let her face that alone, and I won't flee Antalis because I love her. I can't let her worry about me anymore, it's time for us both to grow up and that includes letting each other go.

I don't want to be her weakness, even though she'll always be mine.

· · · • ◗ ● ◖ ○ ● ◗ ● • · ·

Present

"You truly are a stubborn fool, Thylas." Turning my head, I see Siphonie walking toward me, and she doesn't look happy. I stand outside of Carnaxa's tent trying to decide how to approach her. I've heard her stomping around inside and huffing, I'm sure because of me.

"*Bêlit* Siphonie," I greet her as I bow. "To what do I owe the pleasure of your company tonight?"

Siphonie stands with her hands on her hips, pursed lips, and irritation written across her brows. She punches my shoulder; I don't know if it's from when we were kids or if Rhenor's been teaching her – she can still throw a punch.

"Go shuck a shell, Thylas! How dare you leave that mark on Carnaxa! Do you know what would happen if Ereon were to see it?"

"I'm sure he would be rather agitated, if I had to guess." I rub my shoulder. She's not as scary as she wants to be, at least not to me. Once you grow up with someone, it's a bit hard to be scared of them, especially when you've seen them go through their teenage years.

"Foolish, absolutely foolish," she huffs and runs her hands along her purple dress.

"Your husband has already berated me today, I'm well aware of what you will say. Yes, I'm a fool. Yes, I shouldn't have. But no, I'm not sorry. I'm not sorry for what I did and I'm not sorry for stopping it. Because it was me who stopped it, Siphonie. Not her, I could have had her. I know the position that would have put her in, especially in Shaston and I will not put her in danger, ever. So can you please save whatever speech you were planning to waste your breath on?"

She stares at me, opening her mouth to say something before closing it again. She ponders something and it's then I see what King Clennom does. The spirit behind her eyes as she organizes her thoughts. She would make a great ambassador, and one day I plan to give her the title. She nods and starts to walk, leaning in close as she passes me, her voice lowering to a whisper.

"You have to decide, Thylas. Either give her a night of pure bliss or leave her alone. She can't keep doing this. It's killing her with curiosity, along with trying to maintain her duty to Ereon. Figure it out. Enjoy the moment for what it will be and make sure you both know it can never be anything else, or leave her alone. If you decide not to pursue her, let her get close to Ereon. She won't admit it, but I can see her wanting to grow closer to him. He will be her husband, so make up your mind on what you are willing to do."

Twenty-Nine

EREON

The sky is grey, the sun barely starting to crest along the horizon. Standing and looking up at the sky, it's not a good sign. The *khind* will be out if the weather stays like this. Maybe I should delay the journey and see if the weather improves, but I want to get back to Anara. I need to see what he's done to her, if I can save her ... again. I chuckle a bit to myself, she's strong all on her own, she doesn't need me, and nothing will break her.

Carnaxa emerges from her tent, her guard appearing tense as he stands outside. The Captain nods her way before turning and begins to break the tent down. I respect his loyalty to her, I really do, but the marks he left on her neck were unnecessary and stupid. If I was anyone else in Shaston, they would have both been dead. If someone saw the marks now, they still could be, but I've already started a rumor that Carnaxa and I shared a night in Midaeliea to cover for them.

Carnaxa's doe eyes look at me and she smiles, pulling her hair around her shoulder. Deciding I should go say hello, I take a few steps toward her and rub my hand through the hair on my chin. It's grown longer since we left Antalis and soon I'll need a shave.

"Good morning, Princess."

A horrific sound stretches across the wind. My head snaps toward the mountains, and my arm immediately wraps around Carnaxa, pulling her into me. She doesn't need to hear this, not when we are going to be walking through there so soon. Placing my hand on the back of her head, I slide it over her ear and push her head into my chest. My heartbeat picks up pace while goosebumps pebble her flesh. I hope I'm muffling the sound, and the goosebumps are perhaps from being so close to me and not the howl of the *khind*. She doesn't move an inch and keeps her eyes pinched shut. Her smell of coconut and vanilla takes over my senses, momentarily making me forget how we found ourselves in this embrace.

Finally, the *khind* stops, and I release Carnaxa, sliding my hands to her waist and peer down at her. "Are you okay?"

She shakes her head, tears lining her eyes, and a few strands of her uniquely blue hair fall into her face. Her voice is barely above a whisper as she shakes in my hands, "What was that?"

My fingers twitch to touch her hair – "The *khind*." – and without reason, I find myself doing exactly what I wanted. She takes a sharp breath and I let my fingers trail down the side of her neck – the same place that he made his mark, continuing down to her hip, wanting to pull her even closer. "Hopefully going to their caves inside the mountains. I remember the first time I heard them, it can be frightening."

Realizing I'm still holding her, I let her go and take a step back. The first time I heard the monsters, I was barely sixteen and on the way to my first summit. I almost pissed myself. However, hearing one is easier than seeing a *khind* for the first time.

"Hopefully?" She bites her lower lip and I have to suppress a moan at the thought of what it would be like to taste her mouth. Shaking my head, I try to collect my thoughts. What is happening to me? I came here with a plan, a mission, and now ... I don't know anymore. It's not like the feelings I had for Anara are gone, no ... I miss her so much and I would still gladly die for her. But Carnaxa

...

"Yes ... hopefully. It seems as though the rain won't let up for some time. Don't worry, we will probably stay another night here until it passes. I don't like postponing our travels, but we will do what we must to keep you safe." I glance behind her, Thylas is gazing in our direction, his eyes darting to the dark path between the mountains. The call worried him as well, he steps subtly back and forth as if debating whether or not to check on Carnaxa or let her be. "It appears your captain wants to speak with you."

Her soft, small voice gives my heart a jump, "Thank you, Ereon. For this, and …" – her hands dart to the fading bruise – "for not bringing this up." She turns and starts walking back the way she came, her dress swaying in the soft breeze as she does. My heart lurches toward her so hard I have to put my hand on my chest. Trying to catch my breath, I recollect myself. *What the fuck was that?*

I have to focus on today's problems before worrying about more. Figuring out how to get Carnaxa, and the rest of the men through the pass, is my priority and I don't think it is safe enough to travel through today. Something my father will not be happy with.

•••••◐●○●◑•••••

The sun is starting to peek through the clouds and I can hear the thunderous steps of the beast on the trail ahead. While the rain has let up for the foreseeable future, we've made the decision to stay the night, having already lost most of the day.

I sent a message to my father by hawk when we left Antalis, letting him know we were leaving. He'll be expecting us soon and the more I'm late the more she will suffer.

Walking along the edge of the camp, I see Thylas speaking with *Bêl* Rhenor. Both Thylas and *Bêl* Rhenor have their hands behind their backs and their faces show a comfortability and cameradie as they talk among themselves, something I am almost envious of. Rhenor's eyes glance over to his wife. *Bêlit* Siphonie rests on a pallet on the ground outside of their tent, her forearm covering her eyes as she seemingly takes a nap. I've heard those two are a product of an arranged marriage, something unusual in Antalis, or so I'm told, and their relationship seems to be a fairly positive one. Maybe there is some hope in all of this after all. No ... not for me, never could I have that happy ending. Carnaxa is much too good for me. And I fear the ceremony alone will break her. Speaking of my betrothed... where is she? This is not the time to be disappearing, and yet, once again, the blue-haired beauty seems to be missing.

Thylas' eyes keep drifting to a spot behind him, on his left side. Ahh ... there she is. I would bet my last gold piece that's where she is. Alone, but not alone. Clever girl. I want to see how she is doing after this morning, and the fear that she held inside. She thought I would be the one to tell of her dalliances with the guard. I won't. I'm not without my secrets, I keep up my appearances for my own reasons, but I don't think I could ever expose something that would hurt her. I let my men know I had already had her, so if the marks were seen no one would think anything. It's the only kindness I can give her, at least before she realizes the kind of man I truly am.

I walk under large trees that create a canopy above me, the leaves on the branches cast shadows along the deep greens of the grass where florals are crushed beneath my feet. Carnaxa lies below a tree, her light-blue hair spread around her. Her feet are bent at the knees, her skirt's split showing off the entirety of her left, tanned leg. The dress is a beautiful yellow and compliments her in so many ways, and on closer inspection, I notice it is a dress from Antalis, not one of the heavier ones she wore in Midaeliea or even this morning. Surely, she didn't think this dress was appropriate to arrive in Shaston in, or maybe, she's already heard we are waiting. Her top has blue crystals, the same color as her hair, around the edge catching what little sunlight shines through. A brilliant rainbow seems to encircle her, much like the one that was once in our sky.

Walking softly toward her, she doesn't budge and I notice she's sleeping. I hear the slow rhythm of her breath as I get closer. I hesitate and consider walking back to camp and just leave her be, but I also want to talk to her again. I like how she smiles and laughs, I like the look in her eyes when she struggles with her desire to argue with me or give in. I want to see more of that ... fire, I know she's holding inside.

She stirs suddenly, lunging forward, her hand clutches her chest as she sits up straight. "Ereon. I'm so sorry ... you startled me."

"Oh, no Princess, the fault is mine." I sit down beside her and face her. "I wanted to check on you when I noticed you weren't with the rest of camp, I thought you had run off again. When I saw you resting, I was fixing to head back that way." Looking up at the sky, I let her know, "We've decided to stay the night, if you haven't heard."

She rubs her eyes, slightly smearing the charcoal on her lids, then proceeds to run her hands through her hair. "It's quite alright if you would like to stay. I was just wanting to clear my head and found myself out here. Thylas knows where I am. He gave me strict instructions on how far I could stray from his sight. But, I realized I have never truly felt what it is like to sleep under a tree this large and thought I should try it before we leave."

I can't help but smirk, both at her trying, and failing, to place distance between her guard and herself, but also because I know the feeling.

Folding my arms across my knees, I bend down chuckling softly, "I had to do the same thing on my first trip to a kingdom summit. I had never seen anything so beautiful as these trees. Coming from a land of sand, our trees are different and not at all like this. I made sure I slept under one as well." I smile at her. "Princess ... you look amazing." The words spill from my mouth as they used to when I was a teenager, before I realized my lot in this life.

A blush creeps across her cheeks and the bridge of her nose as she looks away from me for a brief moment. She breathes deeply, turning her face to me once again. "Thank you." She presses her hands along the folds of her dress, stretching out the wrinkles. "I realized I probably won't be able to wear many of my dresses from Antalis in the near future, and wanted to wear my favorites while I could." She puts her hand over her mouth and speaks quickly, "I'm sorry. That probably came out wrong. I'll be honored to wear the styles of Shaston, of course."

I want to roll my eyes at her determination to portray herself as an innocent princess. Willing to do what she must for her kingdom, but I know one day her act will fail her. That act will crumble. Because I've been there. Regardless I reach out, running my hand along the edge of her skirt. "Oh, trust me, Princess, I will miss seeing you in these dresses as well. The styles and traditions of Shaston will absolutely be a change for you but maybe we'll be able to find a way for some exceptions."

What a dream that would be. To be out from under my father's rule. Maybe, the two of us could actually usher in goodness to the kingdom of Shaston. It would be hard, I'm one of the men who help maintain its current status. But our kingdom, as it is today, isn't the dream my mother had. She believed one day, I could make a change. A change for the betterment of all people.

"Not while your father is still king," she blurts out, her face changing to an expression of fear as she tries to back away from me. I grab her hand, pulling her back toward me. She scrambles for her words, "Forgive me. Again. I'm sorry. I guess my mouth has a mind of its own after I've just woken up." My fingers trace the back of her hand, loving the coolness of it. Everyone I've ever been with has always been so hot, it's nice that she is cool.

"It's fine. If I am to be your husband, I want you to be honest with me. Only me." I can't trust anyone else with her, not with the way her mouth gets away from her. I let go of her hand and run my hand through my hair in agitation, no. No, I can't protect her. Not now. Not from here.

The silence surrounds us awkwardly and I notice her hand graze a leather-bound book at her side. Squinting slightly, it's titled, *The History of Shaston.*

"Where did you find that monstrosity?" I dip my chin toward the book as she picks it up, crushing it against her chest.

"I brought it from Antalis. I'll admit it is a rather boring read, but I need to learn what will be expected of me when I get there."

I laugh, grabbing a piece of grass from beside us and gently roll it between my fingers. "I was raised in the kingdom, it is boring to learn about even when it's my homeland. I can't imagine choosing to read it. It must be what put you to sleep."

"It's not all boring. It seems like everything is so ..." She searches my eyes, looking for a hint of anger maybe? She carefully selects her words as she licks her lips. "Brutish."

She's not wrong there. As far as the rest of the continent is concerned, we are brutes. Partly due to the battles fought in the northern part of Shaston along with the line of succession that bred my father. It is awful bad luck that all other heirs die leaving only one male to assume the role of ruler. It's been recorded many times throughout our history. Obviously having to kill, or having your blood brothers die would make any ruler bitter. I have never had to experience that as my mother never had any other children. I guess, if I was to have perished, my father would have continued to rape my mother until she bore him another son. I'm surprised he didn't, just so that he could have spares. He never had the chance to consider because she took her own life after I was weaned from her breast. I used to carry a lot of guilt about her death, but now I think she's better off. I'm his son, I can't imagine what it would have been like to be his wife.

"It's just different, as your kingdom seems to me. You'll learn our ways I have no doubt. The people will love you and when it comes time for us to rule, you'll know how to be a true queen consort."

She stiffens and runs her hands along her skirts again before picking at her nails, anxiety filling the space between us. She was brought up to be a queen, not a consort. I'm sure I would be frustrated if our roles were reversed, but this is out of my hands for now. Her father signed the contract, he knew what she would be. Even if he wants to play dumb now. It's not our fault he made bad choices in the wake of his wife's death.

"It's not in Shastonian nature to have a ruling queen other than a queen consort. Even my mother was never a full queen. It is nothing against you, you know this right?"

Her bright-blue eyes meet mine and there is a small flicker, the tiniest bit of hope behind them. As the sun shines down on her, I realize she's the most beautiful woman I've ever seen. My fingers twitch to push her on her back, to kiss her mouth and see what her skin would feel like against mine.

"I have read as much," her words pull me from my thoughts. "I don't understand though. Why is it that women are not of equal stature in your kingdom? Simply because we don't have cocks? How does your stave become more important than my cave, when in fact my cave is what produces the heirs you surely dream of?"

"I, um ..." I clear my throat. My father taught me that men are superior because of their strength, size, and ability to produce so many children in a short time. Women are nothing more than a bed for our seed to come to fruition, much like the grounds are for the harvest. He constantly told me, women are weak, small things. It was Anara who helped me see women are so much more than that, and Carnaxa is reminding me so, even now. They should be protected, they can be fierce and stronger than some men. Maybe not in physical strength, but in their resilience. But I can't let her know any of that. I will have my part to play just like she will. "We should be getting back to camp. I thought the rain was gone, but the sky seems to be darkening again with an impending storm. Plus the night will be settling in soon."

She sighs a little, probably from having to leave this peaceful place. I don't blame her. She must trade the large green trees for sand so hot we can't touch it. A world that will change her, mold her by melting away everything good in her. And I'll be the reason, trading one life for another.

She gets to her feet, dusting off the backside of her sun-colored dress when I notice a piece of grass stuck in her hair. My hand drifts upward to pluck it out, her eyes blink at me. She looks at me like Anara used to. Full of hope, thinking maybe I am a nice man. Maybe I will be a good husband. Maybe there is something good inside me. There is nothing left that my father hasn't twisted, nothing left of the man I once wanted to be. Although, being away from him has me more confused by the day. But it doesn't change that nothing I do now can right the wrongs with Anara, damning myself and Carnaxa in the process. We are the lambs to be sacrificed, but I won't regret giving Anara her freedom.

"I'll just gather my things and be right behind you." She turns, shuffling her belongings together. As much as I want to stay, she'll be along shortly and I want to give her these last few moments of peace, of beauty, and of happiness. I walk back the way I came only glancing behind me once more. I see her staring up at the trees once again, and a smile escapes me before I return my expression back to neutral and my feet back to camp.

THIRTY

CARNAXA

Ereon walks away and I drift to the side. I told him that I need to collect my things, but in truth, I just need a moment. The closer we get to the Shaston border the more my nerves bloom and take over. The book isn't helping anything either; I thought knowing what was to be expected of me would help. Instead, it has me worrying even more.

"Women shall not show any skin from the neck down," is one of the rules of this kingdom. The dresses will cover everything from my fingertips to my toes.

"*Women shall not be permissible to speak without being spoken to,*" is the second one I know I will have a hard time with. They must not understand how a woman's testimony can be valuable for many reasons.

I was reading all of these things when I decided I had had enough and wanted to take a nap. The trees of Midaeliea are huge, and I'm told their size represents their age. They tower over me and the sun, when it slowly peeks out from behind clouds, makes shadows along the ground. I told Thylas where I was, but that I needed to be alone. I'm surprised he is respecting my request for solace, even after he insisted I be watched by others today. After their conclave, one in which I still think I should have been a part of, he came back and I could no longer take the tension between us. I needed the space.

Sitting back down under the tree, I flip through the leather-bound book before putting it in my pack. Another book catches my attention, one I didn't realize was there before. Pulling it out, it's heavy but also feels as if one wrong move will completely destroy it.

On the cover are four circles interlocked in the middle. There is a divot in the middle of the circles as if something is missing, but the circles contain images of fire, water, earth, and wind. I've heard these are the elements of the Ashonera. It takes all of them to create a world, and that's what the Goddess used to make the first Antalians.

Touching the cover softly, I begin to slowly flip the pages. The smell of paper between the binding is one of my favorite smells and

I would happily sit here without even reading it, just soaking up the rich scent of comfort. The writing it seems is mostly in the old language, in Antihana. I'll have to talk to Rhenor, or Thylas I guess, to figure out what most of it says. But toward the back, I notice the language changes. Slowly, it seems the old language changes to something else that I've never seen. But on the last two pages is the language we speak now.

I pull my legs underneath me, pulling my skirt over them and getting more comfortable. Running my fingers over the lines, I notice the handwriting – it's my mother's. Maybe this is a queen's account of ruling Antalis. I know my father said that some rulers prefer to write down their thoughts before changing rulers. It's helpful in knowing everything that has happened before.

"I will not be here long. I don't have the time to write like I once did."

My mother's words bring tears to my eyes and it's only the first sentence. I flip back again, but no, it's a different language, this is the only one that is still in my mother's hand.

"This sickness is taking over me and it's taking longer than I expected. I knew the plan laid out for me- I've always known that one day I would have to go. I just didn't expect it to be today. I wanted to finish watching Carnaxa grow. I wanted to watch her find her drop, even though I know she'll be stubborn. I wanted more time with Clennom, I don't think he will fare well with what's to come."

Tears fall to the page and I quickly move it out of the way, blowing on it so the wetness doesn't ruin the ink. My father didn't fare well, but it's the mention of my name that has my heart remembering the pain of the night she passed. The pain I felt, the way my throat was raw from screaming so loudly. I brush the remaining tears away, taking a deep breath.

"The prophecy will come to pass. It has to. I don't have any control over fate at this point, but I can try to have influence, even from the other side. But even now, I wish I could do things differently. I didn't know what else to do, but I wouldn't have put her in the middle of this if I knew what was to come."

"And who do we have here?" a gruff voice calls out before whistling, and three male figures step out from the woodline.

"Looks like the Antalian harlot," one snickers from beside me. I grab the book, shoving it back into my pack. "Hard to forget her bloodline with her hair the color it is."

I stand. "That's right. I am Princess Carnaxa Althister of Antalis, betrothed to your prince, Ereon." My fingers begin to shake as the men circle around me like vultures. Their eyes are hungry.

"Our prince?" questions a man who is missing his front teeth. "Oh, darling. He's not our prince. Not yet. Is he Lonny?"

Another, his belly hanging over his pants as he adjusts them, smiles at me. "Nope. Not at all. Why, I don't remember taking an oath yet do you, Calen?"

Them talking around me has me spinning in a circle. This one, Calen, would almost be attractive if it wasn't for the look in his eyes that bores into me. His black eyes show no emotion as he licks his lips. From the way he stands, even though he is the younger one of the three, I can tell he's the leader. He takes a step toward me and I step back only to be reminded that the one they call Neol is behind me.

"No, he's not. We aren't from your continent and have not taken any oaths of loyalty to any king or" – he dips low in a mock bow – "any princess."

"Very well. I'll just be on my way then, my guard went to fetch some water and is on his way back." The one time, the only time that both Ereon and Thylas give me a moment of peace, and this is what happens. I should have let Ereon escort me back to camp, I thought I was safe. I always think I'm safe.

"Now, now ... we are already starting this out with a lie? Your guard is back at camp, at the edge of the forest, and we were watching as the Prince of Shaston just left you here ... all alone. No one is expecting you just yet. We've heard the rumors of the princess who 'constantly walks off by herself.'" Calen steps forward, motioning with a jerk of his head to the one who spoke first, but I don't know his name. "Neol, why don't you help our princess out with an escort."

Before I can even scream he has his sweaty palm covering my mouth. I scream anyway. The muffled sounds stop as he wraps his arm around my waist, keeping my arms pulled in beside me. I try to grab anything – anything that can help me but I find nothing. Leaving the dagger again in my belongings instead of keeping it on me.

He holds me still as Calen walks up to me, wiping the tears that escape down my cheek with his thumb. He takes it and sucks it off. "I would save those for later sweetheart. It's been a long time since we've had a woman, and so I expect tonight will be rather unpleasant for you." He reaches into his back pocket and pulls out a vial and a handkerchief and my eyes widen. No. It's nightlock oil, one used by healers for those in pain to be put to sleep.

As he lets the oil soak into the cloth, he whistles and it's the same song I hear as he shoves the cloth in my face and I lose consciousness.

····•••◑●○●••••··

Drip ...

Drip ...

Drip ...

The rain trickles onto my forehead and I wake in a panic. My mouth is dry and I try to smack my lips together to help bring back the moisture but it's pointless. Slowly remembering the events that led me here, I move to pull my hands from above my head, but I can't. The ropes wrapped around them cut into my skin as I struggle against them. I try to scream and then notice that a gag is also there. Kicking my legs around I feel nothing but the grass beneath them, the grass that I expected to be resting in-not being held captive in.

"Well, good to have you back. It's no fun if you aren't awake," Neol says, bending down beside me. "Lonny and I are waiting for Calen to get back so that we can appreciate what you are about to give us." He slides his dirty finger down the side of my cheek before roughly grabbing my throat and pulling me up. My wrist burns as he licks from the side of my neck to the base of my ear. His stench infiltrates my nose and I gag against the cloth in my mouth. "It's been much too long since we've gotten to enjoy a woman. Who knew coming here would bless us with a princess, isn't that right Lonny?"

Lonny squats on the other side, cupping my breast roughly. "Exactly. It's almost like a reward for all that we were banished for in Lidiens."

I fight as best I can squirming along the ground, pulling against the ropes, even biting down on the cloth hoping I can somehow rip it. But it's no use. *Please, Goddess ... do something.* They stand back up and I take a shallow inhale. A little more time, maybe I can figure something out. A little more time is all I need – hopefully. If I can just get my hands untied then I can possibly find a way to fight them off. I used to play-fight with Thylas all the time, but this isn't that.

I watch as they walk away from me, and back to the log circle they seem to have made camp around. I scoot my feet up, able to get into a semi-sitting position, it's the best I can do for now. I don't know where I am, nor does anything look familiar. How far have they taken me from Ereon's camp?

Calen comes back, where has he been? I don't know but he throws a bag at each of them. They rifle through them, the one they call Lonny grabbing a piece of bread out before popping it into his mouth. "That should do us for a couple of days, they haven't even noticed she's missing yet."

My heart jumps into my throat, no one has even noticed I'm missing? Maybe I was too adamant to be alone if no one has noticed; I thought at least Siphonie would have gotten worried. I twist my wrists again, trying to find relief. Breathing through my nose is getting easier as I try to calm my heart. Calen walks toward me, his sword hangs at his side as he squats next to me. "Glad to see the boys didn't get ahead of themselves before I got back, sometimes they get too excited." He reaches out to touch me and I turn my head trying to get away.

He grabs my chin hard, forcing my face back to his. "Now, now ... I think you should learn to like my company because Neol over there will have just as much fun killing you if you don't cooperate." Tears threaten to spill again and when he lets go I exhale through my nose with relief. Before I can take a breath in, the sharp sting of the back of his hand has my neck twisting. I hear laughter from where the others sit and the rain starts to pour down much faster this time, forcing its way through the thick treetops.

"Well, fuck!" Calen looks up, covering his eyes from the rain. "One of you bring the tarp over here and set up some shelter. While you do that, I'll remind our princess of who is actually in charge."

He runs his hand up the length of my leg and I begin to shake. Muffling through the rag, I beg him to stop. I don't want this to be my first experience, I don't want this to be the end of my story. I kick out toward him, getting enough momentum to hit him in his groin and he falls over with a grunt.

I may not remember much about fighting, but I know hitting a man there is always painful. I pull against the ropes, rolling as much as I can in the dirt. I can feel the knot loosening. I pull down again, even harder, when heavy hands grab my biceps and push me down. Neol straddles me, smiling. "Oh, I do love it when they squirm."

Calen is still lying on the ground, but he mumbles, "Just take care of her."

Neol gets inches from my face and sneers, "With pleasure."

The last thing I note is his fist as it connects with my face, and I see stars.

THIRTY-ONE

THYLAS

I flick a stick in the fire as I sit staring at the flames. She should have been back by now. The sun is starting to set, but she asked for space. I watched as Ereon came back from where she was and I knew she was safe or he wouldn't have left her. I don't want to admit it, but I know things are changing for him. I don't trust him, not at all, but if he kept the secret of her marks – it's not for my benefit. It's hers.

I run my hands through my hair, pulling it into a high knot on the top of my head. The clouds threaten rain once again and

I don't want to be walking around with damp hair. The soldiers are starting to settle down for the night and I can already tell some have found the ale and wine. The sparring matches will start soon, maybe I'll join them. I could use the physical exertion to let out some of my pent-up energy and frustration.

I stand up and wipe the back of my leather pants. I make my way toward where the ale is starting to flow when Ereon's voice comes booming from behind me.

"Captain!" He walks toward me, almost out of breath. "Where is she?"

I turn quickly and look at him, maybe he has changed his mind about keeping her secret. I palm my sword, I'm badly outnumbered but I would try anyway. "She's still in the woods."

He looks around before walking that way, motioning me with his hand to follow him.

"What is the problem? She asked —" I catch up with him, our strides matching.

"We have missing men," he chokes out, pushing past the branches in front of him, almost ripping them from the trees. "They aren't my men, not yet anyway. But they were from Lidiens."

"Lidiens? Did you hire those who are banished to be a part of your *Prel*? They were supposed to be headed back from whence they came. King Clennom has stated he will no longer take Lidiens' trash."

"Shaston accepts everyone. We don't have as much of an inflated ego as your people." I don't correct him because regardless of my birth, Antalis is my home. He stands in the middle of the clearing where Carnaxa was resting, turning circles.

She's not here. I run toward the tree I saw her under just a bit ago but there is nothing to show anyone, at any point, napped beneath its branches. No sign of her. I kneel down trying to find anything to clue us in as to where she could have gone.

"Maybe she's just ventured out. We don't know that your missing soldiers have anything to do with her not being here. She loves to walk around, you know this."

He runs his hand through his hair and huffs loudly. "These particular men have a certain ... reputation." Bending down, he picks up one of her bangles. A matching one to Siphonie's. He grabs one of his curved swords in his hand, holding tightly to the bangle. "They are rapists," his words are a soft whisper as the air picks up around us.

"And you brought them along on a trip with Carnaxa! What in the Goddess' name is wrong with you?" I try to keep my voice calm, but my heartbeat picks up and my fingers itch to swing at him. "She is a princess and your betrothed. How could you even feel comfortable knowing they were around her at all? Do you just not care for her safety?"

"Do not think I don't care for her," his voice echoes through the glen. He lets out a slow breath, looking around. "Please, just help me find her."

We scour for what feels like hours but I know it was only minutes, only finding the bangle. We thought that would be all, until Ereon caught sight of her pack and then I found her books a bit farther into the forest. Her belongings were leading us deeper into the woods. We quickly and quietly entered the wooded area at the same time the sky opened up and the rain began to fall heavily to the ground.

As we walk through the brush and thorns we have only one thing in mind. Finding her. Ereon curses under his breath as the thorns snag his pants, but he doesn't stop. And I respect that. He looks genuinely worried. My boots sludge through mud. The longer it takes for us to find her, the more my hope that we will starts to diminish. We should have noticed something was wrong before now, I should have noticed. I won't blame this on Ereon, not all of it anyway. It is my job, and once again I let my feelings get in the way. This is exactly what I didn't want to happen. I didn't want her to become the weakness that got in the way of my duties. And yet, here we are, traipsing through this gods-awful rain shower because I did.

I grab my sword from my hip, swiping at the vines that cover the path we've decided to walk. We have no idea if we are going in the right direction or not, but this is all we have for now. I can't imagine what is happening to her at the moment and I pray, again to the Goddess to save her. Keep her safe, I'll do anything to keep her safe.

"I know you love her," Ereon's words are heavy as he barely turns around to glance at me. "And I know you were the one who put the marks on her neck in Midaeliea."

I stumble over a limb I didn't see, but catch myself before falling completely on my face. I knew he knew I was the one to leave the marks but to say it so openly is something else. I want to choke, the rain falling in my face not helping my breathing.

Wiping the rain from my face, I respond earnestly, "I promise, I did nothing that she didn't want." It comes off more boastful than I mean it to, but I don't want him to think I forced myself on her. I would never force myself on someone and would prefer that to be known now.

"I know." He stops, grabbing a canteen at his hip. Taking a sip he wipes his mouth with the back of his hand. "And I know she loves you. But right now ... I just want you to know, I understand what it's like to love someone you can't have."

What is this? He is truly concerned for her, otherwise I don't see him wanting to have a bonding moment. Maybe it's because, regardless of titles, we are equal in our fear for her, and that matters. For once we aren't competitors, just two soldiers who want the best for our princess.

"But you can have her," I say under my breath. The images I don't want filter through my head. I've tried often to forget that one day, her scent of vanilla and coconut will be mixed with his, he will taste her and she will be his.

He rolls his neck and puts the canteen back in his pack, before motioning for us to continue. The sun is setting and I know the time we have to find her is running out.

"Carnaxa. Yes, I can have her. But that's not who I'm talking about. Her name is Anara, and she's in Shaston – waiting for me." I walk a little faster trying to catch up to him as he continues, "I couldn't save her, not when it really mattered, but I will save

Carnaxa tonight. I've prayed to your goddess since we started this trip, if I have to give my life to save hers, I gladly will. My only request is that someone helps Anara too. I made her a promise years ago and I failed her. I don't want to fail Carnaxa too. But I know, at some point, I will."

"Why tell me this?"

"Because, if I am to die tonight, I want someone to know that I didn't want to develop feelings for Caranxa. I wasn't trying to take her from you, well maybe in the beginning because I could only focus on Anara and what I must do to protect her. But now ... my father is the King of the lands we are going to and it's his command we must follow. I want someone to know these were never truly my decisions to make. And my father, under no circumstances, can know that Carnaxa loves another. He will kill her."

I don't know why I need to tell him this truth, but I do. Maybe it's so we understand each other. "She's never lain with anyone, not even with me. And I know exactly what your kingdom is like." I shake my head, water scattering from my hair. "I was born there. My mother was a slave for one of your *KiTors*. I don't know which. My father was a builder."

He stops, and turns to look at me. "That's unexpected. I assumed the two of you ... But I was told that you washed up on the shores of Antalis. How does one find themselves on the shores of Antalis? Shaston is landlocked, the kingdom has no direct route to the sea."

I just shrug my shoulders. "I don't know. I remember my father and mother arguing; he attacked me with some of his friends, and the next thing I remember, I washed up on the shores of Antalis, Carnaxa staring down at me."

He looks away and nods his head as if he understands why we keep our secrets. No one from the Kingdom of Shaston would want to tell anyone from the Kingdom of Antalis that they are from the northernmost kingdom, even if Antalians are a peaceful people. I would never have had the opportunities given to me if they had known where I was born. I don't remember that night, but what child wants to remember their father trying to kill them?

He walks quickly to our right and hunches down. Gesturing at me to come close and stay silent. Quietly pushing the leaves from in front of my sight, I can see her. Three cowards surround her. Her dress, the beautiful yellow, is now covered in mud and dirt. She's bleeding from her wrists that are tied above her and I see a gash on her bicep. She's squirming as one of the men straddles her and punches her. My hand immediately grabs my sword and I lunge forward, but Ereon's hand catches me. He shakes his head no and pulls me backwards.

"We have to be smart, Captain. We are outnumbered and they could just as easily slit her throat before we can get to her."

"So your plan is just to let them have their way with her while we wait for the right opportunity? I'm going now!" I push past him as he grabs me by the shirt before throwing me to the side. I can't imagine a world where her laughter is never heard again. Even if I can't have her again, I can't live without her.

"Thylas! I promise we are going to get her. But don't make this a fight between us, we have to be united for her."

I notice then, the look in his eyes. He's scared. Just like I am. And he's right. We have to do this right or they'll kill her. I pace around in a circle before finally asking the only question that matters right now. It's the question that will change everything. I need to know if he is really going to help keep her safe- or if he just wants the Kingdom of Antalis. But the way he speaks of her, I think I hear the desires of a twin drop.

"Do you love her?" He shouldn't, not really. He's had few inter-actions with her, but I know what I see and hear from him.

He looks at me before sighing and grabbing his swords from their place on his back. He steps toward me. "Honestly, Captain, I love them both. I can't help but love her, just like I can't help but love Anara. Now ... let's go get her."

THIRTY-TWO

EREON

The moment Ryul told me that three men had not shown up for the head count I knew something was wrong. I could feel it in my bones. I should have made sure she left the glen, but I didn't. I looked toward Carnaxa's captain as he sat around the fire but she was nowhere to be seen. I told Ryul to keep quiet. I didn't need any more of the soldiers getting any ideas. The only person around who I could trust was him, Thylas. So I threw my pride aside and here we are. I'm telling him too much information but he is also revealing more than I expected. How would everyone feel if they knew where he was born? Would it matter? Maybe ... maybe not.

We stand here watching, just watching. After they punched her and she passed out they haven't made an attempt to assault her, yet. They will, I have no doubt. What are they waiting for? I don't know. The rain has lightened for now, but with the rumbling in the distance, it will be back with a force. Maybe they are waiting on that, to cover the sounds of the screams they hope she'll make. She won't because they'll be dead if we do this right, before they even realize we are here. We are slightly outnumbered. Thylas wants to blow our cover now; he needs to learn to separate his feelings from fighting. Sometimes they are helpful, but mostly feelings just get in the way. This is one of those moments where they are clouding his judgement, his logic.

We will wait a bit longer, we need the shadows that night will provide. We are as ready as we can be. I brought Thylas a Shastonian hood, complete with a mouth covering. They are black and we will blend in perfectly with the shadows. I just hope he is as stealthy as he is hot-headed.

I sit watching the three vagabonds eat their apples, smiling every so often behind them at Carnaxa and I gnash my teeth. It's interesting how, only moons ago, I was sent to Antalis with a clear mission. My father explained it to me in detail and then used Anara to ensure I understood his expectations. I sit, waiting for the darkness to envelop us, and remember the words my father spoke to me that night.

·‧•◗◉○◉◖•‧·

One Lunar Year Ago

I could lay here forever, just like this. Her hair, smelling of jasmine, tickles my nose. When Father brought her to me many years ago, I didn't know what to do with this little demon, or as she likes me to call her, myach myomi. She says it sounds nicer coming from her peoples' ancient language. The nickname fits her well.

My father wanted me to use and abuse her, in all the ways he has done to so many others, but I couldn't. As soon as I saw her, I loved her. Something pulled in my heart, a small, golden current rippled outward to her, something so small I almost missed it. She didn't love me though. I would offer her food and she would throw it in my face. At one point, I offered to help her take a bath because she was in the chains only my father had a key for, she said she would rather I throw her outside to burn in the heat. It took a long time for her to trust me, but I think she always saw the real me, the me I was forced to hide. The me I wanted to be, not the me my father formed and forced.

We found love in this desolate and cruel kingdom. If my father found out that the reason I asked for her key was to provide her relief instead of, "finding more useful things for her hands to do," he would be furious. He's always furious, I'm used to that. His fury is scarred across my skin, leaving my soul in shambles.

He taught me how to take pain like a man. He would chain me to the wall and beat me with anything in reach until he was satisfied with his cruelty. He would burn my sides with iron pokers, just enough to leave dots along my skin, forming cruel constellations. He beat me when I cried because I wanted a mother, a caretaker, until I could no longer stand. I was too young when she passed to remember her and in my early years, when I would dare to ask him about her, he would say she was weak like every other woman, and would punish me just for asking.

Anara now runs her hand along those faint scars in her sleep, the ones along my ribs. She doesn't know that she is the one who saved me. Before the night she came into my life, I wanted to end it. I wanted to die. I wanted the torture to stop. I wanted to escape.

One look at her and I knew, if I killed myself, I would be leaving Anara to his rage, just like my mother left me. He hasn't concerned himself with Anara's whereabouts for some time now, proud to hear from the guards outside my door that they hear "screams" coming from my bedroom every night she visits. He has a full harem of women he keeps, he wants to believe I'm as cruel as he is. She screams as if in pain and we throw things to play the game, and then later I have her scream my name in pleasure. They think she's faking it, but they don't realize which part is the lie.

"What time is it?" her soft voice filled with sleep jars me from my thoughts.

"Not the time for you to leave this bed." I kiss her forehead as she rolls over to look up at me. Shadows dance across the room from the flickering light still burning in the hearth. I pull the covers around her shoulders, keeping her warm since she claims I'm always cold to the touch. Our days are hot enough to blister skin, our nights cold enough to freeze off toes.

We know our time is limited. Any day now, my father will demand I marry my betrothed, the daughter of King Clennom, the only heir to the Antalian throne. I've known I was betrothed for years; Father took advantage of Antalis' weakened political state when their former queen passed. I recently heard from my father at the last meeting that the Princess celebrated her twentieth sun cycle. It was agreed upon when she was sixteen and I was twenty-one that we would wed on what her people call the "strawberry moon" of her twenty-first sun cycle.

"What's the stress line for?" She runs her finger across the crease on my forehead.

"Tomorrow ... every time you ask, it will be tomorrow."

She leans up, pushing me back down as she straddles my hips. "But we don't know what tomorrow will bring, how can tomorrow cause you such concern?" She leans down lightly grazing my chest with soft kisses as she does.

"Because you know, as well as I do, that one day he's going to force me to go." A moan escapes from my lips as she kisses the soft spot under my ear, her hips slowly grinding against me. It's hard to focus when she does that.

"Yes. But that moment is not right now. "

Her hand slides down my stomach, my skin pebbles as she reaches that ticklish spot right below my navel. Her hand slinks lower as her hips gyrate. The covers slide down around her waist and I grab her there. Without clothes from the first part of our night, she easily finds, and grabs me tightly. She teases herself with the head on her slit. No, she's teasing me. She smiles down at me as she wiggles, getting her point across.

I grab her hips roughly, flipping her over so she is positioned on her arms and legs. Moving myself behind her, I can feel the heat from her core as she giggles. I drag my hand down her spine and she shivers beneath my touch. These moments are the ones I know we are taking for granted, hoping they will never end. Her neck is begging to be held as she lifts and arcs her head up further. I indulge her, grabbing her neck as she laughs again.

"Always playing games, Anara."

She smiles. She likes her games, at least with me she does. She likes to see the power she has over me and I enjoy seeing the power I have over her. Our moments are always a clash of power – fast and raw and always mutually satisfying.

Finally, I thrust myself into her as my grip on her neck tightens, and a moan escapes her lips. Ever so slowly, I slide into her, pulling all the way back. If she wants to play this game, I'll play. She only lasts through four more gyrations before she pushes her ass against me, turns over, and pouts. I lean down resting the weight on my forearms and kiss her neck and find her again. She buries her face in my neck, trying to hide the screams that are unmistakable pleasure, but she doesn't stop from dragging her nails down my back. I may have a lot of scars, but the ones she leaves are my favorite.

Her breath picks up and I run my hands along her waist, as she lets go of my back and grasps at my hair, locking her legs behind me. She's asserting her control from the bottom, and I would gladly give her anything. Power, protection, freedom ... She could have my soul and I would do whatever she asked.

Our sweat mixes together and the bed makes a steady thump against the stone wall as we find our release together.

"I love you," I tell her, looking down at the eyes I want to get lost in, as we convey the silent promise we make as the moon watches somewhere overhead. I can't imagine not being with her, not having her in my arms and then the thought strikes me. "What if we run?"

She laughs and I roll off her as she wraps herself back around me, her leg over mine and her head on my chest. "And where would we go? I could disappear, but you ... you are a prince. The only Shastonian Prince, might I add."

"And I've told you before, I will help you leave at any moment, all you have to do is ask."

Her hand softly touches my chest and I grab it kissing her soft fingertips.

"I don't want to leave Ereon. I have nowhere to go. I can't make it through Shaston and the mountains by myself, I can't make it back to San'doma. Not without ..." She stops, pulling her hand from mine and turning it like she holds something in it before putting it back on my chest. "I can't."

"Well isn't this a lovely sight," calls a voice from the darkness.

Jumping for the swords I keep next to my bed, she grabs for the covers pulling them over her body. A man, still cloaked in darkness, emerges from what we call "the whore road" – tunnels inside the palace for the servants and my father's secrets to travel. They aren't worthy to walk through the palace halls, but worthy enough to home his dick in.

"I really wanted to think better of you, Son," my father's deep voice booms through the room. I stand in nothing but my skin as he makes his way toward us, his eyes flickering between Anara and me. "When the guards told me she was the only one coming to your room … I thought maybe it was because you had her trained. Imagine my horror when I found out it was because you are in love with her."

Calming my features, I stand up taller but put down my blades. "The things we tell our whores to make the fucking better is all … don't tell me you've never said things to get your way." I find my pants and slip them on quickly. Anara hasn't moved, her hands fisted in the silk sheets that drape across the bed, but her head hangs low and I can see tears already starting to spill. How quickly our daydream has changed to a nightmare.

"Oh, Ereon" – he sits down in a chair beside the bed, the side closest to Anara, crossing his legs – "I've said many things to many people … but never have I let those three words be said to a whore." He twirls something in his hand, and my body starts to sweat. It's a whip, the black leather glaring in the low light of the flickering flame. "I gave her to you as a present. To use, to own, but never to love. You'll have a wife soon or have you forgotten?"

I don't know how long he's been there, lurking in the shadows. The doors are made for silence, for easy access or disposal, should that be the case. But I can't do anything but let him think I'm exactly what he wants me to be.

"I know well the duties I have with the Antalian Princess." Stepping toward him in an attempt to keep him separated from Anara, but he just raises his hand.

"Tsk ... tsk." He stands, his steps quick as he crosses to the bed and grabs Anara by the hair, pulling her to the cold, stone floor. She lies there, her body exposed, but her eyes ... her eyes will never cower. She's already stopped the tears. Her face shows pure hate across her features. *"What a predicament you have put me in. I heard the soft whispers of treason, of running away. For her to commit such a crime, well ..."* He pulls her hair and she screams from the pain. *"She could be given to the Prel, to let them do with her what they please."*

It's a fate worse than death, I've seen what the men do to the women who are "given" to them. The women never come back alive.

"Or better yet ..." He throws her down, her chin hitting the sandstone floors. Blood drips from her chin as she pulls herself up as best she can before he stomps on her hand. *"Stay put."* He throws the whip and it lands right in front of me. *"Give her ten lashes and we will call it even, and then I'll find you a new one tomorrow."*

I've whipped many men, even women, due to my father's commands. But I can't. I won't. She nods at me, giving me the okay. Even now, she would sacrifice herself, allowing me to be the one who causes her pain. She would take those lashes, but it would never be enough for him. What would he do to her if he found me a replacement? Use her himself?

"No."

He drawls, *"Okay then."*

Taking his boot off her hand, he walks to the whip and picks it up. He tosses it in the air and then he strikes. It hits me across the face, a gash forming immediately as my head turns to the side, fast enough to cause my neck to pop.

Before I can take my next breath, I hear a whoosh and a scream as he whips her across her back. I charge at him and two guards, I didn't realize were nearby, grab me from behind. He raises his hand and this time the sharp sound of the whip is mixed with grunts from his men as I struggle against them. They kick my knees and I land with a solid crack against the floor.

He raises his hand again and comes down hard, her back already a bloody mess. She's crying and it will be a sound I hear for the rest of my life. This is all because of me, because I fell in love with her.

"Stop! I'll do anything," I beg my father.

He raises his hand and stops, turning on his heels.

"Anything?" He runs his hand along his wide jaw, pretending to contemplate. He's known about us for a while, I can't believe I didn't realize it sooner, and now he wants something. He wants something I won't want to give him.

"Yes, anything. Please, just don't hurt her." I know it makes me sound weak to him, but what else am I supposed to do? Making a deal with him is all I have left, he likes deals.

"It's time you go fetch your soon-to-be wife."

"It's not time yet. We aren't supposed to wed until the summer after next."

He punches me, more blood spewing from the gash across my face and my mouth. "It's time now ... and you aren't going to wed there.

You'll bring her here and be blessed by our god, not their goddess."
He spits on the floor beside him at the mention of her. "You'll bring
her here, it has to be done here. No other ruler has ever been wed
anywhere else."

Anara catches my attention, she's trying to push herself up. But her
arms give out and she falls down again. I nod my head toward her,
afraid to ask, "And what about her?"

"Bring the Princess here, intact and preferably in love with you,
and I'll make sure your whore is safe when you return, she's yours to
do with as you please. Keep her, kill her, fuck her. Have them both,
but if you mess up or take too long ... well ..." He grabs, and adjusts
himself through his pants, "Maybe I'll see why her pussy turned you
weak."

I nod my head and he gestures for the guards to let me go. I push
myself up and start toward her, my own pain not even registering as
I push past him, grabbing a sheet from the bed. I kneel, wrapping it
around Anara as she curls in around my feet, shaking and crying.
I'll clean, and tend to her wounds and we will leave this place, I
don't care how far we have to run. We will leave tomorrow after I
can get her bandaged up. She'll need to sleep, and I'll need time to
gather supplies.

"Oh and Ereon" – he stands tall, his dark hair blending with the
shadows – "you leave in the morning."

···•••◐●○●◑•••···

Present

"They've lit a fire. This is as good as it's going to get," Thylas' words register as I remember the plan. Staying lost in the past is a fool's game. I can't change what already happened, but I can change what's happening here.

I wrap my hands with a leather strap and grab the handles of my swords. If it starts to rain again, I want to ensure I have a good grasp on the swords. I nod toward him, as we simultaneously pull up our hoods, at the exact moment a gut-wrenching scream comes from the trees. Forgetting all our plans, we run into the darkness.

Thirty-Three

CARNAXA

The pounding in my head is the first thing I register as I bat my lashes lazily. My vision is hazy and I feel water sliding down my chin before it drips onto my chest. I pull my hands to wipe it away when I notice I can't feel my hands at all.

Everything floods back to me. The men. The clearing. The beating. I pull my arms, but they are numb, just like my fingers, from being above my head for so long. I notice the rag that gagged me is now gone and I lick my dry lips. I try to control my breathing as I do my best to stay silent. I see the three men sitting on stones in front of me, their fire is barely illuminating me. The sun has set and now, any hope I had of being found feels like a distant dream. Maybe if I stay here, silent, they'll think I'm dead and be on their way. They could leave now and go wherever they want, abandoning me for someone else to find. They could just go ... but as Lonny turns to look at me, a sadistic grin takes over his face.

"Looks like our princess is awake," he laughs, pushing off his knees to stand. He claps Neol on the shoulder as he too, turns in my direction. Calen, who I'm assuming is the trio's leader, doesn't move from the fire.

"If you touch me," my voice is rough, but I push through the burn, "not only will the Kingdom of Antalis forever be looking for you, but the Kingdom of Shaston as well. Do you really think Prince Ereon would allow this to happen without consequence?"

Lonny pulls up his pants, the underside of his stomach still showing beneath the hem of his too-short shirt. "Oh from what I've heard, Shaston men don't care much for women. No matter how nice they look." He spits at the ground before he reaches up above me and my arms drop to the dirt. Neol grabs them with his burly hands and I scream. I scream as loud as I can, ignoring the searing pain in my throat. I scream as if I can call out to *Mohasha* myself. I kick my legs, I kick toward anything within reach. I twist, I turn. I do everything I know to do, and the pain in my arms starts to become more noticeable as feeling starts to return. I hear my once yellow skirt rip, and a sharp kick to my own ribs takes my breath away.

My hands are free from their grasp again, Neol must have let them go. I roll over to the side and pull my legs up to my chest trying to hide from the impact of another boot connecting with my back. I hide my head between my elbows, trying to protect what I can. One of the men grabs my ankles, pulling me to my back. I hear my skirt rip more and I feel rough hands sliding along my calves. "Look here, fellas. Our little princess thinks she can put up a fight."

I throw my hands around hoping to hit anything, but they secure them back above my head. Neol grabs my ankles, pulling them slightly apart. And it's at this moment that I make a promise to the Goddess. If I should ever find my way out of this, I will never be this helpless again.

"If you like your hands, I would suggest you take them off *my* princess," a voice, I'm not expecting, breaks through the thumping pulse in my ears. The men stop and turn as Ereon emerges, the flames' flickering light casts shadows all around him. One of his curved blades in each of his wrapped hands. His face is hidden mostly behind a black mask and hood. He looks intimidating and my heart quickens at his presence.

"And who might you be?" Calen stands up, cocking his head to the side and smiling at Ereon. "We don't mind sharing." He flicks his hand and Neol turns his back to the trees, releasing my ankles and inching towards Lonny still near my head.

Lonny leans down, keeping his eyes on Ereon, and grabs at the top of my breasts with a free hand, ripping the fabric as he does, but before he can tear it fully, blood splatters on my face. He releases my top and grabs his neck as he gargles.

Looking behind him, I notice emerald eyes, the ones that have always promised to be my safety. Thylas kicks Lonny to the ground and points the tip of his shining blade against Neol's throat. Neol's eyes flick back and forth between Calen and Thylas, sending a silent plea to his comrade for support. And all is still. The whole world seems to fall into a hush.

Then everyone moves at the same moment. Thylas looks down at me for just a moment, a subtle nod to get up and move closer to him. But it's then that Neol sees his opportunity to attack. He knocks the sword aimed at his jugular to the side and lunges at Thylas, taking him to the ground hard. I scramble to find my footing. And I run, for the first time in my life, not away from danger, but to it.

Ereon charges Calen, but my kidnapper turns quickly and jumps over the fire, a smile on his face. The sounds of Ereon's blades sing as he prepares to pursue him. As I run toward Thylas who wrestles with Neol on the ground, Ereon screams my name, fear lacing his voice, but I ignore him as I gather what strength I have left and jump on Neol's back. I take my bound hands and place them over his head.

I pull as hard as I can trying to put as much pressure on the rope around the man's neck as possible, his breaths becoming shallow. Finally Neol rolls to the side and off Thylas. Thylas jumps to his feet before kicking the man in the gut and Neol staggers backwards, falling to the ground, taking me with him.

"Let go, Naxa!" Thylas grabs his sword from the ground, but it's hard to move. My leg is stuck under Neol and my hands are still tied and around his neck.

"I can't!" I yell and Thylas looks at my hands and raises his sword, I pull my hands as far apart as possible, hopefully creating enough space for whatever Thylas is about to do. Thylas doesn't hesitate. He slits the man upwards, from the middle of his stomach to the tip of his chin, slicing the rope around my hands in the process.

Thylas bends down quickly, rolling the man off of me, and pulls me into his arms. His heat instantly warms me. Looking over my shoulder, Ereon circles Calen and Calen sneers.

"So if that is the Captain. This must be Shaston's prince." Calen lunges toward Ereon, but he jumps out of the way. His hood is still firmly on his head, but in an instant, he reaches up and jerks it off.

"And if I am" – he rolls the pommel of his sword in his hand – "will you cease this? Or do I have to kill you too?"

The man's hollow laughter filters through the trees and Thylas pulls me back into him. I push his arms down trying to run to Ereon, not sure how I will help but I refuse to stand by and just watch. Thylas' hands grab my wrist and he wraps his arms back around me, stronger this time.

Suddenly the man stops moving and drops his sword. He holds up his hands and flatly states, "I surrender."

I stop trying to pull away from Thylas, his strong arms still holding me. My eyes dance between the pair as Ereon's shoulders relax and he places one of his own swords in the baldric on his back, before taking steps to close the distance between him and Calen.

Ereon smiles, Calen clasping him with one of his hands on the shoulder before Ereon rams the other sword he kept in his right hand through the man's sternum. Ereon mumbles something I can't hear and twists his sword a half-turn before pulling it back out. Ereon tosses Calen to the side.

His eyes are full of fury until he turns to me. He drops his blade, running to me and Thylas lets me go. Ereon wraps an arm around me, lacing the other through the back of my hair. His heart is racing as my head rests against his chest. He pulls back, running his hand along the dried blood on my face. He pulls me in again and kisses the top of my head. "I'm so sorry, Princess."

"It's not your fault, I should have ..." my words escape me and I try to take a deep breath as I back away from him. I turn around and find Thylas directly behind me. The heat of his skin clashes with the coolness of Ereon. I fall to my knees and I cry, a deep guttural cry. My hands shake as everything that's happened tonight threatens to overtake me. They both kneel down beside me.

Ereon rubs his hand down my back and Thylas rubs my thigh. This could have turned out so differently. I could be dead, or worse. I could be many things, but right now I am thankful for the second chance. The chance to not sit on the side anymore, the chance to stop letting everything happen to me. I control my life, no one else.

Thylas touches my chin, slowly lifting my face to meet his. "Let's go back to camp and get you cleaned up."

I nod my head, and try to stand. My knees buckle before I can straighten and I slam back into the ground. The adrenaline from the night fades away into exhaustion. Ereon lifts me up with one hand behind my knees and the other around my back. "I got you, Princess. Just relax. We've got you." I should protest, but right now I don't care and I let exhaustion take me, feeling safe once more.

·····●●●○●●●····

"It's getting worse," Siphonie's voice whispers. "Rhenor told me the messenger said as much. My uncle, the King, has been secluded in the castle, in an effort to prevent anything happening to him. Great Goddess, please protect them. Protect us."

Rubbing the sleep from my eyes I mumble, "What?" This can't be, my father would never separate himself from his kingdom. We love our people.

Siphonie flinches, jumping up from her knees where she prays and turns. "Naxa! I didn't know you were awake." She rushes to me, kissing both of my cheeks. We tried to bandage you up the best we could, but you'll probably be sore for a few days."

Raising up on my arms, I groan as my bicep strains and a sharp pain laces through my ribs. My arm is bandaged with a pink cloth and I eye Siphonie questioningly. She shrugs.

"Ereon wanted discretion. All I had were my things or the boys' dirty things to bandage you with. I thought, at least this looks pretty with your hair." She chuckles and pushes a pillow behind my back to help me sit up. She tries to sound apathetic, unconcerned.

She was scared, and her way of dealing with trauma is to lighten the emotional load with humor.

"Thank you very much, but why is Father separating himself from the people?"

She sighs and looks around the room. "Because there have been seventy-five new cases of the deluc since we left."

Seventy-five? We've always had about thirty a year for the past two years, but seventy-five, it's inconceivable. It's true, the Goddess has officially left us, we are no longer her people. My mother was always so sure, she told me stories. The stories of Her love, but right now— all I feel is anger toward her for letting this happen. Our people are good people.

Siphonie scoots closer to me. "Your father has sent envoys to the Southern Continent; he's been told the people there know more about the *Mohasha* realm and plagues. Hopefully, they'll find answers soon."

"But if they are all going to die anyway, why am I going through with this marriage? Is it better to die by sickness than the sword?"

"I ..." – she rubs her hands along her upper arms before pushing the hair off my forehead – "I can't answer that. We just have to believe it's all in the plan of the Goddess."

I jerk up in surprise. "The Goddess? The one who almost let me get raped in the woods? The one who has cursed our people? The one who took my mother for no reason except to show the world we are no longer favored? That Goddess?"

I don't know why I am so angry, but I am. What is the point of all this? What is the point of leaving my home, hoping to keep people from war when the deluc is taking them anyway? And in a prolonged sort of way. I saw the deluc take away my mother and it wasn't quick nor pleasant. She was a shell of the woman I once knew. This can't be the Goddess my mother told me about. The one who loved Her children, the one who gave them twin drops, and the one who, even some myths said, walked among us.

My hands grip the sheets in anger at my sides. "Where was she tonight? Because she certainly wasn't with me. The only people who were with me were Thylas and Ereon. It's because of them that I am safe, not the Goddess. I prayed to her and she didn't listen. She would have let me ..."

The words catch in my throat and the tears escape, "She would have let them take the only thing I have control of anymore." My body begins to shake and my ribs hurt from it. I lean over as sobs rack my body. Siphonie grabs me and pulls me close.

Siphonie sits, holding me against her chest, rocking slowly back and forth. I don't want to be this person, one who says nothing, I don't want to believe in someone who may not be there. I'm ready ... ready to make my own choices, at least the ones I can.

···•◦◉○◉◦•···

At some point, I must have fallen back into exhaustion, because the next thing I know, I'm waking up in a dark room. For a moment I panic, putting my hand over my heart, thinking I must be back in the woods and my rescue was nothing more than a dream.

Then I see a small, lit torch — I'm inside my tent. I look around for Thylas and don't see him anywhere. That's odd.

Standing on shaking legs, I do my best to find my robe and wrap it around me. The familiar comfort bringing me even more peace. Underneath it I wear just the nightwear I brought with me, someone must have changed me. Which I'm glad for, I hope they burned the dress I was brought back in. I don't want any physical reminders of this night. Well ... except for what I'm about to do.

I don't know when exactly I decided to pursue this, to take something back. I want to be the one in control of the one thing I still have. I don't fully get my kingdom and I don't get to choose my husband, but I do still have a piece of me that will be mine to give. My cheeks flush as I remember the feeling of being in Ereon's embrace and the way his eyes softened toward me.

I slip on my sandals and leave the safety of my tent. Most soldiers are asleep, but I notice Thylas and Ereon at a table near the center of camp. Both of them look relaxed, their legs stretched out in front of them.

Thylas throws his cards across the table, standing up, frustrated, "I'm done with this. It's late."

Well, I thought they looked relaxed, but obviously something is on his mind or they were arguing. I'm not sure which. Ereon raises his head and looks in my direction, a smile lighting his face. "Princess ..."

Thylas turns and walks my way. Emerald eyes take me in and I fidget with the hem of my sleeve, feeling much less confident then I did a moment ago. "I'm alive."

"That's always good to hear, *Nohæ*. We have been checking on you, but we were also letting you get your rest." He reaches up, running his hand down my arm before wrapping it around my waist and leading me back to where he was sitting. He motions for me to sit down in the chair he just occupied. My legs still are sore so I oblige.

"Careful Princess, you've had a long day. Maybe we should get you back inside." Ereon leans back in his chair, running his hand through his beard. His eyes glance up at Thylas, an understanding passing between them before he says, "We were done here anyway." He motions for his men who are hidden in the shadows. How did he get away from them to come find me?

Maybe he sees the surprise on my face because he lets out a low chuckle. "They aren't too happy about me disappearing. But when we brought you back to camp they realized why I left. Although, I doubt I will escape their notice anytime soon."

I glance back at Thylas, a feeling I understand too well. He always watched me more closely the days after I successfully escaped his dutiful eyes.

"Siph ..." I cough, grabbing someone's water from the table before taking a sip. "Siphonie said the deluc is getting worse? My father is secluding himself from the people?"

They look quickly at each other, whatever happened when I was taken has changed their interactions. They are different and I don't know why.

Thylas kneels beside me. "Yes. I'm sure she told you that your father sent people to the Southern Continent. Try not to worry, your father is just being cautious, that's all."

"Yes, well, he may be, but his kingdom's subjects are not. Ereon" – I look back at him, his honey eyes drawing me in as he leans in, resting his forearms on the table – "we need to discuss the deluc with your father soon, develop a plan to help Antalis. I will not let my people suffer."

"We ... can try," he answers honestly and in a hushed tone. His eyes search mine, probably looking for something to better understand my true motives given I've been silent up until now. "My father may prioritize other plans in the Kingdom of Shaston, but we can try. You will have to try not to draw attention to yourself, you will have to follow the laws of Shaston. No questions asked."

Seems a fair trade, his father is set I'm sure, in the tradition of his people. When we reach the Shaston border what will be expected of me will be so unfamiliar, so foreign, and so suffocating. But I'll do what I must. "Fine. I'll trust you in this. I'll trust you'll help me help my people. Our people." A look of doubt flashes across his eyes before he sits back up straight, nodding his head.

I start to stand when a slight pain from the night's events reverberates through my side and I stumble, both Ereon and Thylas are on either side of me in a moment.

"Don't worry, Princess, I got you," Ereon confirms, as he holds on to me.

Thylas nods his head toward my tent, "Maybe, we should get you to the bed after all huh, *Nohæ*?"

Ereon's mens' boots thump across the ground behind us as we make our way to my tent. The crickets are chirping loudly tonight, almost like a song. I can still smell the rain, even though it has stopped. I can do without the rain, but I won't go without one last night of freedom. Tonight, I'll take control of the only thing I have left that's mine.

Thirty-Four

CARNAXA

The mens' presence fills my tent with tension. It's wrapping around the three of us, and I once thought that my tent was of decent size, but with both men in here, I'm not so sure anymore. The guards stayed outside, three steps away from what I heard Ereon tell them.

And now we stand here, oddly, everyone unsure of what to do. Would Thylas want to even stay in here after all that's happened the last few days? We still have so many things left unsaid, and Ereon for once looks like a small, shy boy. He sways from one foot to the other. Meanwhile, Thylas' eyes match the same ones that he had the night we almost found ourselves in each other, the night I wanted so badly. The night I still want.

"We'll let you rest," Thylas is the one to speak through the silence. I don't want to be alone. Not tonight, I don't want to remember the things that were done to me, I don't want this to be my last memory before I step onto foreign sands. Not that Midaeliea is home, but at least here, it feels familiar. When I cross the border, all sense of comfort will be stripped away.

"Don't go ..." my voice comes out breathy and I try to regain my composure. I clear my throat and stand up straighter, trying to appear braver than I currently feel. "I don't want to be alone tonight, not after everything that happened. I don't want *that* to be my last memory of this place, I want something more."

Thylas stops and takes a long sigh. I know he's fighting with himself, even with his back to me. Fighting because if he stays, he knows what I want. I want him to stay, I've always wanted him to stay. Ereon takes a breath and his face becomes one of resolution as he walks up beside Thylas. He's probably going to remind him that it's not his place to stay with me, because I'm not Thylas' woman.

Instead, I hear his deep voice soften, "Go to her." Thylas turns around looking past him, at me. His eyes are full of desire and want and then he looks at Ereon once more.

Ereon palms Thylas' shoulder. "Go to her. Have your night because it will be the last one you can have. But know, I can't leave this tent with my men outside until you do, not if" – he grins softly, looking back at me – "she can't stay quiet. I can't let them know that she was with you, they'll believe I shared her but would never believe that I turned a blind eye. Do what the both of you wish, and I give you my word not to interfere."

His words shock me and goosebumps flicker across my skin. I run my hand along my wrist, missing the bracelets that were once there. Ereon's eyes linger and take me in from head to toe and I can't help the heat that blooms from just his stare. "Her first time should be special, she's too beautiful for it to be any other way." I blush as the two exchange words that I was never meant to hear.

He releases Thylas' shoulder and shuffles to the corner of the room, moving a chair with him. Turning to face the wall. His shoulders slump as he runs his hand through his hair. He'll hear everything and I suddenly do not care; he will be my husband soon. I know he is more than the cold exterior he wears. He hides his secrets, but who doesn't have thoughts and fears they keep to themselves? I can't explain the way my feelings for him have changed, the way I feel just as safe with him as I do when I'm with Thylas.

I run my hands along the tie of my robe and take a deep breath. "Come lie with me." I hold out my hand and Thylas grabs it gently. He pulls me into him, kissing the top of my head. As we walk toward the bed I let my robe fall to the floor, left only in a thin night dress. Feeling exposed, more than I thought I would, I quickly find the bed and burrow under the silk sheets.

I want this, but I'm scared. Scared of what this will mean. Will I be able to have this one night with Thylas and never again? Maybe if we can both have this moment, we can both move on.

Thylas takes off his tunic, letting it drop to the floor and I smile. He's beautiful. His solid abs and lean frame. His tattoos trail across his tan arms and shoulders and I find my fingers itching to trace them. He's not small, not by any means, but he's not as large as the man who sits silently in the corner, trying to look anywhere but at what's going on over here. Thylas crawls into bed beside me, and puts his arm behind my head pulling me into him with his other. He's comfortable and safe, he's always been with me. I take a deep breath, the smell of sage and sandalwood taking over me. Reaching out to him, I rub my hands along those scars. The scars that changed everything for us, because he thought that by staying away he would keep me safe. Keep us both from feeling exactly what we feel now. He shivers, goosebumps pebbling his skin beneath my touch.

I lean in further against him, and feel his desire against my thigh. I ache to know what he feels like without the barriers between us. There are still words I should have said before now, and before this goes any further I have to tell him.

"I'm sorry I didn't tell you before."

He leans back, looking down at me, confusion etched in his features. "Tell me what, *Nohæ*?"

"That I was untouched. I thought if you knew, you wouldn't want me. I'm not experienced like the other women you've been with."

A chuckle from deep in his chest fills the tent along with a matching one from Ereon. "Naxa, trust me. That was not why I didn't let things go any further that night. I didn't want to be a mistake when you're marrying ..." his words trail off. Ereon's own chuckle dies down and his boots scrape the floor across the room.

"You were worried that *he* would kill us." And we were. We all thought Ereon would – never did I think he would give us this night. Even if it is to be our only. It's a gift and one I'm happy to have. "He knows about the marks. When he saw me that same night, I didn't have them covered."

"I know." His fingers trail my thigh, pushing the material up with it and back down. "He told me, when we were looking for you. We have ... an agreement of sorts. But don't worry about any of that." He reaches up, pulling the leather band in my hair. Running his hands through my hair softly, letting the braids out. "Just tonight, baby girl. We have tonight."

I lean up kissing the hollow of his neck. "I want this." I push my hand into his hair and pull him toward me.

"Are you sure?"

I glance back at Ereon, who's smoldering eyes are staring at me, he's turned his chair around. My heart wants to jump from my chest to him and I tighten my thighs, craving friction just from his look alone combined with Thylas' fingers lazily dancing across my skin. Desire must show through my eyes because Ereon winks, heat filling my core, and it's then I know. I truly do want this.

"Yes" – I look back to Thylas – "I can't describe it, but I know this is right. I can feel it." The pull of my heart is undeniable now. It's pulling toward both of them, and I'll give into it, just for tonight.

Thylas pulls me to him and kisses my neck, the same place his previous marks have since disappeared from. I can't help but hope he leaves them again. I reach down, running my hand along his length and a moan escapes him. I greedily pull the ties from his leathers and his full length spills forward. It's as big as I thought it would be, big enough to understand why all the women want him.

Pushing him onto his back, I kiss down his chest before licking him from tip down his shaft. I may have chosen to be untouched but that doesn't mean I haven't learned a few things in my time. As I grab him with one hand and part my lips, he pulls me up by my arms, flipping me onto my back, positioning himself between my knees.

"I will not last long if I let you do that." His hair hangs down around his face, shielding me from seeing anything but him. My chest rises and falls and my heart is about to explode from how hard it's beating.

His hands find the hem of my night dress and pull it up slowly before pulling it over my head and tossing it on the floor. On impulse, I pull my arms up to cover my chest but he quickly grabs my wrist, pushing them above my head.

"This is a better place for your hands. Don't use them to hide from me, I promise I want to see all of you."

I smile as he kisses down my neck, his tongue licking across the freckles there. He moves down and nips at my breast before kissing it gently. A loud moan falls from my lips and now I understand why Ereon couldn't leave. I won't be quiet. Thylas' tongue circles one nipple before going to the other, fully enjoying taking me to the edge.

When he releases my wrist, I bury them in his hair. Pulling softly on the strands as he peppers kisses down the middle of my breast and down my stomach. He stops just at the apex of my thighs. He smiles up at me. "So wet already, baby girl. We've barely started." He runs his hand along my calves, as he leans down, resting them on his shoulders. He lies down like a man about to devour his last meal and I laugh at the notion before a broad sweep of his tongue makes me moan once again. I pull his hair harder and arch my back. A shiver radiates through me with each swipe of his tongue. He inserts one finger and I rake my teeth across my lower lip at the sensations that spread through me. Slowly he circles inside of me, alternating his finger and his tongue.

The scrapping of a chair catches my attention. I glance at Ereon, a bulge clearly in his pants as he leans his arms on his knees. Watching us intently, a look of debate passing over his features. I want him too. Taking one hand from Thylas' hair I motion for Ereon to come over. Ereon's eyes flick to Thylas, who looks down at me as I motion again. Thylas dips his chin, running his hand down the inside of my thigh.

Ereon stands up suddenly, walking over to us and I want him too. Ereon leans down, cusping my chin before devouring my mouth with his. And I erupt. Wrapping my legs around Thylas as he leans up, rubbing my entrance with his swollen cock. And I grab onto Ereon's shirt, pulling him further into me. Tongue and teeth clash and euphoria fills me as I've never felt before, here between these two. Thylas softly thrusts inside me as Ereon bites my bottom lip. Thylas on his knees stays still, letting me adjust around him. I close my eyes, stars forming behind them as the fullness and slight pain takes complete control of me. Ereon licks the side of my neck and it's then, as I look between the two men, I see them.

I feel in my heart the current I've so often been told about, as it starts to circulate inside me and build before swirling around me. The currents of gold and silver that ebb from me to each of them, a matching golden current from Ereon rippling with mine. Barely there, a much softer silver ripple flows towards me from Thylas. I gasp, unable to fully comprehend what I see. I start to pull away to make sure I fully understand, but just as quickly as I glimpse the ripples, they are gone and Ereon pulls away.

I lean forward to reach for Ereon again and bring him back when he grabs my wrist, kissing the inside of it. "It's not our night, Princess." He kisses me one more time, this one soft and sweet before looking back at Thylas. "Worship her."

Thylas nods before leaning down over me, but this time I push his hair away and watch as Ereon leans against the wall. I don't want to be hidden from Ereon. He undoes his own leather, pulling his manhood from the prison he wouldn't give me keys to moments ago as he leans against the wall, trailing the length with his own fingers.

"Are you okay?" Thylas asks, calling my attention back to him, and I run my hand along the ridges of his back as I nod softly.

"Yes." I wrap my legs fully around him again, grinding against him. "I want this, I want you," I tell him again. He kisses my hairline, down my forehead and then the tip of my nose.

"As you wish, *Nohæ*."

Thylas leans down, running quick kisses between my breasts before his tongue flicks my erect nipple and tingles pulse through me. He grasps my other breast roughly before his eyes stare back into mine. He never looks away as his thrusts get quicker and my moans get louder. Those outside must hear me, but I don't care, the pleasure is too much and I tremble beneath his touch. I feel myself begin to tighten around him, seeking my climax and I push against him wanting him deeper.

Ereon's breaths from the corner of the tent unite with ours becoming the music for this Goddess-blessed night. Looking at Ereon, his deep brown eyes take in everything happening before him. His hips flex forward as his hand roughly slides back and forth against his long length. He winks at me as he increases his pace. Thylas kisses my chest, my neck, everything turning into a blur as I let my fingers leave my own marks across his marred skin. I turn back to Thylas as he lifts his head to meet my gaze. I move the inky strands from his face again, cupping his cheek with my palm and kiss him deeply. He sucks on my bottom lip and my legs pull him tighter against me. If all I have is one night, then I will enjoy it enough for a lifetime.

He smiles down at me and slowly glides himself out of me before pushing into me again deeply. "Come for me, baby girl," his voice is gravely and the command in his words has me withering as he continues his strokes.

The pressure builds deep inside me, begging to be released. My moans become screams as they mix with my tears, all from a happiness and a pleasure I've never felt before. I have so many emotions all at once and I can't contain them anymore. I grab the back of his neck, pulling him down onto me as his hips push into me once more and I do as he requested.

He finds his own release as he grunts into my neck, pulling my hips impossibly closer to him. My legs tremble from the after effects, and while the soreness is there – the pleasure is what I feel the most. Our breaths are heavy against each other. Ereon's groans fill the air. His eyes sweeping me from head to where Thylas and I are still connected and back. He grips the chair with one hand as he holds himself up. His hand pumps two more times before he growls his own climax.

Thylas nuzzles my neck and kisses the three freckles there before slowly pulling out of me and laying beside me. He pulls me into the side of his body and I lay my head on his chest. His heart beats erratically as he tries to calm down. He kisses the top of my head and rubs my shoulder softly with his rough fingertips. I lie here in bliss amazed at what just happened, until I remember the dancing currents between us. I don't have just one twin drop ... I have two.

THIRTY-FIVE

CARNAXA

I'm still wrapped in Thylas' arms as the sleep leaves my eyes, the sunlight slowly leaking into the tent. Last night was not how I had expected things to happen. When I was younger though, I always knew Thylas was to be my first. I wanted him to be. Thylas holds me closer pulling me into him, his warmth wrapping around me as I trace my fingers along his cheek. A soft snore from the corner of the tent reveals Ereon stayed like he said he would. In the haze of memories from last night, I remember him coming over and pulling a blanket over me, Thylas already asleep beside me. He kissed my hairline and returned to the corner of the tent, falling asleep in the chair.

Heat instantly flames my cheeks as I remember how Ereon's kiss felt. That wasn't the Ereon I would have expected a few short moon cycles ago. He was cold and rude, and while at times he still is. Last night, I watched his eyes. I saw the currents connecting us, and I see now, why his walls slip around me. I saw the longing in his eyes that matched what I felt, and I wanted more from him. I still do. I know he's hiding things, I've known it for a long time. He has already hinted he has someone waiting for him in Shaston. Sadness takes hold of me for a moment, I'll be breaking someone else's heart, but maybe Shaston has a way we can make a *Shæwi Koki* anyway. I've never heard of such a thing in their kingdom, but times are changing. I can't let the gift of him letting Thylas and I have our night not be repaid. He didn't have to let us have that moment, but he did. He knows what it's like to love someone you can't have.

Ereon groans again, shifting in the chair and I roll over softly still wrapped in Thylas' embrace. I know what the ebb and flow of our currents meant last night, but I'm not ready. Everyone dreams of finding their drop, I always did, but now... everything is different. I thought finding my drop would mean finding my happiness, but now that's not the case. Now it's a complication. Why would the Goddess bestow me with two? Two on opposite sides of conflict; two who until recently, couldn't even be in the same room with each other. I know a twin drop can be denied, and that's what I'll do as soon as I get to Shaston. I'll perform the *Neni,* the ceremony to deny a drop, to provide closure to the individuals involved in the hopes that everyone can move forward in their lives. It's usually done only in agreement, but I don't have a choice. I don't want to have my allegiances swayed. I need to keep my eyes set on saving my kingdom.

I run my hand over my face, sighing softly. I am here, still covered in sweat and sex, and my people are dying. My father is secluded and yet here I am, euphoric and confused. The deluc could quickly take my father and then it would be Ereon's father who rules my kingdom. Something I do not want. Something I hoped could be avoided until Ereon is king.

"I can hear your thoughts from here, Princess."

Thylas tightens his hold around me, kissing my neck softly. "Her thoughts are always loud."

So much for hoping I wouldn't wake them. I push back into Thylas and shut my eyes. Maybe I can ignore the real world for a few more moments and live here in this bed. I could be happy here. I could just stay and dream.

Ereon stands up, stretching tall and it's then I notice he's not wearing his shirt. His body is riddled with scars, more than even Thylas wears across his back. They mare him everywhere that can be hidden from sight. I study him ... burns, perhaps? From here the scars along his ribs look like constellations across his warm ivory skin.

He catches me looking before grabbing his tunic and throwing it on. Someone outside scrapes the canvas of the tent and Thylas' hand tightens around me, his face nuzzling into the back of my neck. Ereon walks to the opening, turning his back to hide the bed and those who lie in it, only opening it enough to be seen himself.

"What?"

"Prince Ereon, we've heard from a scout. The *khind* seem to have retreated to their caves now, and your father is getting anxious about the lack of our arrival since we have not sent him a message since —"

"I know when I last sent a message, we will arrive when we arrive. Things changed as we traveled. Gather the men and get everything prepared. We will leave soon."

He lets the fabric fall back into place. His eyes lazily dance over me. Thylas runs his hand down my body and breathes in deeply. We know when we leave this tent, everything must change. I hope neither of them realized what I saw last night. I am not sure how either of them would feel knowing what I know. The question still remains as to why Ereon would allow this. For Thylas and me to have to have such an intimate experience when I am betrothed to him. Even when he knew I wanted him, I am the one who brought him to us. I wanted him here, with us. I wanted to be entangled between them, but he didn't.

Ereon leans down and kisses my forehead. "We have to go."

I nod my head as Thylas pushes up and pulls me to him. His lips crash into mine. I wrap my hands one more time in his inky strands and breath in his scent. Breaking the kiss, he kisses my nose before whispering, "This can't be the last time I have you, *Nohæ*. But it is ... for now." Getting out of bed, he stands trying to find his own clothing, leaving me feeling cold without his body heat encircling me.

Ereon stands at the door, fully dressed with his swords attached to his back. Thylas and Ereon share a glance between them. "I'll be outside. Hurry it up Captain, but I'll give you a few moments." He fixes his features as he resumes the facade of the cold prince everyone expects, and leaves.

Instantly, Thylas kneels beside the bed pushing hair from my face, leaning his forehead to mine. "Are you okay, Naxa?"

"I think so ... I'm sore." I glance down and he leans back, a smile tugging on his lips.

"Yeah, that's expected." He licks his lips. "I didn't mean for it to have worked out like this. When I dreamed of this. I always expected it to be just us."

I pull the covers around me, sitting up more on the bed. I'll have to leave it soon.

"How did this happen? I mean, you and Ereon? What happened?"

He grabs my hand and kisses the back of my knuckles. "We have an understanding. I can't really explain it, except we thought we lost you. When fears are heightened, well, the truth seems to come out. I would still rather punch him than speak to him, but we have called a truce, for now."

Ereon, I'm assuming, taps three times on the side of the tent. Our time is up.

"I have to go, *Nohæ*." He pulls me forward and kisses me deeply. His scent, his taste, his heat. I don't want to let him go, but when Ereon taps the side again he releases me.

As he heads out for the day, I have to know one more thing. "Thy, what does *Nohæ* mean?" He's called me it for so long and has always refused to tell me, but I need to know now.

Running his hands through his hair to tie it up once again, getting ready to show the world that he is the Captain, he smiles. "It means 'my dream.'"

And with that, he walks out the door.

··•••◐●○●◑••··

There is a chill here among the shadows of the mountain, even with the sun shining high overhead. Thylas explained as we were packing, that we would move quickly without the use of the carriage, and so now Siphonie and I are riding horses, something I've not done in a long time. I was given a pair of leather pants that Rhenor found somewhere, because no one likes to ride a horse in a dress. Thylas gave me one of his tunics to wear as a top and every time he sees me in it, he smiles. The memories of last night replaying just as much for him as they do for me. He likes seeing me in his clothing. After they left this morning, I grabbed the jeweled dagger from my trunks and attached it to my thigh. It's not hidden as it would be in a dress, but I don't care. I want people to know that I am no longer the prey. Siphonie returned my pack this morning, saying Thy and Ereon found it before they found me. I was overjoyed to see the journal still intact, but it did get wet. I haven't looked at the damage yet. I was even more excited to also find my bangle inside and slipped it on quickly.

Siphonie wears a pair of Rhenor's pants, although she has them tightened with a rope around her waist. She made some joke about how being in another man's pants was behind her and she would have to find someone to loan her a pair; Rhenor didn't find it as funny as I did. So he found a rope and a pair of his.

We've been inside the pass for not more than an hour and so far it's been uneventful but the air is getting hotter with each step. Thylas' hair is still piled high on his head, his normal style, but it looks like he's been swimming from all the perspiration.

Thylas makes sure I feel safe, never leaving my side from the time I left the tent this morning. He keeps his horse on the right side of me, while Rhenor stays behind me right beside Siphonie, who trots behind Thylas.

Ereon is on his stallion to my left. Maybe the heat isn't from the atmosphere but simply being placed in the middle of the two who had me moaning in pleasure last night, and now we must pretend nothing happened. But I feel Thylas' heat as it fights with the coolness of Ereon's aura, the heady mix has my body feeling so many things.

The trail is simple — rock, and at times dusty — but simple. Nothing seems extremely dangerous but it is a narrow passage only fitting three horses across. The sides of the mountains stretch high into the sky, in fact, I can't see anything but them. I've never seen anything so tall, I can understand how the stories of Shaston being banished by the Goddess came about. This landscape contributes to the feeling of being completely cut off from the rest of the continent, and I guess they are. I shudder because soon enough, I will be too.

"Are you okay?" Thylas rides a bit closer to me, his brown mare keeping in step with mine.

"Hot ... but okay. You?"

"Besides the fact that my ass is numb, I think I'm okay." He adjusts in his saddle.

"We still have about three more hours, trust me, your ass won't be the only thing that's numb. It'll take you a minute to remember how to walk when we stop," Ereon mumbles riding up on his mountain of a horse.

"Three more hours?" Siphonie whines, "Aren't we going to stop and stretch our legs?"

"Can't risk it until we near the end of the pass. The weather has been working in our favor now, I don't want to jeopardize our party, unless you would like to meet the *khind* face to face?" He smirks at her and I smile too. He's actually talking to us, and not the arrogant Ereon, but the Ereon that he's let me catch glimpses of.

"Where are they?" she asks.

"In their caves, for now. If you look up" – he points his hand to the top where small craters line the sides – "that would be where they are."

As if conjured by our thoughts, a howl rattles the rocks around us. The sun slides behind a dark large cloud and all the men look up quickly. Thylas' hands tremble as he directs his horse even closer to me. He's never witnessed these creatures either. We feel the vibration of the mountains around us as the creatures seem to wake from their slumber.

"Calm ... the cloud will move." Ereon holds his hand up, stopping the entire convoy. "Just try not to make any noise," his voice is barely above a whisper, but he grabs one of his swords from his back.

Suddenly feeling very cold, I wrap my arms around my chest, barely grasping the reins between my fingertips. I want to look back at Siphonie to check on her, but I don't let my eyes move from the caves Ereon just pointed out. A deadly silence surrounds us, as if the world itself just went mute. Then rocks trickle from the top, rolling down the mountains, as giant paws appear on the ledges above us.

Thylas slides off his horse getting even closer to me as Ereon cuts his eyes toward us. "Stay ... calm," his words are clipped, and Thylas just rolls his eyes.

A beast appears from the shadows, the head is as big as my horse and its fur has fire at the tips. My heart races and my whole body shakes as it sniffs the air with its wolf-like snout.

Thylas runs his hand up his sword, grabbing the handle before pulling it from the sheath, a swooshing sound echoes through the pass. The *khind* looks right at us from its perch and snarls showing its long, pointed teeth.

Pebbles scatter beside me, as Thylas once again tries to get closer to me. Ereon growls under his breath, "If you move one more time

Captain, I will finish you off before these creatures get to us. Stand still." Surprisingly, he doesn't move again. My eyes remain on the beast as it slowly lets out a howl, and I flinch.

"Princess ..." Ereon's voice is the only thing I can hear over the pounding of my own heart. "Look at me, look at him ... just stop looking at them. I can hear your heart from here."

I jerk my eyes down trying to focus on my breath. One breath in. One breath out. In through the nose, out through the mouth. The *khind* lets out another shrill shriek and I wince at the high-pitched sounds, my eyes darting back to the creature who is staring right at me. It stops and tilts its head.

I want to look away, I want to stop staring into the soulless eyes staring back at me. It starts slowly descending and is now roughly sixty-five paces from us, on another ledge where pebbles scatter away from its large paws. Soldiers try hard to not move as the small rocks shower down on them. More creatures appear around the edges of the mountains and begin descending. The soldiers who have never traversed the pass begin to fidget pulling their swords and I hear more whispers of "stay calm" being issued. It's hard to look away when death is clearly staring at me.

The one that has its eyes on me jumps down and it is only fifty paces from us now. Ereon grabs his sword as do the rest of the men. This must be it. There is no longer any hope that staying quiet will save us. The fire on the tips of the *khind's* fur causes what few plants there are around us to catch fire, and smoke begins to fill the area.

Thylas' hand touches my thigh and slightly squeezes. "When I tell you, you don't look back, you don't wait, you ride as fast as you can in any direction. Just get out of this pass." He grabs the dagger in the strap on my thigh, and grabs my hand from the reins, wrapping my fingers around the handle. "You are the last, and only heir to Antalis, you have to be the one who survives this. The rest of us do not matter."

I can't leave them. I can't leave any of them. I won't. I'll fight if I have to. I'll probably die, but I've lived long enough being a coward who hides behind the crown.

One step forward from the monstrous creature and the ground beneath us shakes. I can feel a scream wanting to burst from inside me.

Two steps and every man around me gets ready for battle, the pressure in my chest buildings.

Three steps and I let it go with everything I have in me.

The scream is something I can't control. The confusion of everything happens all at once: the pain and fear from being taken; the heartbreak that comes with the realization I have a drop I can never love; understanding I am just a pawn and will never truly rule my kingdom; missing my mother and wondering what she would want me to do - how to best serve myself, and my people. Everything gets thrown into this scream. I watch as everyone's breath becomes visible and they breathe deeper as the air around us cools. Tears run down my face, turning to ice as the temperature gets colder. But I keep screaming, my throat turning raw. The sound of my despair, dread and worry reverberates all around us, and every creature stops and turns its head toward me. The largest one, in front of us, stops and tilts its head once more and I stop, closing my mouth and grip the dagger even tighter.

The *khind* lets out a howl that sounds of sadness as it takes a step back. Then another. The others follow suit retreating back up, into the caves. The leader remains, just staring at me until it decides to ascend the mountain as well. With a final flick of its tail, its huge body is swallowed up by the rockside surrounding us as the sun starts to peek through the clouds.

A collective sigh is heard coming from the entirety of the group as the air around us warms. A few "it's a miracle" can also be heard from the men, some praying and thanking the Goddess for her safety. But the eyes that stare at me aren't praying. Ereon, Thylas, Siphonie and Rhenor say nothing, they all saw the same thing I did.

My hands shake as I replace my dagger in its sheath. I have no answer to the questions those closest to me may have from what they saw or felt. I have no idea why the *khind* stopped. Maybe they sensed the coming sun. Perhaps it was the Goddess intervening. Either way, I'm glad they are gone.

As if everything comes back to life, Ereon jumps down from his horse and bares his teeth toward Thylas. "You could have gotten her killed for disregarding my order."

"They were coming this way anyway!" Thylas steps toward him, the vein in his neck popping.

Ereon breaches the distance between them before shoving him back. "They can't distinguish color! If you don't move they don't notice you as much! Even their smell isn't that great! They rely on sound from fools who panic."

I slide from my saddle and start toward them when Rhenor grabs my elbow pulling me back and rushes between them instead. He puts his hands on Thylas' chest and leans in. I can't hear what he says but Thy huffs loudly in response before kicking a rock and walks in the other direction.

Rhenor bows. "I am sorry, Prince Ereon. Thylas is very protective. He did not mean anything against you."

Ereon just sighs. "He knows, as should you, *Bêl* Rhenor, that I do not want anything to happen to her either." He rubs his hands together. "I've been through these mountains, I know what I'm doing." His eyes flick to me. "Or, I did."

"Thank you for your understanding." Rhenor turns and walks back to Siphonie. He doesn't know what all has happened, he's still worried Ereon will hurt Thylas. But I don't think so. Not now.

Returning his attention to me, he runs his hand down my shoulders. "Are you okay?"

"I'm ... " I shake a little to try to clear the nerves still pulsing. "I'll be okay, but why did they stop. What was that?"

He shrugs his shoulders and runs his hand through his beard, trying to find the right words. We both know whatever happened wasn't normal. He strokes the mane of the white horse I ride as he speculates, "I don't know, Princess. But I think it had something to do with you, but most didn't seem to notice. Keep it that way. This is not the time to be running off, do you understand?" He lifts my chin with his finger. "I mean it. I will not allow anything to happen to you"

I nod my head as Ereon turns and faces his soldiers. Rhenor has made his way back to Siphonie, holding her as she's crying into his chest. He runs his hands through her soft-pink hair, holding her close. I turn and look for Thylas, but I don't see him. He's cooling off somewhere and I know he will be back soon.

"We'll take a break to regather our bearings, but not for long. This will give everyone the opportunity to change their pants," Ereon calls out to the men and smirks, his princely mask back in place.

A chill sweeps across my spine and I can't help but look up again at the crevices holding the creatures. I know it saw me, each time it stared directly at me. I felt it. Ereon says they are color blind, but I know what I felt.

Thirty-Six

CARNAXA

The last couple hours have gone by slowly as we made our way through the pass. The creatures stayed inside their dwellings and we moved relatively quietly. Thylas came back, shortly after Ereon announced our brief respite, calmer now than when he left. He was quick to apologize and I forgave him easily because we were all scared. I know how he feels for me. I know he is my drop, and I figure I am his too. But he's never said as much before, in fact I know he has told people he can't have one since he's not from the shores of Antalis. But if the Goddess granted me two, she must have blessed them as well.

Siphonie rode the rest of the way beside me, feeling better being in a circle of the soldiers, and I feel better with her here as well. She has run her hand back and forth across her stomach for a while now. She told me she knew right when the monsters showed up, she would have done anything to stay alive for her baby. Siph has never been a fighter, but I have no doubt she would have fought if the encounter had gone differently, just like I would have.

As we crest the last hill, the mountains stop and the sun is beginning to set in the distance. The orange sands shine like fire through the opening of the mountains and I breathe in deeply. Shaston. We are finally arriving on their sands. We are still in the shadows of the mountains, but according to Rhenor, we will stop to "dress adequately" for this new culture we are about to step into.

What my mother must think of me. Her daughter she raised to be a queen, finding herself in the heat of the sand instead of the Goddess' seas. I just hope she's proud of me, maybe it wasn't what she wanted but maybe, someday, I can be more. I was raised by her caring heart. I was raised to be strong. I was raised exactly for this.

Ereon raises his hand once again, signaling us to halt, casting a long leg off the saddle to hop down. "We'll stop here." He grabs a bag from his saddle, pulling out similar clothes to the ones he saved me in. Thylas has already dismounted and is putting on a matching outfit to Ereon's. They both look breathtaking in the black, loose attire, but I instantly miss the colors of home that were just on Thylas and I panic. I knew this was coming, but I don't have any

Shastonian clothing. I didn't even have the horse riding clothes I'm wearing now. Quickly I scurry down from the horse, giving it a pat on the head as I walk over to Siphonie.

"Do you have clothes?"

She chuckles a response, "Obviously. You know I love shopping."

"No" – I roll my eyes, gesturing to all the men exchanging short sleeves for those of long – "I mean Shastonian clothing."

"Oh ... no." She looks around just as lost as I am. She pulls her hair up in a tight knot on the top of her head as she calls Rhenor over. "What are we" – she points to the two of us – "supposed to wear?"

"I have some items," Ereon speaks up from behind, making us all jump. "I ... wasn't sure what size you were when I left Shaston so I brought a few to choose from. I knew Antalian's don't usually make clothing like we do." He holds out his hands, displaying heavy, cotton fabrics in a variety of neutral colors.

"Thank you." Reaching out and grabbing them from his hands, a spark shoots up my arm from where our hands touch, and how I long to be back somewhere where it's just us ... and Thylas. Just one more night, perhaps. I know he told us it could only be one, but I don't think I can accept that. "Do you mind if Siphonie tries on some pieces? She didn't bring appropriate attire either."

He shakes his head. "They are yours to do with what you wish." He starts to walk away before turning on his heel. "I almost forgot, here are your cuffs. I've already passed the others out to those in the entourage who need them, including the Captain and *Bêl*

Rhenor." He holds out two black leather cuffs with silver thread stitching.

Siphonie and I look at each other with quizzical looks before looking back at the bands in his grasp. I reach out and rub the smooth leather between my fingers as I take it from him. "Our cuffs?"

"Father's rules to keep those of prestige distinguished from the others of our kingdom. It's law to keep them on at all times." He holds his arm up, showcasing his own cuff. "See, I have to have one too. I didn't wear it often in Antalis, the humidity gave me a rash where it rubbed my skin."

Siphonie takes hers as well, and shrugs. "Well, it's not the most beautiful bracelet I own. But I'll make it work." Fumbling with the fastenings, she huffs and holds her wrist out to me. "You'll have to help me."

I lace the cuff around her wrist and turn to Ereon, asking, "Do you mind?"

"Of course not." He smiles and helps put the cuff on the opposite wrist that holds my bracelets my mother gave me. "There you go, a princess of two kingdoms now represented on your wrists. One to remember your past and one to symbolize your future."

My wrist falls from his hold and I stare down, the cuff much heavier than I expected. It already itches, but I'll do what I have to.

Siphonie is beautiful in the muted-orange fabric wrapped around her. She could make a fishing net look beautiful though. The dress is a bit large on her small frame. It took us forever to figure out how to wrap the scarves around our heads. Finally, we found a way to make each one stay. I decided to wear a white one, a bit of my hair framing my face. My long, flowy skirt twirls, but the boots I'm wearing underneath look odd. I already miss the sandals my feet have always known. The top is slightly fitted along the waist but has long sleeves that reach past my fingertips.

We walk back to our traveling companions, Rhenor with us as he kept watch while Siph and I changed. He remained ever the gentleman keeping his back turned, even though Siph tried hard to get him to turn when it was her turn to disrobe.

"Can you smell the difference?" she asks randomly.

"The difference in what?" I respond, trying to adjust the sleeves of the top. I don't like these at all.

"The air. You can't smell that? It smells like burnt food here." She sniffs the air again. "Oh Goddess, is this a pregnant woman thing?"

We burst out in laughter together, and she links her arm with mine. "If it smells like burnt food," I say trying to catch my breath, "I'm glad I'm not pregnant."

We continue to laugh and she talks about how many other things she can smell, and I never realized grass had a scent until she said it was all she could smell in Midaeliea. I'll miss this, our carefree laughter without fear, because soon, I know it will have to stop.

Ereon stands, talking to a soldier, and he glances at us. He stops, mid-sentence, and a smile spreads across his face as he greedily takes me in. He licks his lips before walking toward us, leaving the soldier looking confused.

"Well, he certainly likes what he sees," Siphonie whispers. "I'll let you two talk." I blush, one because of his unabashedly staring, but also because of everything else happening. I have yet to tell her what has happened between us. I smile and look down for a moment, she'll never believe me. I fidget with the hem of my sleeve as his eyes bore into me.

"Princess ... you look ... beautiful." He reaches forward, grabbing my hand and pulling me to him. "If I may." He motions at the scarf and I nod.

"We don't want the sun getting jealous of your beautiful face. Even though the sun will be setting soon, the heat doesn't disappear until the cold sweeps in with the darkness, and I don't want you to burn." He pushes the hair I had left out and pulls the cloth around the lower half of my face, securing it behind my ear. "There, now you look perfect. Go ahead and find your captain, he's still mad and keeping his distance from me. We'll leave soon." He leans down, kissing my cheek.

He walks back to his men, finding his own black scarf, wrapping it gracefully around him.

I walk clunkily back to Siphonie, still getting used to these boots. I hate them, but apparently, they help keep the burning sand from my feet. I put my dagger into my right boot. "I hate these boots, how can anyone wear these all the time?"

"I agree, *Nohæ*." Thylas comes to stand beside me, his emerald eyes blaze against the fabric that covers his own face.

"You seemed to have a better idea of how all this cloth works than we did." I laugh and twirl in front of him. I've never felt so weighed down.

He chuckles. "Well, I had Rhenor teach me before we left and Ereon showed me again last night when ..." his words trickle away and we both just nod. He looks around making sure no one is looking at us before he cups my face, "I thought I would worry about all of this cloth hiding your beauty, but it seems nothing can do that."

I lean into his hand and look up at him. We have a long road ahead of us, but I'm glad that at least now, he's back to being my friend, if not more, than what he was in Antalis. When he was still too scared to get close.

· · • ◑ ● ○ ◐ • · ·

Just a few more feet and I will touch Shaston's sand. I'm already having to squint as the sun's light becomes almost blinding, bouncing off the red sand ahead. The sand seems to shift in color from red to orange as it comes closer into view. Instead of being in the rear of the convoy as we have been most of the way, Ereon and I lead now.

Ereon stops just before the mountains open to take in a long breath. "Well, here we are. Welcome to the Kingdom of Shaston."

He leads his horse forward and mine follows behind. The coolness of the mountains dissipates and scalding heat overtakes everything. It feels like fire in my bones and I clutch my chest because my breath leaves me. I struggle to take a single breath. "Something is ... wrong," the words feel like needles as I grapple for breath.

Straining to find anyone, I look forward to where Ereon once was, he's trying to speak, his mouth opening and closing as his eyes squint in pain. He clutches his own chest and bends over his stead, holding on by only his thighs. A heavy pressure builds inside of my chest and I have to close my eyes to try to find my breath. A deep breath in, and a deep breath out.

Pain shoots from my heart, radiating all over me. I can feel the pain in my fingertips to the bottoms of my feet. I curl inward, grabbing onto the saddle horn to keep from falling over when images invade my mind.

Images I've had from nightmares over the years. A man burning at a stake, fire engulfing everything from homes, to stables, to people. The metallic smell of blood takes over everything, there is so much blood everywhere. The cries of children and women are ear-splitting. The war yells of soldiers fighting and swords clashing. A woman in the middle of it all, ice surrounds her as fire blazes outside of the boundary she seems to keep.

"*Nohæ*!" I can hear my name being yelled. Calling me in the distance to retreat from these horrific visions, but I can't. I just stare at the woman. Her body shaking as she stands, tears staining her face and blood dripping from her fingertips. She looks broken and defeated.

She turns and meets my gaze, her words barely audible. She holds something in her hands, but I can't make it out. "*A læ t neni pe, o a læ pengæ pe wæ lomo popo ra læ*"

"Is she even breathing?" Siphonie's siren voice sings to me this time.

"Keep her face covered! Find something to make us shade, hurry," Ereon's voice is like thunder in the background of this scene. "Princess, come back."

I'm not ready to leave, not yet. There is still more to see.

"It's time, Daughter." I watch as the woman brings a dagger to her neck and I flinch as she slices her throat. Crimson ribbons run down her dress as her knees buckle and she smiles, looking right at me. I move away from the scene and feel as if I slam back into my body.

People around me shuffle and scream, and I feel them shaking my body but I can't reach them. Stuck in some sort of in-between, my body too tired to find anything but the darkness waiting for me, not knowing if it will keep me in the nightmare I just saw or let me go in peace. I give in, letting it pull me like the tide, away from everything and everyone around me.

THIRTY-SEVEN

THYLAS

Following behind them, I nudge my horse to cross the boundary. Hopefully letting the nightmare of this mountain pass stay behind us. I'm home, in the land of saffron sands that still haunt my dreams. The past I thought I had left behind. The memories of an angry father and a loving mother swarm me until I see Carnaxa clutch at her chest. Her other hand is gripping the reins tightly as she starts to scream. I kick my heels into the sides of my horse, urging it closer to her when the pain filters into my own heart and veins. I keep urging the horse forward, riding through the pain. If I can take a lashing and not cry out, I will get to her.

She falls from her horse, her face just barely hidden in the shade from her scarf as she tumbles through the sand. I push through, ignoring the pain blooming inside of me, and yell, "Ereon!" When he turns to look back at her, his face contorts in pain. Ereon falls from his horse, landing face down in the sand, clutching his chest. My breaths are rigid as I can no longer withstand the pain echoing through my body. No longer able to hold on to the reins, I also greet the sand in agonizing pain

Just as quickly as the sharp pain arrived, it passes. I crawl across the rough sand to get to her. She's screaming and thrashing about in the sand. "*Nohæ!*"

Siphonie jumps down from her stead and runs to Carnaxa, trying to remove her face scarf. "Is she even breathing?"

Ereon, seemingly past his own pain, runs toward her, his boots leaving imprints in the hot sand as he does. "Keep her face covered! Find something to make us shade, hurry." Soldiers scramble around us, grabbing bedding to stretch across tent poles to provide shade. He leans down and grabs her face, fretting, "Princess, come back."

I knew the other night, but now everyone can see the feelings he truly has for her. His eyes are full of fear, but also with love for her. No one here can deny his feelings for her. I move to her other side and grab her hand. Rhenor looks at me with a questioning look and then looks back and forth between us all. He knows, he can see it too. He knows the Princess' desire mirrors my own feelings for her, but he can also tell that there is more between Ereon and her too.

We scramble looking for the source of her pain, anything we can find to help calm her and get her back to us. We hope to find an injury we can treat and will heal. There is no such wound.

"*A læ t neni pe , o a læ pengæ pe wæ lomo popo ra læ,*" her blood curdling scream surrounds us, with words I know she doesn't understand. Words only a few of us here probably do. It's the old language. Rhenor's eyes glance at mine as he shakes his head at me. Don't translate. Got it. The words are formal and for right now, they don't make any sense at least not right now. It would not do anyone any good to know, so I nod in agreement back to him.

She continues to scream over and over, the horror shreds through her as her hands dig into the sand. Her fingertips burn as she does. We pull them out, trying to keep her safe and unharmed as much as we can. When suddenly, she gasps loudly and falls silent

I don't know who grabs her first, but both Ereon and I pull her scarf down, now that the shade is providing safety from the sun's rays. He leans down and checks her breathing while my fingers check for the pulse in her neck. Her breathing is slow, it's labored but steady. It's there. That's what's important right now. My *Nohæ* is still here. She's still fighting, and there is nothing I can do to help her. I don't know how much longer we have till we arrive at Shaston's castle, I don't have a way to get her to a healer aside from the one in our *Shayi* who is already shaking his head saying he doesn't know. So I sit with her, wrapping her in my arms as

Ereon starts yelling something at his men, and I continue rocking her back and forth. Holding her, hoping to keep her here.

"Captain ... there is a small village, we need to get her there now." Ereon's hand lands on my shoulder drawing my attention. "Let us get her there. I'll carry her on my horse, make sure you keep up."

I nod softly, picking her up and placing a kiss along her hairline, before gently securing her in Ereon's arms. His black stead starts to trot in a different direction than where we were originally headed. Siphonie is trying to ask me something as I mount my horse, but I ignore her. Right now, I have to keep up with Ereon.

"Just go. I know where he's going." Rhenor slaps the back of my horse and we gallop behind Ereon.

····•◑●○●◐••···

People greet us, noticing their prince riding up. He never stopped, he never slowed down and she looks so tiny in his arms. He clutches her with his hands, keeping her face buried in his chest as best he can. The people start parting as they notice him barreling into the village, not slowing down in the slightest.

Jumping from his horse, Carnaxa still in his arms, he yells, "We need healers!" He carries her into a building, laying her on a bed.

"What is wrong with her?" I yell at Ereon as the healers flock around her. We may have all felt some pain, but everyone else seems to be awake and unharmed, so why isn't she? I put myself between her and the men and women who are flooding this room. I don't know them, what if they aren't even true healers? What if they are enemies of Antalis?

"Why do you think I would know any more than you do? You were with us when this happened." He punches a wall and mutters under his breath. "I don't know what happened. But I promise, these people will help her, but we have to let them." He pulls my arm, trying to get me to leave her.

"No! I will not leave her in this strange place. I'm sworn to protect her and by the Goddess, I will kill anyone who stands in my way and that includes you, Prince."

"If you think you could kill me and walk out of here alive, you are mistaken, Captain. Did you forget that I love her too!?"

One of the older healers walks between us before she admonishes, "We are trying to save Princess Carnaxa and do not need whatever this is" – she motions between us – "happening here. Get out, both of you." Her wrinkled hands push us toward the door.

I know I should leave, I'm being irrational, but my legs feel like trees rooted to the ground. She pushes Ereon again, emphasizing, "We need the room."

He huffs and pats my shoulder. "Thylas, let them do their job."

I run my hands down my face and let out a loud sigh, but I follow him from the room. My anger and anxiety twist into a heavy knot in my chest. I need her to be okay. He leads me to a vendor and grabs two ales – passing me one. I drink it quickly hoping for some relief. His eyes dart around watching those among us but his eyes are riddled with worry. We walk back to the healing room and wait outside. Ereon sits down with his back against the wall, running his hands through his hair. I sit down beside him and stretch out my legs. The people passing side-eye us and talk in hushed breaths.

"They've never seen me show so much emotion," Ereon confesses.

I rest my forearms on my bent knee, adjusting the sword at my side. Where are Ereon's swords? Did he drop them, it's the first time I truly notice how distraught he is. He doesn't have his swords or his guard. He's just a man who is worried as much as I am.

"For a woman or in general?" I take another drink, realizing it's already empty.

"Both."

I look back toward the room. The healers have not come out, we have received no status update on Carnaxa. My palms sweat profusely with each passing moment . Is it from this horrid heat or my nerves? Probably both. For once, Ereon does not boast or make comments. We just sit in silence, waiting.

"Prince Ereon ..." The oldest healer, the one who shoved me out, finally appears in the doorway. We quickly stand. "She's still asleep; we've done all we can. She, from what we can tell, is stable. We'll send someone to get water and liquified food for her. I don't advise either of you to be here when we provide nourishment to her."

"Will she wake?" my words come out more clipped then I mean for them, but her not waking up is not an option.

"We do not know the plans of the gods, boy. She may wake up tomorrow or she may never wake up."

Ereon pops his neck. "Thank you," the words come out gritted and his fists clench at his sides. The healer turns back into the room.

I look around trying to find some sort of comfort in anything. So I fall to my knees and raise my hands, the way the priestesses always do. "*Neshæ pekæ ra , lengo ra , noko ra,*" reciting the same prayer I said to her the night her mother passed. Ereon joins me, "Watch over her, guide her, love her."

I look at him shocked, but we continue to chant here on our knees for what feels like hours. As the healers leave, we stay and pray. We pray until the sun starts its decline and we can no longer feel our knees.

When we are finally done, we go into the room and look at her. Carnaxa's hair is splayed around her like a divine being, she looks so much more peaceful than she was just a few hours ago. Ereon moves to stand beside her, sitting on the edge of the bed. But I can't sit so I pace the room. "What are we supposed to do?"

He runs his hand down her arm. "We wait, Captain. We wait and we pray to her goddess. That's all we can do."

Thirty-Eight

ANARA

The days have blended together, the small window at the top of the wall barely lets in any light, only enough to tell day from night along with the briefest glance of the sun and moon. I don't know how long Ereon has been gone. I can't remember what it is like to feel a ray of light other than a flicker of a torch skimming my skin. I can't remember anything but pain at this point. Pain that the King swore I wouldn't succumb to if Ereon did what he was commanded. Atlas promised I would be safe ... and I guess I am, if I'm still alive. Regardless, Ereon will blame himself for this.

He always does. It's not his fault, he had no choice but to do what he did – what he will have to do.

For a moment, I thought King Atlas was truthful in what he told him. He had never touched me before so why would he now? I was wrong. So very, very, wrong. My body aches from the beatings, but when physical abuse didn't break me ... he thought forcing himself on me would. He was wrong. With each thrust, he made me stronger because I would not break- not to him. Not when I remember who I am and where I am from.

My people never asked to be stolen from our lands. I've heard this misdeed has come to a stop as of a few lunar years ago when they realized we hold no value to them here. If I had been stolen, I would have been broken, but I wasn't. I was sold by my father who was left with me, his only daughter. A daughter with flames in her veins who couldn't be controlled. A daughter born with wisdom and beauty. He was scared of what I could do. So when he saw the Shaston army, the *Prel,* on our shores, he willingly sold me. The voyage to Midaeliea and then to Shaston was tough, but I was bought for the King, so none of the Shastonians dared to touch me.

No one took my innocence, that had been given to a kind boy one night under the stars. When I was presented to the King I watched him stare at me, I knew then that he would try to take everything away from me. But he couldn't, I may not have access to it – but it is still only something I can give freely.

I listen for any sounds from the dark, damp corridor outside my prison. He's not visited me in a couple of days and I know he will soon. The obsidian chains clink as I try to find a comfortable place to sit. Having nothing but a bed and being chained to the wall, comfort is hard to find.

Looking down at my hands, I can barely make out their shapes in the dark but I know what they could do if only they had the chance. I won't always be here. I won't always be trapped and the King will meet his end. By my hand if not someone else's. He threw me at his son, only for his son to fall in love, but I made the choice to use the feelings between us.

I smile as I remember my first time with Ereon. His face still had a boyish look to it. I close my eyes, letting the memory take hold, giving me a reprieve from the hell I'm in.

·· • • ◍ ● ○ ◐ ◍ • • ··

Seven Lunar Years Ago

"Can you stop moving so much?" I push him again to turn around so I can put the salve on the marks across his ribs. The ones his father made with a heated iron this time. For six months now, Ereon's had me. For six months, I've been engaged in a dangerous game with the King. For six months, we've been each other's reprieve from the horrors of this world. I expected him to take me by force but he never did. In the beginning, I fought off even the smallest tokens of kindness. I would accept nothing until that first night his father's guards dropped him off at his door. They brought me through the "whore road" and told me to be ready for him. I wasn't prepared for

the shattered body that was delivered that night, expected to clean the mess his father made.

"It fucking hurts!" he hisses through clenched teeth as I put more ointment on.

"I'm trying to be as gentle as I can." I run my hands along the burns, touching softly. "The stiller you are, the quicker I can get this finished."

"For a tiny person, your hands feel like they are the weight of a boulder. I think you are pushing down for fun to make this hurt worse." He chuckles softly to himself. "I think you are a demon in disguise sometimes. Something here to torture me."

Distraction with humor, I smirk. He always does this. It's our routine. He bears the pain but tries to joke it away anyway. My hands linger on his side, grazing the muscles there. Heat blooms inside of me as I long to be touched by him, but that would make things worse. Make it worse when he finds out who – what – I am.

Smiling up at him, I tell him, "I'm a myach myomi. Tiny demon. That's what you would say in my home."

He turns his head from me and I gather the gauze to wrap his wounds.

"I'm sorry you are here."

I nod my head, I know he is. He's told me time and time again. The chains that bound my hands strike together, a reminder that I am not here by choice. Finishing with the gauze, I go to stand up but let my fingers linger longer than they should on his skin. It's enough for him to notice my hesitancy.

He grabs my fingers with his calloused hand, pulling me back down beside him. "Anara," he says my name like a prayer, a wish that the world was different. That we met through different circumstances. His eyes show the longing behind them. I don't miss the way he looks at me when he doesn't know I'm watching or the bulge in his pants when I'm around. His eyes now seek permission, he wants me to say yes. But I can't. He's not the only one who carries secrets.

"Don't." I turn away from him but he doesn't release me. Tucking a piece of hair behind my ear. "Don't make it more complicated. Don't pretend I have an option here."

He grunts, pulling his hand from mine and standing, groaning in pain as he does. He grabs his ribs.

"If you didn't have an option, I would have taken you already. I haven't done that. I won't." He walks barefoot across the stone floor throwing on his black robe.

I stand up, the chains jingle again and I hold them up showing him. "What do you think we can accomplish here, Ereon?" I scream at him, "I am in chains! I am away from my home! I can't…" Tears of rage and despair slip down my cheeks. "I can't fall in love with you because then … " he turns back toward me and crosses the distance between us. I promised myself I wouldn't love him. "Because then I won't leave if I get the chance." And you'll hate me even more when you know the truth.

Before I can blink his body is pressed against mine, pushing me into the wall behind us. He runs his hand across my cheek and into my hair. His lips push against mine igniting the fire inside me, one I haven't felt in so long even if it is useless. I run my hands up his chest, the chains keeping me from doing more.

I want him. Great God, or maybe Goddess, whoever listens to the prayers of the broken, I want him. He pulls his hand from my hair before kneeling before me. His mouth leaves a trail of sparks along the waistband of my skirt, his eyes looking back up at me. He's once again asking permission and this time I give it with a nod and a smile.

He reaches up, grabs hold of the chains on my wrist, and kisses the inside of my wrist. "I promise you, myach myomi, I will find a way out of these for you. I will find a way to get you out of Shaston."

He pulls down my skirt, his eyes never leaving mine as he does. He puts his hands behind my thighs, lifts me up and I wrap my legs around his waist. His bandages brush against the underside of my knee.

"What about your ribs?" My hands are in between us awkwardly, but he never lets me go, never lets me fall.

He looks down while walking me to his bed before he growls, "If they hurt more than my want for you, I'll let you know."

· · • • ◗ ● ○ ● ◖ • • · ·

Present

The rest of that night was when I knew I would forever stay where he was. I will endure him being married to someone else and

I will do what is needed because my heart belongs to a prince. We just have to find a way to escape his father.

It's still day out, just barely, the sun slowly sinking into the horizon and my room becoming filled with shadows once again. As I start to prepare for the night, the moonlight catches my attention, slipping through the paltry window. The full moon shouldn't be so high up this early in the evening, brighter than it naturally should be, warring with the sun as bringer of light. It shouldn't be up, not at this hour. It's far too soon and much too bright. If I was outside these walls I imagine I could reach up and touch it. I smile slightly as my mother's words come to mind, a story shared among our people. A story that got me out of one type of trouble, only to find myself in another. Tilting my head to get a better look outside, I start to speak the words, "Upon the day the moon turns bright ..." Before I can finish I lose my breath and crumble to my knees.

Pain emits from inside me, my heart quickening in a way I haven't felt since I was five. The long-dormant fire surges through my veins, the obsidian chains combating what they can. I roll to my side, clutching at the pain that spreads from my heart. Everything feels as if I'm burning and I roll harder on myself needing to scream out. And I do. I scream so loud, I know any guards must hear me but no one comes running. I scream as everything flashes through my mind. The memories of the past and images of the present and visions of what's to come. My mother's smile, my father's sneer. The way he looked when I first found my true form. The happiness I felt when I would run in the flames.

I breathe through my nose as best as I can, trying to remember how to control what I feel, but the darkness is trying to grab me, but I won't let it. I won't let it take this from me – not again. The pain rages inside my head, songs and words fusing and my ears pounding.

Suddenly it stops. Everything is quiet. Everyone is quiet.

Still shaking, I sit back up. And for the first time in a long time, I smile. I look up at the torch's flame and move my fingers, the chains cutting me deeper, a fail-safe the King placed on me years ago. At first, the fire does nothing, but then, ever so slowly, it sways the way I command it. I flick my wrist and the flame grows brighter.

My laughter fills the room. I don't care who hears me. I don't care if the whole castle can. Because I am one of the few who knows exactly what has happened. The Antalian of prophecy has touched Shaston's sand.

Magic is awake.

To Be Continued ...

"Like a mermaid in seaweed, she dreams awake,
trembling in her soft and chilly nest."
~ John Keats

Acknowledgements

How do I even begin to thank everyone who has helped me in this journey?

First, my husband Brian: You were always jumping in to help with the kids or household chores. You were always reminding me I could do this; and you always made sure I felt supported in my times of doubt, even though you probably had no clue what I was talking about. I love you so much and am forever proud to be your wife. You are forever my *nohæ* come true.

My kiddos: You can't read this until you're 35 but just know that Mama did this because of the love you give me and the strength I feel every time I look at you both. I wrote this book in part, to show you that your dreams are worthy of giving it your all. My greatest joy in life is being your mom and I love you both so much.

My mom: You have always called me your "free spirit" and always supported my many adventures, never once doubting I couldn't accomplish what I put my mind to. You're my best friend and I know I would not be the woman, wife, or mother that I am today if I did not have you to look up to.

My best friends: Veronica and Jessica, thanks for listening to me ramble without stopping and being some of the biggest supporters. Thank you both for being there before this story was even an idea. My hope is we will be around for each other even later in life, when we are old and in wheelchairs, laughing about that one time I wrote a book. I love you both so much.

Sam: Where do I even start? The peanut butter to my jelly (yes I stole that from you); my wifey (also stole that); and my PA. My friend and my un-biological sister. I don't know what I would have done without you. You truly helped me break out of my shell, understood when I cried, and never once doubted me. It's funny to think that something like Instagram connected us and here we are closer than two peas in a pod. You have no idea the impact you've had in my life and I'll forever be grateful for our friendship.

Fellow authors: Lauren Leasure, Fay Bec, Morgan Gauither, Sabrina G., Ryana Hunter, and L.R. Friedman, y'all will never ever know how much it meant to have your mentorship and help in the early book writing stages and throughout my entire publication journey. When we first met, I was just fangirling over your work and couldn't be happier at the friendships I've forged with each of you! Each of you was willing to answer my questions during both night and day - this book would not exist without you!

My alpha, beta, and sensitivity readers: Y'all really did stick it out through some of the muck and dirt! From my alphas who were the first ones to say "You have something here!" and to my betas who helped make this story even better! Every single one of you means so much to me.

The Bad Bitches Group on IG: Kels, Antonella, and Jacquie, I love you and the late night chaotic conversations we always share.

The Bound By Mischief Family: Boss Daddy loves you and I am so thankful for your support!

The Midnight Tide Family: Thank you for accepting me and this story. Thank you for the support and virtual-hand holding that I needed. Each of you are so important to me!

To my followers on Instagram: Thank you for being here from the beginning. I love the community support and I'm excited you're finally able to read THOS.

Cover artist, Shae: You took my idea and created a cover insanely beautiful! You are amazing!

Joyce: Editing was one of my biggest fears and one of the things I always told myself I couldn't do. You proved me wrong. You will never know how truly thankful I am for you. You are not only my editor, but my friend and someone who I will cherish for the rest of my life. You would call me out when I stopped believing in myself; told me I could do better when I would half-ass something; and always – always listened to me. I went into the editing process expecting to cry and yet I found myself excited when I saw there were comments waiting for me from you. Thank you so very much for everything you've done. You'll forever be someone who changed my life ... thank you for being you (I had to add an ellipsis for you somewhere).

To my readers: Thank you for giving The Heat of Seas a chance. Thank you for believing in me and my book. I truly wouldn't be here without you. Oh, and this book ends on a cliffhanger - don't say I didn't mention it.

About the Author

DeAnna Hill is a Dark Fantasy Romance Author who specializes in forbidden love and messy relationships. Prepare to be drawn into a world where love and darkness collide, where passion ignites in the shadows, and where the boundary between fantasy and reality fades away, leaving a lasting impression long after the final page is turned.

As a homeschooling mom of two boys and wife to her husband of many years, she understand the importance of balancing work and family life. She loves to immerse herself in her work, usually with a fresh cup of coffee in her hand. When she's not typing away, she can be found indulging in her favorite guilty pleasure, Taco Bell, with a warm and cozy blanket wrapped around her.

Find Out More

If you're looking for something that is both thrilling and emotional, then look no further than her work.

MORE BY MIDNIGHT TIDE

A woman on a mission...

Rose Gardner never thought she'd leave the small town of West Ridge. But when her husband dies at war, she must return his arms to his place of birth to set his spirit to rest. After traveling into enemy territory, Rose falls into a trap. Held captive in an enchanted manor, she finds herself face to face with a beast who is equally horrifying and kind. Will she manage to complete her quest or be pulled in by the secrets of the manor?

A man haunted by his past...

Trapped within his own home and in the body of a hideous beast, Kris never wanted to share his prison with another. As much as Rose may draw him in with her beauty and stubborn strength, he knows she must escape before the next full moon. After all, he remembers all too well what happened to the previous caretaker. The dead won't let him forget the blood on his hands.

Sometimes, the beauty does claim a beast.

Aeryx is a warrior in Morozko's army, yearning to destroy those who brought ruin to his home. But when duty brings him to the human world, he encounters a problem. An intoxicating problem he wants nothing to do with.

A problem he can't resist.

Noel has rebelled for most of her life, and college is doing nothing to change that fact. Until one sorority night, when she witnesses the unthinkable and stumbles upon a monster from another realm. A monster who makes her question everything.
Including her desire for the beast.

I live in a magical world. A world filled with vampires, shifters, and mages.

Mysteriously, I was born without powers.

After living the past two years in a personal hell, enduring abuse from a fiance I didn't choose, I finally snapped. An act of self-defense against my fiance angers my father, and in retaliation for

my actions, he creates the ultimate contest. One that only the most powerful magicals can compete in to win my hand in marriage.

It sounds bleak, but anything has to be better than my current situation. At least, I thought so, until *they* appeared in the middle of the night to whisk me away.

A vampire prince.

A wolf without a pack.

A powerful mage.

My three captors do everything they can to win the contest, and as the attraction between the four of us grows, so does their desire to keep me safe.

When the mystery of my birth comes into play, we begin to question everything I thought I knew about my life. Am I just a human with no magical powers? Or am I something else entirely? One thing is certain, if my captors cannot keep me safe, more than my heart is at stake: my life is on the line.

www.ingramcontent.com/pod-product-compliance
Lightning Source LLC
Chambersburg PA
CBHW031435200726
48289CB00001BA/99